GOLDEN

GOLDEN

ANDREA DICKHERBER

For Knox, Quinn and Rooney.
Follow your bliss, always.

CONTENTS

GOLDEN

FRESH

1

———

THE SUMMER BEFORE

The piece of this story that matters the most began in the summertime, when Midwestern air conditioners groan with overuse, the balance of chlorinated water and urine in pools everywhere takes a disastrous turn and the clichéd fantasies that plague teenage minds while they lie awake at night in their bed, or in someone else's bed, stand the greatest chance of coming true. It began the summer before we went off to high school. The summer my parents spent traveling in Europe. The summer I spent living with Rudy.

I awoke the first morning of that summer staring at Rudy's hair, a tangled mess of shiny espresso strands, stretched out across her pillow until they almost tickled the edge of my nostril. Buttery sunlight was melting through her velvet curtains, but she was still sound asleep, her mouth parted slightly to let breath move in and out. I leaned back against the soft leather headboard and rubbed at the crusts of sleep in my eyes with closed fists. It was barely eight.

There's something special about the hours after midnight at a sleepover. In the dark, the restraints that bind your personality loosen their hold and the most secret bits of yourself come bubbling to the surface and ooze out of your mouth.

We stayed up, lying under the covers in Rudy's queen size bed, our elbows bent to prop up our heads and the volume on the TV turned down low, the screen casting eerie blue light over the foot of the comforter. Under the cover of darkness, with the reward to my revelations being a gleam in her green eyes and a friendly laugh tumbling from her mouth, I told Rudy about my excessively sweaty armpits, my love for the metallic, greasy taste of fried chicken livers, the time last year when I'd gone searching for a new razor blade to shave my legs and accidentally walked in on my parents together in the shower. A sleepover was the place where it was safe to spill your secrets, and I always felt an irresistible pull to ingratiate myself to other people by laying out my own flaws for a cheap laugh. When we fell asleep, both of us snuggled beneath her down comforter, our shoulder blades pressed together, my heart was still fluttering with anxious excitement. But in the clarity of morning, I felt scraped raw – my insides a hollow of embarrassment. I scolded myself for revealing so much so soon, for leaving the impression that I was one of those loud, annoying girls who forces herself on your lunch table in the cafeteria with her cheap plastic lunchbox of weird smelling food and her poor hygiene.

I sighed quietly, cupping my hand over my lips and breathing into my palm. I winced at my sour morning breath. Why couldn't I have been born more dainty and less disgusting? I breathed with my lips parted, airing out the rank cave of my mouth.

Rudy's bedroom was decorated in shades of purple, the furniture a rich color of wood I couldn't identify. Her comforter was white and floral, and the first thing I did upon awakening was check to make sure my unpredictable period hadn't arrived in the middle of the night and bloomed out upon the white fabric. It hadn't, thank God. On the surface of Rudy's desk sat a shiny silver computer, a white lightning bolt dancing back and forth across the solid black screen. There were no posters tacked to the walls, no glittered or sequined collage picture frames sitting on the dresser. I worried that I had no idea how to be a teenager at all.

My eyes throbbed behind heavy lids. I just wanted to sink into the pillow and sleep forever, but my mind itched with activity. She would wake up soon, I reassured myself, and I waited for nearly an hour, my eyes closed so that if she opened hers she wouldn't find me staring at her face.

"Rudy," I whispered finally. Her head jerked, and she rolled toward me, long black eyelashes still pressed shut over her light green eyes.

"Rudy?" I felt self-conscious just saying her name out loud. I pressed my cold fingers against the warm skin of her shoulder. Her eyes twitched beneath her eyelids, and she pursed her lips.

"Hm?" Her eyes fluttered open and she squinted at me, disoriented.

"Sorry." I blushed. "I was just going to say, I think I'm going to go eat breakfast, if that's okay?"

Clouds of sleep cleared from her eyes and she nodded.

"Yeah, of course. I'll come with you."

"You can sleep if you want. You don't have to get up."

"No, it's okay." She smiled a pearly-white smile. "I'm starving anyway."

RUDY LIVED down the street from my family, in what was easily the largest house on a street of huge homes. They had a pool and a four car garage and a housekeeper who cleaned their three story spread, excluding the basement, which primarily housed an enormous wine cellar that, months later, Rudy and I learned to raid inconspicuously.

My parents and I were the newest to move to the gated neighborhood, following my father's promotion and rapid climb up the corporate ladder, and our new house still didn't feel like a home to me even after a full year of living there. Everything was made of granite and stainless steel, and my bedroom was on the east side of the house, where the vents were extra gusty and it was always too cold. Three quarters of the year my father was absent from our sparkling new home, out of the country on business, and my mother, who when we were living in our modest two story colonial in Boston had pined desperately for this life of luxury, now alternated between moping around the house in her collection of silky bathrobes and coordinating house slippers, or spending a few days at a spa being botoxed or strategically removing and injecting plump fat cells into another part of her body, to entice my father to stay home more often or to bring her along as arm candy on his next trip across the world (something he hardly ever did). And while they were gone, they would leave fourteen-year-old me in charge of the homestead. Our housekeeper, Helen, would pick me up from school and be at our house a few hours of each day, but she left by six o'clock to go home to her own family, to cook greasy, comforting fried chicken and macaroni and cheese dinners and kiss her rowdy children's foreheads. I was left all alone inside this massive marble structure. I didn't get a lot of sleep those nights, huddled in the living room with all of the lights turned on, watching late night television with my comforter wrapped around me more for protection than warmth. It wasn't a tortured existence, and I suppose I shouldn't complain; my parents were always around when it counted, when they were to be seen – before school proms and at awards ceremonies and to see me off to college – and they lavished me with any material possession I could have asked for, but those nights by myself, terrified of the dark, endless corridors of our lonely new house, I would have given up every single meticulously hand-stitched pair of designer jeans in my closet just to have a family that was *present*.

That wish began to unfold in early September, after our first summer in St. Louis, at a neighborhood "picnic". It was far from a picnic – no red and white checkered tablecloths, and no one would have considered sitting on the ground. My parents were both in town, my mother sporting a freshly tucked chin and a new dress that slipped over the small curve of her waist, having dragged my father and I along to keep up appearances and prove we belonged with the wealthy, tennis-bracelet-wearing neighbors who now surrounded us.

The Goldens had hosted the picnic in their own sprawling backyard, and I had gazed up incredulously at the enormity of their house through the tinted glass of the back window of our car as we pulled onto the brick pavers of their circular drive. Their house was a matching dark brick, jutting angles and almost comically massive fall flowers in multi-colored blooms sprouting up anywhere they had the space (but still tactfully, of course). The grass was a shade of green I had previously only seen in artificial sources, like food dye or children's crayons, and it hugged the flat yard as snugly as a fitted sheet. A valet stepped out from underneath his little white tent to greet us, a drop of sweat trickling down the side of his neck. He must have been dying in the heat of that late summer weekend, dressed in a full black tuxedo and a matching hat perched over his closely cropped black hair. He was young, though not too close to my own age – twenty or twenty-one, I thought. I often found myself making a game out of studying people around me, imagining in my own mind what I thought their lives were like (because at that time I thought that any life that I imagined was invariably more interesting than my own). He could be a college boy, trying to squeeze the last few bucks out of summer before he went back to school. He was good looking, and his eyes were soft and kind, so he probably would have a girlfriend, a nice, pretty, but not beautiful girl, and maybe he was even saving up all the money he made parking rich men's cars so that he could buy her an engagement ring. He would most definitely drop down on one knee to ask, I thought, as he took my father's keys and held the car doors open for my mother and I to step out, and he directed us toward the copper gated path that led to the tinkling party noises emanating from the backyard. I glanced back to see him hop into the front seat of the car and drive it off to its own party, sitting in a row of similarly shiny, expensive automobiles (ours was, though not obvious to me, the least impressive of them all), and I decided he wouldn't propose in a restaurant or something obvious like that – a park, maybe. He looked like the outdoorsy type. As we rounded the side of the house, me teetering perilously on three-inch heeled sandals that didn't agree with the bricked pathway, the expanse of the yard came into view like flipping a page in a magazine. Like Alice entering Wonderland.

There was a huge tent, the obese mother tent of the one the valet had waited underneath, and professionally decorated tables were laid out beneath it, splashed with linens in all the fashionable fall colors (this particular year, that included burnt orange and a deep shade of purple). There were even more flowers in back, both growing from the ground and floating in pretty vases. Candles glittered everywhere I looked, despite the fact that it was still very much daytime. On the edges of the tent, the catering staff stood behind long tables filled with finger foods – shrimp satay and stuffed olives and peppers and bruschetta – their hands gloved in plastic, their eyes looking both bored and slightly intimidated. I was still getting my bearings, gazing around at the party and at the glittering water on the uncovered pool that lay several feet behind the tent, when my eyes landed on Rudy, the only other picnicker I had spied under the age of thirty. She was standing beside one of the round purple tables, laughing as she spoke to an older couple, the woman in a brown pantsuit with hair pulled back severely, the man just beginning to bald at the crown of his head. In contrast to the visible aging of the couple, Rudy was awash with youthful beauty in every sense of the description: long, dark hair pulled loosely into a shining braid, a brightly colored dress flowing effortlessly over her thin curves, never-ending, tanned legs growing out from underneath her dress. Her eyes were so expressive, so attentive, that even though the gross older man's eyes were devouring every inch of Rudy's youthfulness, it seemed she either was too naïve to notice or too self-assured to care (this was one of Rudy's mysteries I never did figure out).

"This way, dear." My mother threaded her arm through mine so we were linked at the elbow and pulled me in another direction, steering our family toward the beaming man and woman who were clearly the host and hostess, the owners of this castle, the king and queen of our neighborhood.

"Mr. Golden, Mrs. Golden." My mother, because she was the initiator of all things social, as my father and I retreated into the background, reached out cordially to shake the man's hand, and offered the woman a dainty, unfeeling hug.

"Please, call me Kat," the woman said, smiling warmly up at the three of us. She was plumper, soft and rounded in all the womanly places, and a good four inches shorter than I was in my heels, but she still radiated beauty in a way I couldn't quite describe.

"This is a wonderful party. We're so happy to have been invited. You have a lovely home," my mother continued, with the appropriate degree of reverence, though careful not to appear overtly impressed.

"Thank you!" Mrs. Golden smiled again. Her husband had fallen into manly conversation with my quiet father, and she reached for his wrist, giving it a little squeeze. "Charles had quite a bit to do with the design of the house. The gardening's my forte, however." I learned later that unlike many housewives on our street, she truly meant this – Mrs. Golden spent days and days every summer laboring over her gorgeous flowers. The lawn-care company tended to the grass and the trees and the bushes, but no one but Mrs. Golden touched the flowerbeds.

"And who is this beautiful young lady?" She tilted her face toward me, and I blushed suddenly at being acknowledged.

"This is my daughter, Jillian." My mother placed a thin arm around my shoulders, her fingers lighting softly on my arm. "She's about to begin her eighth grade year. She'll be a freshman at Ogden Academy next fall."

Ogden Academy was the most prestigious (and by that virtue, most expensive) high school in our area, and though I had a full year before I would enter high school, my mother took great pride in telling people, even people to whom it would mean nothing, that this is where I was going to attend school.

"Fantastic!" Mrs. Golden clapped her small hands together, and the gold bracelets around her wrists clanged against one another. "Have you met my younger daughter, Ruth Ann? She'll be attending Ogden for high school next year as well."

I shook my head politely, still smiling at her.

"She's just over there, in the blue dress." She pointed toward where Rudy stood, now alone, talking with one of the caterers as she bit down on a piece of shrimp. "You should go join her. Save her from us old folks." She winked at me, which was normally something that made me cringe, but she managed to do it without being obnoxious.

I obliged, parting from my parents and walking across the yard to where Rudy stood.

"Hi." I came up behind her and stuck my hand out shyly to shake hers. "I'm Jillian."

She wiped her fingers on a gold edged napkin, and then grasped my hand in her own. "I'm Rudy. Nice to meet you."

"Yeah, you too." I was so painfully shy, so utterly intimidated by the entirety of the two months since we had moved into this opulent neighborhood, and it seemed to all culminate in this one, singular experience. I had met no friends thus far, and yet I could think of nothing to say, nothing at all, and I was sure I would remain friendless.

"Your family just moved here, right?" Rudy picked up a glass of lemonade from the table nearest to us, and took a sip.

"Yes. We moved in July," I said. I'd never met her before, but now, suddenly, I imagined her watching me in my sweaty t-shirt, hauling boxes into the house, and I immediately felt both embarrassed and flattered that she had noticed.

"Where are you from?"

"Boston." I felt a familiar pang in my chest for my old friends and our old house and my old, less-lonely life.

"I've never been to Boston. Do you miss it?"

I nodded. "I miss my friends."

We had agreed to write old-fashioned letters, and I lived for the days when an envelope arrived in the mail, my name scrawled across the front in girlish cursive and a Boston post-mark in the corner.

"It'll get better. I promise it's nice here," Rudy smiled.

One of the caterers, a man with orange-red hair and freckles covering his face and neck, appeared at our side, pushing a silver tray of food between us. "Appetizer, ladies?"

"What are they?" I stared down at the bits of food – green lumps coated in a layer of oily, crumbling beige, cradled inside little paper cups.

"Jalapeno poppers."

"Sure. Thank you." Rudy took one, and I did the same, eyeing the pepper skeptically.

Rudy lifted it in her dainty fingers and bit off half. Cheese and clear juice trickled from her mouth, and she cupped her palm under her chin to catch it before it dripped onto her dress. Watching, I resolved to avoid any embarrassing mess by eating the entire thing in one bite.

"This is spicy," Rudy warned, but it was too late. I'd already crammed the entire pepper into my mouth. It couldn't be that bad, could it? I bit down and it oozed over my tongue, hot and gooey. "Really spicy."

Rudy wiped her face and gulped from her glass of lemonade.

It was like an oven in my mouth, the temperature rising by the second. My tongue itched like crazy. I chewed twice and swallowed the pepper whole, feeling it blaze a spicy trail down my esophagus.

"Oh my God." The sides of my nose were collecting tiny beads of sweat and my eyes were watering. I reached for the nearest drink, bringing it to my lips just as Rudy opened her mouth to speak.

"Wait, no!"

I gulped an enormous mouthful of the bitter amber liquid and cringed helplessly as it flooded my assaulted taste buds. I gagged, spewing flecks of beer out onto the front of Rudy's dress.

"That's beer," Rudy finished her warning.

My face was so hot with embarrassment I wasn't sure I could speak. "I'm so sorry," I squeaked.

Over the years, I've thought of this moment often – my adolescent anxiety, the intense desire to impress this stunning girl, the tenderness of my own humiliation, softened by age and humor – and it never fails to make me smile.

"I'm so glad you moved," she said. "Finally, someone I can hang out with in the neighborhood."

I HAD EXPECTED it to be easy from there – to glide into best friendship – for my life to instantly bounce back to how it had been in Boston. But it didn't. School had already begun, and Rudy and I went to different junior high schools (hers was a private middle school my mother had been unable to secure me a position in this late in the game), and we saw each other only a handful of times over the course of the year. She was always friendly, and I was always awkward in a way I agonized over for days afterward. She was like a crush, but not in that manner. I idolized her from the beginning in this way I can't quite explain, not that I would have tried explaining it to anyone if I could. At my junior high school the cliques were firmly established, and I was not charming enough to force myself into any of them; I remained on the edge of friendlessness, participating in only a marginal way, despite my mother's attempts to host slumber parties at our new house or push me into activities like ballet, cheerleading or girls tennis (the right sort of activities, mind you).

It wasn't until my mother convinced my father, probably under threat of divorce or tantrum or withholding of sex, to take her on a summer vacation to Europe following my semi-miserable eighth grade year that I finally got the friendship I had wanted all along. My mother informed me over our breakfast of exotic fruit the weekend before they left for Spain, the first leg of their journey, that Mrs. Golden had offered to let me stay with them for the summer. For the *entire* summer. At first I had balked, unsure that I wanted to be pushed onto another family – tagging along behind Rudy when I still wasn't so sure she wanted me around. But the prospect of spending another year alone, on the periphery, threatened to break me. I had already lost so much of my old self, sunken into this shell of self-conscious self-reflection that was exhausting and all-consuming. Finally, I consented. And I resolved I would spend the summer making myself as likable to Rudy as possible. I would win her over, completely and totally, and I would ride through the next four years of high school with a gorgeous, enviable best friend by my side.

If only I had known I didn't have to work so hard at it, I could have saved my young self a lot of worries. For a reason I still can't place, Rudy loved my self-conscious teenage self at first sight.

———

THE FIRST TWO weeks of summer consisted of several hours spent lounging beside the pool in Rudy's fenced in backyard, soaking up rays of sunshine and watching it darken and swell up in our skin. We would wait as long as possible, testing our endurance in a game of chicken until one of us would give in, begging for a relief from the heat. Then we would dive into the cold, silky water of the pool, feeling it glide over our necks and backs, between our toes and through strands of our unwashed hair. We would stay in the pool, swimming back and forth across the length of it underwater until our lungs felt like bursting (Rudy could always hold hers the longest), and doing dives and handstands and flips in the water of the shallow end. At lunchtime we climbed out and sat on the edge of the pool, dangling our feet through the crystal water, droplets streaming out of our hair and down our backs onto the sweltering brick beneath us, and Mrs. Golden would bring us lunch – salami and crackers, blueberry muffins, sliced fruit and homemade potato chips – on individual wooden platters. High school may have been the last time I was comfortable eating in my bikini, or maybe it was only in Rudy's company that I felt a swelling of her abundant self-assuredness seep into me, enough to show off the skin across my stomach, pulled taut over ribs and young muscles. My stomach never swelled over my waistband, never became anything other than a strict, flat line despite how many calories I dumped down into its depths, but sometimes I looked down at my lunch – the soft brown of the muffin's rounded top, speckled with oozing blue lumps – and I imagined it, as my mother would, sitting on top of my own jeans.

Mrs. Golden never ate with us – almost every afternoon she was off to brunch or coffee, at the Country Club or the Ladies Gardening Group, with one of her many housewife friends who kept a schedule almost identical to her own, but a few times Imelda, the Goldens' housekeeper, would have her lunch with us beside the pool. Imelda was fat – much fatter than Mrs. Golden – with an even deeper skin tone and tight, black ringlets of hair she kept pulled back with a bandana while she was cleaning.

"You better be careful, girls, or you'll turn as black as me," Imelda would say, rolling up her linen pant legs and dipping her swollen, red painted toes into the water. I loved the sound of her voice – it always seemed like she was on the verge of bursting into laughter, giggles tucked into the creases between her words.

She teased us about our tans and our floppy, disheveled hair – bunheads, she called us – and she probed us with questions about how we kept the boys away. Rudy always laughed the loudest when Imelda was around, and I envied Imelda's easy-going nature. I wanted to make Rudy laugh like that, to be someone she could be effortlessly comfortable around (although, truthfully, Rudy was effortlessly comfortable with everyone she met – at least it seemed that way to me).

In the afternoons we walked to the country club a few blocks away to play tennis (Rudy always won this too), or we went for long, sweaty jogs around the neighborhood on the afternoons Rudy became antsy and itched to be away from the house. We would fly down the sidewalks, our tennis-shoed feet slapping against the scorched pavement, heat radiating off of our sun-soaked skin. We ran in only our neon sports bras and slick shorts that covered just half of our thighs, and if there had been anyone around to look, Rudy's lithe body and my long, whirling white-blonde ponytail surely would've elicited stares. We always finished our runs with a sprint back up the hill to Rudy's house, and we fell over in the prickly, freshly cut grass, panting up at the blue sky above us. Running was the only thing I discovered that summer I was better at than Rudy. I could run faster and for longer intervals, and I always found I had more breath left in my lungs when we were finished, so running became one of my favorite afternoon activities, despite the deep, sore burn it left in my calf muscles the day afterward. When we caught our breath again, we would jog around to the back of the house, covered in salty sweat and speckled with pieces of grass and dirt from the yard, peel off our bras and socks and shoes and dive into the pool in just our running shorts. I had never, *never* been topless in public before that summer, and the sensation of the cool liquid on my bare chest, the possibility (though very slim, considering the tall white fence that enclosed the Golden property) of a stranger seeing us both thrilled and terrified me. Rudy's father was always irritated when he came home from work and found clumps of soggy grass collecting in the pool, but he never told us in person, just left Rudy notes on the kitchen table before he departed in the morning (over the years I knew him, the years that I practically lived in his home, I came to know Mr. Golden as a reasonable and stoic man – I spoke to him only a handful of times and when he did speak, the words stayed with me for years). Mrs. Golden always brushed off her husband's scolding.

"Don't worry about him, girls," she would write in bubbly cursive underneath her husband's pin straight words. "You're strong, active women! Grass can be cleaned, but don't you ever let go of those beautiful spirits."

———

WE WERE at the country club tennis courts, standing fifty feet apart on opposite sides of the net and dripping with sweat as we finished the final game in our set of five, when we met Ian for the first time. Rudy smacked the ball out of bounds and I ran to chase it toward the fence; when I returned, wiping stinging sweat out of my eyebrows and carrying the fuzzy ball in my clinched fist, she was angling her racket casually toward the concession stand on our far right, nodding her head in his direction. I turned to see him leaning on the counter, watching us. He quickly dropped his gaze the moment we made eye contact, and I did too. I dropped the tennis ball into the pocket of my shorts and met Rudy in the middle of our court.

"Who is that?" I asked her over the net.

She shrugged. "I don't know. But he's been staring at you this whole last game."

My interest piqued, I stole another glance in his direction, but he was still looking down at the supply of snacks beneath the counter of the bar.

"But you don't know who he is?"

"Nope." Rudy twirled her racket in the palm of her hand.

Beside us I heard the thwack of someone's racket connecting with a tennis ball. "Maybe he's new. I've never seen him before."

I considered this. We had spent at least one afternoon each of the past five weeks here and the only concession stand worker we had encountered was a pale, pudgy woman whose clothes were far too tight for her bulging stomach and who often left the snack stand unattended while she snuck off behind it for a smoke break.

"Let's go talk to him," she said, pulling the pink visor off of her head, leaving a thin line an inch above her eyebrows.

We crossed the length of the line of courts but the boy didn't look up until we were standing directly in front of him, underneath the shade of the black and white striped canopy. When he turned toward us I could see that he was jarringly handsome, with short brown curls and deep-set brown eyes.

"Hi," Rudy said, leaning against the counter. "Could I get a Gatorade, please?"

He nodded, then looked toward me.

"I'll just have a bottle of water. Please."

He turned to the refrigerator behind him, and Rudy and I exchanged a glance. She wiggled her eyebrows up and down.

"Thanks," I said as he slid the bottles to us across the white countertop.

"No problem."

"Just put it under Golden, please," Rudy said, twisting the cap off of her bottle and taking a long drink.

"Are you new here?" I asked, swinging my water bottle in my hand. I was suddenly unsure of how to control my arms. "We haven't seen you before."

"No, not really," he said, typing Rudy's name into the computer beside him. "I usually work on the golf range though, but someone called in sick today."

"Oh," I answered dully. I sipped from my water bottle,

unable to follow up my question with anything remotely intelligent.

"What's your name?" Rudy filled in.

"I'm Ian."

"I'm Rudy."

They both looked at me.

"Jillian," I said. "So, do you go to school here?" I felt like a police interrogator. Why couldn't I just hold a simple conversation?

"Yeah, at St. Louis High." There were only two things I knew about St. Louis High school. The first was that it was a public school and the second was that, according to the kids in my eighth grade class, it was the easiest place to score weed.

"Cool," I said. "We start at Ogden this fall. We'll be freshmen."

"So, Ian, are you doing anything later tonight? Some friends bailed on us and we were looking forward to doing something fun," Rudy asked, and I shot her a very blatant look. We had just come over to talk to him, to flirt perhaps, and to leave. I had never intended to follow through on anything, but she was already taking another long drink from her Gatorade and it was apparently up to me to complete the social transaction.

"I get off at six, then I don't really have any plans." His cheeks had turned slightly pink through his tan and he was looking back and forth from me to Rudy.

"Do you want to hang out? We could go see a movie or something?"

"Um, sure." He blushed even deeper. "What's your number? I could call you when I get off work. Maybe at seven or eight or something."

I wrote down my phone number on a little square cocktail napkin and he folded it into fourths and stuck it into the pocket of his khaki shorts.

"We'll see you later tonight, then," Rudy called over her shoulder as we turned to walk away.

"See you tonight," I repeated awkwardly. "Bye."

My arm reached up to wave before I could control it.

He smiled, and his teeth were small and white. His left front tooth was just barely crooked and I wanted to squeeze him for having that one small physical imperfection that made it possible for me to believe that a boy could be interested in me.

"See you later."

WHEN MY PHONE rang at seven thirty that night we told him to meet us at my parents' house, because it would be empty. And we asked him to

bring a friend, to which he happily, even eagerly, obliged. When they arrived, Ian's old Honda slowly rolling down the length of my driveway, Rudy and I were waiting for them outside on the front porch, swinging in the woven hammock beside the front door, our thighs pressed together through our jeans.

"Hi," Rudy called, waving as the boys got out of the car and walked up the sidewalk, both of them with their hands shoved in the pockets of their shorts.

"Hey." Ian looked up at my home behind us. "Nice house."

"Thanks," I said, and I shifted so he could sit next to me in the hammock. It had been unclear to me earlier how we would split into pairs, but now it appeared that because it was my number Ian had been given, it was me who he would sit beside. It was me who he would pursue, though bashfully, judging by the way his face flushed when he sat down and our sides smashed together. Inside, I was drowning in a hot puddle of happiness.

"I'm Jake." His friend, who had a blonde buzzed hair cut and was not nearly as good looking as Ian, remained standing, leaning against the iron railing of the porch.

"My name's Rudy." She didn't get up to shake his hand or hug him, or even to allow him room on the hammock. For a brief second I feared she would revoke her apparent decision to allow me Ian and because his friend was sort of ugly, she would choose Ian for herself instead (because surely, if given the choice, he would pick Rudy over me). But, of course, nothing like that happened at all.

That night we watched a movie in my family's basement, on a television that was so new it had not yet been set up properly (the boys did this while Rudy and I popped popcorn in the basement's small, similarly unused kitchen). The couches were cushy and deep seated and smelled of new leather. Ian and I shared one couch while Rudy lay sprawled across the other and Jake sat by himself in the matching armchair, looking at Rudy nearly as often as he looked at the movie. It appeared Rudy had not intended for this to be a double date at all; she and Jake were only vehicles to aid in the union of Ian and me.

In the middle of the movie – a horror film we selected from my parents' mass library of DVDs – I got cold and Ian offered to get me a blanket, but because it was my house and I was fearful that if left alone to wander in the dark Ian would stumble into my room and find something horribly damning, like a stray pair of dirty underwear or a tube of pimple cream, I was the one who scurried off to find one in the hall closet. When I brought it back and he spread it over both of our laps, his hand accidentally brushed against my knee for a moment – it was warm and clammy with sweat. We both blushed.

The rest of the movie went by in a blur – the important things I would remember were that during a creepy scene, Ian shifted so that his fingers brushed up against my own. A minute later, he wove his fingers through my own with such caution I could actually feel the question within the gesture. I tried to smile at him in response. And at the very end of the movie, when Rudy and Jake were both consumed completely in the unfolding action on the TV, he cleared his throat softly and I turned my head to look up at him and he pecked his lips against mine, my very first real kiss, and the fluttering sensation in my chest lasted the whole rest of the evening.

After the boys left, Rudy and I locked up my house and crossed the street to hers. I was so exhausted and spent by the way I had felt too alert and over-sensitized by all of the physical contact– it was as though each nerve ending that had touched Ian had been charged with enough feeling to fill my entire body – that I knew I would fall asleep the moment I crawled into Rudy's bed.

"So, did he kiss you?" Rudy asked finally, her voice foreign in the stillness of the summer night.

"Yes," I said, and a little smile crept over my face.

"I thought so!" She was squealing now, and she grabbed my wrist in her hand. "At the end of the movie, when that girl was running away? I didn't see it, but you looked so...I don't know, your face looked different when I looked over at you guys."

My heart plummeted and I felt a diluted wave of panic wash over me.

"Great," I said. "So I make weird faces when I'm around guys? Especially when they kiss me?"

Rudy laughed. "No, stupid. You're being ridiculous. You just looked happy. And I could only tell because I know you."

This comment put me at ease – not so much because I felt better about my facial expressions post-making out but because it implied that I had a friend, a real, true friend who knew me.

———

I was just settling into our relaxed summer routine, getting accustomed to another person's constant and welcomed presence in my everyday life, when Rudy threw out the first of many obstacles for me.

It was a Friday morning and we were laying poolside, sprawled out on our stomachs, determined to bronze equally on both sides, though we agreed that laying face down gave us kinks in our necks and made the blood rush to our faces. Our stomachs were full with cream cheese and cinnamon bagels, our bathing suit tops untied and hanging loosely off our shoulders. It was hot that morning, so stifling hot and windless that whole summer. The surface of the pool was completely placid, and I could already feel the skin of my thighs sticking to the navy cloth chair.

"A guy from Ogden is having a party tonight." Rudy turned her face toward me when she spoke, and I opened my eyes a crack to look at her. The woven pattern of the chair had pressed indentations into her cheek.

"Who is it?" I asked, though surely I wouldn't recognize the name.

"Skyler Warren. He's a sophomore."

Panic began to rise in my chest, and my heart rate picked up. There had been so much agonizing change in my life the past year that I feared any deviation from the norm, anything that threatened to rock my fragile boat of sanity.

"Do you want to go?" Rudy asked, politely.

"Okay. Sure," I said slowly.

"It's okay if you don't want to," she said. She was always so accommodating of my feelings, and that fact almost always guaranteed that I would do whatever it was she wanted to do. "It might not be that great anyway."

"No, let's go," I replied quickly. "We haven't really done much yet this summer. I mean, with other people. You know."

"Right. You can invite Ian, too, if you want." Rudy said, then lay her head back down on the chair and closed her eyes again.

I blinked and continued to stare at her face, thoughts swirling in my head. She breathed softly, her nostrils flaring the tiniest amount with each exhale. My heart pounded against my ribcage with increasing speed and my throat felt so constricted I was sure that soon I wouldn't be able to breathe at all.

———

LATER THAT NIGHT, after we had been fed (Mrs. Golden, though exasperated by our insistence, allowed us to have a pepperoni pizza delivered and eat it in Rudy's bedroom), Rudy had dressed me and, per my request, styled my stick straight hair into soft waves resembling her own. We paraded down the stairs in front of Mrs. Golden, who planted her hands on her hips and clucked pleasant admirations at our outfits.

"Oh, Jillian, your hair looks so pretty with that shade of red! And those eyes!" It was the compliments that first made me fall in love with Mrs. Golden.

"Don't they look beautiful, Charlie?" She prodded Mr. Golden, who had come up from the TV den, his man cave, to see us off.

"You both look very nice," he said. He wrapped one arm around Mrs. Golden's shoulders and looked at both his daughter and his wife proudly.

We posed together in front of the huge marble staircase in their (largely unused, I came to discover) formal foyer, our arms placed around the smalls of each other's backs, while Mrs. Golden snapped our photo and grinned at us, her face partially obscured by the camera. I've still got my copy of that first picture we took together, enclosed in a frame that Rudy bought me as a part of my fifteenth birthday present.

"What time is our curfew?" Rudy asked through her smiling teeth as Mrs. Golden took another photo.

"I don't know, Rudy. Who's driving you?" Mrs. Golden lowered the camera from her face and pressed a button to review the photo she'd just taken.

"Can we just take a taxi?" Rudy slipped her feet through the straps of the flat, silver sandals she had set by the foot of the stairs.

At this, Mrs. Golden looked up at Mr. Golden. She returned her gaze to Rudy and her facial features sharpened into a sterner, motherly look. "You know I don't like you out by yourself like that late at night."

"But mom, it's the summer before high school. And it's only a ten minute ride away." Rudy wrapped her thin arms around her mother's neck and lay her head on Mrs. Golden's shoulder. Rudy, even in flats, was already several inches taller than her mother. "Trust me. Trust *us*. Please."

"They'll be fine," Mr. Golden added, giving his wife's shoulder a gentle squeeze.

Mrs. Golden stood contemplating for a few more seconds, but it was obvious that Rudy would have her way. "Fine. Fine, call your taxi. But be *careful*."

"Thanks, mama." Rudy planted a kiss on her mother's cheek and pulled her cell phone from the purse hanging against her left hip.

"And be home by midnight. No later," Mrs. Golden added, and Rudy nodded, the phone already pressed up against her ear.

———

WHEN WE PULLED up to the front of Skyler Warren's house it was clear, even to someone as inexperienced as myself, that the party was already in full effect. Light spilled out from cracks in the thick window draperies, casting yellow lines out across the dark grass. Cars lined the curb – BMWs and other shiny, new cars – parked bumper to bumper, most with navy Ogden Academy parking tags hanging from the rearview mirrors. Ian had agreed to meet us there – we had been on a handful of "dates," from Rudy and I visiting him on his lunch break at the country club to more movie nights at my parents' empty house, but tonight was the first time we would be out together in public. I could make out his shadowed, lanky figure leaning up against the door of his old mustang, punctual as always.

Rudy pushed the taxi door open, and we stepped out onto the sidewalk leading up to the house. Outside in the cooler night air, I could feel the soaking wet armpits of my silky shirt cold against my skin. I pressed my arms into my sides and crossed my forearms over my body. I felt even more out of place than I had inside the stale, smoky, yellow cab.

Ian met us at the open gate and as we approached the front door I could feel the throb of the music against the soles of my feet through my shoes. He let out a low whistle, gazing up at the face of the house. "This place is freaking huge."

I felt my cheeks go warm.

"You can stay with me, if you want to," Rudy said, combing a dark wave of hair away from her eyes with two fingers. "I don't know everyone, either."

I nodded; the lump in my throat had grown so large that I felt it would

be difficult to speak.

She pushed open the right side of the huge double doors, and we followed her into the crowded foyer. It was my first glimpse inside another Ogden student's house and while I would never whistle, I wasn't unimpressed. The walls were papered with an elegant scrollwork pattern stretching all the way up to the vaulted ceiling twenty feet above my head.

Creamy marble covered the floor and a burgundy and teal embroidered rug was spread in the center of the entryway. It looked old – *antique* – and expensive. I watched as a boy stepped back onto the rug, his shoe grinding chunks of mud into one of the embroidered roses. He didn't seem to notice.

The room was packed – dozens of kids pressed up against one another as they stood talking loudly over the pounding music, clutching red plastic cups in their hands. The girls wore jeans like mine, with the same meticulous stitching on the back pockets, the same distressed holes gaping over their knees. Hanging from their tanned shoulders they wore neon halter tops or pastel polos with a little animal embroidered beside the buttons –usually a horse. I took a mental note.

Rudy pushed her way through the crowd that was semi-circled around the door, leading with one arm and pulling me along with the other until we had reached the threshold of another room. In the kitchen were a handful of guys crowded around a center island, where a boy in a button down shirt and backwards baseball cap was manning a beer keg. Puddles of spilled beer speckled the granite countertop at random, like landmines on a battlefield.

On the opposite side of the enormous kitchen was another circle of kids packed around a long wood table watching two pairs of boys lobbing a ping-pong ball into more red plastic cups across from them.

"Rudy Golden?" I barely heard someone shout her name. I turned my head away from the game. It was the boy with the keg who had called out to Rudy.

"Hey!" Rudy yelled, stepping closer to him. I followed so closely behind her I could smell the hint of shampoo in her hair. He wrapped her in a one armed hug, their sides smashed together for the briefest of seconds before they both pulled away. "This is my friend Jillian. She just moved here last year. And her boyfriend, Ian."

This close – standing just inches from his face – I could see this boy was very good looking, with dark eyes and dark hair and a sprinkle of freckles across the bridge of his nose. My heart pounded; it didn't help that without prior discussion, Rudy had called Ian my boyfriend.

"Hey, Jillian. Ian. I'm Skyler." He nodded.

"Nice to meet you," I yelled, my voice ringing strange in my own ears.

"You guys want a beer?"

Rudy glanced at me and I arranged my face in a way that I hoped conveyed ambivalence.

"Do you have anything else?" Rudy asked.

"Nope, not tonight." Skyler shook his head and smiled. "It's beer or bring your own. Sorry, ladies."

"Beer's okay then," Rudy said, and he filled three cups with foamy liquid and handed them to us.

"Thanks," I said, gazing down into my cup.

"Oh, none for me, actually." Ian held up his palms to ward off the proffered cup of beer. "I have to drive later."

"A responsible one, huh?" Skyler clapped him on the shoulder. "Most of these drunk idiots are just planning to crash in my basement. Where do you go to school, man?"

"St. Louis High. I'm working at the country club golf course this summer, though. That's where we all met."

"You go to High, huh?" Skyler paused then held out his cup exaggeratedly, as if to cheers then took a big gulp. "Go Rams."

Ian thrust his hands into his jeans pockets and looked down.

"We'll see you later on." Rudy squeezed Skyler's forearm and took a small sip from her cup before leading us down carpeted stairs and into a large basement, far less crowded than the floor above us. A different song was playing on this level, at a slightly lower volume, and a group of girls was dancing together in the corner. A few guys sat on cushy leather couches. The television was turned off and they weren't speaking to one another, just staring very obviously at the dancers as they slithered around to the music.

Sometimes, at fourteen especially, I thought that the easiest thing in the world would be to be a man. Being a girl required so much showmanship – you had to buy the right clothes, you had to wear the right makeup, you had to impress the other girls but you couldn't be too impressive, lest they decide you were someone to envy. You had to give the right compliments in public and the right insults in private. You had to always long for something you didn't have. And you had to play the game, or you risked becoming something worse than being enviable or disliked – being unknown completely.

But boys could be crude, they could be lazy or stupid or ugly or fat, and they could still be loved and respected. They said what they thought, and they asked for what they wanted. They fought with their fists and then they slapped one another on the back and forgot what they had been fighting about in the first place. They stared at the girls they wanted, and then they got them.

"Do you like beer?" Rudy leaned in close to my face to ask me.

"I don't know," I admitted, lifting the cup close to my nose.

"Don't smell it," Ian said. "You definitely won't want to drink it after you smell it."

I tipped the cup up to my mouth and took in a mouthful. It was bitter and the color reminded me of urine. I struggled not to grimace.

"This is disgusting," I said, and Rudy and Ian laughed.

"I know. I'm still getting used to it. My brother used to dare me to finish his beers when he had friends over, so I got a head start."

Rudy had two older siblings, both old enough that they had moved out of their parents' house. I hadn't met either of them yet, (her sister, Marta, was spending the summer at an internship in New York City and her brother, Kent, was a freshman in college, living on campus for the summer and retaking a prerequisite calculus class because, Rudy had told me, his grade was bringing down his GPA, which he needed to improve if he wanted to get into a decent law program three years from now), but I heard about them constantly from Mr. and Mrs. Golden. When Rudy had given me a grand tour of their home the first week I was there, I had seen pictures of them hanging in the large hallway between the formal foyer and the dining room. Rudy had called it her parents' trophy room, and she had rolled her eyes in fake exasperation as we passed through. But a few times in the past weeks I had found myself drawn to that hallway, fascinated. There were pictures of Mr. and Mrs. Golden's wedding, when Mrs. Golden's waist was nearly as tiny as Rudy's, and a family portrait of the five of them when Rudy was only three or four, dressed in a poofy black dress and patent leather buckled shoes. There were photos of her siblings' high school accomplishments and thick shadow boxes full of medals they had won. Kent had been a wrestler in high school and I was shocked to discover that he was also quite handsome; I thought the two were mutually exclusive. And Marta, who was beautiful but very serious looking, was president of the student council and debate teams. Finally, there were photos of them in cap and gown, grinning at their high school graduations. I couldn't explain what drew me to that hall, but something about the memories encapsulated there filled me with a warm feeling.

"I'm going to need a lot of practice," I said, taking another large gulp of beer, this time while holding my breath, hoping I wouldn't taste it.

Rudy clinked my cup with her own and drank as well.

The three of us mingled amongst the kids in the basement, and most of them seemed to know who Rudy was even though a lot of them were a year or two older than us. I wasn't surprised that Rudy attracted more attention from the boys than the girls. The boys always touched her, wrapping her in big hugs to greet her or resting their hands on the small of her back, or on her waist, and leaning in even closer than necessary when she spoke to them. In contrast, the girls didn't approach Rudy; some of them looked at her through sideways glances and whispered to their friends when Rudy wasn't watching. But she handled all of it with grace, easing away from the boys when they clung to her too tightly, and smiling kindly when another girl looked her way.

When we had both finished our beers I felt slightly light-headed, my face flushed with heat while I stood awkwardly beside Rudy, fiddling with the lip of my cup while she talked to another polo-clad guy beside us. Ian was across the room, playing a game of darts with two other boys, and I watched them with bored eyes. I felt an odd swelling of pride when he said something that made the other guys laugh, and I wondered if this was what it felt like to be half of a pair – your partner's social wins were your wins, and their social missteps your own as well.

"Hey," I heard someone say, and I ignored it because it obviously wasn't meant for me.

"Hey." This time I felt fingers grasp my arm, though not harshly, and I turned toward the voice. "Have I met you before?"

The voice belonged to a guy with shaggy brown hair that hung down to his eyebrows. He was very tall, and he stooped over a little to speak to me. His breath was sour.

"I don't think so," I said.

"What's your name?"

"Jillian."

"Jillian," he repeated, without giving me his own name. "I'll remember that." He grinned a toothy grin and his eyes slipped quickly from my face down to my chest and back up again. Gross.

Someone walking past knocked into his arm and beer sloshed over the rim of his cup and splashed onto my jeans. I jumped back, and Rudy turned.

"Oh, no." She glanced at the wet stain spreading across my thigh.

"Shit. I didn't mean to." The guy lunged toward me, stooping over to wipe at the wet spot with bottom of his shirt. I could see the coarse brown hair around his belly button and my cheeks flushed bright red.

"It's okay." I pulled my leg away out of his predatory grasp.

"Don't worry about it," Rudy swatted him away. She met my gaze. "Let's go get refills."

"Sorry." The guy stood as we turned to leave. I couldn't meet his eyes. I waved, limply.

We pulled Ian away from his darts game and fled up the staircase into the kitchen. This time Skyler was gone, and Rudy began to refill our cups herself. The foyer had cleared and from the kitchen I had a clear view of the front door as it swung open and three guys in baggy jeans and long t-shirts walked in, their eyes scanning the crowd as they stepped into the room. The first boy was tall and slender, his jeans hanging low on his hipbones, exposing green plaid boxers. He wore his hat backwards over thick black hair and cold black eyes. The second boy was shorter and squattier, with a stern brown buzz cut and a matching fuzzy mustache. The third guy was black, and he carried an open beer can in one hand, pausing in the doorway to swig from the top. There were two girls in the foyer and they turned as the door slammed shut. Both girls gave them a once-over and immediately turned to walk into the kitchen. The guy with the hat smirked as he watched them go.

"Who are they?" I nudged Rudy.

She handed me my cup, now full and cool against my fingers, and she peered into the foyer. "I don't know. Not from Ogden."

"I've seen those guys around school," Ian added. "Or at least I used to – I think they dropped out or got expelled."

They walked past us toward the kitchen and the plaid boxers guy stopped and tipped his chin up in Ian's direction. "I seen you before, man."

Ian blushed. "Yeah. Yeah, I go to school with you."

The guy kept walking. "Shit, man," I heard him say as he disappeared into the kitchen crowd. "You traded up."

Ian and I followed Rudy into what I presumed was the living room and we all squeezed onto one open cushion on a crowded leather couch. I drank my second beer much faster, my taste buds slightly numbed, and I took in the activity around us with wide, attentive eyes. In the corner of the room was a grand piano and two girls with straight blonde hair sat pressed against each other on the shiny black bench, all twenty of their fingers dancing sloppily across the ivory keys. A boy stood beside them holding two cups in his hands and waving his arms like a music maestro, spilling beer on the floor, the girls and the piano, though none of them seemed to care much. I couldn't hear their performance over the music that blared from the ceiling speakers but judging by the faces of those sitting nearest to the piano, it couldn't have sounded good.

Though it was stifling outside and hot inside the house, someone lit a fire in the fireplace and several boys were throwing their empty red cups into the flames, prodding at the mound of melting, oozing plastic with the end of the fire poker.

The couch shifted as the boy beside us stood up and left. His spot was quickly filled by a couple. The girl leaned her head against the boy's gingham-clad chest and he leaned his face down to hers. They started kissing, his sloppy lips on her pretty pink mouth. I turned away from them quickly and finished the rest of my beer staring down into my own lap, feeling sticky and claustrophobic and awkward. Ian's arm was resting across my shoulders on the back of the couch and I could feel his body pushing closer against mine. 'Not here,' I wanted to say. 'Not in front of them!' I leaned close to Rudy, my hair falling like a curtain across our faces.

"I think I need to go to the bathroom." I had been holding it since we arrived. Wasn't there some saying about breaking the seal? Regardless, I feared leaving physical evidence of myself in the house.

"Are you feeling sick? I'll come with you," Ian stood and helped me off the couch.

But on the way there we got lost, circling the main floor twice and still unable to find a bathroom.

"Let's just go upstairs," Rudy said, finally. "It's not a big deal."

She led the way up the stairs, past poster-size portraits of the Warren family. Mrs. Warren was thin and pale and sour looking. Mr. Warren had a thick beard and red cheeks. I wondered what they would think when they came home to stained carpets and plastic mounds in their pretty fireplace.

At the top of the staircase a marble hallway split in two directions. There were five doorways; three were open and led to bedrooms, as neat and tidy as guest rooms in a fancy hotel. The remaining two doors were closed.

"We'll check this one." Ian nodded toward the closed door at the far end of the hallway.

Rudy turned in the opposite direction and Ian wove his fingers through mine and led me down the hallway. His other hand reached out; his fingers closed around the gold door knob and he turned it. The room was dark, lit only by a desk lamp in the corner of the room, but right away all of their faces whipped toward where we stood frozen in the open doorway. The non-Ogden boy – the one with the sleazy mustache and buzz cut – was slipping a small plastic baggy into Skyler Warren's hand. Skyler jerked in surprise at our intrusion, and the bag fell to the ground, spilling half of its powdery white contents onto the plush carpet.

"Fuck." The mustache guy ripped his arm away. "That was you man, that was all you."

At the same time, one of his friends, the black friend, pointed at us, eyes narrowed. "Who the fuck's that?"

I couldn't speak. All I could do was stare, mortified, as Skyler dove to the floor in a desperate attempt to scoop up the escaped powder as it sifted through the carpet threads. Another Ogden boy dropped to the floor to help him.

"Who the fuck's these clowns," the friend repeated, his brown and tan index finger burning a hole in the middle of my chest from ten feet across the room.

Skyler looked up from where he kneeled on the floor, and our stunned eyes met for the briefest second before he turned to Ian. He stood and stepped toward him, their chests a few inches apart. Skyler's bloodshot brown eyes narrowed.

"What the hell, man." He shoved the middle of Ian's chest with an open palm and Ian tripped backwards, his face red and naked with surprise. "I know you're from the hood but don't you know what a goddamn closed door means?"

"What the fuck do you know about the hood, rich boy?"

Mustache guy shoved Skyler in the back and I watched in horror as Skyler toppled forward, knocking Ian over onto the carpet and landing on top of him with a thud. Ian struggled beneath Skyler's weight, his legs flailing as he tried to stand.

Before I could think about it, before anything more mortifying could happen, I was stumbling backwards out the doorway and slamming the door shut behind me. I ran down the hall, my fallen curls whipping against my back. I ran straight into Rudy as she stepped into the hallway, colliding against her side. Her elbow jabbed into my bladder.

"I found the bathroom." She gestured behind us.

"We have to leave."

She cocked her head to the side, her eyebrows drawn together. "What about Ian?"

Before she could say another word I had grabbed her wrist and started dragging her down the stairs.

"Jillian?" Her voice was muffled by blood pounding in my ears. At the bottom of the staircase I pushed through the crowd, clearing a path to the front door and out onto the porch. I didn't turn around until I had pulled her all the way out onto the sidewalk in front of Skyler Warren's house. I dropped her hand. Mine was clammy and warm.

"What happened? Are you okay?"

I nodded. My throat was dry. "Will you call the cab?"

"Okay."

She punched in a phone number, shooting worried glances in my direction while she repeated the Warrens' address into the speaker. I glanced back toward the house, half expecting to find all five of them chasing after me, but of course they weren't. A rush of relief washed over me, followed immediately by a smothering blanket of embarrassment. How could I have left Ian in there? Why had I brought him here in the first place? Why had I acted so stupid?

When I glanced back again, Ian was walking out the front door. I was shaking, my heart in my throat as he walked across the lawn toward us. I couldn't look up to meet his gaze – what if he had a black eye or a bloody nose or some other physical representation of my horrendous mistake? He stopped just in front of me. His black Converse sneakers were wet with dew or maybe with spilled beer.

"Can I talk to you?"

I nodded. I still couldn't manage to look up from the ground as I followed him toward his car.

He unlocked the passenger door and the interior lights flipped on as he held it open for me. I ducked my head and climbed in. It smelled like peppermint and men's body spray; a half empty bottle of Mountain Dew sat in one of the cup holders while the other was occupied by a handful of loose change. He walked around the front of the car to the driver's side and I glanced up for the first time while his face was turned away from me. It was dark and I could see him only in profile, but he didn't appear to be gravely injured.

He opened the driver's side door, and I stared at my hands as he got into his seat. This was the first time I had been in his car. He had come to my house several times that summer, but he had never driven me anywhere, and now it seemed clear he never would. I could feel him looking at me but I couldn't speak, and I picked idly at a chip in my thumbnail polish until the lights finally went off after an agonizingly long period of time. I waited patiently for him to yell at me, to acknowledge how badly I'd treated him, to deliver my first post-party break up speech on a platter laced with spilled cocaine. He had been a good first boyfriend, a boy to have my first kiss with, but we should have known it would never work.

"Hey," he said finally. He wanted me to look up at him, and I did. "I'm really sorry about what happened in there."

I was taken aback. "But I'm the one who left you in there. Aren't you mad?"

"Well yeah, that wasn't great, but you were scared." He reached across the console and took my hand. "I get it. I'm sorry I got you into that mess."

"It's okay," I found myself accepting his apology, bewildered.

"So you're okay? We're okay?"

"It's okay," I repeated, and he leaned over and pressed his mouth against mine. It seemed the subject was closed. All was forgiven; all would go on. That was a good thing, right?

I didn't realize my hand was still limp in his until he squeezed my fingers, and I remembered I should hold his hand in return.

———

WHILE RUDY and I waited for the taxi, I told her the whole excruciating story. My face was bright red; I could feel it as it smoldered. At the end of my recounting, she wrapped her arms around my shoulders and pulled me into a bear hug.

"Don't worry about it too much. Skyler's a nice guy – I've known him since we were kids. He'll forget about it."

"But *I* won't forget." I looked down at my lap. "This was the first party I've ever been to, and I embarrassed myself in front of everyone."

"Can I tell you something?" Her voice got softer and she gave me an extra squeeze before she pulled away. "This is my first real party, too."

I looked at her then, in case she was joking.

"Why didn't you tell me that before?"

Rudy shrugged and smiled a small smile. "I just wanted you to think I was cool."

"You could have told me," I said.

We were both quiet. The house thumped behind us, and someone deep inside let out a girly squeal.

"At least Ian forgave you. He's a really cool guy, you know."

"Yeah," I said.

"It's ten past midnight," Rudy looked at her watch as a yellow car pulled up to the curb. "My parents will probably be up waiting. That's what they always used to do with Kent and Marta."

Inside the taxi I wallowed in all sorts of self-indulgent guilt. I remembered the baggy falling over and over again, Skyler's face as he looked at Ian with disdain and Ian's soft-voiced apology as we sat together in his car. And now the dread of Mrs. Golden's disappointment was compounding my guilt. I could see her, her gold-bangled arms crossed over her ample chest, worry lines creasing her forehead, watching out the front window for our safe return. I could see Mr. Golden, silent and serious, his mouth an angry straight line. I imagined being grounded to their house (which, truthfully, would be no punishment at all, especially considering the new discovery that I couldn't handle myself in public). Mostly I hoped they wouldn't see me as a bad influence on their daughter.

But when the taxi driver pulled up in front of the Goldens', all of the windows on the face of the house were black. Mr. and Mrs. Golden had gone to bed without waiting up for us.

I LEARNED SO many things about Rudy that summer, and about how to live in a world of privilege, but the thing that struck me the hardest was that Rudy lived only in extremes. I saw her either fresh-faced and damp-haired from the shower or the pool, sauntering around the house in her pajamas bottoms or a pair of jean shorts, or she was styled like a magazine spread, pink gloss on her lips and eye shadow sweeping over the crease of her eyelids, hair cascading in beautiful curls down her back. There were mornings she would sleep past noon, when I couldn't wake her no matter how hard I prodded, and I ate breakfast alone in their quiet kitchen, listening to the sounds of Imelda's heavy breathing as she lumbered around the house with her dustpan and broom, and other mornings Rudy would be awake as soon as the sun popped up above the horizon. She would jump on top of me, straddling my waist, and dig her fingers into my sides, tickling me until I screamed for mercy. Some days she loved every tiny thing about her life, from the extra marshmallows gracing her bowl of Lucky Charms to the name her parents had given her to the way a white-haired angel had stumbled into her life (she once called me this, in those exact words). It was those days I cherished the most, hoarding them in a secret place in my heart until the time I knew I would need to retrieve them, when I had to move back into my own home upon my parents' return from Europe (they called me once every week, and we spoke for fifteen or twenty minutes, mostly about the castles they had seen, or the spectacular food and wine they had eaten and drunk, and I indulged my mother's need for approval, for envy from her own daughter even, by ooh-ing and ah-ing at all the appropriate moments). The Goldens were so sweet; the loving, caring family of my dreams, leaving one another sweet notes on the whiteboard of the refrigerator, sharing a leisurely family dinner at least once per week, the three of them (plus me) seated around one end of the eight person table, bumping elbows while they all reached for the same bowl of pasta. I received hugs from Mrs. Golden every time I saw her – despite how greasy I was with suntan lotion or sweat – and kisses on my cheeks before we went out, leaving the faint hint of her orangey-red lipstick on my face so that I had to scrub it away before we could leave. It was these casual displays of affection that impressed me the most – the ability to love your family, to physically show them love, even while no one important was watching.

But on rare occasions, often when I least saw it coming, Rudy would wake up filled with a displeasure that I now assume simmered continually far beneath her surface. She would shrug off all the activities of our daily routine, refuse to consume anything but coffee for breakfast and brood until the afternoon when she would finally concoct some insane plan for our day, and her mood would brighten in a way that wasn't quite normal but sparked with some flavor of sinister beauty. Once, she decided we would hitchhike across the state to Kansas City and I went along with it because Rudy was her most convincing in this mood and because I was still afraid that to disagree with her, to deny her what she wanted, would be to lose her as my best friend. So we left her house on foot and walked until we were near enough to the highway, and we stood at an empty intersection (thank God we at least had the presence of mind to avoid impeding on a corner already occupied by a homeless man with a crumpled cardboard sign) and waited, with our thumbs jutting out toward the street (we were undecided on whether or not this was still necessary, but ultimately concluded that if we were hitchhiking, then we were playing it by the rules). After half an hour in the bright sun with the heat of car engines and the smell of exhaust permeating into our skin, a half hour of receiving concerned or predatory or unsure glances from each person who drove past, a man in his late twenties or early thirties stopped and let us into his truck. We rode the entire four hours with him, Rudy in the front seat and me in the back, my heart beat pounding within my chest the whole time. Each time he moved, to turn up the radio or to redirect the airflow from the vents on the dashboard, my heart would seize up and I would be sure, with every fiber of my being, that this was the moment he was going to pull out a knife and kill us. But he didn't and Rudy talked to him the whole long ride – about his hobbies, his girlfriend, the small town where he grew up – until we arrived on the opposite side of the state, in a neighborhood foreign to us both. We got out of the car in front of a Starbucks and my legs felt like jelly holding up the weight of my body. We both ordered cold drinks, used the bathroom, then returned to the I-70 on ramp to hitch a ride back. For our second trip we traveled with an older woman, her grey hair in a long, thin braid that stretched down her back, and she didn't speak much. By the time we arrived home the sky was a deep black, scattered all over with the pinpricks of gleaming white stars. Mrs. Golden asked us what we had been up to all day, and we told her we had gone to my house to watch movies, and she believed us, or at the very least, she pretended that she did.

———

THROUGHOUT THE REST of the summer I went out with Ian a few more times but it didn't last, and I think, in my gut, I knew the whole time it wouldn't. He was nice, kinder than my idea of a typical high school boy, and he made it easy to talk to him about things, like my family and my life in Boston. And he never, ever compared me to Rudy, which is one of the characteristics I now most deeply appreciate about him, and that I wish I had recognized at the time.

Physically, things never got past the stage of making out, sprawled awkwardly on the couch in my basement, both of us lying on our sides, our knees and arms jabbing each other in the side or shin while we kissed. Once he had placed a clumsy hand on the zipper of my shorts but before I could stop myself I had recoiled back, and he must have noticed because he never tried again.

One night at the beginning of August, as we were standing on my porch, surrounded by the deep, warm quiet of a late summer evening, I told him I thought it would be better if we just remained friends. He looked at me inquisitively, his thick, straight eyebrows scrunched together. In the dark it was hard to read his face. When he asked me why, I told him we were going to different high schools in a couple of weeks. It would be hard to stay together. And plus, I had added, weren't there girls at his school he'd probably fit better with?

It took a few moments, the two of us standing awkwardly a few feet apart, my arms crossed over my chest and his dangling at his sides, before a look of comprehension dawned in his eyes. He nodded once and I could see, in the firm line of his mouth, that though he may not have agreed, he understood – he *got* it. I had a lump in my throat as I watched him walk out to his car and drive away without saying anything else.

His phone number remained in my phone until I finally had the strength to delete it during my junior year of high school, but we never spoke again.

———

On August 20th the hours of our last summer afternoon ticked by as Rudy and I lay next to the pool, soaking in the last drops of sun, our bodies swollen with heat and our skin browned and greasy like rolls fresh out of the oven. We had resolved to lay out as long as we could, our last time before school began and brought with it the chill of fall, but the day was so blazing hot I couldn't imagine it ever being cold again. By three in the after-noon we were sweat-soaked and couldn't stand the heat any longer, and we dragged ourselves into the house and stumbled into the formal foyer where we sprawled out on our backs underneath the huge chandelier, possibly my favorite feature in the Golden house, an intricate mass of gold and crystal that hung high from the ceiling three stories above us. The cold granite floor pressed into my pores like ice and I could hear blood thumping at my temples as air-conditioned air rushed into my lungs, filling my chest as it expanded and contracted. The glittering pieces of the chandelier overhead blacked in and out of view. I glanced over at Rudy lying beside me. Her eyes were closed and her lips slightly parted; the tendons in her neck lay slack, and though she was only a foot away from me, I was confident Rudy belonged to a world vastly different than my own. More than anything else, I wanted to be in that place too.

2
———

FRESHMAN FALL

In Boston I went to an all girls Catholic school where the most well-liked girls played 6th grade basketball and there was no such thing as a cheerleading squad. But when I moved to St. Louis, because virtually all movies about high school portray cheerleaders as popular and pretty – the ideal embodiment of all that the quintessential high school girl wants to be – and because I was, at that point, still very naïve, I convinced Rudy to try out for football cheerleading our freshman year. We were bad – too inflexible to be good at toe touches and too weak to be good bases for stunting – but somehow, when the final lists were posted, we found we had made the JV squad along with two other freshman girls and a handful of sophomores and juniors. Initially, I was ecstatic (and so was my mother, a former college cheerleader with the old uniforms hanging in the back of her closet to prove it), and the feeling lasted for days – until our first official practice.

Cheerleading, it turned out, was not all I had hoped it would be. We had practice for an hour and a half every day after school and because the volleyball team used the gymnasium for their own practice, we were forced into the floor-to-ceiling windowed lobby between the locker rooms and the gym. Intermittently throughout practice boys would walk by, gawking at us while we jumped and shouted. Often (only if it was a group of boys, never one boy on his own) they would yell things or whistle and Rudy and I would turn our heads and get distracted by their handsome smiles or their boyish hair flipping and Kendell, the Varsity cheerleading captain, would scold us for our inattention.

Kendell was a senior and she was short and muscular and pretty, with blonde hair that kinked naturally into tight spiral curls (and when she ironed it straight, it was nearly three inches longer than normal and she looked like a completely different person). And Kendell was, for lack of a better word, an enormous, intimidating bitch. Both JV and Varsity practiced together and Kendell spent the entire hour and a half berating the underclassmen on the squad – singling us out to do jumps, making us recite all of the words to the school fight song, at top volume, often in pairs or all alone – and being especially cruel when boys from the football team would walk past on their way to the football field. Once she made Natalie, a quiet junior who despite trying out every year was still on the JV squad, hold the splits until she cried and two other girls had to usher her into the bathroom so she could regain her composure. It seemed like Rudy was the only girl on the squad who wasn't completely terrified of Kendell, and because of this, Kendell hated her. By association I could tell that she hated me too (though not with the same passion – a watered down, residual form of hate). What she didn't know – what none of the other girls on the cheerleading squad, who all thought I was as fearless and stubborn as Rudy knew – was that in reality, defying Kendell petrified me. When she called out my name, my heart would lurch in my chest, though I willed it to stop. When Kendell's back was turned, as she was teaching us the moves to a dance or taking a drink from her water bottle during a break, Rudy would catch my attention and make faces at me, mocking Kendell's drill sergeant gestures. Sometimes the other girls would see her and laugh. I always smiled back at Rudy when she did her impressions though I lived in silent, paralyzing fear that one day Kendell would turn around and catch us.

Aside from suffering under Kendell's dictator-like captainship, cheerleading was hard. I wasn't good at remembering the dance steps, my arms shook when I was basing a stunt and practices made me tired and cranky, yet unsatisfied, unlike how I felt after a long, tiring run. The best part of cheerleading, perhaps its only saving grace, was that we got to ride the football boys' bus to all of the away football games with the junior and senior boys. Rudy and I always shared a seat, and we always ran to the front of the line to board the bus so that we could sit as close to the back as possible (the football team sat at the back of the bus and the cheerleaders in the front with the football coaches). This was yet another thing that seemed to irk Kendell, who sometimes tried to sabotage our efforts by putting us in charge of carrying the heavy bags of pom poms, thus ensuring we would be the last girls on the bus and would have to sit beside the hairy, grim-faced coaches. Rudy endured it like a champion. On those nights we would sit cross-legged in the front seat of the bus, hunched over a piece of paper that Rudy held between us, playing games to predict which guys we might marry and the cities where we would live. But Kendell had a vendetta. One afternoon, cursed by the gods of high school misfortune, I jammed my school locker, inside which sat my cheerleading shoes, and to go to practice without the appropriate shoes was a first-degree offense in Kendell's book. Rudy and I yanked at the metal handle of my locker, spinning the combination over and over again in frustration. Finally Rudy shoved a pen into the edge of the door and managed to pry it open and we hurried down to the sports lobby while the squad was in the middle of stretching.

"You're late," Kendell yelled, and my face burned bright red.

"I'm sorry." Rudy glanced at my beet red cheeks then shrugged her shoulders. "I couldn't find my socks."

I avoided eye contact with Kendell because it actually caused me physical stomach pain, but Rudy stared her dead in the face while Kendell's lip twitched in fury. The rest of the girls raised their heads from their knees to watch the feud between the fierce captain and the fearless freshman.

"Go run laps," she said. "Around the entire school. You too, Jillian." I was, of course, an afterthought.

Five times over the three-month-long football season we were sent to run laps around the campus, first two, then three, then four, but it never fazed Rudy, or me for that matter, at least not once we were out of Kendell's presence. We would talk while we jogged, cursing Kendell and her "hillbilly Southern accent" (she had moved from Texas the year before she started at Ogden) or the ridiculous, over-sized navy bows she wore in her hair on game days, and when we ran past the football field some of the guys would turn to look at us, and we would smile and wave and speed up a bit as long as they were still watching us, and all of these little things made running seem to me a reward, not a punishment.

———

BOYS WERE ALWAYS DRAWN to Rudy, obviously because she was beautiful, but also, I think, because there was a part of her personality that appealed so strongly to them. She was like them in a way – confident, sporty and honest – and unlike the other beautiful girls at Ogden, Rudy's allure was uncomplicated. She didn't need make up or fancy clothes – she was just as remarkable in a t-shirt as she was in a formal gown. I think the most important element was that she *knew* this, which was something most teenage girls, me included, could not be convinced of regarding their own looks. So it was Rudy, the freshman girl in her jeans and hooded sweatshirts, who attracted sidelong glances from all the boys in the school. They were always coming up to her in the hallway between classes, throwing one bulky arm over her thin shoulders and pulling her into their chests in a way that was both crude and boyishly charming. They would smile at her and shout down the hall when they were too far away to touch her, and they would offer us rides home from school. That whole first year of high school, before either of us could drive, Rudy and I never needed to take the bus or walk (though sometimes we did it anyway, just because we wanted to). To my great surprise, some of the older boys would talk to me as well. They would tease me the same way they teased Rudy, rubbing their open palms on the top of my head to mess up my hair or coming up behind me in the hall and picking me up off my feet when I wasn't expecting it. I was in awe, in pure delight, just to have so many boys (good looking boys too, as many of the boys at Ogden were) around me. Rudy enjoyed it too. She was always happy at school. Particularly, I learned in late October of that year, in the company of Houston Jones, the junior quarterback for the football team.

It seems weird to describe a boy as beautiful, but that's the word that always came to my mind when I saw Houston. He was tall, with dark hair and sinewy muscles that popped up when he flexed his biceps or when he threw a long pass to one of his receivers. He had big, straight, white teeth and the longest eyelashes I had ever seen on a boy. I thought he was doing a disservice to Ogden girls, wasting so much of his time covering up his handsome face with a football helmet, but to each his own, right?

We were at a home football game, standing on the sideline in our short white skirts and tops emblazoned with "Ogden" across the chest in thick, navy letters, and instead of watching the game, I was paying attention to how, because it was already dark out, the lights on the field bounced off of my pom poms, which lay on the ground in front of my feet. For the most part I found football to be utterly boring. But something had happened – apparently, we had scored – and suddenly everyone in the stands was on their feet, stomping the bleachers and clapping their hands and shouting until all the noise combined into one low rumble. I grabbed my poms off of the ground and thrust them into the air in my fists, and I kicked and cheered along with the other nine girls in formation around me. As the noise died down, Rudy leaned toward me.

"What do you think about Houston?"

"Houston Jones?" I was confused. I looked out toward the field, where he was standing with several other players huddled around him, mud and grass clumps streaked across one of his shoulders.

"Do you know any other Houstons?"

I did not. "Like, in general?"

"Sure," Rudy answered.

I shrugged. "I don't know. Why?"

"He asked me to the Fall Ball yesterday."

The first thing I felt, before I felt surprised, was deeply hurt that she had waited a full day to tell me. "Seriously? What did you say?"

"I haven't answered him yet," Rudy said. "But I think I'm going to say yes. Why not?" She smiled, hopefully.

Before I could answer, one of the girls began a cheer, and Rudy and I both sprung into action as though someone had flipped a switch to activate us, swinging our arms in unison with the other girls.

The Fall Ball was Ogden's fall semester equivalent to the prom, though it wasn't quite as formal. It would be held on a Saturday night, two weeks away, and I had not yet been asked. Rudy and I had talked about it, about who we'd like to go with and how we would wear our hair, but it had not seemed imperative that we secure dates yet – not real, live ones anyway. We still had weeks to think about that. Now, with the dance two weeks away and Rudy with not just a date, but one of the most coveted dates in the school, I felt cold panic start to settle against my chest. It remained there and grew throughout the rest of the football game, and when we won and the girls went wild, I waved my arms but was unable to yell, my throat constricted with anxiety.

———

THERE'S little to say about how the Fall Ball turned out other than to note I found a date (one of Houston's friends from the football team), and I was extremely nervous and, as a result, drank too much at the party afterward. As a whole, it was fairly uneventful. The most interesting thing about the Fall Ball was that it created a deeper and more significant layer of loathing between Kendell and Rudy because, apparently, Kendell had a crush on Houston too. This we discovered when we were both left off the guest list for the end-of-the-season cheerleading sleepover at Kendell's house and Deena, one of the other freshman girls on the squad, called us from the sleepover, put her phone on speaker and we hunched over the other end of the line and listened in as Kendell ranted about Rudy – about how she had only made the squad because her sister had been the coach's favorite student, how Rudy was so skinny it was almost disgusting, you could almost see her ribs and her shoulder blades poking through her skin, how the boys only talked to her because they thought she was a naive, easy slut and how Houston Jones would break up with her as soon as she slept with him because that was all he was after with her anyway. We didn't get to hear the entirety of the conversation but we heard enough, and when the phone line went blank we looked up to meet one another's eyes. Mine were wide and incredulous; hers were narrowed. Thank God, I had thought, football season was over and we were free from cheerleading, free from Kendell's company.

"What a bitch," Rudy had said, her voice small and injured.

"I can't believe she'd say that about you," I added.

"I'm kind of surprised, too," she said softly. She flipped her phone shut and slid it across the carpet. "But whatever. It doesn't matter – she can think what she wants."

This was true; she wasn't just saying it. I believed Rudy literally took nothing negative to heart, not that I could see. We were silent for a few seconds, sitting on the carpet in her bedroom, staring at the phone several feet away from us now.

"I have to go home tonight," I said, finally, looking at my watch. "My mom wants me to play tennis with her early tomorrow morning."

"Let's watch a movie before you leave. And ice cream sundaes?"

My stomach growled beneath my sweatshirt. "Oh my God, you read my mind."

———

THAT AUTUMN WAS ALSO the first time I met Rudy's sister, Marta, and her brother, Kent. The week of Ogden's five day Thanksgiving break (private high schools, I discovered after I went off to college, were also blessed with longer breaks than most public schools), Kent came home to visit his parents for the first time in nearly a year. When he'd called in the middle of a Wednesday night dinner to tell them he would be around for the holiday, Mrs. Golden had nearly shrieked into the phone, her face split wide open with an enormous smile, one hand clutching her chest, just like in a movie. Mr. Golden had been less impressed, or at least less theatrical, but the corners of his lips had turned up into a small smile beneath his bushy gray mustache and he had beckoned the phone from his wife at the end of the call and confirmed his son's flight schedule and arrival time, something that seemed to me a distinctly male way of expressing emotions you felt you could not say in words.

One morning, a week after his phone call, I was in the Goldens' kitchen, bare foot in lace trimmed pajama shorts and with un-brushed teeth, rummaging through the pantry for some breakfast when I heard the doorknob wiggling, the soft suctioning of the door as it opened, and footsteps on the hardwood floor. I froze with my arm in midair, my hand outstretched to grab a box of Frosted Flakes, and I strained my ears to listen. If it was a burglar, I thought, I could outrun him, and I mentally mapped the fastest route out of the house.

But as the footsteps proceeded toward the kitchen, I did not move. Then Kent popped his head in through the swinging kitchen door.

"Hey, mom." His face flashed with a big, sentimental smile for half a second before it crumpled into confusion. "You're not my mother."

He stepped into the kitchen. He was thinner now than in the photos that hung in the trophy room, and he had a layer of dark stubble covering his chin, but I could recognize him instantly as Rudy's brother.

"Sorry, no," I said. "I'm Rudy's friend. Jillian."

"Nice to meet you." He didn't reach to shake my hand;

instead he turned to pull open the refrigerator door and peer inside.

He didn't say anything more, and I reached again for the cereal, preparing to retreat back upstairs to the safety of Rudy's room, where she still lay sleeping and where I would probably finish off the half empty box of cereal all by myself and hide the empty box at the bottom of Rudy's trashcan.

"Hey, don't leave because of me," Kent said from inside the fridge as I tried to slip past.

"Oh, it's okay," I shrugged one shoulder to further emphasize my nonchalance.

"You're going to eat that without milk?"

"It's fine that way."

"No, it's not. Nobody likes cereal without milk." He emerged from the fridge cradling a gallon of milk and a bottle of orange juice in the crook of his elbow. "Here, sit with me. I guess nobody else is around?"

I shook my head. "I don't think so."

"Figures." He rolled his eyes, which were a brilliant shade of green, an even more vibrant version of Rudy's. "I tell them I'll be here this morning and they make plans anyway."

"Actually," I said, taking a seat at one of the stools that nestled up to the long kitchen bar. "I don't think they were expecting you until Wednesday or something." It was Sunday. I knew the Goldens' schedule by heart. It was the calendar by which I planned my life, and not only was I more than confident Rudy's brother had arrived days earlier than planned, but I felt a prick in my chest at his insinuation that his parents were negligent or forgetful or uncaring.

He had picked up the cereal box that I'd placed on the counter and started pouring it into two over-sized bowls, but he looked up when I spoke.

"Oh, yeah? So I see you're privy to all the family business, huh?"

I was taken aback a bit, embarrassed by the seriousness of his tone, but then he was smiling again.

"Chill out, I'm just kidding." He drizzled milk over one of the bowls then passed the jug and the second bowl to me.

"I wasn't worried," I said.

"So," he said through a crunchy mouthful. "You're one of Rudy's friends? You a freshman at Ogden, too?"

"Yes."

He nodded while he swallowed. "What'd you guys do last night? Big party?"

"Um, yeah, sort of. Why?" I ate some of my cereal.

"You smell like beer."

I felt heat rise up and color my face and all of the sudden I was acutely aware of my long, bare legs against the cool seat of the stool, of my unkempt hair and the puffiness of my sleepy eyes. "Sorry. I haven't showered yet."

"Hey, no big deal. Just giving you a heads up; I wouldn't kiss my mother with that breath."

At this I knew my cheeks had blushed fully pink, but at the same time I felt flattered, privileged even to be receiving this sort of attention from him. Previously, at sleepovers with my old friends in grade school and in junior high, despite how much we had hassled my friends' cute older brothers – following them around, spying on them with our ears pressed up to the cracks of their bedroom doors (what did they do in there?) – they had paid us zero attention whatsoever. We had been invisible to them, not even worthy of this sort of sisterly-brotherly chiding.

"You're just jealous," I said, emboldened by the peculiarity of the conversation. I crunched down on a spoonful of flakes, milk sloshing around in my mouth. "I bet your morning at the airport was riveting, huh?"

"Oh, absolutely. I bet I got more action than you, too. The guy next to me was curled up on my shoulder the whole flight. I've even got the drool stains to prove it."

"Nice," I responded quickly. I can play at this game, too, I thought. "Did you get his number afterward?"

"Nah, I'm not a relationship type of guy." He looked into my face, considering me. His eyes were so green they practically sparkled, like emeralds under the spotlights in a jewelry store, and I felt a pleasant nervousness in the pit of my stomach. "One night stands are more my thing."

We were still regarding each other from across the countertop, both of us half-smirking, when Rudy walked into the kitchen.

"Hey, jerks." She rubbed one fist against her eye sleepily. "Thanks for waking me for this party."

"Well, aren't you cheery this morning, sleeping beauty?" Kent tipped the bottle of orange juice to his mouth and drank directly from the jug, his Adams apple bobbing in his throat as he swallowed.

Rudy stuck her tongue out and made an angry face at her brother, but then she smiled as she pulled out a second stool and sat, perched with her knees drawn up to her chest. Her butt cheeks were nearly visible, peeking out from her shorts, but she didn't seem to take notice. "What did you make me for breakfast?"

"We ate it all, no breakfast left. Sucks for you."

Rudy reached for the Frosted Flakes and took a handful from the box, eating them dry out of her hand. I crunched down on another spoonful while Kent brought his bowl up to his face and drained the sugary milk that remained at the bottom.

"Well, I'm going to go carry in the rest of my shit," he said, setting the empty bowl back down on the counter in front of him. "Enjoy your breakfast, ladies."

"Let me know if you need any help," Rudy said. "Not."

"Thanks, sis." He turned and glanced at me as he passed through the kitchen door and said "See you later, Jillian," and though Rudy's presence had ruptured the moment – broken the spell – when he met my gaze I could see in his eyes that something had transpired between us, and I could feel in the gentle pounding of my chest that this wasn't the end of it.

———

KENT WAS the only secret I kept from Rudy, the single thing I felt I couldn't share with her because he was her only brother. It might have been different if they had hated each other but they were close, a friendly rapport existed between them, and that seemed to make it physically impossible for me to tell her that I liked him.

On our first evening of Thanksgiving break there was a massive party planned, again at Skyler Warren's house. After my immediate refusal on the grounds of mortification, Rudy launched a counterattack and after a week of assuring me the cocaine incident would be completely forgiven and forgotten, I reluctantly agreed to return to the Warren's house. Mr. and Mrs. Warren were leaving for a quick trip to Seattle, and in the cafeteria at lunch I heard upperclassmen debating whether or not it would be the best party of the semester. It seemed to me that Skyler's parents were always both absent, which struck me as extremely sad, even though my own parents weren't consistently present. Not that it was absolutely necessary to have a parentless house for a party – it had become obvious to me over the last few months that many parents didn't discourage their teenagers from drinking. In fact, several of my classmates' parents would drive them to parties and return to chauffeur their drunken children home. Once Rudy and I even got a ride back to her house from the father of one of the girls on the cheerleading squad, and he had made me feel slightly uncomfortable with the way he would swivel around in the front seat and stare at us (but not at our faces). He had promised us (pinky sworn, as a tipsy Rudy had requested) that he wouldn't say a word about it to either of our parents, who he saw regularly at Ogden Parent Association meetings.

The word around school was that this party would be even bigger, with three kegs this time, but the thought of another night drunk on beer made my stomach turn. The taste made me pucker my mouth and cringe, the sheer quantity of liquid made my stomach bloated and bubbly, and I always felt like I would surely throw up, though that had never actually happened.

"We'll get Kent to buy us something else," Rudy said in her bedroom after school. She was sitting on the carpeted floor, her legs spread so she could bend over to paint my toenails.

At the sound of his name, my heart had leapt. "Will he?"

Rudy nodded her head but her hand remained steady as she painted a line of pink polish down my big toenail. "I think so. He has a good fake ID. We should probably ask him early though; I don't know if he has plans tonight."

I considered this for a moment, what plans he might have; if they would include a woman, a girlfriend perhaps, or some gorgeous girl he had gone to high school with, both of them back home for the holidays, both of them lonely and looking for the sort of attention a person could seek from a one night stand with an old acquaintance – the familiarity that would make it easy to slide straight into kissing without introduction or the uneasiness of silently communicating what you wanted to the other person, yet the knowledge you would both be leaving, that this was only temporary in the best sort of way. In reality, of course, I had no idea what a one-night stand was like.

"What do you want to get?" I asked, my own knowledge of alcohol extremely limited.

"I don't know, maybe vodka. Or rum?"

"Okay. Does that go with soda?" I asked.

"I think it can." Rudy had finished one foot and set it aside to dry, propped up on one of her outstretched legs, as she moved on to my second foot.

"Houston will be there tonight, right?" I said. For the past month or so, ever since the Fall Ball, Rudy and Houston had been some sort of bizarre couple. They weren't always together – they didn't hold hands walking through the hallways, or sit together at lunch or anything – but he drove us to school occasionally and sometimes, on the weekends, Rudy would make plans with him to go see a movie or to hang out at his house, and I would be left alone with my mother to bake a batch of low-carb brownies or spend the evening rearranging all of the clothes in my closet. I wasn't even sure they were exclusive (Houston was precisely the type of guy I could imagine seeing multiple girls at once) because Rudy didn't talk about him often, and because she didn't bring it up, I had never thought to press for details.

"Yep. He said he could give us a ride there, too."

I hated riding with Houston because I always had to sit in the backseat, alone with his piles of sour, sweaty smelling football practice clothes (football season was over, which made it all the more disgusting), but I nodded my agreement anyway.

When my nails were dry, shiny hot pink against the faded tan of my toes, we knocked on Kent's closed bedroom door. Through the walls I could hear the loud bass sounds of rock music. Rudy banged hard against the door; finally it swung open and Kent's head popped out.

"What?" He said.

"Will you take us to the liquor store?" Rudy flashed him her best shit-eating smile. "Please?"

He sighed and rolled his eyes. Behind him, as I peeked through the doorway as covertly as I could, I saw dark blue, sparsely decorated walls. His bed was covered in a burgundy and blue plaid comforter and beside it sat an oak dresser, the top scattered with loose change and dollar bills, tiny glass bottles of cologne and a half-crushed, empty soda can. One of the drawers was open, revealing white pinstriped boxer shorts stacked one on top of the other. I looked away, directly into the strands of beige carpet beneath my own feet.

"Do you have cash?"

"Yes," Rudy said.

"Give me a second." Kent closed the door and within seconds reappeared, keys jangling in his hand and a Florida State sweatshirt covering his plain t-shirt. "Let's go, kids."

On the ride there I sat in the backseat of Mr. Golden's car staring at the back of Kent's head, his perfectly disheveled brown hair sticking up from his scalp in all the right places. No one spoke much, and I sat back and inhaled the strong smell of Kent's cologne mixed with the clean scent of the car. In the parking lot of the liquor store, Rudy handed him two twenties from the pocket of her jeans and he disappeared inside the store. While he was gone, Rudy changed the radio station and turned up the volume and, free to give myself entirely to fantasy considering that the real object of my affection was hidden out of my sight, I imagined Kent holding my hand, taking me to dinner, kissing me softly on the lips. He came back minutes later, two plain plastic bags hanging from one hand.

"Set these back there, will you?" He passed the bags to me in the backseat and I cradled them like a precious gift. A newborn baby or fragile china. He climbed into the driver's seat.

"What did you get?" Rudy asked.

"A handle of Congress and some vanilla rum. And some stuff for me."

Rudy made a face at him, and he threw his hands in the air.

"Hey, you only gave me forty bucks. Did you expect Grey Goose?"

———

WHEN OUR CARAVAN arrived in front of Skyler's house that night it was already past eleven. I was wearing a black skirt and high heels that showed off the length of my legs, and I'd spent extra time agonizing over smoothing the cowlick in my hair, but much to my disappointment Kent was already gone when we came downstairs, dressed and ready to leave for the evening. Though I was flattered by the compliments Houston's friend, Jack, gave me on the ride across town, I could already feel my good mood slipping away.

Walking up the sidewalk my energy drained with each step. In front of me Houston had his arm wrapped carefully around Rudy's waist, his fingers cupped against the side of her hip, and behind me Jack was glued to his cell phone, chanting one word answers over and over to whoever was on the other end of the line. In the middle I felt lonely and isolated and frumpy, clinging to my purse, which was heavy with the bottles of liquor hidden inside.

Inside the kitchen I filled a plastic cup halfway with Coke, then wrestled the seal from the top of the rum bottle. Were you supposed to do half and half? Was that enough rum? Beside me Rudy had already mixed her vodka drink and was timidly sipping from the cup. I should have watched her, I thought to myself.

"It tastes pretty good." She shrugged.

As I lifted the bottle Houston swooped in behind Rudy,

planting a kiss on her cheek, which she met with an enormous grin.

"Come be my beer pong partner?"

She looked at me, for my consent, and I nodded as casually as I could. Just because I was lonely and miserable didn't give me a right to come between these lovebirds.

"I'll find you as soon as the game's over, okay?"

"Okay."

When her back was turned, I tipped the bottle into my cup, watching the clear liquid gurgle from the neck of the bottle out into the dark soda until the cup was filled to the brim. When I brought it to my lips I nearly gagged. Either I'd done the math wrong or I hated hard alcohol. Regardless, there was nothing I could do about it now except suck it up and force it down. I took another bitter sip then swept both bottles into my arms and shoved them awkwardly into my purse, hugging it against my hip.

What was I supposed to do now, I wondered. I gazed around the kitchen, the tasteful granite countertops and stained wood cabinets, the silver pots and pans hanging from a contraption over the island centered in the middle of the room. Traffic flowed in and out of the kitchen doorways – girls parading in to make their drinks, complicated concoctions of liquor, juice and soda, empty-handed guys wandering inside to peer into the doors of the stainless steel refrigerator, eyes glancing over their shoulder as they reached for a beer that either they'd hidden or they were stealing, then hurrying from the room before they could be discovered. I watched with growing curiosity as one boy rifled through drawer after drawer in the kitchen, and when he pulled out a black handled knife, the blade sharp and glinting along the edge, my breath caught in my chest. But he pressed it into the side of his beer can, puncturing the aluminum as he clutched the can horizontally. He tossed the knife onto the counter then opened the top of the can and shoved his mouth over the jaggedly cut hole, enveloping the side of the can with his slobbery lips, beer rushing out and down his throat, past his bobbing Adam's apple. When he was finished he left, a puddle of spilled liquid marking the place where he'd stood.

I leaned against the countertop as casually as I could, holding my glass halfway to my mouth so that if anyone happened to make eye contact with me, I could lift it to my lips as fast as possible to avoid conversation. Or if I grew bored. No one stayed in the kitchen long, and the movement, chaos and noise gave me camouflage.

It wasn't long before, with nowhere else to divert my attention, I had finished my drink, and Rudy was still no where to be seen. I fidgeted with the strap of my purse, shifting my weight against the cabinets. I crossed one leg over the other but it was hard to keep my balance with just one high-heeled shoe against the slippery tile. I uncrossed my feet and hugged the purse to my stomach. Maybe I just needed to drink more.

I poured several glugs of rum into the cup and topped it off with soda. The knife boy returned, this time with two friends trailing behind him, and we made eye contact as he entered the kitchen. He smiled and my cheeks flushed. I had to get out of the kitchen before anyone else recognized me – the lonely kitchen lurker, the creepy girl who stares while you make your drinks.

I left my kitchen haven and wandered cautiously out into the dining room where four long, plastic folding tables sat in the place the dining table would have been. Three were occupied by couples teamed up to play beer pong against each other. The fourth held three kegs, its cheap plastic middle buckling under the weight of all the beer. I found Rudy at the far table, and I weaved through the crowd to stand at her side.

"You found us," she said, raising the ball to shoot. She missed.

"Yeah. I got bored by myself," I admitted quietly.

"We're almost done."

There were two cups left in front of Rudy and Houston while the other couple, who I recognized not because I'd ever spoken to either of them, but because they were popular juniors and I'd studied them with their friends in the hallway and at football games, had just one.

"Did you finish your drink?" I asked. Rudy was drinking from one of the beer cups now, her soda and vodka nowhere I could see.

She nodded. "We won, so this is our second game. God, you go through so much alcohol playing."

"Hey." Houston nudged her with his elbow, his mouth stern and his eyes clouded with concentration. "Pay attention."

She turned back to the table, and I stepped back to stand against the wall and wait for the end of the game. After Rudy missed again, Houston took the ball in his hand, spinning it around in his fingers before he raised his arm, poised over the table. He bent back his forearm and sent the ball sailing across the room, where it plopped with a splash into the final cup.

"Yeah!" He pumped his fist in the air and Rudy turned to me with an apologetic smile. Houston was already setting the table for another game and, not wanting to be a nuisance, I left them alone.

In the living room I found an empty seat at the end of one of the overstuffed leather couches, and I busied myself with finishing one drink after another until finally, Rudy materialized in front of me. Her head was spinning, but I thought maybe mine was spinning, too. Either way, I grasped her forearms to steady us both.

"Are you ready to go home?"

My head was pounding and I'd spent the last half hour avoiding

eye contact with the creepy freshman guy who kept smiling at me from across the room. I nodded with enthusiasm. I didn't remember how we'd arrived at Skyler Warren's until we were already outside, shivering on the porch in just our skirts and sweaters against the bitter-cold November air.

"Where's Houston?" Outside, the music thumped with slightly less force, but I still had to yell to hear my own voice.

"Gone." Rudy wiped at the corner of her eye, smudging a tiny trail of mascara onto the edge of her nose. "We got in a fight and he left."

"How are we going to get to your house?" I hugged myself, rubbing the goosebumps that had sprung up on my biceps.

"I'll call someone. I'll call Kent."

I sat down on the steps to the porch, hugging my knees to my chest while she stepped further into the yard, phone pressed to her ear.

"Kent," Rudy yelled into the mouthpiece. "Will you come pick us up? Our ride left us." Her eyebrows drew together angrily and her voice was warbled, shaking with the threat of tears. "Seriously, Kent, please just come get us? I don't want to call a taxi, it'll take forever and it's cold. Please."

She spent another minute arguing with him, and I tapped the heels of my shoes against the step to distract myself and to create body heat. My head felt detached from my body.

Finally she seemed to have convinced him and she gave him the directions to Skyler's house.

"What an ass," she said, and I didn't know whether she meant Houston or Kent. She sat down next to me on the step, pressing her side to mine and we huddled together in the cold to wait.

When Mr. Golden's car pulled onto the street we stood and

ran (ran as much as you can run when you're drunk and wearing high heels) into the street. Rudy yanked open the back door and climbed inside and I, in my state of drunken boldness, got into the passenger's seat. It was warm inside the car, hot air billowing out of the vents.

"Where's your boyfriend?" Kent tilted his head up toward the rearview mirror to look at Rudy without turning around.

She shrugged her shoulders. "I don't know."

"What a good guy," Kent mumbled under his breath. I felt a throb of affection toward him for this display of big brotherly protection.

None of us spoke, and after a few minutes I twisted around in my seat to glance at Rudy. She was lying across the backseat, her legs propped up on the car door, asleep. I turned back around.

"She's sleeping," I announced to no one in particular.

"Yeah," Kent answered.

I leaned my arm against the plastic console that divided the front seats, my fingers dangling off into the empty cup holders. A few moments later I felt Kent's arm join mine, our forearms pressed together, the heat of his skin against my goosebumps. I didn't dare look down at our arms for fear our touching was an accident and if I acknowledged it, he would move. I stared ahead, out the windshield into the darkness, my heart pounding.

A few more seconds passed and I felt his warm hand close around my cold fingers.

"Your hands are freezing," he said casually, like holding hands was something normal for us.

"Yeah," I said. I laughed, and it came out more like a croak.

The skin on his palm felt pleasantly rough against my smooth hand, and I suddenly felt thankful for my thin, girlish fingers. He rubbed the pad of his thumb against the palm of my hand, and I felt like I was melting into the back of the seat. Clearly it was not an accident. We remained this way – Kent holding my left hand, me turning into a roiling vat of liquid – until we pulled into the driveway of the Goldens' house. Only then did I dare to glance across the seat and meet Kent's gaze, mostly because it would have struck him as odd if I refused to look at him then. He smiled at me, gave my fingers one final squeeze and then he let go and got out of the car, and I abruptly felt his absence. I wanted his skin to be touching mine again; it felt unbearable to me at that moment to be alone, to have all of my body parts to myself.

Kent opened the back door of the car, reached inside and scooped Rudy, still asleep, into his broad arms. I climbed out of the seat and followed him to the door and into the house. He carried Rudy all the way up the stairs and into her bedroom, laying her on top of the covers in her bed. When her head hit the fluffy pillow her face scrunched up like she was going to speak, but she said nothing. I dropped my purse inside the door and as he stood to leave we made eye contact again through the shadowy light. On his way out of Rudy's room he walked very close to where I was standing, and I felt his fingertips brush very lightly against my bare thigh.

The next morning Rudy was miraculously un-hung over and I, now in a fully sober state, went out of my way to avoid any contact with Kent. The mortifying thought came to me that maybe I had dreamt up the entire strange interaction between us, and the further the day progressed, the more likely this seemed. It was only when that night at dinner his foot bumped against mine underneath the dinner table and I looked up to catch his brief but significant smile that I became certain the event had truly happened.

———

I SPENT Thanksgiving Day at my own house. Both sets of my grandparents flew in for the holiday, and my uncle and his family came from Chicago to spend the day at our house. My cousins were young, five and eight, and they ran around the house in their socked feet, sliding across the slick floor and giggling when they lost their balance and fell down, bouncing onto their knees and elbows and butts. In the morning I joined in, chasing them down the hallway as they screamed with childish glee, until my mother retrieved me to help set the table for lunch. At one o'clock we sat down at the long mahogany table in the seldom-used formal dining room and while I filled my plate with mashed potatoes and stuffing, I thought of the Goldens. Marta was supposed to be flying in that morning from New York, and I imagined all of them reunited as a perfect family unit, laughing as they sat around the dining room table drinking hot cinnamon cider (one of Mrs. Golden's special recipes). Even in my family's best moments, I always imagined the Goldens surpassing our warmth.

By six o'clock, when the sun had begun to set behind the fence in our backyard and my youngest cousin had fallen asleep on the couch, everyone began to leave, to retreat back to their hotels (though our house was large enough, my entire family's need for privacy meant that no one ever stayed the night with us when they visited). I wanted to go to Rudy's, partly to feel myself an integral piece of their family dynamic, and partly just to be in Kent's presence. Though he hadn't been at the forefront of my thoughts, whatever had happened after that party had been lingering at the back of my mind the entire day. But my mother refused to let me leave the house, insisting that I not interrupt the Goldens' family holiday. So I stayed, brooding in my room, well aware that I was being selfish and adolescent yet not caring a bit, while my parents sat together in the living room sipping what was left of the wine they had served with dinner.

FOR THE REST of Thanksgiving break, I stayed glued to Rudy's side like a permanent accessory, a bracelet or a skirt or one of her appendages that had somehow become unattached from her body. I went shopping with the Golden women on Black Friday and ate left-over turkey sandwiches with them for dinner, but it wasn't until Saturday night that I got what I had been after, though I don't think I really knew what it was I wanted, or at least I hadn't believed I would truly go after it until after the moment itself had already passed.

Rudy and I had gone to another party, this one to mourn the end of our holiday break, and we were sloppy drunk again (to be completely accurate, Rudy was sloppy drunk. I was in a state of meticulously planned drunk – drunk enough to water down my good reason, but not enough to render me obnoxious), and Kent had agreed to be our ride again. It was the night before he would return to Florida.

As we walked to the car, I wrapped my arm around Rudy's waist to help steady her while she bent down and climbed in the back. When the car pulled away from the curb, I was pulled into a strange alternate universe where Kent was my husband and Rudy our child; it wasn't two in the morning, it was mid-afternoon and we were going home after a long day at the park. This is what it would feel like to be in a relationship, I thought. This is what it would feel like to be connected to people by love, not obligation. Emboldened by my own fantasy, I reached across the seat and, in the real, live universe, placed my hand on top of Kent's hand, which was resting on his knee.

He glanced down at my hand, and he looked at me from across the car, and this time I was the one who smiled. Looking back, these details shock and amaze me. Was it the alcohol?

Who was this girl, this freshman in high school, who made moves on her best friend's much older brother?

Before I knew it, we were at the Goldens' again, and he was lifting Rudy from the backseat, and I had a striking and appropriate sense of déjà vu as I followed them up the stairs and watched him put Rudy to bed in her room. But this time, with just a hint of hesitation, he grabbed my hand and pulled me out into the hallway with him, pulling Rudy's door closed behind us.

He led me down the dark hall and into his bedroom and without turning on the light (if he had turned on the light, if I had seen all of the features of his face and witnessed this moment for what it was under the brightness of a light bulb, my shaky confidence would have deflated and I think I would have turned around and left), led me to his bed.

He pushed me, gently, onto the mattress and he lay down beside me. His sheets were unmade, and a wadded up roll of comforter lay uncomfortably under my lower back, but I didn't try to scoot away. He was kissing my face, and then my mouth, and he tasted vaguely of beer, even though he was the one who had driven us. He probably weighed nearly twice what I did, but he felt as light as a feather on top of my chest.

We stayed like this for ages, for eternities, until it felt like there was nothing to do but to go further, and that's where we stopped, both of us, simultaneously (probably not simultaneously, but this is how I will always remember it happening). I don't know if it was because he was nineteen and I was only fifteen, or if it was because I was his little sister's friend, or if it was because he just didn't like me that much (this crossed my mind, and I think I believed this reason the most, especially when I was feeling most insecure), but we never went any further than lying there, kissing. It was the best possible outcome, the only way I could see for us to escape the situation we had put ourselves in without any irreparable consequences. I could keep this, this relatively innocent drunken make out session, a secret from Rudy but if we had had sex, if her brother had taken my virginity, that secret would not have been manageable. At that point, Rudy and I both still held our virginity cards, clinging to them with all our might against the tornado that was male adolescent concupiscence. If I had handed mine over, she would have known. It would have been evident in my mannerisms and especially when I looked her in her eyes.

When I got up from the soft blue sheets of Kent's bed at three-thirty in the morning, I straightened my dress and crept across the carpet holding my shoes in one hand, and neither of us spoke a word. I opened the bedroom door, then turned and looked at him across the darkness, our eyes locked for an instant in a wordless pact of silence before I stepped through the threshold.

I'm not sure what all Rudy hid from me, but that night remained my one big secret, my single act of treason upon our friendship.

$$3$$

FRESHMAN WINTER

Fall in the Midwest was subtler than fall in Massachusetts. Though the colors – the reds and oranges of the leaves that fell from tree branches and blanketed the ground and the golden yellows of the sunsets and the contrast between the light of summer evenings and the light of fall nights – were muted, I still thought autumn was beautiful to watch. When winter crept in though, its fingers digging into my sides beginning the second week of November, it was far different than it had been in the East. Midwestern winters were bitterly cold, with strong, biting winds that whipped at my hair and blew up into my jacket no matter how tightly I had it buttoned. The sky remained an unyielding wall of grayish-white and though it wasn't always snowing like it had seemed to in Boston, the sidewalks and parking lots were marked with a perpetual layer of dirty, gray sludge. Yards turned into soggy brown puddles when they weren't covered in a layer of white snow, and even the snow itself never seemed to hold the same virginal beauty in St. Louis that it had in Boston, against the backdrop of stone buildings and national history. That was the best way to describe winter in the Midwest, I thought, sitting in math class at the beginning of

December, my head propped up on my arm, staring out the dirt smudged window as wind bent the branches on a bare tree in the courtyard. Long and dirty and freezing.

Math was the only class that year I didn't have with Rudy – she was in freshman Geometry with most of the rest of our classmates, and I was taking Advanced Algebra because my score on the math section of Ogden Academy's entrance exam had not been high enough to bump me up to Geometry. This had infuriated my mother, once she found out there were only two sections of Advanced Algebra offered at the school (compared to the six Geometry classes), placing me firmly, if not permanently, in the bottom quarter of my class. She had spoken first to my math teacher, and then to the principal, both of whom had referenced my math scores and then, taking in a deep, anticipatory breath, told my mother that there was nothing they could do – I would have to remain in Advanced Algebra. Maybe, they said, mostly to appease her at least a tiny bit, to give her some hope, and to get her off of their backs, we could "revisit the situation" after seeing the grades for my freshman math class. It appeared that money couldn't get you anything you wanted. Or, in a school brimming with wealth, we just didn't have the kind of money or clout that would get you that sort of influence.

By December I could already tell (I did not share this with either of my parents) that if there had been any truth to the idea of revisiting my math proficiency, I would definitely not be moving up. We had taken three exams over the course of the semester, and I had earned C's on all of them. At my school back in Boston, and at the junior high school I had attended the year before I hadn't been a stellar student, but I had mostly brought home A's and B's, and this had suited my parents just fine (grades weren't the sort of thing that impressed my mother, unlike designer purses or naturally straight hair). But at Ogden it seemed that the workload was considerably more difficult. Or, I thought as I twirled my pencil around between two of my fingers, possibly it was because I spent the majority of my time in class thinking about what I would do after school or during the coming weekend, and outside of class I spent the majority of my time worrying about boys or how my clothes looked or what I would say if an upperclassman tried to start a conversation with me at a party or at the movies on a Saturday night. My immediate desires seemed most pertinent to me; homework and studying and facts all had a payoff that lurked so far in the future I was either unable or unwilling to see it.

Advanced Algebra was my last class of the day (I'm sure this didn't help with my productivity), and after I had turned in my daily problem sheet (mostly a collection of doodles and scribbling that made evident my mathematical shortcomings) I would rush out of the room and down the hall to the second floor landing where Rudy and I and the rest of the freshman class had our locker assignments. Our lockers were right outside Rudy's final period classroom, but today I had beat her. I poked my head into her class, but they had clearly been dismissed already – only a few stragglers were still standing around talking or shoving notebooks into their book bags, and none of them was Rudy.

I leaned back into the hall, dropped my book bag off of one of my shoulders and swung it in front of me so I could remove some of my heavy textbooks. It was a Wednesday, and I should have been planning to study for my History exam on Friday but instead, Rudy and I were planning on watching a Sex and the City marathon on TV all night. I unloaded nearly my entire book bag then replaced it on my back, then I stood and waited, other kids streaming past me, some even running (only boys) toward the large glass double doors that led out into the icy afternoon freedom. Though I had become more confident, more open and outgoing, since I had begun hanging out with Rudy, I found myself slipping into my old, shy shell at certain moments. Especially when I was stationary and when I was alone. People walked past me, some of them waving or calling out to say "hi" across the river of bodies, and I would wave back and smile timidly, but I could feel myself drawing inward. I looked up and down the hallway for Rudy. Finally, once most of the rest of the student body was gone, I found her, walking slowly toward me, her hands shoved into the oversized pockets of her sweatpants.

"Hey," I said cheerily. "Where were you?"

"I went in the bathroom to call my mom back." Phones weren't allowed anywhere in the school. She bent over her lower level locker and twisted the combination lock. "My grandma died this morning."

I abruptly wiped the smile from my face. "Oh. I'm so sorry."

Rudy looked up at me while she dropped a book into the bottom of her locker. "Thanks." She smiled sadly. "I didn't really get to know her very well. You know what I mean?"

I nodded, unsure of what to say. These situations always made me feel incompetent.

"I wish I could've spent more time with her. I only got to see her a few times my whole life." Rudy shut the metal locker door and stood.

"Your mom's mom?" I asked. We started walking toward the stairs. "Your Greek grandma?"

Mrs. Golden was part Greek, which helped explain Rudy's beautiful, dark features. Her family had moved to the United States when Mrs. Golden was a child, so that she and her four siblings could go to school in America. In college at Dartmouth, Rudy's parents had met and her mom had decided to stay here and get married. Two of Rudy's uncles, as well as her maternal grandmother (her grandfather died sometime before Rudy was born), still lived in Greece. They were wealthy, owning some large company, I think. I was never quite sure how people acquired their fortunes.

"Yeah. The funeral is in Greece, on Friday. We're leaving tonight."

Selfishly, I felt a pang of disappointment and panic. Rudy would be gone for several days, and I'd be all by myself.

At the bottom of the stairs we pushed through the heavy glass doors and were hit with a gust of cold, blustery air. I pulled down on the sleeves of my sweater, covering my hands in the fabric.

"How're you getting home?" I asked.

"My mom's coming to pick me up. We can take you home, too."

I was unsure whether I wanted to be so close to Mrs. Golden right now, after she had lost her mother – my ineptitude would surely rear its ugly head, and possibly I would say something insensitive or stupid – but I had no immediate alternatives and it was very, very cold. Before I could answer, Mrs. Golden was pulling up in front of us in their black SUV, and I was climbing into the back after Rudy.

"Hello, girls." Mrs. Golden turned to smile weakly at us from the front seat. She was wearing large black sunglasses, though there was virtually no sun in the sky. She took them off as we were situating ourselves, and I could see that the skin around her eyes was puffy and red. She wasn't wearing any eye make-up, or she had cried it all off.

At first, none of us spoke. I didn't dare say anything. I just stared out the tinted window, out at the leafless trees and dirty sidewalks as we cruised down the street. It was odd riding in the car with Mrs. Golden. I had literally never seen her driving; I hadn't even been positive that she had a driver's license, though in retrospect it seemed ignorant of me to think she wouldn't. But still, the back of her head, far below the tall headrest of the driver's seat, her ringed fingers clutching the big, leather steering wheel seemed out of place, almost comical.

"Rudy, I packed up your bag," Mrs. Golden said, glancing back at us over her shoulder. "Daddy's coming home early; he should be there when we get back, and we're going straight to the airport."

"Are Marta and Kent going?"

At this, Mrs. Golden sniffled. "Kent left this afternoon. He should meet us when we arrive. But Marta can't be there. You know, she just started on this project, and she's new at the company. She wishes she could be there..." she trailed off, her voice wavering. I could see that her chin was beginning to quiver.

"It's okay, mom." Rudy scooted up to the edge of the seat so that she could reach over the back of the driver's seat and hug her mom around the shoulders. Mrs. Golden put one hand over Rudy's. "I love you."

When Mrs. Golden pulled into my driveway, I picked up my book bag and climbed out of the car. "Mrs. Golden," I finally spoke, just before I closed the door behind me. "I'm very sorry for your loss."

She smiled at me, tears glistening in her bare eyelashes. "Thank you, sweetheart."

———

It didn't snow in St. Louis at all over our Christmas break, though there was a chance of it in the forecast nearly every day. My family flew to Boston for a few days, to celebrate Christmas at my grandparents' house, and it felt eerie to be back in my old neighborhood, to see the Frank man's house across the street, and to drive past my old school on our trip back from the airport. In Boston it was a snowy Christmas; big, fat, picturesque flakes tumbled down out of the clouds beginning in the morning, when we crowded around the gigantic Christmas tree, and lasting until dinnertime, when we crowded around my grandparents' antique dining room table. We ate glazed ham (except my mother, who had currently gone vegetarian) and I gorged myself on sweet potato casserole because it was so cold outside and I felt empty and moody and wanted to be filled with something. Winter was always my least favorite season – it still is, to this day, the time when I feel the deepest sadness, almost in the marrow of my bones.

It was the first family Christmas I was allowed to sit at the adults' table instead of at the children's table with my younger cousins (my dad was the oldest of his siblings, and I was the oldest grandchild). Also, for some reason that Christmas my mother was absolutely insistent I spend time with her. She woke me up early to eat breakfast with her, and she invited me to go to yoga class with her at the gym down the street from my grandparents' (I gave her a look before I flat out declined). Most important to her was that I spend one full day of my vacation shopping with her, something I hated to do because she would whine that I didn't listen to her and I made fun of her clothing choices, which was true, for the most part, though I wouldn't admit it to her.

"We'll get manicures and pedicures, too," she begged, after we had finished Christmas dinner. "Please, Jill, just this one little thing for me. It's Christmas. I want to spend some time with you."

Reluctantly, I had agreed and on the day after Christmas I found myself riding shotgun beside my mother as she drove wildly through busy Boston traffic on snow-slicked roads. I buckled my seatbelt and clung tightly to the armrests, my knuckles turning white, something I had never thought actually happened in real life.

"So, what do you want to do first?" She smiled cheerfully from behind the steering wheel.

"I don't care."

"Shopping? Or the spa? We could do facials too, if you want."

"I really don't care." It was early morning and I was irritable. "Either is fine with me."

"Honey, it's your day. Pick whatever you want."

"No, mom, it's your day. You're the one who wanted to do this." My voice had come out with sharper edges than I had intended, and my mother pursed her lips, looking slightly injured.

"How about shopping first," I offered after a few moments of silence, an apology for my transgression. "Then we can do the spa when we're tired. It'll be relaxing that way."

"Sounds great," she perked up again. "Good idea."

I had hoped that because this was all her big plan, my mother would be less demanding and opinionated on our girls' day shopping trip, but perhaps I had set my expectations far too high. It was naïve of me, knowing my mother, but even in the car on the way to the mall I had envisioned us walking among the throngs of shoppers, blissfully swinging glossy shopping bags from our arms, pointing at dresses we liked in the store windows and sharing mother-daughterly laughs. But that was Rudy's mother I was thinking of, not my own.

In the first store we visited, I wanted to stop and look at the sweaters, but she dragged me to the shoe department and immediately began picking up pointed stiletto heels and handing them to me as I stood there, baffled.

"Mom," I said. "These are way too high. I can't walk in these."

The pair I was currently holding, electric blue and almost five inches tall, would put me at a height taller than some of the boys at Ogden.

"Just try them on," she pleaded. "They would be so cute on you, with your long legs!"

I sighed under my breath, and sat down to pull the boot off my right foot. My mother was still bumbling around the tables of shoes while I slipped the blue heel over my bare toes.

"Here," I said, standing up to model for her. "See, there's no way I could go anywhere in this. I'd fall all over myself." I took a few exaggeratedly wobbling steps.

"Oh, they're so adorable though." She was not discouraged. "Here," she picked up another shoe, this one brown leather and fringed on the sides, but just barely shorter than the one I was wearing. "Do you want to try these on? They're cute, too."

"Gross," I said, changing back into the shoes I owned. "Those are ugly."

My mother put her hands on her hips, and I could feel an argument brewing between us, but she said nothing and it seemed to pass, at least for the moment.

"Can we please go back and look at the sweaters?" I asked, a small peace offering. "I don't really need any shoes right now. I can't wear those to school, anyway."

Reluctantly, she followed me back to the junior's department and stood nearby as I thumbed through racks of colorful sweaters, all of them soft and pretty under my fingertips. She waited outside the dressing room as I modeled each shirt for her, and she nodded noncommittally and paid for three sweaters before we moved on to another store. For an hour, things went successfully, both of us polite and slightly deferential toward one another, the way you would act toward a new friend, or a crush you were trying hard to impress. She even took me to get coffee and bought herself a drink as well, a latte with real milk (though the syrup was sugar-free). But as we were sitting at the coffee shop, sipping our drinks and resting our feet, the tenuous balance between us began to crack.

"So, where to next?" My mother asked, looking at the mall directory she held in her hands.

"I don't know. I don't really need anything else. We've already bought a lot of stuff." I took a drink of my hot, sweet beverage. "Thanks, for all the clothes, though. And for taking me."

"You're very welcome," she smiled. "Come on though, we're not ready to go home yet! We've barely covered half the good stores."

I drank some more and did not say anything.

"We should look for some other things, some 'party clothes'." She actually made quotations marks in the air with her fingers as she said this. "I know you and your friends go to parties and things sometimes. What do you wear then?"

I was literally shocked that my mother knew I went to parties. We always, without fail, went on nights we would be staying at the Goldens'. My parents would have enforced a curfew; they would have stayed up waiting for us to return home (my mother, so she could prod us for information about the social scene at the party, my father, if he happened to be home, to smell our clothes and our breath for signs of alcohol and to examine our eyes for pupil dilation). Sometimes, before I left the house, I would tell my mother that Rudy and I were going to hang out with friends, but I had never actually told her we were going to a party.

"They're not exactly parties." I mirrored her dorky air quotes. "I mean, it's usually just some friends hanging out." I spoke carefully, delicately, afraid I was stepping into a trap. My mother was not someone in whom I felt I could confide.

"Okay. Well, what do you wear to these hangouts? Not the same clothes you wear to school, right?"

"No," I said. "Usually I just borrow something from Rudy."

My mother cringed a little. "Well why don't you let me buy you some things, so you don't always have to borrow."

"It's not a big deal. I like sharing clothes with Rudy." If I agreed to what she was offering, I knew she would expect me to divulge.

"Wouldn't it be nice if she could borrow your things, too? If you could return the favor?" She was clicking her fingernails against the tabletop, and I couldn't block out the annoying sound.

"No," I said. It was only one word, but we could both hear the layers of attitude beneath it. I suspected that even someone sitting nearby, maybe the balding man two tables away reading a newspaper, could discern all of the hidden messages in my 'no'.

Abruptly, my mother's facial features changed. They relaxed, went smooth and flat, then tightened again into a far less friendly formation.

"Fine," she snapped. "I guess daddy and I can't provide you with things that are as nice as the Goldens'. I'm sorry we don't have enough money to impress your friends, Jillian."

This, her explicit mention of money, and most of all, her insulting Rudy's family, made my blood boil. I narrowed my eyes at her across the table.

"That's ridiculous. You're being stupid."

"I'm your *mother*. You shouldn't speak to me that way."

"Well, maybe if you acted like my mother, not my bitchy older sister, I would treat you that way." As soon as the words were out of my mouth, as it was happening even, I wished I could take them back. But it was like when you were about to vomit – you could will the contents of your stomach to settle, you could cover your mouth with your hands, but once it was projectile, nothing you did could reverse it.

She leaned back against the curved bars of her chair as though I'd slapped her across the face with the palm of my hand

(I think, perhaps, it may have been easier to take if that's what I had done).

"Well," she said quietly, after a few seconds passed, seconds during which I became saturated with guilt. "I think that's enough for the day."

On the walk back to the car my shopping bags hung like anchors from my arms, weighing me down. I wanted to return it all, the gifts my mother had bought me before I said rude and irrevocable things to her. I was sorry, truly sorry, but even during the twenty-minute car ride back to my grandparents' house, I couldn't make my mouth form the words to make an apology. I'm not sure I could have said anything in that moment, in the aftermath of calling my mother a bitch, that would have been sufficient. By the end of my Christmas vacation, the freshness of the incident had worn off (as far as I know, she never said anything to my father about what had happened), but, as atonement for my mistake, I was more patient and kind with my mother for the remaining years I lived under her roof. She was not a bad mother – she made mistakes, lots of mistakes, and she often approached situations from a direction that did not appeal to me, but she loved me and I denied her the credit she deserved. But this was my small penance: often in the years that followed, I got irritated or frustrated with her, but never again did I lose my temper so badly. Never again was I so cruel.

———

ON OUR FIRST snow day of the year Rudy called to wake me up at 6:30 in the morning, a full half hour before my alarm was set to wake me for school.

"Wake up," she called cheerily from out of the speaker. "It's a snow day! School's cancelled."

"It's six-thirty," I said groggily. My mind was still half asleep. Possibly three-quarters.

"Come over. And bring your snow stuff."

She hung up the phone before I could answer, and I lay underneath my warm covers, still clutching the phone in my outstretched hand. After fifteen minutes, I crawled out of bed and pulled back the curtains from my window. Outside our yard was blanketed in white, and tiny flakes were still pouring down from the sky, obscuring the houses across the street.

When I walked downstairs my father was sitting at the kitchen table, drinking from a steaming mug of coffee and casting angry glares at the screen of his laptop.

"What're you doing here?" I asked, reaching for a banana from the fruit basket on the table.

"My flight was cancelled." He didn't look up from the computer.

"Sorry," I said, peeling back the banana's yellow skin.

He glanced up at me. "So, I guess school got cancelled too, huh?"

I nodded.

"And you're going over to the neighbors', I presume?"

I nodded again. My father and I were not particularly close either, but we did not mince words as I did with my mother.

"Well, be careful. And don't ride anywhere with anyone, especially not anyone your own age."

"Okay," I said.

After I had dressed, bundled up in so many layers I could barely move, I trudged out the front door and through the snow to Rudy's house. The snow on the ground was a foot deep, slushy and thick as my boots pushed down into it.

Mrs. Golden opened the front door after a single chime of the doorbell, and she ushered me inside, where I stripped off my top layer of clothing.

"You must be freezing," she exclaimed. "But it looks beautiful outside, all covered in white, doesn't it?"

"Absolutely." I nodded my agreement.

Upstairs on the second floor, Rudy was in her bedroom, yanking clothes out of her closet.

"What's up?" I said, throwing myself onto her unmade bed.

"Hey." She turned around, an enormous pair of sweatpants in her hands, and began to pull them on over the pair she was already wearing. "Your first proper St. Louis snow day. Are you excited?"

Rudy clearly was. Her eyes were bright and she was smiling from ear to ear.

There had been a few snow days the year before, the first winter I was there, but I did not correct her. "Sure, I guess. What exactly does that entail?"

"Sledding." Rudy stuck her hands through the arms of a sweatshirt and pulled it over her head. "And a snowball fight in Forest Park."

"With who?" Inside the Goldens' well-heated house I was beginning to sweat underneath my bulky clothes.

"Not sure. Just people from school. Houston said he'd pick us up in an hour."

I harbored extreme doubts about Houston's ability to drive in inclement weather, and my father's warning was still fresh in the back of my mind, but an hour and a half later (teenage boys, it seemed to me, were incapable of showing up for anything on time) I followed Rudy into the backseat, where we squished up against another guy already seated behind Houston.

"Did you bring your hot chocolate?" Houston said from the front seat, over the thump of music rattling the car.

Rudy and I brandished our thermoses. "We came prepared," she said.

"Yeah, so did we," the guy in the back with us – Patrick – said, and Jack, the guy in the passenger's seat, laughed.

Patrick pulled out a bottle of Bailey's and, in the backseat of the moving car, poured a generous amount into each of our thermoses, spilling on my arms and on the floor of the car in the process. The drive was slow and Houston drove with more caution than I had expected. I thought maybe I had underestimated his skills. Then, as we pulled into the parking lot at the park, he threw the emergency brake and the back end of the car slid around and I was tossed into Rudy's shoulder as the car spun in a circle. My hot chocolate sloshed into Rudy's lap.

"Do it again," Jack cried when we slid to a stop, all of the boys laughing and grinning, and Houston hit the gas pedal again, then repeated the process and we went sliding across the icy pavement a second time. This time I squealed with glee as well, my heart pounding in my chest. When we got out of the car I saw four other vehicles parked in one corner of the lot. I recognized two of them as belonging to kids from school, but there was no one inside the cars and we didn't see them nearby either.

"Watch out," Houston said as we walked out of the parking lot and into the park. "They're probably hiding somewhere waiting for us."

The second the words were out of his mouth I heard something zipping through the air and before I could move a snowball slammed into the side of my face.

"Holy shit!" Jack yelled, and all three guys bent to the ground and began frantically scooping up snow to pack into ammo.

Wet slush dripped down my cheek.

"Are you okay?" Rudy grabbed my arm, but when she saw I was laughing, she started to giggle too.

Packing snowballs, I quickly learned, was not one of my strong skills. No matter how much I smashed the snow between my gloved palms, it failed to form a nice, smooth ball. But the boys were fast and efficient at it, so they would crank out snowball after snowball and stash them in a hole at the base of a big tree where Rudy and I would retrieve them, folding up the bottoms of our coats and holding them to our stomachs so we could store dozens of pieces of ammunition at once. Then we would take off running, sprinting the distance from one tree to the next, crouching behind the trunks if anything came flying in our direction, then standing to retaliate, throwing one of our own balls when we glimpsed a flash of color – the tails of someone's puffy winter coat or a logo on their stocking cap. I sucked at making the snowballs, but I had surprisingly accurate aim.

"Crap," I muttered as another of my balls crumbled to powder in my hands. My fingers were cold and soaking wet (my gloves got ripped off when one of the boys tackled me to the ground and pummeled me with snow) and too stiff to treat the snowball delicately. My shoulders were sore, and I could hear the rasp in my voice as I panted. We had been in the park for almost two hours, I guessed, and looking around at the way everyone else was moving, slower and with less purpose, huddling in on themselves against the cold, I could tell that the others felt similarly exhausted.

"Truce?" I yelled to one of my teammates, Jack, fifty or sixty feet away from me. He didn't hear me, so I cupped my hands around my mouth. "Truce?" I yelled louder, and he turned to me and nodded, I think, though it was hard to tell beneath his scarf and ski mask.

"Truce!" He repeated, his voice bellowing out over the snowy park. "Truce! Come out, you assholes, we're done!"

From all around us people popped up from behind trees and bushes and we walked back toward the cars, dragging our tired feet, making long tracks through the snow. When we'd first arrived at the park the ground had been untouched, a perfect white barrier across the grass, but now when I looked back over my shoulder it was blemished all over with footprints, patches of dull green and brown visible through the trampled snow. This part – the rapid defilement of that immaculate winter canvas – was the part of winter that made me the saddest, and I felt a pang of disappointment strike me at that moment, even around all of those people. Even when I'd been exhilarated and happy just minutes before.

Someone behind us launched another snowball and it hit Houston in the back.

"Hey!" He whipped around but couldn't tell who had thrown it. "Fuck off, we called a truce." He sounded angry but he was smiling. His white teeth were almost translucent between his red lips and pink, wind burned face.

When we reached the parking lot all twenty of us collapsed against the hoods of the cars, or on the ground below us, sprawled out to rest. My calves burned under my long underwear and sweatpants and I felt cold dampness leaking in from somewhere, though I couldn't pinpoint the location.

Rudy and I sat on a snowdrift, where the city truck had pushed all the extra snow when they'd cleared the parking lot early that morning, and we drank from our thermoses, which were miraculously still a little bit warm. I could feel the lukewarm liquid – and the alcohol mixed into it – warm my insides as it traveled down my throat. Beside me, I heard Rudy's stomach growl.

"What time is it?" She said, laying one arm across her stomach. "I'm about to die."

"It has to be almost noon. I'm starving, too."

We left the park to drive back to Rudy's house, all of us fairly quiet in the car. The roads were mostly cleared, and it had stopped snowing, and I wondered absent-mindedly if my dad had been able to get a different flight. At the Golden's, all five of us sat thawing at the kitchen table, our cheeks red and our hair flattened against our foreheads at odd angles from our hats, while Mrs. Golden made us fat grilled cheese sandwiches and steaming bowls of tomato soup, and I ate two of each before I felt my stomach start to expand. After lunch we went back out into the snow and unloaded plastic sleds from the trunk of Houston's car and we dragged them up the street to the big hill that ran down from one of our neighbor's backyards to the community pool (which was largely pointless because most of the houses in the neighborhood had their own pools). There were only three sleds and five of us, so we took turns pairing up, two or three of us smashed together, our arms and legs entangled on top of the tiny plastic discs, while someone else shoved the sled down the hill. A few times we tried stacking all five of us onto one sled, lying on our stomachs, our arms spread out to the sides. As the smallest I was always on the very top, lying with my face pressed against someone else's back.

"Ready?" I would cry, and all I could hear below me was moaning and laughter. "Let's go!"

I would push off the ground with the tips of my boots – the only part of me that could touch – and the person on the bottom would drag us along, pushing as best as they could with their hands.

Most of the time we toppled over immediately and all went rolling down the hill on our own, stopping at various points when our momentum ended, laughing hysterically until we couldn't breathe. But once, the last time we tried it, we managed to make it three quarters of the way down the steep hill with all of us together, my mouth aching as I grinned and screamed against the wind, my heart bursting with the biggest happiness, and I thought how lucky I was, how unbelievably lucky I was, that this was all mine.

4

FRESHMAN SPRING

The last week of February marked the beginning of spring sports season at Ogden, even though it only hit forty degrees outside on a lucky day, and it would still be weeks before any of the coaches would consider having us practice outside. Rudy and I joined the track team, and when we showed up at 3:30 the afternoon of our first practice I scanned the gym for familiar faces in the relatively large crowd. Track was a popular sport at Ogden because it was so diverse, with sprinting and distance races and field events. It appealed to people who weren't really all that athletic because you could blend in easily, not like with basketball or volleyball, and because the track team did not make cuts. Also, Coach Kline, the head coach, was one of Ogden's most popular teachers because he was genuinely funny and he was really good looking (he was probably only in his late twenties, which seemed ridiculously old to me at the time; but he was a runner and he was trim and muscular and had a strong, masculine jaw and I could understand, though I couldn't quite agree with, why many of the girls at Ogden had crushes on him).

Rudy and I weaved through the crowd and stood beside Natalie, one of the girls from the JV cheerleading squad.

"What do we usually do for the first practice?" I asked, snapping the hair band on my wrist.

Natalie was a junior and she was pretty, with long brown hair and soft features, but pretty in an unobtrusive way. She was quiet and didn't draw much attention to herself, though she was nice and actually very funny when you got to know her.

"Today they'll probably just give us all the information. Forms and the meet schedule and everything, you know?" Natalie wasn't an especially good cheerleader but I had heard that she was a fast sprinter, that she had advanced past the district meet the year before.

"Do we even run? I need to shed some of this winter flab, man," Rudy joked, grabbing a handful of t-shirt around her waist.

"You think that's bad? Check out my sagging butt." Natalie rolled her eyes and turned to give us a better view of her not at all saggy backside. "Too much of my mom's pecan pie at Christmas."

Throughout high school and college, I was fascinated by the tendency of all girls to follow another woman's self-deprecatory comment with one of their own. It was like an invitation you could not decline – you had to RSVP by revealing your own self-consciousness, the things you hated about your own body. Though I certainly didn't love everything about myself (I thought my blonde hair washed out my complexion, my knees turned in and made me look bow-legged, my hips were too narrow and the freckles on my nose and cheeks looked like pimples), I didn't really feel compelled to air all of my grievances. I thought about my faults constantly, particularly in the company of boys, but deep down I hoped that maybe I was just imagining these flaws. I feared if I spoke them out loud, they would somehow become more prominent. But when someone else started it, you had to follow suit – to not, to seem self-assured and confident, would be a gross betrayal of the female population, not to mention cocky.

"Hey." Coach Kline was yelling over the rumble of the crowd in the gym, trying to get our attention and quiet us down. "Hey, everybody!" He flapped his arms, as if he were physically patting the noise down, like smoke in the air. "How about we get quiet so we can get this season started?"

Someone, a boy, in the back of the crowd hooted and pumped his fist in the air.

Coach Kline smiled. "That's right, it should be a kickass season, huh? Whoops, I probably shouldn't have said that, right?" This was part of the essence of his popularity – that he could curse in front of us, that he would joke with us and because he was still close enough to our own age, it didn't seem creepy or over-exaggerated.

"So," he continued. "I'd like to start by thanking everybody for coming out today. We've got a lot of returning seniors, juniors and sophomores, and I know I see some new faces out there as well."

There was more cheering, from the seniors, and I began to tune out, gazing around at the faces in the room as I often found myself doing in classes or assemblies or even at a party or a movie theater. It wasn't necessarily that I was uninterested in what Coach Kline was saying, just that I found the people around me to be so much *more* interesting. They were so alive, and their lives so much more compelling than flat, unfeeling words or pictures in my textbooks or actors and actresses on a movie screen.

Ogden was a small school - there were only about 800 of us in all four grades combined, and that year's senior class would graduate only 178 students in the spring, according to what would be printed in the graduation program. That was their entire class though; it was virtually un-heard of for someone at Ogden to drop out of high school.

The school was small, but there were still many faces in the crowd I didn't recognize. It's a cliché for high school to be cliquey, but at Ogden it seemed that the groups were so well defined, they became solid boundaries you physically could not cross. I had 200 classmates, and I only ever really spoke to one third of them. But sports were huge, and they drew everyone together. There were kids of all races (though Ogden was still 85% white, something they did not highlight on the fancy school website), clumped together under the fluorescent bulbs in the gym. There were scholarship kids, in slightly more worn tennis shoes, and to my right, a pair of girls with black painted finger-nails and neon streaks in their hair listening attentively to Coach Kline. I didn't actively dislike anyone who was different from me. Actually, I often found myself either fascinated with them, with imagining the circumstances that made their lives unique from mine, or intimidated by them and thus I averted my eyes when I passed them in the hallway. No one at Ogden was ostracized; there weren't any "bullies" (at least not any general, black-leather-jacket-wearing, knuckle-cracking bullies; bullies existed, but they existed within each clique, and they were often your former friends), we just associated with those most similar to us. We refused to exit our comfort zones, and in that way, we were the blandest portrait of teenagers possible.

But that's not how I saw my classmates and myself while I was still attending Ogden. Standing in the gym, which was less than five years old, with fancy features that made it look more like a college gymnasium than one meant for a high school, or walking through the school, I often felt a swell of pride rise up in my chest. We were more than ordinary, I thought, walking through the columns that flanked the front of the school, or past the marble lobby where the school secretaries sat behind glass paneled windows. The school was special, and we were special by virtue of our attendance here. In high school I rarely felt pride in myself as an individual, but it wasn't hard for me to feel proud of a group I was a part of.

I was looking at the ceiling, at the large blue velvet championship banners that hung from the rafters, when Coach Kline stopped speaking and everyone around me began to stir.

"Well, that was a bust," Rudy said beside me.

"Huh?"

"Weren't you listening? No practice today. Soccer reserved the gym for four and it's too cold outside."

"Oh. Sorry, I sort of zoned out. That sucks." I was following her into the lobby that faced out toward the sports parking lot.

"Natalie said she'd drive us home," Rudy said, sitting down on one of the gold plaqued benches, donated by an alumni class. "She had to get her stuff out of the locker room first though."

It was a Friday and because we had no tests coming up the next week, Rudy and I had sworn off of studying for the entire weekend. We left our backpacks in our lockers, to further commit ourselves – not that it was a tough commitment, not for me at least.

"Let's wait outside. Something smells in here." Rudy stood and walked toward the doors.

"It's freezing outside."

Rudy shrugged. "It doesn't look that bad. Come on, I want some fresh air."

She pushed the door open and reluctantly I followed her outside.

We were only wearing shorts and t-shirts and the wind whipped through my ponytail, slapping it against my back. The hairs on my forearms rose instantly, and I wrapped my arms around my body.

"Do you think I can walk on my hands?" Rudy had her back to me, but there was no one else outside (probably because it was barely 40 degrees out) so I knew she was speaking to me.

"I don't know. Can you?"

"I bet I can walk all the way to you." She turned around and wiggled her eyebrows at me.

I scoffed. "Bottle of Patron that you can't."

This expression had been widely used amongst the Ogden seniors that winter and it had just begun to trickle down the totem pole to our freshman class. It felt a little false coming out of my own mouth, but I felt a bit proud for coming up with a reason to say it aloud, even just to Rudy.

"You're on."

She kicked into a handstand, her long legs up straight above her head, and when she began to stagger forward on her hands her t-shirt slipped down over her face, exposing the red fabric of her sports bra. She moved about three tiny steps, then fell over onto her back with a scream. She was still several feet away from me, and she was laughing hard, her eyes pinched closed.

"You're insane," I said leaning over and offering my hand to help her up. "Plus, you owe me a bottle of Patron now."

Rudy grasped my palm, but she stayed limp and let me yank at her, trying to lift her dead weight off the ground.

"Totally insane," I added.

"Yeah." Rudy opened her eyes, but she kept giggling. "But you love me, don't you?"

And I did. I really, honestly did.

———

THE SECOND WEEK OF MARCH, before spring sports schedules got seriously underway, Ogden had a weeklong break from classes, sports and any other school activities. It was the only time all year, aside from the summer (and even then, there were unofficial practices and camps), that everything at the school shut down completely to give us a rest. Officially, it was our spring break; unofficially, I learned, it was called "Dead Week," and for every day of that week, someone from the senior class held a party at their house and everyone spent the entire week getting drunk for a last time before the really serious athletes gave up alcohol for the next three months. It was an Ogden tradition, Rudy told me. When Kent was a senior, her parents had let him stay home for the break while the rest of the family left for vacation; when they'd returned the house had been trashed, with broken bottles all over the place, and an enormous red stain across one of the living room rugs. Mr. Golden had been livid. But Rudy said her parents wouldn't stop us from going to the Dead Week parties, though it seemed that all of the parents were vaguely aware of what happened at them. They mostly turned a blind eye, probably just thrilled the party would be out of their hands and away from their valuables.

The fourth party, on Thursday night, was being held at Kendell's house. Though the intensity of their feud seemed to have died down, there had been no reconciliation between Rudy and our pompous senior cheerleading captain, and I had assumed, though I didn't confirm my assumptions with Rudy, that we wouldn't be attending. But Thursday night, after we sat through pasta dinner with Rudy's parents, still slightly hungover from Wednesday, Rudy started rifling through her expansive closet again, while I lay sprawled out on the bed, my hands folded over my full stomach.

"We're not going to Kendell's tonight, are we," I asked, unable to keep the surprise out of my voice.

"Sure, why not?" Rudy called from the closet. "Did you not

want to?"

"No. I mean, yes, I would go. I just thought, since she basically hates us…" The situation had seemed so cut and dry to me that I couldn't even explain my train of thought.

Rudy appeared in the closet doorway holding a dress in one hand, her other hand on her hip. "It's Dead Week though. You don't think she'd be that petty, right?"

I shrugged my shoulders against the mattress. "I don't know."

"But we don't have to go if you don't want to."

"No, I'll go." I said these exact words in similar conversations with Rudy probably a thousand times. "I just didn't know we were planning on it, that's all."

"It should be fun." Rudy pulled the dress off its hanger and held it flat against the front of her body so I could give her my opinion. "I hear Kendell has a gigantic house."

———

RUDY HAD HEARD CORRECTLY. When we arrived at the gates in front of Kendell's house a few hours later, I found myself literally speechless at the sight of its hulking mass. The exterior resembled a castle, with grey stones and pointed roofs over little rounded towers, and inside everything was cloaked in rich red and black furnishings. People spilled out from one room into the next, and we pushed our way through, collecting our bearings, waving to people who waved at us first and searching for our friends. This was largely how I survived crowded upperclassmen parties – seeking out a group of people I knew, attaching myself to them like a magnet on a refrigerator, and hoping what I was doing would help me remain inconspicuous.

We found Houston with his friends in the den, four of them circled around a plush leather ottoman, passing something around the circle in their fingertips. They had their shoulders pressed together, blocking the view of whatever they were passing, but as we got closer one of them shifted and I could see it, whatever it was. It looked like a fat, brown cigarette and it smelled like the wind outside the car window when you're on the highway and you run over a skunk. Of course I didn't recognize it was a joint – I had never actually seen one in person before.

Rudy snuck up behind Houston and wrapped her arms around his waist. He was holding the weed in his hand and when she squeezed him, a thin trail of smoke seeped from his mouth.

"Hey, you," he said. His eyes were red around the edges, I was fascinated to observe. He looked down at his hand, then held the joint up toward us and raised his eyebrows.

"No, thanks," I shook my head. I was curious what it would feel like to taste the smoke on my tongue, and I might have taken him up on his offer if the circumstances had been different (if the room was darker, if it was only Houston, Rudy and I, if I had felt more confident that I wouldn't erupt into a coughing fit). But here, in this moment, with four junior and senior boys at a crowded party, I declined.

Rudy shook her head too.

"Suit yourselves," Houston shrugged and passed it on.

I followed Rudy and Houston out of the den and toward the heart of the party in the living room. There was a bottleneck forming, people trying to shove their way into the room, and I stayed close behind Rudy so I could squeeze through the path they cleared. I always felt a hint of shame tagging along as their third wheel, but the feeling was never strong enough to make me detach from them. Inside, the living room was huge, with tall ceilings that arched over the hardwood floor beneath us. Paintings taller than me adorned the walls. All of the furniture had been pushed aside, lining the walls of the room, to clear enough space for a dance floor in the center. There was a deejay (an actual deejay, with flashing lights and microphones and a swanky advertisement for his services taped to the front of his table) mixing music, and a knot of people danced in the middle of the room.

"I don't want to dance yet," I could hear Rudy yell into Houston's ear. Her eyes were on the dance floor, where Kendell was snaking around in the middle of the crowd of people. She was wearing a silvery shirt that just skimmed the waistband of her jean skirt, and her short legs were elongated by the added inches of high heels. "Let's go get a drink."

Houston obliged, and I followed them into the kitchen. There was a full bar set up and Rudy mixed us both drinks. I took a sip from my cup and the taste of liquor was so strong I nearly spit it back. I looked up to make a comment, but Rudy's eyes were closed, her own cup tipped back so that the contents spilled into her open mouth. When she lowered it, half the drink was gone.

I was hardly surprised when, an hour and two similarly strong drinks later, Rudy announced loudly that she was ready to hit the dance floor. But by now, Houston was wrapped up in his third game of beer pong. He was on a winning streak, and he wouldn't leave the table.

"Let's go dance anyway," Rudy tugged at my arm. "I just want to move." Her eyes were sparkling, wet green jewels beneath the arches of her eyebrows.

"Yeah, okay."

The dance floor had grown, expanding toward the edges of the room as more and more people had flocked to the thump of the music. The paintings on the walls shook slightly, knocking against the drywall with each drumbeat. Rudy pulled me into the center of the crowd and she wove her fingers through mine, thrusting our arms high above our heads as she moved with the music. Someone bumped into me from behind, and I was pushed up against Rudy, our faces smashed together at the cheeks.

Out of the corner of my eye, I saw a flash of silver and suddenly Kendell was at my side, reaching across my body to grab Rudy around her wrist.

"What're you doing here?" Kendell's eyes were squinted and they locked on Rudy's face. Two of her friends, girls named Amber and Dominique, stood close behind her, their arms crossed on their chests. Their posture reinforced Kendell's anger.

Rudy yanked her arm out of Kendell's grasp.

"Don't touch me."

"What the fuck are you doing in my house?" Kendell was screaming now, her eyes glowering. A guy beside me turned to look. I could feel the situation rapidly spinning out of control, and the feeling was disorienting.

"No one invited you here!" A dot of spit clung to Kendell's bottom lip.

Rudy gave her a cold glare but said nothing.

What happened next, I could not have anticipated. In fact, the possibility of a physical fight was so far from my mind that when Kendell threw the first punch, I was actually confused as I watched her arm straighten out until it was horizontal in front of her, her fingers balled up into her palm, all of this occurring in slow motion in front of my eyes. It wasn't until her fist connected with the side of Rudy's face, just below her ear, that I recognized the movement as a punch.

Rudy, however, must have expected it, at least on some level, because the instant Kendell hit her she lunged forward, knocking Kendell over. Her back hit the ground, her head banging against the floor, and the people behind them scattered wildly, scrambling out of the way like a bomb had been detonated.

I had never seen a fight in person, but I had imagined that it would resemble boxing, which I had watched before on television with my father. I thought the two would face one another, bobbing up and down slightly, trading punches and jabs until one of them clearly had the upper hand. I had envisioned something orderly and civilized, but I saw now that I had been wildly, stupidly wrong.

Rudy was on top of Kendell, straddling her torso, and she drew back her arm and hit Kendell in the face with the knuckles of her fist. Kendell was thrashing below her, kicking her heels wildly and yanking at the long tendrils of Rudy's hair that hung down in her face. Finally, (it seemed like finally, though in reality it was probably only a few seconds) she pushed Rudy off of her chest and with one of her arms, swung aimlessly and connected with Rudy's shoulder. Both of them flailed on the ground, their fists drawn to one another like magnets, and everyone in the room watched raptly, giving them an increasingly wide circle of space, until three senior guys burst from the crowd and into the circle. One of them grabbed Rudy by the shoulders and yanked her back; the other hauled Kendell away, one big arm around her waist, while the third stood in the middle, his arms spread wide to separate the two girls until several feet of open space existed between their still swinging arms. Kendell's curls stood up from her head like a crazy blonde fire, and one of her eyes was beginning to swell, the skin around it puffy and pink. Rudy's dress hung askew. One strap had slipped down her shoulder, and there was a thin red line on the side of her face where one of Kendell's rings had cut her skin. Both of them appeared visibly dazed.

Once they were separated, both of their chests heaving as they drew breath and calmed down, the crowd around them exploded. Everyone was talking at once, their eyes wide with incredulity. A camera flashed white light.

"Here." The boy holding Rudy motioned to me, and I stepped forward from where I had been standing, frozen. "She's your friend, right? Take her outside."

He passed custody of Rudy off to me and I held tight to her arms for a second before I realized her muscles were flaccid beneath my hands – she wasn't a wild animal trying to escape. I loosened my grip, and she followed me out of the room.

Outside, in the chilly night air, my heart was still thumping furiously against my breastbone.

"Holy shit," I breathed, finally. "Holy fucking shit. You just got in a fist fight with Kendell."

Rudy brought her hand up to her face, touched the cut and examined the trace of blood on her fingertips.

"You punched her in the face! Did you see her eye? Holy crap."

Rudy looked up and met my eyes, but her mouth was still an unreadable straight line.

"Oh my god, I can't believe that just happened." I couldn't stop talking, adrenaline flowing from my mouth in the form of words.

"What happened to her eye?" Rudy asked finally, her voice strange.

"It's all swollen! You gave her a black eye!"

"I did?" Her face was so shocked, so innocently surprised, that I began to laugh. She stared at me, bent over at the waist as I laughed, until she began to giggle too.

She held onto my shoulders, both of us howling with nervous, incredulous laughter alone in Kendell's backyard, oblivious to the cold air stinging our bare skin, until we could catch our breath again.

THE FIGHT WAS the most popular topic of discussion at Ogden in the weeks following spring break. You could hear people whispering about it (or even speaking loudly about it – it was no secret) in the halls between classes, and at lunch, speculating about what had started it and who had thrown the first punch. Someone had videotaped the entire thing on their cell phone, but the video quality was poor and the camera operator had moved the phone around frantically, so you could only catch glimpses of the fight, of Rudy knocking Kendell over, of Kendell grabbing for Rudy's hair. Occasionally, when I was walking with Rudy to class that first week back, I would feel someone glaring at us, but they would turn their head when I looked. Other times, someone we hardly knew would come up to Rudy, their arm held high, palm out to offer Rudy a congratulatory high five. This surprised me most; not necessarily that other people disliked Kendell, that they wanted to see her get her ass kicked (the outcome of the fight was decided later that night, and the vast majority of people who had seen it go down came to the conclusion that Rudy was the victor), but that because it had already happened, it was now acceptable to blatantly acknowledge this happiness.

By the end of our second week back in school, as March was coming to a close and the branches on the trees in the school courtyard were beginning to sprout little white buds in anticipation of spring's arrival, no one was talking about the fight anymore. The freshness of the event, the excitement it had spawned, had died off. And also, the fight seemed to mark the end of the feud between Kendell and Rudy. They didn't become friends, of course, but they were no longer hostile to one another, at least not publicly. They were on the same 400-meter relay team during track, and they could run side by side at practice without an argument igniting. I was utterly shocked by this reversal at first. But this, apparently, was the way that Ogden functioned. There were so few of us at the school; by the end of the year we all knew one another, by face if not by name. We saw each other trip in the hallways, spill milk on our pants during lunch or stand around half-naked in the locker rooms before sports practice. We were intimately familiar with one another and because of this, we often clashed like siblings. But similarly, because there were so few of us, we couldn't permanently hate one another. Relationships, friendships, courtships and enemy-ships were so tenuous at Ogden – they could change before your eyes in just a matter of days. It was amazing to me, the sense of possibility. But I was also struck with the fragility of it all. At Ogden, nothing was permanent.

———

THAT YEAR, our very first prom was held at a ritzy hotel downtown. They served snacks and punch from real glass plates and engraved martini glasses on the roof of the building, and you could see the St. Louis Arch in the distance, with the river a dark, swirling mass behind it. We arrived by limousine almost two full hours after the dance had begun and we only stayed for an hour, enough time to have professional pictures taken with our dates, them in their black on black tuxedos, Rudy and me in sparkling floor length gowns that must have cost our parents hundreds of dollars (prices are the types of things for which I have no memory). I remember thinking how stupid it was that we were late and we didn't stay. I wanted to see the King and Queen crowned, but Houston and my own date were impatient. They wanted to get back to the limo, loosen their ties and drink some more before their buzz wore off. I didn't yet understand the whole point of prom wasn't the dance (the dance was just to be seen, briefly, before you went on your way). And the boys, like seventeen and eighteen-year-old boys in all decades, wanted *us*. They wanted to take off our sparkly dresses and they thought that, because it was the prom, we would let them. But we didn't; at least not those boys, and not that night.

Rudy was always in the company of boys, all kinds of boys, and I think that's what made it so hard for her to get along with other girls, particularly girls like Kendell. To be a freshman girl and receive so much attention from the older boys – it made sense that the junior and senior girls were jealous. But Rudy let everything pass over her, the whole mixture of good and bad feelings, of new friends and new enemies, without leaving so much as a scratch on the surface of her exterior. Later, in college, when my friends and I would get distracted from studying and find ourselves reminiscing about the high schools from which we had come, I was thoroughly shocked to find that everyone's high school experience had not been as easy as mine. They had agonized over themselves as freshmen, groaning about their timid naiveté, the ridiculous clothes they wore, how they tried *so* hard – too hard – to fit in. I learned freshmen in high school were supposed to be socially awkward, to say and do the wrong things. But I had no horrifyingly embarrassing mistakes to share with my college girlfriends, because Rudy and I had transformed into high schoolers seamlessly, effortlessly even. They shook their heads and rolled their eyes and told me how lucky I was, how nice it would have been to have escaped all of that tedious adolescent agony, but sitting with them in a study room, over our open chemistry books, what I felt wasn't exactly a feeling of luck, or a feeling that I had dodged a bullet. Until then, I had assumed my high school experience to be almost ideal, but this gave me pause. Maybe, I thought, this was what had gone wrong. Maybe Rudy and I had needed that friction, the difficulty of the transition. Maybe if we had been gawky and awkward freshman girls, holed up in Rudy's bedroom gushing over yearbook photos of senior boys we were too scared to speak to and stuffing our faces with ice cream and potato chips while we watched reruns of old sitcoms and did our homework, things would have turned out differently.

SCREWED

5

SOPHOMORE FALL

My sixteenth birthday fell on the last Friday in August, the week before Rudy and I returned to Ogden for our sophomore year. I woke up early that morning, excitement and nervous energy filling my body, and my mother drove me to the DMV office because I feared driving there myself, with her beside me in the passenger's seat, would jinx things. I would rear-end a police officer or side-swipe an old lady or something equally horrible. The instructor who administered my test was a big man, his stomach bulging over his belt, and he was bald with the exception of a wisp of thin grey hair combed over the top of his head. To compensate for his missing head hair, he sported a massive, bushy grey mustache and he did not smile, not even when we pulled back into the DMV parking lot and he congratulated me on passing the test.

When my mother and I arrived home, this time with me sitting behind the wheel, I could see my father's car still parked at the end of the driveway, just in front of one of the garage doors. We were still easing down the length of the driveway, me with a puzzled expression on my face – my father was never home past nine in the morning on a week day – when the second garage door lifted, slowly revealing first the tires, then the front grill, then the entirety of the new, shiny black car inside. My father was leaning against the hood of the car – my car! – a bouquet of pink roses in one of his hands, and when I saw him, I accidentally pumped my foot on the gas pedal and we jerked forward suddenly.

"Jillian!" My mother cried beside me, but I had already hit the brakes, shifted into park and I was unbuckling my seatbelt. I was out of the car before she could say anything else, running down the remainder of the driveway and leaping into my father's arms. He grabbed me around the waist, the flowers tickling the back of my neck, and he laughed a bit, nervously. I did not hug my father often.

"Congratulations, Jill," he said. "Happy birthday, from your mother and me."

"Thank you so much, Dad," I breathed into his shoulder. He still smelled like mint and tobacco smoke, like he always did when I was a child. The way he still smells today, somehow, though he gave up smoking long ago.

The first place I drove was, of course, across the street to the Goldens', and I sat in the driveway honking the horn until Rudy pulled back the curtains and peeked out her window. From the look on her face and the way her mouth opened, I could tell she was screaming.

———

CROSS COUNTRY WAS the second fall sport Rudy and I tried, having come to an unanimous decision (there had been no need to even discuss it) we would never again go out for cheerleading. Even then, from the perspective of only one more year of age, my glee at having made the squad and my visions of myself in a blue and white striped skirt, raptly watching football games from the sidelines, cheering in earnest and celebrating with the team when they won, other girls envying me my cute uniform and my popularity, seemed stupid and childish.

The cross country team was small, a tight-knit group of fifteen runners (ten of whom were boys) who intimidated me slightly because they were outspoken and quirky and because they seemed to know and take pride in the fact that they were outspoken and quirky. I loved to run – I had thrived as a part of the track team the spring before and had kept up my own training over the summer – but there was also something about the dynamic of the team that drew me to it. They were like Rudy, in a way, with their confidence and self-assuredness. I still find myself intrigued by this type of person, people who are fully comfortable in their own skins, and when I was in high school and college, I would attach myself to people like this in the futile hope the quality would somehow rub off on me.

Cross country was serious though; there was practice every day we didn't have a meet, even on Sundays, which drove my mother completely nuts. Though we weren't religious, when I came downstairs on Sunday mornings in my running shoes, she would sigh and lament that Sunday was a day of rest, and was the school even allowed to hold practice on the weekends? I would remind her this was a voluntary practice, that our coaches wouldn't be there. We just wanted the extra exercise. She would sigh again, and ask, "what about church?" "We don't go to church," I would say, and she would counter with, "What if we wanted to? I've been thinking maybe we should start," and typically, this was the point where I would simply walk out the door, waving over my shoulder as I left.

Sunday runs were our longest and slowest – endurance runs and team building runs where we all stayed together, trotting along at the pace of the slowest runner on the team (this was

Rudy when she made it to Sunday practice, though she didn't always). Sunday runs were also when we stole signs.

The first thing Rudy and I had discovered on our first hot, sweaty day of practice, was that the cross country locker room (all of the sports teams at Ogden had their own locker rooms featuring a side for the boys, a side for the girls and a "conference room" in the middle, with wooden benches for team meetings; all of the locker rooms were separated by a long, tunnel-like concrete hallway that cut through the middle of the school basement and was often used by students for secret, public hook-ups) was covered in stolen traffic signs. One short wall was half covered with rows of street signs, most of them green with white trim around the edge, some of them white and blue or red, all of them lined up perfectly, end to end. The ceiling was peppered with caution, no U-turn and huge, red stop signs. Some of them I couldn't even discern the meaning of (surely these weren't on my driving test? I couldn't remember). I was highly impressed by their size though, almost as wide across as I was tall, far larger than they appeared from inside a car on the road.

How we got away with this, I had no idea. The coach was cool – he rolled his eyes and warned us that if we were ever caught, he would feign ignorance and throw us to the wolves (he was also the only male coach at Ogden who wore his hair pulled back in a six-inch long ponytail, and the rumor among the students was he had been a decathlete at the University of Oregon but had been kicked off the team for smoking too much pot and performing poorly at meets). The administrators hardly ever went down into the locker rooms (even at a prestigious school like Ogden, the locker rooms were still locker rooms; they smelled like stale sweat, and it was difficult to imagine our principal, in his expensive suit, wandering around the blue painted cement floors amongst lockers that housed jock-straps), but the janitorial staff cleaned several times a week, and I found it hard to believe we never got into trouble (they did, eventually, years after I had graduated).

For the new team members, Rudy and I and a freshman boy and girl, the initiation rite was to steal a sign, any sign of our choosing. We wouldn't be alone – we would have the help of our teammates – but we had to select the sign, remove it from its post and carry it while we ran back to the school. We took turns, the freshmen each obtaining their signs the first and second weeks of school, then Rudy, and then it was my turn, the day after our first meet.

I had placed well at the meet the day before, finishing just thirty seconds after the top female runner from our school, Tawny Barrow, a junior. When we crossed the finish line, I bent over, exhausted. I braced my arms against my thighs and ducked my head, panting, afraid I was going to vomit. I had felt the contents of my churning stomach, the smooth muscles starting to contract, ready to propel up through my esophagus. Then, I'd felt Tawny come up behind me, her breathing heavy as well. She placed a dry palm (I don't think there was an inch of my own body that was dry) on my back, and rubbed her hand in a slow circle, standing there until finally I stood, the park around us spinning in circles in my cloudy vision.

"You okay?" She was still touching the small of my soaked back, and looking up at me as though she were bracing herself to catch my weight if I toppled over. It was attention of this sort that made me unbelievably uncomfortable – I never cried in public, not because it was particularly embarrassing, but because it would invite the sympathy of others, and to have people patting my back and whispering words of pity or encouragement, watching me with cautious, sad eyes (girls, especially, were so quick to jump to your aid), would always make me cry harder and harder.

"I'm fine," I wheezed, my legs jiggling Jell-O beneath me.

"Nice race," she smiled. "You totally kicked ass back there."

Tawny was, befitting of her name, dark tan all year round. She was gorgeous, despite (or maybe this even enhanced her beauty) wearing her long blonde hair in dreadlocks. She was the only girl I had ever seen with the hairstyle (and the only men I had seen with them were homeless), and I was endlessly fascinated watching the tangled-looking chunks bobbing from her ponytail when I was running behind her. How long had it taken her to get them to do that? Did she wash them? When I asked her, she had laughed long and hard, and told me of course she washed them, a few times each week, with a special shampoo.

I had soaked in my parent's Jacuzzi bath tub the night after the meet, letting the jets drum water into my exhausted muscles, and now they ached dully as I pounded softly against the pavement, Tawny's tan legs peddling a few feet in front of me. I was sore and tired, but I still felt strong, buoyed by my second place finish.

"Lead the way, Jill," Peter Scaggs, the tall, lanky, boy's team captain waved back at me after we had run a couple miles. "It's your catch this week."

My heart began to thud in my chest as I pushed to the front of the pack. I ran another half mile, winding through side streets, where the buildings were worn down, the brick crumbling in places. There were "For Sale" signs popping up on the corners of each block, and there was a lonely, yellow plastic slide at the end of the street, the fossil of a forgotten playground.

"Hey, slow down turbo!" I could hear Rudy yell from the back of the group. In my anxiousness, it seemed I had picked up the pace.

"Sorry," I yelled back, slowing. There was a sign at the top of the street, weather-worn green with the street name, "Weedley Avenue" printed in all capital letters across it in white. There was no one around, only a few empty cars flanking the sides of the street. This was the one.

I slowed to a stop several feet from the sign, and I could hear the footfalls of the others behind me slow.

"Weedley. Nice," Tawny laughed, and I laughed nervously with her as I slipped a small bag from my back. I unzipped it, the sound of the zipper cutting loud through the air, and pulled out our tools, the set that was kept in one of our empty blue lockers.

"We've got guard," one of the twin junior boys on the team volunteered, punching the other twin softly on the arm. The other boy (I think the one who had spoken was Easton, and the one who had agreed was Ellis, but I was never sure) nodded his consent to this arrangement, and they jogged off to the points where other streets would intersect this one.

I was tall but not tall enough to reach the top of the sign to see what I was doing.

"Here, let me climb on your shoulders."

I waved Rudy over, and she bent down to let me climb up her back. I swung my legs around her neck and she hugged my shins. Tawny and Peter helped her to stand all the way back up.

I worked fast, twisting the bolts from the back of the sign, my biceps twitching with activity. My heart was beating in my throat now. I had been present for three other sign snatches, but I had been a bystander. To actually touch the sign, to steal it with my own fingers, made my stomach flip. A bead of sweat ran down my face, the sun beating down from overhead. I was unscrewing the second bolt, twisting it out of its rusty hole and dropping it to the ground below, when I heard someone yelling. Rudy had heard it too, and she turned beneath me, twisting her shoulders so the sign was no longer within my reach.

We could see Easton (Ellis?) sprinting toward us from the west side of the street, waving his arms above his head and shouting. I couldn't make out what he was saying; his lips were a jumbled mess.

"Shit!" Someone yelled and, simultaneously, someone else cried, "Let's get out of here".

Rudy jerked, and I pitched forward and squealed. "Wait!" I screamed. "Wait, hang on!"

She steadied herself, and swung around to face the sign again, and I grabbed onto it with both hands and yanked, while our teammates ran past us up the street.

"Hurry!" Rudy mumbled from between my legs. I yanked a final time and the rusted sign came off in my hands. The force of the pull threw me backward, sending both Rudy and me tumbling onto the sidewalk, where we landed with a smack on our backs.

"Ow," I cried, the point of my elbow striking the hot concrete. Sharp pain shot through my arm. But then we were up again, onto our feet, and I was shoving the sign into the bag and pulling the zipper shut, and we were sprinting after our teammates. The wind whipped at the sides of my face and blood thumped in my ears.

"Hey," someone hissed. An arm shot out and grabbed mine, and we were pulled into a narrow alley. I crouched beside a dirty yellow brick building, weeds growing up the side of the wall, and I tried to catch my breath.

"Did you get it?" Someone else whispered, and I nodded my head, pointing at the bag in my hands.

"Good shit," Tawny grinned, holding her long arm up toward me. I reached out, my arm still stinging all over, and slapped my palm against hers as hard as I could, and the noise rang out all around us.

———

I first met Celine in my sophomore Geometry class (as I had predicted, I had not excelled enough in freshman Advanced Algebra to skip ahead). She was a transfer student, new that year from Seattle, and she sat in the seat beside me on the first day of class.

"Hi, I'm Celine," she had dropped her bright yellow book bag on the tabletop we shared and stuck out her arm.

Surprised, I looked up from my unopened textbook (I had been examining the Technicolor shapes dancing across the front of it)."Hey," I said. I shook her outthrust hand, and her palm was soft and a little damp. "I'm Jillian."

"Jillian, your hair is so pretty." She plopped down in the chair next to mine. For a second I thought she was going to reach out and run her fingers through my hair, but she did not. "Is it naturally that color?"

"Thanks," I smiled politely. "It's been this color since I was a baby."

Celine had a soft, pretty face, with tiny features: a little pointed nose, thin arched eyebrows, a short bowed mouth. Except for her ears, which were round and stuck out from the sides of her head through her pale brown hair.

"You're lucky." She smiled at me, and a dimple formed on one side of her mouth. "I'd kill to be a blonde."

I laughed, unsure how to respond, but before I was forced to say anything else, the bell rang and Celine was pulling a notebook from her book bag. During class, I noticed she studiously took notes on every single thing the teacher said, even though it was only the first day and Mrs. Touk, our plump Geometry teacher, was mainly going over the format of the class and the syllabus she had printed for us. Celine wrote in big, curling letters, with a hot pink pen that, interestingly, also featured hot pink ink. In contrast, I spent most of the class either watching out the window (a freshman gym class was out on the lawn doing jumping jacks and some sort of sprint drill in their matching grey and navy gym clothes) or studying Celine herself. She was wearing a plain red t-shirt, tattered jeans that hung loosely on her thin legs and colorful woven bracelets lined both of her arms. She laughed at all of Mrs. Touk's stupid, first day jokes (and she seemed to be laughing genuinely, which Mrs. Touk rewarded with appreciative glances every so often) and her laugh was deep, unlike her soft, girlish voice. When the bell rang at the end of the class period my stomach was growling and I didn't even bother stuffing my math book back into my bag before I bolted from the room, hurrying to the cafeteria.

"Hey." I heard someone call from behind me as I was pushing my way through the hall, and it took several tries before she finally caught my attention by grabbing the back of my book bag. I stopped and turned.

"Hey!" Celine was grinning and she stepped up beside me. We started walking again. "Do you have lunch now, too?"

So, I reasoned, she had decided she liked me. She had decided we were going to be friends. Though I hadn't made any clear decisions about her yet, I ceded to her resolve.

"Yeah," I offered. "Do you want to sit with me?"

The previous year, Rudy and I had sat in the back corner of the cafeteria, at one of five round tables, with a small group of girls from our class. When Celine and I exited the lunch line carrying sandwich-laden trays, I looked across the crowded room to see Rudy already seated at the table, two girls sitting beside her. She met my gaze, and seeing Celine walking beside me, raised her eyebrows in curiosity. I raised my own and shrugged one shoulder in answer.

"Hey," I said as I took my seat beside Rudy, setting my tray down on the marbled plastic tabletop. The lunches Rudy and I had selected were identical, turkey sandwiches with mozzarella and lettuce, small bags of tortilla chips and crisp red apples. "This is Celine. We just got out of math together."

I offered no further explanation, mostly because I didn't know anything else about Celine. But she picked up the slack, extending her hand across the lunch table toward Rudy first, then each of the other two girls.

"Celine Donner," she smiled widely. "I just moved from Seattle. It's so different here! So weird." She bit into her sandwich, which, I noted, was really just several slices of cheese stacked high between two pieces of bread.

"Seattle? That's cool," Deena, the girl sitting beside me, who I knew from cheerleading the year before, said.

"Yeah, it was really nice. I liked it there." She opened her bag of potato chips, lifted the top of her sandwich and layered chips on top of the cheese. "My dad's in the military, so we move around quite a bit."

"How long did you live in Washington?" Rudy asked.

Celine closed her eyes for a second as she thought. "About five years. That was the longest we stayed anywhere. Before that we were in North Carolina, California, Florida. And Germany and Korea, overseas."

"Geez," Rudy was eating her chips first, sliding them into her mouth one at a time and crunching down with her teeth. "I bet California was a cool place to live. I think I want to go to school at UCLA."

The Goldens had spent a week at the end of the summer in Los Angeles, and since then, Rudy had been obsessed with the idea of moving to California. "The beaches were gorgeous," she had gushed, while we sat in her room and ate ice cream the night she got back. "And the people there were so interesting. Kind of...eccentric, I guess. It was like they didn't exactly care what other people thought of them, but at the same time, they were showing off for someone. Plus, I tried surfing, and it's so much fun."

I shook my head and rolled my eyes at her, but I could see it too, Rudy fitting seamlessly into Hollywood. Shopping on Rodeo Drive with the waves of her dark hair blowing in the breeze, or laughing as she played on the beach – her long, tan legs were perfect in a bikini. But I did not like to think about growing up, going to college or leaving St. Louis, even though I'd only lived there for two years. I was sure Rudy and I would go to college together, but we were only sixteen! I didn't want to think about anything past the next weekend.

"California was pretty," Celine agreed, noncommittally. "But we were mostly in the desert there. I didn't get to see a lot of beach."

"That sucks," Rudy said, and I couldn't gauge her opinion of Celine. The five of us sat and talked through the rest of lunch, though I mostly ate and listened, watching the other girls' faces and studying their reactions to one another. Usually I ate lunch so slowly I only had time to finish half of my tray of food, but when the bell rang – three short bursts to send us on to our next class and send the next lunch shift into the cafeteria – I had polished off my entire sandwich and bag of chips and my stomach felt stuffed.

"See you in bio," I said to Rudy as the five of us cleared the table and stood. This year we had only two classes together, and one of them was biology, our last period of the day.

"Right." Rudy sipped the last drops of her soda from the can and swallowed. "I heard she's showing a movie. No syllabus."

I smiled. When we watched movies in class, Rudy and I would sit in the back of the room and pass a notebook back and forth beneath the table playing tick tack toe or hangman or writing funny stories about our classmates as superheroes or cartoon characters.

"Thanks for letting me sit with you guys," Celine said, dumping her empty sandwich wrapper into the trashcan. She slung her yellow backpack onto one slim shoulder and gave us a dimpled smile. "See you tomorrow in math, Jillian."

"Yeah, no problem," I said. "See you around."

———

RUDY AND I HAD ALWAYS, for the year and a half that I had known her, been a twosome. We had other friends, but they were more acquaintances than anything, really. Girls we played sports with, girls we were partnered with for science labs or history projects or the other Ogden girls who lived near our neighborhood and occasionally came over on a Friday night to ride to a party with us and use sleeping over at Rudy's house as an excuse for their parents' benefit. No one else ever really stuck, though, and I had taken pride in this, thinking Rudy had chosen me to be her best friend because I fit all the qualities she liked best and everyone else around us had fallen short. But there was something about Celine that Rudy was drawn to as well (and it didn't help that Celine had no other friends in the state, and was unafraid to be the third wheel). So, beginning that fall, we became an awkward threesome. Or, at least, awkward to me.

That first time I met Celine in math class, I had found no reason to dislike her. In fact, she was the type of person who normally would have intrigued me. But once she began to infiltrate my friendship (that's what it had felt like!) I began to pick her apart, usually only in my own mind, but sometimes out loud in front of Rudy when it was just the two of us, in the form of snide but subtle comments. Celine was a vegetarian, something I thought of as fake and showy and disingenuous. She bought strange clothes sometimes, expensive clothes made by special companies who touted, in large words on the tags of their products, that they did not test on animals or employ child laborers, but looked remarkably similar to the clothes you could buy from JCPenney at the mall. And, most obnoxious of all, in my mind, she was the type of person who had a personal anecdote for every conversation. If Rudy and I were talking about a boy, she would bring up a past boyfriend from one of her previous schools. If we were wishing we could go to Vermont with the rest of our class for a ski trip over Christmas break, she chimed in with something from her collection of travel experiences. She thought she was world-wise and charming, and I, at sixteen, found this utterly intolerable.

6

―――――

SOPHOMORE WINTER

In November, my cross-country season ended with a personal best at the district meet. The boys, as a team, had won the district meet and sent four individual runners – Peter, the twins and an exceptionally talented and shy freshman boy – to the state meet, while Tawny had been the only Ogden female to advance. Afterward, because the weather had grown colder, and because I now had to compete with Celine for Rudy's attention, I started to neglect my running. Instead, I would sit around the house with my mother on Saturday mornings, drinking coffee and reading the newspaper (realistically, I only read the entertainment and crime sections, but it made me feel adult to share the newspaper with her), waiting for Rudy to call me when she woke up.

In early December, Rudy clipped an ad from one of my magazines. It was one of those perfume advertisements with the sticker you peel off, and underneath, there's a sample of the perfume. Rudy loved the smell of it, and she'd taken the clipping home with her and set it on her dresser, and before we went out one Saturday night, I saw her press the paper against her wrists, rubbing off some of the sampler smell. For Christmas, I gave her a huge bottle of that perfume, and she had squealed and wrapped me in an enormous hug. Celine gave both Rudy and I homemade drawstring purses, wrapped in matching butcher paper. Rudy hated carrying a purse, but she smiled and thanked Celine for the gift, and she brought it with her once when we went with Celine to a movie. She wore the perfume I gave her every day of Christmas break. I felt more secure than ever in my position as Rudy's best friend.

By late January, when we returned to school, Ogden's boys basketball team still held a perfect 18-0 record. Rudy and I had never really attended basketball games (we had gone to a grand total of three home games our freshman year, largely so Rudy could have an excuse to see Houston). Rudy and Houston had broken up months before and, consequently, we had not been to a single game the first semester of our sophomore year. But this was the best the team had performed in a decade, and the school became electrified with an anticipatory energy that was hard to ignore. The cheerleaders had begun to hang handmade posters on the lockers that belonged to basketball team boys and on game days, when the boys wore their uniforms the entire day at school, it wasn't uncommon to see someone run up and slap one of the players' a high-five or hoot and applaud them in the hallway. I even heard a group of three or four junior girls had spent the weekend before a Monday night game baking plates of cookies that they had then delivered to each member of the Varsity team at their families' homes.

The first week of February, I found myself at my first basketball game of the season, pressed between Rudy and Celine in the crowded bleachers of the student section. We were three rows up from the court, in the first row of seats open to the general student population (the first two rows were unofficially reserved for student spectators – primarily boys – who had earned their coveted seats by attending every single game, wearing ridiculous costumes and generally making fools out of themselves cheering on the team). We cheered with the rest of our classmates, and we got thoroughly wrapped up in the game itself.

Ogden won. And basketball fever went rampant.

———

It was a dreary, rainy Sunday in February when the idea of Zach Smith first developed. Rudy and I were sitting at the Goldens' kitchen table finishing homework, textbooks spread out in front of us. We were both quiet, the faint hum of someone else's TV show on the other side of the house the only sound besides the rain beating softly on the back porch. I was playing with the edge of the blanket wrapped around my legs when Rudy put her pencil down and looked up from her history study guide.

"You know what we should do?"

"Hm?"

"What if we made a fake person? Like a profile on chat."

I waited, confused, but she appeared to be waiting for my response.

"Why?"

"We could see what people really say about us. And I bet we could find out all kinds of hilarious stuff about other people," Rudy said. "It's not like we'd be mean or anything. It would be funny. Just for fun."

"But how could we do that? How would anybody know her?"

"I don't know. I didn't plan it all out or anything," Rudy shrugged. "I just thought it'd be entertaining."

I looked over her shoulder out the window, where the rain was picking up, pinging off of the brick sidewalk like ricocheting bullets.

"What if we said it was my cousin? Like from Boston?"

Rudy perked up, the corners of her mouth twitching into a smile. "Yes! That's perfect. And we could say he's thinking about coming down for the summer, so he's trying to get to know people."

"He?"

Rudy nodded enthusiastically. "Girls will be more willing to talk to a cute guy than to a girl they don't know. They might find her threatening."

"Okay," I said, befuddled. "How do we set it up? Do we need an email address?"

"I can't remember," Rudy said. "Hang on, I'll go get my laptop."

She dashed out of the room, and I closed my math book and pushed it aside to make room on the table. It was things like this, I thought briefly, that made me a C student.

"Here, scoot over," Rudy set the computer down in front of me, and I moved to the edge of the chair to make room for her beside me.

"What should his name be?" I asked. The momentum of the idea was shaking me out my rainy-day-induced hypnosis.

"Bond. James Bond."

"Bradley Pitt."

"Theodore Bundy."

"You're really creepy," I said, and Rudy laughed.

"Seriously though," she said. "What about Ryan? Or Zach?"

"I like Zach. What's his last name?"

"Your last name?"

"No, that's too weird. Make it my mom's maiden name. Smith."

"Zach Smith, it is," Rudy opened up a web browser window and started typing.

We sat, squeezed together in one oversized kitchen chair, while we picked out "Zach's" hobbies – soccer, weight lifting and

Scrabble (the last one had been at Rudy's absolute insistence) – his school, his favorite movies and books. We picked out a photo of an attractive looking guy from some obscure modeling website. He had white-blonde hair like mine, and if I had met him in real life, I would have been too intimidated by his good looks to speak to him unless he spoke to me first.

"Who should we suggest he make friends with?" Rudy traced over his face with the cursor as she thought.

"Callan and Jen. And the rest of those junior girls," I said. "And guys on the soccer team. And Celine."

Rudy snorted. "I bet Jen won't even accept it. I don't think she talks to people she doesn't already know."

"Make sure you hide his friends list, too, so nobody can see he doesn't have any friends yet."

"Right." Rudy nodded.

"Hello, girls." Mrs. Golden pushed through the kitchen door carrying an empty popcorn bowl in one of her hands. Instinctually, my heart leapt like I'd been caught red-handed, and I felt the urge to shield the computer screen with my hands. "How's the homework coming along?"

"We're taking a little break," Rudy said.

"Mmhmm," Mrs. Golden smiled and stopped behind our chair. "And who is this cute boy? Should I know him?"

Both of us burst into a fit of giggles. We shared a look, and I laughed so hard I nearly slid off of the seat of the chair.

"What?" Mrs. Golden's face was the picture of confusion. "What? What does that mean?"

"It's my cousin," I said, giggling.

"From Boston," Rudy added.

"Oh, okay." Mrs. Golden still looked unsure as she took her empty bowl to the dishwasher and placed it inside. "What's so funny about him? He looks like a very nice boy to me."

Laughter bubbled out of us again, and Mrs. Golden left the

room shaking her head without waiting for an answer. When she was gone, we closed the laptop and Rudy returned to her own chair and flipped back to where she had left off on her history guide. I reopened my math book, but now I felt too stimulated to return to my geometry problems. The rain outside had stopped, but the clouds still hung low overhead in the sky, and I alternated between staring out at their hulking, grey masses and staring down at the tiny black numbers printed in my textbook. We had intended to come back to the profile later, to see if anyone had accepted our online friendship requests, but as the afternoon dragged on it slipped further and further from our minds. By the time my mother called me to come home for dinner, Zach Smith had been completely forgotten.

———

"What'd you guys do yesterday? I tried to call you, but you didn't pick up." Celine stared at me from across the lunch table the next day at school.

She bit into an apple, and I felt my cheeks flush. I had ignored her call while Rudy and I were studying.

"Sorry," I said. "I think I left my phone on silent. We were just studying, though."

Celine nodded. Her feelings appeared totally intact.

"So," she said between bites. "Your cousin added me online."

For a split second, I had no idea what she was talking about. Then I remembered. I felt Rudy's foot tap against mine underneath the table, reminding me to speak.

"Um, yeah. Zach. He's trying to meet some people here," I mumbled.

"He might come stay with Jill's family this summer, for a month or something," Rudy added.

"Oh, that's cool. Is he single? He's really hot," Celine glanced at me. "Sorry if that's weird to say."

"No, that's okay. I mean, we grew up together." What did that even mean? I was making no sense, I thought to myself. "Yeah, he's single though."

"He just seems so cool. I saw he was into soccer, and obviously I am too," Celine continued.

I literally could not believe my ears. I stole a glance at Rudy and the look on her face convinced me I couldn't be hallucinating. She widened her eyes quickly so that only I could see, and I gave her a weak smile intended to convey the message that I had no idea what the hell was going on either. Beside us, the other girls at the table were listening as they moved food around their lunch trays.

"Yeah, he's a pretty cool guy," Rudy said, and then she shoved a handful of fries into her mouth.

"You've met him before?"

Rudy nodded with her mouth full. She was chewing extra slowly.

"Zach came down for Thanksgiving," I improvised. "With his family. That's when he met Rudy."

"You didn't have a thing with him, did you?" A flash of guilt flickered over Celine's face, until Rudy began to shake her head. "Oh, great. I think I'm going to try to talk to him. Maybe we could get to know each other before he comes."

"Yeah, sure." I took a gulp of water.

"If I'm even here this summer. I might go back to Washington, to help with that environmental campaign, you know," Celine said.

"What's that for again? I mean, what would you be doing?" Rudy jumped at the opportunity to embark on another subject, and Celine dove into a description of her passion to prevent the pollution of the ocean. To my great relief, it lasted until the end of our lunch period. We dumped our empty trays onto the conveyor belt beside the dishwashing room and Celine said goodbye and dashed out of the cafeteria, still nibbling the apple she'd been eating all hour. I turned to Rudy.

"What just happened?" I asked.

Rudy took a deep breath. "I think we're in some serious shit."

————

CELINE HADN'T HAD a single boyfriend over the year she'd been at Ogden (neither had I, but in my mind this fact revealed less about me than it did about Celine). She hadn't gone on a date, and she went to every dance alone. When Rudy and I talked about guys in her presence, she didn't even seem to be particularly interested in anyone from our school, and I was beginning to harbor the secret suspicion that Celine was a lesbian. Never in a million years had I expected her to be interested in Zach, my fake cousin, a random photograph on the Internet.

That Monday after school Rudy and I had gone straight to her house and pulled up his profile on the computer. Immediately, we were bombarded with friend requests and friendship acceptance notifications. It seemed as though half of the school had developed an interest in him, and my stomach sunk down within my abdomen.

"Good Lord," I said, wide-eyed. "That really spread fast."

"Zach has more friend profiles than I do," Rudy laughed. She pulled up the first message from Celine, and as we read it, I felt dirty, though it contained nothing more intimate than a simple greeting and some questions about Zach's soccer career.

"What're we going to do? Tell her it's fake?"

"If we tell her he's fake, she'll probably freak out. After she said all of that at lunch and we went along with it," Rudy answered.

"But we couldn't tell her then, in front of everyone else."

"Yeah, but that's not what she'll think. I don't want to hurt her feelings." Rudy bit her lip and paused for a second. "I think we should just keep going with it. It'll die out soon, and she'll forget about him."

"Yeah, I guess," I agreed hesitantly. "So, do we message her back?"

"It can't hurt, I guess. We don't want to make him seem like an ass."

"We don't?"

"I don't think so."

Our response was nice but short, and after a few days without hearing back from Celine, we thought we had dodged a particularly unpleasant mess. But that Friday Zach got a long, hopeful message from Celine, and when she met us at Rudy's that night to leave for a concert, she started asking questions. The entire thirty-minute drive Celine leaned up from the back-seat of my car, her elbows perched on the backs of both of our seats as she inquired about Zach's childhood and his family and even his plans for college. She was obsessed. Rudy and I plied her with answers we made up off of the tops of our heads, digging ourselves deeper and deeper. By the end of the car ride I was so weighed down with a guilt I hadn't expected to feel, I could barely enjoy the concert and when I looked over at Rudy midway through our favorite song, I could see on her face that she felt the same.

The thing was, there was no way out. At least no easy way.

———

THE DISTRICT BASKETBALL game was scheduled for a Wednesday night and by that time, Rudy and I had been sucked into the hype. We painted navy blue stripes on our faces and wore tall navy socks with shorts even though the temperature had fallen again and it was only twenty-five degrees outside after the sun went down. I sat at Rudy's vanity while Celine curled plastic ribbon into long spirals with the open blade of a pair of scissors and tied it in bunches around my ponytail. We pulled into the school parking lot nearly half an hour before game time. It was already packed. Rudy circled the lot for ten minutes before we gave up and parked down the street, running and skipping all the way into the sports lobby, partly because of the excitement and partly because of the cold. My socks chafed against the goosebumps on my calves while we ran.

The game turned out to be a blowout. In the first quarter, our boys pulled ahead by twenty points. By the end of halftime they had extended their lead to thirty, and the opposing team's players looked dejectedly at the scoreboard as they wiped sweat off their brows with the backs of their hands. Their coach screamed at them, his meaty face red all the way up to his hairline, but they never gained any positive momentum. The second half of the game was just a showcase of Ogden's best basketball skills.

The game ended 87-55 and when the buzzer sounded Rudy and I rushed out of the bleachers and onto the court with the rest of the students, celebrating wildly with our team.

The team advanced through the sectional tournament, though they won no more of their games by a point margin greater than ten. Rudy and I drove to every single game, some of them more than an hour away, and I learned everything there was to know about basketball in a single month (or at least it felt that way). Ogden's last game before the state championships was decided by a single basket, shot from outside the three point line by a senior named Rusty Phelps. He wasn't a starting player, but after our star had fouled out in the middle of the fourth quarter, the coach put him in and left him for the remainder of the game. Rusty had bad acne, white capped pustules, angry red scabs and faded, healing brown marks. It covered his forehead and the sides of his mouth and though I felt sorry for him, every time I saw him I couldn't help but think how awful it would be to kiss him. The potential of my lips brushing against one of the infected bumps made me feel like I could throw up. I assumed the same went for all the girls at our school; I had only ever seen him talking to boys. And he wasn't a particularly great basketball player either; he wasn't one of the boys whose jersey number students would paint on their chests or faces and as far as I could tell, he spent most of his game time sitting on the bench cheering on his teammates. But somehow, as the final seconds ticked off the clock, Rusty ended up with the ball in his hands, and he was steadying it, then he was raising his arms, then he flicked his wrist and sent it spinning through the air. I could feel the crowd around me, all of us taking one collective intake of breath and holding it as the ball hit the rim of the basket and when I saw it fall through the hoop (really, all I could see between the shoulders of the students jumping and flailing in front of me was a tiny flash of orange in the white of the net) I threw my arms around Rudy and squeezed her so hard she squealed, and I was so happy for our team – I was ecstatic – that as I soon as I saw Rusty Phelps get swallowed up by his teammates, I forgot him entirely.

"I knew he could do it. I told him he'd get his moment, eventually," Rudy said later that night, as we'd made our way through the parking lot toward her car.

"You knew who could do what?"

"Rusty. I told him he'd get the chance to have a big moment like that."

I stared at her, smiling to herself.

"Since when are you friends with Rusty Phelps?"

She shrugged. "We talk sometimes, at school. He's a really nice guy."

We were quiet for a second, the sound of muted celebration still audible from across the parking lot.

"So," Rudy said when we'd reached her car. "Do you want to stop for burgers or something? I'm starving."

———

"Want one?" Rudy tipped her open bag of chips in my direction and just as I reached across my lap, the bus driver hit a bump on the highway and half a dozen chips fell out onto the speckled brown seat between us.

"Man," Rudy murmured. She swept them off the seat with the back of her hand. "Guess I won't be eating those."

We were on our way to the Class 3 Championship basketball game and because it was held more than two hours away, Ogden had commissioned school buses to drive any willing student-spectators to the game (the basketball team would be riding in style, in their own coach bus, complete with TV). Because it was easy, because it meant you could ride in the same vehicle as the person you secretly liked and sneak glances at them for a whole two hours and then maybe, if you got lucky and Ogden won, you would summon up enough bravado to ask them to share a seat with you in the dark on the bus ride home - almost everyone who was going to the game was riding one of the three Ogden buses. Shared successes like this created a situation where there was just enough general camaraderie that anything was possible.

I pulled three chips out of the bag and stuck them in my mouth one at a time.

"Do you guys want any?" Rudy turned around in her seat

and offered the bag to Deena, from our lunch table, and Celine, who were sharing a seat behind us.

"No, thanks. I'm trying not to eat carbs," Deena frowned.

Celine stuck two chips in her mouth and reached down to wipe the orange BBQ dust on the bottoms of her jeans.

"What, are you doing Atkins?" Rudy asked. "That's what it's called, right?"

Deena nodded. "For prom."

"My mom tried that one time," I added. "Don't you have to eat only green vegetables for the first two weeks or something? And no soda or coffee?"

Deena nodded again, the corners of her mouth turning down. "It really sucks. But they only had a size 4 left in the dress I bought."

"My mom lost, like, ten pounds. I guess it works," I shrugged.

"I hope so," Deena sighed. "I need to lose five pounds. I just want a freaking chocolate bar."

Rudy and I laughed, and up toward the front of the bus came a series of unidentified girly squeals. Our chaperone, the swim coach, turned to survey the bus with a grumpy stare.

They had tried to filter the busses by grade level – one for freshman and sophomores, one for juniors and one for seniors – but we had snuck onto the juniors' bus, along with a group of other sophomores, without any problems. Between snippets of conversation, I was letting my eyes drift toward the back of the bus where Drew, a blue-eyed, blonde-haired, straight-white-teethed junior was sitting.

Drew was handsome. Preppy-handsome. When I laid eyes on him for the first time during the district basketball game, I couldn't believe I hadn't noticed him in the hallways before (later that night, after I was at home in my bedroom, I had pulled out my freshman yearbook and flipped through page after page until I found him smiling up from that year's sophomore class photos). On the bus he was sitting with a group of boys, all of them wearing white t-shirts beneath old Ogden basketball jerseys. He leaned over, laughing, and his long bangs fell into his eyes. He flicked them out of his face with a quick shake of his head, and my stomach flipped.

"You bought your dress already?" Rudy was saying.

"I ordered it last week."

She lowered her voice the slightest bit. "Do you have a date yet?"

Deena blushed and shook her head. "No. But Stephen and I just broke up, so I'm not really surprised. I'm not worried about it yet."

"Oh, right." Rudy looked relieved. "Has anyone been asked yet? Besides the obvious couples?"

"I know Isaiah Staples asked Marissa Johnson already." Deena chewed her bottom lip. "But that was a giveaway, too."

Rudy nodded and I turned my head toward the window, but there was nothing outside but billboards and tall, dead grass.

"Jillian, when is Zach coming for the summer?"

"What?"

Celine had looked up from the magazine on her lap and she was staring at me over the back of the bus seat.

"When is Zach coming for the summer?" She repeated.

"Um, I'm not sure yet if he is." I stole a quick glance at Rudy but she turned away quickly, avoiding my eyes.

"Do you think he'd go with me if I asked him to prom?" At Ogden, all four classes were allowed tickets to the prom. It was very diplomatic.

"Yeah, maybe," I blurted.

Rudy pressed the tip of her shoe against my toes and I looked down. She had left a faint, dusty mark on my suede boot.

"Zach's your cousin, right?" Deena piped up. "Celine, you have a thing with him? Doesn't he live in Boston?"

"We've been talking a lot, lately. He's supposed to come visit this summer."

Celine wasn't even whispering. She was practically yelling, professing her love on a bus crowded with kids just waiting to judge her!

"So, you haven't met him yet?"

"No," Celine said. "But we've talked on the phone a couple times."

On the phone? I elbowed Rudy covertly, behind the shield of our seat back, and she raised her eyebrows. That was a lie. A flat out lie. And we hadn't messaged her for weeks. I could hardly open my mouth to speak.

"Actually, I forgot, I don't think he was thinking about coming until July," I managed. "If he comes, I mean."

"Bummer," Celine frowned. "I guess I'll be going to the dance solo, then."

"So, you really like him then?" Deena – oblivious Deena – pressed.

"I do. I think he really likes me, too. We have a lot in common."

"That's awesome." Deena didn't look entirely certain of that awesomeness. "Well, if I don't find a date, we can go together. Two single ladies, out on the town."

———

WE WERE SAVED from further conversation when the bus pulled into the parking lot at the University of Missouri basketball complex. We gathered our purses and filed down the steps and out of the bus behind a group of boys whose stomachs were painted navy and white and who were hooting and chanting already, though we hadn't even made it into the gymnasium yet.

The place was enormous. Rudy and I hurried through the

curved concrete hallway along with the group. A section of seats had been cordoned off for the Ogden student body and across the court was the opposing team's crowd, all of the students dressed in matching red t-shirts and some of them holding hand-drawn posters.

"Let's go this way." I was watching Drew as he followed his friends to their seats, and I pulled Rudy by the wrist in the same direction.

We pushed into the row directly behind him; he was only three seats to my left and if I had really stretched, I could have touched his shoulder.

"Why'd you want to sit over here?" Rudy was situating herself in the hard plastic seat and she didn't look up to see my cheeks flush.

For two weeks I had been obsessed with the idea of going to prom with Drew, but I had yet to mention my interest in him to Rudy and I didn't really know why. Or, more accurately, I knew why – Rudy was direct and forward and sometimes very pushy – but I didn't want to admit that I was indirect and timid and terri-fied of approaching boys I found attractive. I would learn their routine and carefully place myself within their grasp – I would eat at their lunch table in the cafeteria or dance directly across the room from them at a party or sit right behind them at a basketball game – and I would wait. I thought putting myself in their general vicinity was enough; surely they could sense my longing for them. Surely, if the feelings were reciprocated, they would talk to me; they would initiate the conversation. If I told Rudy she'd force my hand, and I wasn't sure I was ready for that just yet.

"It's a good spot. I didn't want to get stuck behind someone tall," I said and she nodded.

Both basketball teams were warming up on the court below us and I watched as Houston Jones shot the basketball. It hit the rim of the basket and bounced away. We were too far away to hear, but I could see him mouth the word 'fuck.' I glanced at Rudy and she was watching him too.

"Can't they get ejected for cussing?"

"Only during the game, I think," Rudy said, eyes still on the court.

"Oh." I picked at the fingernail polish on my thumb.

When the game began we all stood, and I watched Drew pull a blue whistle from his back pocket and put it in his mouth, hanging off his bottom lip. When the referee blew his shiny silver whistle, so did Drew.

The game was tense from the beginning; a nail-biter, hair-raiser, whatever you want to call it. Only four or five points separated the two teams during the first three quarters. I had finger marks on my forearm from where Rudy had been squeezing.

In the fourth quarter, things just got ugly. The other team was from a public school, also in St. Louis, and after one of their players was fouled, they started chanting. At first you couldn't really tell what they were saying, but soon it picked up in volume and was impossible to ignore.

"Trust funds can't play basketball, take your ass back to the mall!"

They were holding their hands up, rubbing their thumbs against their fingers. Pantomiming "money."

They shouted it over and over, until finally one of their administrators caught on and shushed them, but the fire had been lit. The parents in the crowd were shaking their heads silently, but the students were murmuring.

"That's fucked up," I heard a boy behind me say.

When our principal, Dr. Foakley, had his head turned, we would throw up the finger in small sections at a time and though some teachers saw us, they didn't say anything. There were too many of us to discipline. At least we weren't yelling, they must have reasoned. And maybe we should have had a better comeback because our basketball team began to suck. All of the sudden, the other team had pulled away by eight points. We didn't give up yet – the boys were sweating and sprinting down the court with the ball and they managed to get within four points before the opposition pulled ahead again. From the stands, we tried to pull them out of their funk. We screamed for whoever was carrying the ball, and we stomped our feet against the floor and cried out when they scored. My throat was raw by the end of the game. But in the last minute we were still 10 points down and you just knew it was over. I could feel it in the response of the crowd. Some of the girls were on the verge of tears and some of them were already crying, their arms around each other. The boys just shook their heads solemnly and kept yelling half-hearted encouragements to their friends on the court.

When the buzzer sounded, the opposite side of the gym erupted, their surge of energy carrying high over the slumped shoulders and bowed heads of our crowd, but I couldn't turn away from the court where our players stood. Houston had his hands on his hips, staring down at his feet. One of the senior boys was actually crying, his mouth turned down, his hand shielding his eyes.

I looked at Rudy and her shoulders were low, her hands hanging limply at her sides. She was biting her bottom lip and staring at the court.

The teachers began to usher us out of our seats almost immediately, and we shuffled our feet and hung our heads climbing the steps out of the auditorium. Behind us, under the lights of the basketball court, the winners were still celebrating loudly, their cheers echoing through the rafters.

Outside, in the cold, late-February air, we found our voices again.

"That sucked," Celine murmured beside me. "It was so close."

I nodded and shoved my hands into the pockets of my jeans.

"I can't believe that chant they did," Deena shook her head. "*So* racist."

"It wasn't racist," I said. "They weren't talking about us being white."

"You know they meant that, though." Deena lowered her voice to a whisper. "Half of their crowd was black."

"Ogden's not all white. Our team isn't either," Rudy said. It was true; there were three black boys on the basketball team, and there were kids from most ethnicities at our school, though they were definitely the minority.

"Whatever," Deena rolled her eyes. "It was still rude."

We were quiet as we reached the bus. It was locked, and we all stood outside shivering, huddling up against the side of the bus to shield us from the wind as we waited for the driver and our chaperones to return. Drew was nowhere to be seen. Finally, across the dark parking lot we saw the basketball team emerge from the side of the hulking building, their navy duffel bags hanging from their slumped shoulders. Drew and his friends were walking beside a group of players, their heads bent low and hands in their pockets with the exception of one boy who had his arm slung over one of the dejected player's shoulders.

The chaperones were following, and our bus driver rushed to the front of the crowd to unlock the door to the bus. The girls pushed to the front of the line to board and, chivalrously, the boys stepped aside for us to go in front of them. I was climbing the steps when I turned and saw Rudy wasn't behind me anymore.

"Where'd she go?"

Celine shrugged, and I stopped holding up the line and slid into one of the seats in the back half of the school bus.

I saw her out the window, her back turned to me. She was standing beside Houston; they were both standing apart from the rest of the basketball team and the rest of the students in general. Rudy reached up and touched the upper part of his arm, and he smiled a small, polite smile. Then she leaned forward and kissed him on the cheek before she turned and hurried back to the bus, her arms folded over her chest. Houston watched until she was all the way inside before he went back to his teammates.

How did I miss that? I remember wondering how long Rudy had still liked him. I had had no idea. There were signs of course, once I thought back to them – she didn't date anyone else that year, she still had pictures of him in her room, she still talked to him in the halls at school – but I was too wrapped up in my own concerns to notice them.

Rudy slid into the seat beside me.

"Do you care if I sleep on your lap?" she said. "I'm so tired."

I wanted to ask her about Houston, but I felt too guilty. Instead I just nodded, and she bent her legs up in the seat and lay her head in my lap. She closed her eyes, and I leaned my forehead against the windowpane. The glass was cold against my skin.

I shut my eyes and made a silent promise.

I will be less selfish and more observant, I silently swore. I will be a better best friend.

SOPHOMORE SPRING

Rudy and Houston got back together, apparently to no one's surprise but my own. "I knew it," Deena said over lunch. "They're so cute together, aren't they?" And then, once again, it seemed, Rudy was with prom date and I was without. But I told her about Drew, and I pinky-swore her to secrecy.

"He's so nice. I think he's your type," Rudy had agreed, standing in her kitchen as she stirred a bowl of boxed brownie mix. A fleck of the batter slopped out of the bowl, and she wiped it off the counter with her thumb, then ate it.

What did that mean? And how did she know he was so nice; did she talk to him?

"Do you know him? Like, have you've talked to him?"

"No. Not really. I had that one art class with him last semester. He just seems like a good guy."

Oh.

"You have to promise you won't say anything to him," I said. "Or to Houston."

Rudy looked up from the batter.

"Okay. But why not?"

"Rudy."

She turned to retrieve a pan from under the stove, then she lifted the bowl of batter.

"You forgot to grease that," I said.

"Oops." She set the bowl back on the counter. "I'm just saying, if you like him you should pursue him. Talk to him at track practice or something. Ask him to hang out with us some weekend."

"I don't even know him. What if he doesn't like me back? I'll feel like a moron." I grabbed a handful of pastel M&Ms from the candy bowl on the counter. Easter themed.

"Why wouldn't he like you? You're beautiful, you're smart, you're an awesome hurdler. You're a sweetheart." She rubbed a stick of butter across the bottom of the brownie pan.

"Rudy," I pressed. "Just let me do this my own way. Or not do it, whatever I decide."

"Fine. I promise." She zipped her lips, threw the imaginary key into the pan and slopped a thick, gooey spoonful of batter on top of it.

———

FOR THREE WEEKS following our kitchen conversation, where I swore Rudy to secrecy, I pursued Drew "my way". This consisted of sitting as close to him as I could without being conspicuous while we were stretching during track practice. At lunch, I asked Rudy to sit at Houston's table (they didn't normally spend lunch together – even the second time around, they were a strange kind of couple) but she happily obliged so I could be just one table away from Drew. I doodled his name in pencil on the borders of my homework, then erased it and drew it again in a different font. At night, I stared at his black and white photo in my yearbook (why were they black and white, I wondered, when color photography had been the norm for decades?) and sometimes I even planted a kiss over his face before I turned the light off to go to sleep.

It wasn't working. Surprise, surprise.

"I think you should talk to him. Tonight." Rudy wiggled her eyebrows from across her room. I was sitting cross-legged on her bed; she was rifling through her open closet, selecting outfits for the two of us. It was a familiar scene, with the new addition of Celine, perched on the seat of Rudy's vanity.

"I agree," Celine added. "It can't hurt anything, right?"

But what did she know? She was pretending to be in an internet relationship with a guy who didn't even exist. I felt a pang of guilt beneath my snotty attitude.

"Maybe," I said softly.

Rudy disappeared into the depths of the closet, then returned a few seconds later.

"Really, you need to do something tonight," she said seriously. "If you're serious about this, you're running out of time. People are starting to pair up for prom."

For her, things were so black and white, so "do it or don't do it". So *easy*. I hated her just a little bit, but she was right.

"So, what're you doing for prom?" I turned the attention to Celine. "Who do you want to ask you?"

"I'll probably go alone. There's just not anyone at school I'm really interested in."

She stretched her arms in the air and yawned.

"You're not going home tonight, are you?" Rudy popped out from the closet again at the sound of Celine's yawn.

"I'm so tired. And I have a test on Monday to study for."

"Me too. We're studying all day Sunday; study with us then," Rudy reasoned. "Just come with us tonight."

I remained quiet. I was already irritated. I didn't need Celine tagging along to the party tonight.

"I don't know what to wear. Parties aren't my thing, really."

Celine did not drink, Celine did not smoke, Celine did not wear sparkly things or sexy things or things made by companies that tested on animals. Celine was a modern day hippie.

"Borrow something from me," Rudy said. "Just come, please?"

Celine was cracking. Rudy could wear her down, too.

"Do it, or I'll punch you. Do it, or I'll wear my mom's fur coat to the party."

Celine laughed. At least she could have a sense of humor about her eccentricity.

"Fine," she threw her head back in mock exasperation. "I'll go this time. This *one* time."

———

My mood had improved slightly by the time we strolled into the party, buoyed by my new spring dress and my cute strappy sandals and the strawberry daiquiris Rudy had whipped up in the blender as we were getting ready while her parents were gone for the evening. Rudy actually made us link arms as we walked up the sidewalk; we were those girls.

Inside it was warm and bright. Things were good with Rudy and Houston, and she found him right away, sitting in front of a card game over the coffee table in the host's living room. She settled into his lap, one of his big, muscled arms wrapped around the smallest part of her waist while the other hand held his cards fanned out in front of him. Rudy pointed to his cards with one of her dainty index fingers and leaned over to whisper in his ear. He took a sip from his beer and smiled. I couldn't stick around in the living room watching her for long; I was sinking again. I needed to find company of my own.

I got up from my seat on the sectional and made my way out of the room with saying a word. Rudy glanced up as I left, but she didn't stop me or call out. I left Celine sitting with the seniors crowded around the poker game.

In the foyer, I darted into the bathroom to peer at myself in the mirror. I wet my fingers in the pedestal sink and dabbed at the cowlick at the back of my head, pressing it down against my skull. I smoothed the ends of my hair, where it lay flat and white-yellow against my chest. I pulled a tube of sheer pink lip gloss from my clutch and smeared it across my bottom lip, rubbed my lips together and smiled at my reflection. My nerves were boiling over like a pot left too long on the stove. With my sandaled foot, I put the toilet lid down, sat on the fuzzy seat cover and hung my head between my knees. Wasn't this what you were supposed to do to combat nerves? Or was that for nausea? I opened my eyes, and I was staring at my own green underwear beneath my dress. I took three deep breaths and stood. I smoothed my hair again, flushed the unused toilet and ran water in the sink, lest someone think I was doing something strange in the bathroom. When I exited, a junior girl was waiting outside the door and we avoided each other's eyes.

The next space I entered was the basement, where kids were polarized either around the bar on one side or the pool table on the other. My eyes lit upon Natalie, leaning against the bar between two other senior girls.

"Natalie." I set my hand on her shoulder and she turned to smile at me.

"Jill!" She was twinkling. She threw her arms around me and squeezed me around my middle.

"I didn't know you were coming," I said into her hair.

"Me neither!" She leaned back and held me at arms length. "I got my letter from Harvard today. I got in!"

"You got in?" In the fall, she had applied for early admission at Harvard and had been deferred. Ogden was a prestigious school in Missouri, but that didn't change the fact that this was still the Midwest. We weren't exactly groomed to go to Ivy League colleges. "That's amazing! I'm so happy for you!" I hugged her again, this time in earnest.

"Thank you," she gushed. "It doesn't even feel real yet. I feel like I'll wake up tomorrow and find out it was a big joke."

I shook my head and rolled my eyes. "No way. You deserve it."

Really, she did. Of all the people I met at Ogden, Natalie may have been the most sincerely deserving of her success.

"Thanks, Jill." She smiled and the corners of her eyes looked damp, like she could tear up at any moment.

"Well, I'm sort of looking for someone, so I'm going to keep moving." I motioned vaguely toward the opposite side of the room, toward the thwack of pool balls. "We'll talk more later though."

"Definitely," Natalie nodded. "I'll find you and Rudy later."

"Yes. And congratulations, again, Nat."

I made my way to the pool table, but I could already tell he wasn't there. I lingered for a few minutes and watched, standing at the edge of the circle. It was a crowd of underclassmen, of freshmen and my own sophomore classmates, but I didn't really know many of them, guys or girls. The two boys who were playing, bent over the table with their fingers steadying the cue stick as they sent balls shooting across the green velvet into leather pockets, were named Michael Denalby and Trent Calvert. They were both in my class, and I could sum up what I knew about each of them in neat little gossip-filled packages. I knew Michael had been suspended the second quarter of our freshman year for pulling down his pants and flashing his friend "the goat" – a through-the-legs-from-behind view of his genitalia that boys seemed to be fond of one-upping each other with – during his World History class. I knew Michael's dad was a lawyer and I knew that, though I didn't think he was particularly smart himself, Michael was expected to take over his father's practice once he graduated from law school, which boggled my mind. We were only sixteen; graduating college was six years in our future, and law school would be several years past that. To have your future mapped out that far in advance seemed to me like watching a basketball game when you already knew the outcome. Didn't that make the present – parties and football games and math class and deciding which college you would go to – seem boring and unimportant? What if he decided he liked engineering or painting, instead? Or did this legacy make things better for Michael; because he had a guaranteed career stamped across his future, because he was backed by his father's fortune, did that make him feel free to do things like show his penis to an entire class of students without much consequence?

Trent, I knew, was a scholarship student. This fact didn't make him any more or less liked, and it wasn't really something anyone talked about at all; it was just a fact I knew. Trent's mom was a single parent, and the general opinion of the guys in our class was that she was very attractive. The whispered opinion of the girls at Ogden was that she was kind of a slut. Because the two rumors seemed to reinforce one another (I was a disgrace to feminists everywhere), I believed them both. I also knew Trent was a very good public speaker (despite being only a sopho-more, he was captain of the speech and debate team, which was actually a highly sought after position) and he was very smart. In the fall, when most of our class took the ACT for the first time, he was rumored to have scored 35 out of 36. I, on the other hand, had scored 24.

I watched them slowly circle the perimeter of the table, knocking the balls in one or two at a time, until only the eight ball was left.

"Right corner pocket," Michael called. It went in, but so did his white cue ball. He cursed under his breath and he handed the stick off to the next boy in line before he cracked open his beer and proceeded to chug the entire thing as I walked away.

Upstairs, I spotted Drew from behind, recognizing him by his blonde hair and pale blue polo and the curves of his calf muscles as they disappeared up the stairs toward the second floor. I held my breath as I weaved through arms and legs and torsos in the large hallway leading to the second floor staircase. He was out of sight, and I bounded up the stairs after him, my heart pounding in my chest. At the top the light was dim; I stopped and looked left. My heart flattened and dropped, sliding down my spine.

Drew, with his luscious locks and perfect white teeth, his sturdy arms and stomach muscles and his boyish laugh, followed another girl into a dark room at the end of the upstairs hall. She was leading him by the wrist; all I could see of her before she disappeared through the doorway was her slim, bangled arm, her purple fingernails clutching Drew's forearm. But by the way he was smiling at her through the empty doorway, I didn't need to see her to know.

My face fell and just before the door closed with a thud behind the two of them, he glanced back down the hall and our eyes met. I tried to smile a little, nonchalantly. 'Oopsies! Sorry I caught you sneaking off! Don't mind me; I won't interrupt your fun!' That's what I wanted my smile to say, but I'm sure I didn't pull it off. In the split-second that the door was closing, his eyes looked a little confused. But he returned my small smile and then he was gone.

I turned and slunk back down the stairs, my stomach swinging between my ankles.

"Jillian." I heard someone's warbled voice calling my name, but I turned in the opposite direction at the bottom of the stair-case. I just wanted to leave, but first I had to get to Rudy. Before I could reach her, Celine materialized in front of me.

"Hey." She grabbed my arm and I pulled it away. She tried again, this time setting her palm on the front part of my shoulder, just above my bicep. "Hey, will you go outside with me? I wanted to talk to you about Zach."

There were only three or four people besides us in the entryway; two girls sitting at the bottom of the staircase and some other people wandering in and out from other rooms of the house. I still shouldn't have said it; we were supposed to be friends, Celine and I.

"Give it up already," I sneered.

"What?" Her face crinkled in confusion.

"I said, give up. Stop talking about him." I wasn't speaking quietly. The girls on the staircase turned to look at us.

In the morning, I would decide I did it because I was drunk. That's what I would tell Rudy; I was drunk and upset, I didn't mean to say what I said, especially not in front of everyone or at the volume that I said it.

"He doesn't even exist. Zach's not even *real*."

Her face crumpled further. She looked at me like I was speaking a different language. French. Mandarin.

"What are you saying? What does that mean?" She crossed her arms over her small chest and leaned back a bit, distancing herself from my obvious hostility.

"He's not real. We made him up; it was me and Rudy this whole time." I was almost yelling now. In my peripheral vision, behind Celine's head, I saw Rudy rise from Houston's lap when my words reached her ears. But I couldn't take it back now; there was no stopping me. "It was a *joke*. You weren't supposed to *like* him. It was just a fucking joke."

Celine's small, pale features were going pink.

I didn't know how big of a mistake I'd made until I saw it in Rudy's face as she approached us. The moment cracked; my anger melted into a sickly puddle. I looked to the side and I saw the two girls were whispering, staring up at me. A boy had frozen in place on his way into the bathroom, his fingers hovering over the doorknob.

Celine looked like she was going to cry. A tidal wave of regret washed through me so suddenly I thought I would throw up.

"Celine," I said.

"Jillian." Rudy had reached us at that exact moment. Celine shook her head, like she was trying to physically shake sense into what was happening. Rudy reached out for her, but she jerked out of Rudy's reach and stormed out the front door in a half-run.

My face was on fire. I looked down at my feet and heard chatter around me, that distinct brand of talking-about-what-just-happened chatter.

"Let's go." Rudy was pulling me toward the front door. "Let's go home."

I thought we were going to chase after Celine at first, and my gut thumped, but Rudy kept walking down the driveway and I didn't see Celine. Rudy was walking fast and I shuffled to keep up with her. We were going to Rudy's car, I realized. We were really going straight home.

I didn't get the nerve to look her in the face until we were inside the car, her gripping the steering wheel with both hands, even though she hadn't started the engine yet. She didn't make eye contact with me for a long time, and when she did she wore a peculiar look. I looked down at my lap and wanted to disappear.

"What happened?" She sounded, of all things, incredibly sad. "Why'd you say those things?"

"I don't know. Shit, I really don't know."

She started the car and we idled. I let out a loud breath.

"He went into a room upstairs with another girl," I said, biting my lip. "I didn't even get a chance to..."

I couldn't finish the sentence. My chin quivered and tears emerged out of nowhere in the corners of my eyes.

"Don't cry, Jill."

"I'm sorry. Really, I'm sorry."

I met her eyes and burst into tears and she put her arms around me in an awkward hug over the console.

"It's okay," she said. "It seems really bad now, but it'll be better in the morning."

I laid my head on her shoulder and let out a flood of tears. Rudy the angel. Saint Rudy. She had stayed with me, when she could have chosen Celine.

———

THAT NIGHT AT THE GOLDENS, I couldn't sleep. I crept out of Rudy's room and down the long, dark staircase toward the trophy room, where I sat with my back up against the wall and my legs outstretched, my hamstrings and calves pressed against the cold floor. There were sconces at either end of the hallway that were always left on, and their light made the picture frames cast shadows across one another so that parts of all of the photographs were shaded and grotesque-looking. It was cold and I had a stomachache. I wrapped my arms around my body.

There were three new photos on the wall – new since the first time I had been in the trophy room. One was of Marta; a photograph of her sitting behind a desk in her small office at a New York nonprofit organization. It was a clipping from a newspaper story about young world-changers; they picked fifty of the top young professionals in New York City and they had written a whole paragraph for Marta. Mrs. Golden had gushed for a month.

The second was of Kent studying abroad in Portugal the spring before. Rudy had gone to visit him with her parents, even though that meant she'd had to miss the first day of our final exams (Ogden, of course, allowed her to make it up and she got an A). In the picture, Kent was smiling and handsome as ever, but I no longer felt the same stirring when I thought about him. He was preparing for his final year of undergrad and was applying to law school at the University of Missouri. He would be only two and a half hours from home, but he was eons away.

Finally, there was a small photo of Rudy, cheesing in her cross-country uniform, holding a fifth place medal out in front of her body. She had just finished running, and her cheeks were red. Her hair fluffed away from the sides of her head. The picture was from our conference meet, where I had won the second place medal, and I had a copy of the same photo on my bulletin board at home, a copy where I hadn't been cropped out.

———

HALEY HATFIELD. That was the name of the girl Drew asked to his junior prom – the girl he had followed into an upstairs bedroom at Corey Jennings' party. Like me, she was a sophomore. Unlike me, apparently, she went after the things – the boys – she wanted. I heard she didn't have sex with him that night, but it seemed things between them were pretty serious. Serious enough for him to get on the school P.A. system and ask her to be his prom date in the middle of the morning announcements, and serious enough for them to date through the rest of the summer and into the fall of my junior year.

As for me, I threw all of my extra energy, all of the energy I had wasted pining uselessly after Drew, into track. I focused on hurdling, in particular, the event that Coach Kline had selected for me, specifically, the previous year. At first I had been upset – embarrassed that I was being singled out – when he had called my name at the end of warm up one day in the middle of my freshman season. I made eyes at Rudy, and she paused and shrugged before turning and hurrying after the sprint group as they paraded through the parking lot toward the track. As I was walking toward Coach Kline, another coach waved for his attention, and I stopped and waited a few feet away, my arms crossed awkwardly over my chest, until they had finished their conversation and she left.

"Jillian?"

I nodded. What was this about, I thought. The track team wasn't supposed to make cuts. And besides, there were far worse runners on the team than me. I was self-doubting, but I wasn't stupid.

He glanced over my head. The rest of the gym was empty. He shrugged one shoulder toward the door.

"Let's walk and talk."

He held the door open and followed me out onto the parking lot, the gymnasium door swinging shut behind us with a slam.

"Jillian, have you ever done hurdles?"

What? That wasn't a question I had been at all prepared for.

"No," I said, confused.

"How would you feel about giving them a shot in the next meet? You're tall and you've got long legs and a nice stride; I think there's a chance you'd be pretty good at the 100 and 300 meter hurdles."

"Really?" I blushed. "Yeah, sure. I'll try it."

"Awesome." Coach Kline had given me a quick smile, then his face returned to normal. Business face. Head coach face. "I'll have you practice with us today, then. See how things go."

"Today?"

He nodded. "We'll start with some drills. Simple stuff."

"Okay." I nodded as we walked through the huge, arced gates that led onto the track. The sprinters were already out on the track, the whole group of them running down the straightaway. They slowed as they reached the curve, first the lead group of boys, then each person behind them slowing to a brisk jog. I had picked out Rudy in the middle of the pack, knowing her by her neon orange shorts.

Since freshman year, I had grown another two inches, my legs longer and leaner, my body more gazelle-like than ever. I did okay during my first year as a hurdler, but sophomore year I was ready to work. Ready to put in all the effort. I did short sprints down one length of the blue rubber track and hurdle drills running the length back down toward Coach. There were only four of us who competed in the hurdles, but we had Coach Kline's undivided attention for half of each practice as he ran us through drill after drill, learning to run, not jump, over each hurdle, to snap our front legs back down once we'd sailed over one plank and were on to the next. He timed us with the stopwatch he always wore hanging around the back of his tanned neck.

I didn't think about prom again (of course I thought about it – I thought about it every time one of the girls at lunch refused to eat anything other than carrots and celery sticks, or when my mom pressed me about picking a time to go dress shopping – but it didn't float to the forefront of my thoughts) until one day after practice in early May. I was standing on the track with my heel hooked over one of the hurdles, leaning into the stretch until I could feel it pull the muscles in my hamstrings.

"Hey." Rudy walked up in front of me, swinging both of our book bags in the crook of her elbow. The sprinters regularly finished twenty minutes before the hurdlers, but Rudy and I still rode together.

"Hey," I said to the ground, my face pressed into my knee.

"How was your practice?" She leaned against the other side

of the hurdle and it scooted forward an inch. She stood again, crossing her legs awkwardly.

"It was okay." I gave her an odd look. I let my right leg drop and swung my left onto the hurdle. "What about yours?"

"It was good. Hand offs."

"That's cool."

It was a Wednesday and we had a chemistry exam the next morning. She was probably dying to get home and start studying.

"You don't have to wait for me," I said. "We can start driving separately, since I've been getting done later."

"I know," was all she said.

When I stood, Rudy handed me my book bag and we started walking.

"So, I was thinking," she started, then paused.

I waited.

"You still don't have a date for prom yet, right?"

"No. Thanks for pointing that out," I said sarcastically.

"That's not what I meant."

"I know."

"Well, what about Jack?"

Jack was Houston's friend. He was a senior, the one who had gone sledding with us and helped spike our hot chocolate with Baileys the winter before.

My heart beat faster.

"Does he want to go with me?"

Jack was cute. Not Drew cute, but still very cute. And everyone at school liked him.

"Yes." Rudy had changed into flip-flops, and they slapped against the bottoms of her heels as we tromped across the pavement.

"How do you know?"

"That's what Houston said."

"Well, why doesn't he ask me then?"

"I think he's going to. I just wanted to make sure you'd go with him."

"Of course I would."

We reached her car and she popped the trunk for us to throw our bags inside.

"I think we're getting a hotel room after the dance," Rudy said quietly, when we had both climbed inside the car and shut the doors behind us.

"Really?" I shot her a wide-eyed look. Was this why she was acting weird? "You guys haven't had sex, have you?"

She shook her head quickly. "No, I would have told you."

But they were getting a *hotel room*. After prom.

"Are you going to?" I pressed.

Rudy clutched the steering wheel and nodded.

"I think so. I think he really loves me, Jill." She looked at me, her face unsure. "Is that bad? Should I not?"

I was taken aback. She had told me everything she and Houston had done – not in detail, or anything, but discreetly – and I knew she was thinking about it, but I thought she meant in the future. At the end of the summer or something, months away. I didn't know she'd meant *now*.

"No," I said quickly. "I mean, yes, you should, if you want to. I guess."

She bit her bottom lip.

"Sorry, I sound like a moron. It's just," I took a deep breath. "I just wasn't expecting that. You should do whatever you think."

"I know." She started to back out of the parking spot, even though there were no cars around her. She could have just pulled forward and left. "I wanted to know what you thought, though."

I was flattered, if a bit confused still. "I get it. No one's going to think anything less of you – nobody's going to think you're a..."- it was hard to say the word – "a slut or anything, if you're worried about that. It's not like it's a one night thing. You guys have been together a long time."

"So you think I should?"

"I think you should." That was what she wanted me to say, wasn't it? "If you want to, obviously."

"Okay." She dutifully looked both ways before pulling out of the school parking lot and onto the street. "Would you want to get a room with us then?"

"What?" I looked at her again and she returned the look. "Like, me stay in the room with you and Houston?"

"And Jack."

"Oh." Duh. Of course. "Is that what the guys want?"

"I think, so we can hang out together at the hotel," she said to the windshield. "You don't have to if you don't want. We could just go to someone's house afterward."

"Like you'd skip the hotel room if I don't want to go?"

She bit her lip and shrugged. "I told Houston I wanted to ask you about it first."

I swallowed. "It would be fun though, right?"

Rudy nodded. "And, obviously, you don't have to do anything with him if you don't want to. I mean, I don't know if he's even thinking of that, but you know what I mean." She took her eyes from the road; when she said this, she looked directly into my pupils.

"Duh," I said.

My heart thumped in my chest. Maybe, if she hadn't given me permission to back out, I could have refused. But she did. It was all up to me, and that pretty much sealed the deal.

———

THE NEXT MORNING I found a bouquet of a dozen red roses in my locker, a small note attached to them with a one word proposal in bold-faced font across the front. "Prom?" it read. He had signed it on the back.

"That's so cute," Rudy cooed, peering over my shoulder into the locker. "You should wear one behind your ear today," she teased.

I blushed. "Yeah, right. For good luck on our test."

I left them in my locker, of course. I thanked Jack at lunch and gave him my affirmative answer before Rudy and I scurried off to our Chemistry test. But I couldn't concentrate on neutralizing equations. Periodic elements didn't have to worry about what transpired in hotel rooms after prom. Or maybe they did; what did I know? Before I even turned in my test, I knew I had failed.

———

THE DAY OF THE DANCE, we got our nails, make up and hair done, my mom chauffeuring us around town to her favorite spots; this was her area of expertise. I wore mine in long curls down my back; Rudy got an up-do, to showcase the low-cut back of her gown. When I zipped her into the dress, I stood back and whistled.

"Look at you, hot stuff."

You could see the points of her shoulder blades as the black dress curved down her tanned back.

She grinned a red lipstick grin. "Put yours on. I want to see yours."

I don't think I've ever posed for more pictures in my life.

There were photos of Rudy and me on the grand staircase in the Goldens' foyer, the chandelier glittering above us in the background. There were photos of us with our dates when they came to pick us from Rudy's. They were wearing white tuxedos;

their ties and vests matched the colors of our dresses. My mom snapped a photo as Jack unboxed a corsage and tried to slip it over my wrist.

We took more pictures at Houston's parents' home, more still at Forest Park, in front of the beautiful architecture of the art museum, with a big group of classmates. At dinner, Rudy hardly touched her salmon. I ate more than normal, devouring my entire steak, and immediately thought I shouldn't have. My stomach roiled.

At the dance, there were more photos. Shrieks and compliments and posing for individual and group shots every time we saw one of our friends. My cheeks ached, but I smiled my face off.

An hour before the dance ended, we were off to the hotel. Houston was sipping a beer as he drove. Rudy and I sat in our gowns in the backseat. She reached for my hand where it lay, limp in the empty middle seat. I squeezed her cold fingers.

We told our parents we were sleeping at Deena's.

I feel like I should note that the boys were sweet about it. They held the car door open for us. They turned their backs as we undressed, letting our expensive dresses crumple to the carpet where hundreds, probably thousands, of other people's feet had tread. My dress had a poofy skirt, and when I left it behind it kept its shape, rising off the floor like I had left part of myself inside.

As it was happening – as I felt that sharp pain, that dull throbbing in my lower body – I glanced across the room at Rudy, just a few feet away. The lights were off but I could just make out her face. Her pretty hair was limp, smashed up against the professionally laundered pillowcase. She met my eyes for a split second before we both looked away, and I thought I saw something sad there. Something much older and wiser than I felt at that moment. I was probably imagining things.

I was glad I was there with her.

————

ALL THE TIME I hear people claiming they live with no regrets. Celebrities say it in magazine interviews, musicians write it into their song lyrics. Spunky, "cool" high school teachers hang inspirational posters touting the phrase. Well, I call bullshit.

I regret so many of the choices I made during my adolescence, I couldn't even count them on all my fingers. Maybe not even my fingers, toes and teeth combined. There are mistakes I've made that make me wince, choices I wake up thinking about and can agonize over for days still, years after the fact. Then, there are smaller mistakes, smaller regrets whose outcomes I can live with. Pills I can swallow.

Losing my virginity when I was only sixteen, to a boy I barely knew, in an expensive hotel room paid for by his parents' MasterCard – I wish I could say that was one of my worst mistakes.

For the remainder of the school year, the whole two months after that fateful party, Celine sat in the back of our math class at a table by herself. I never tried to apologize, and that summer I heard her family had moved back to Seattle as soon as school was out. I never spoke to her again. If Rudy did, she never told me.

BONGS AND BONGS

8

———

JUNIOR SUMMER

Rudy and I dove into the summer before our junior year like champions. I made it all the way to the state track meet, where I finished 12th out of 16 in the 100-meter hurdles. Rudy was selected to be one of Ogden's junior yearbook photographers for the next school year. It was the first full summer we both could drive; we had no obligations and the weather was getting warmer by the day.

Uncharacteristically, my parents had offered to treat Rudy and me to a trip to Cancun in July of that summer, as an early gift for my seventeenth birthday, and we jumped at the chance. My mother, eager for some sun and "girl time," would be our chaperone. We prepared for the trip by tanning regularly, drinking copiously and shopping for tropical outfits. My mom allowed us margaritas at the hotel on our first night in Mexico and the gates were open wide from there. It was paradise in our teeny bikinis.

Houston dropped the bomb upon our return to St. Louis. We arrived back at home – jet-lagged, dehydrated and sunburned, despite our valiant attempts to stay on the safe side of the tanning/burning line – and Rudy was on the phone with him for nearly an hour. I think I drifted in and out of sleep in her bed, readjusting every few minutes when the sheets scratched at the sensitive pink skin on my shoulder blades. When she began to cry, it was so softly that I almost didn't hear her. I flipped onto my side and there she was, curled up in the seat at her vanity, her phone limp in her hand and un-wiped tears falling down her pink cheeks.

"What's wrong?" I sat up.

Rudy just closed her eyes and shook her head.

"What happened? Did something happen?"

"He wants to break up." Her voice came out steady but upset. Forlorn. Sad.

"Why not?"

She shrugged and fiddled with the phone in her hands. "College."

Ah. College. "But it's only July."

"He wants to "get used to being single" before he leaves." She made the quotation marks in the air with her index and middle fingers. "I guess."

"That's stupid," I said dully.

I wished I were better at sympathy. Another person's tears put me on edge; how could *I* possibly console them? By patting their back? Wiping their face? The right words never seemed to come to me. I was, and still am, uncomfortable with the truest displays of emotion. I pulled at the hair tie on my wrist and let it snap back against my skin.

"Houston's an idiot." I snapped the band again. It made a satisfying slapping sound. "He's an asshole."

Rudy stared at the henna tattoo on her ankle and sniffled.

"You could do better than him, anyway. *So*," I threw my head back and added a whole line of "o's" to the end of my "so". "... much better. Remember how I always sat in back when we rode with him to school last year?"

Rudy nodded.

"His football stuff smelled like death." I took a stab at humor. I just wanted to make her smile again. "Once, I accidentally touched his dirty jock strap. I almost made him pull over so I could vomit. I think it was molding or something."

One corner of her mouth lifted into a half smile. She was still looking at her feet, wiggling her toes against the chair.

"I hope he gets herpes or something. Not something deadly. Just so his balls fall off."

It wasn't really funny, but at this Rudy gave a deflated laugh and I sighed internally in relief. She had stopped crying but a little tear droplet still clung to her jawline.

"We need to find new boys," I offered. Did we really? Truthfully, I thought I would probably be fine with the pool and my magazines and my best friend. "Different boys."

"Like, U City guys," Rudy said.

Was she joking? She must be joking. "Or college guys. That would show Houston," I said, in case she wasn't joking.

"Yes," Rudy said just before her eyes started to leak fresh new tears.

9

———

JUNIOR FALL

Remember how I said Rudy was built from extremes? She might have mellowed, let it all simmer on the back burner or something, for the first two years of our high school career, but feisty Rudy came back. And the first semester of junior year began with an explosion of bad decisions.

You know how they say you rebound from a break up? Well, when Rudy bounced back from her fall, she didn't bounce back up quite the same. Maybe she got scratched by the rough ground at the bottom of the drop or maybe a pebble gouged out a little, nearly imperceptible piece of her. Or maybe at that point she hadn't yet reached the bottom; maybe she had further to fall. Whatever it was, she didn't rebound straight back up to her old self. Instead, she rebounded sideways. She bounced left; out of bounds. And I felt like I had no choice but to chase after her.

We started small. Tiny, in fact, with a trip to the Galleria to have our ears double pierced. We didn't warn our parents (we were so squeaky clean, so new at this rebelling thing) beforehand, and when we left the jewelry store, both of us sporting little cubic zirconia studs beside the usual earrings in our sore, red earlobes, we were inflated with a fresh sense of freedom, individuality and maybe a little bit of recklessness. We strutted through the mall and into the parking garage. I felt, I thought, like an adult. I didn't want to go back to Rudy's where, under the chandeliers and beside the sparkling pool and on top of the freshly cut grass, we would decidedly be kids again.

Apparently, Rudy felt the same. "Do you want to go get coffee somewhere?"

"You read my mind."

"Let's go to Wash U. They have a coffee shop on campus, right?"

I frowned. "Yeah. But where can you park on campus without a pass?"

"I don't know."

We sat. We buckled our seatbelts.

"Your earrings look really good," I told her.

"So do yours," she countered.

"What about the loop? There's a Starbucks there, right?"

"Okay."

Rudy didn't know how to parallel park; she had lost all of her points on the driving test in that one section. We circled the block twice before we found a lot where she could pull straight into a parking space. We donned our sunglasses and got out of the car. It was the first week of September, and we still wore cut-off jean shorts and tank tops. We were both as brown as pecans, and the tops of my toes were rough from a summer of too much chlorine and not enough moisturizing lotion.

Inside, we both ordered vanilla lattes, and I felt proud of my taste for coffee the same way I felt when I drank beer. Like an adult. We settled onto bar stools facing out toward the street. I glanced at a discarded Wall Street Journal beside me, decided I wasn't feeling that adult after all, then turned to Rudy.

"What do you think your mom's going to say when you get home?"

Rudy shrugged. "What about yours?"

"She'll probably try to rip them out. I should've gotten little skulls, just to mess with her."

I sipped my coffee but it was still too hot to drink. I rubbed the burnt tip of my tongue over the backs of my teeth and looked around.

Students with laptops and open textbooks occupied most of the tables. One of them, a boy in a flannel shirt and black glasses was twirling a pencil in his fingers. A girl wearing headphones was staring out the window, mouthing the words to whatever song was playing in her ears.

Outside the window the people passing by carried shopping bags and Styrofoam food containers. It was a Saturday. They didn't look all that different from the people at Ogden, but there were fewer button down shirts.

"I've been thinking," Rudy started, then interrupted herself with a drink from her latte. "We should volunteer for something."

I raised one blonde eyebrow. "Like?"

"Like something to help people less fortunate than us."

"Okay? Like a soup kitchen?"

"I was thinking more like Habitat for Humanity. You know, building houses."

"We don't know how to build anything."

"Not everyone does the construction stuff. They need people to paint and do little things too."

Oh.

"Then, when it's finished you get to see all the hard work you did really amount to something. It's tangible, you know?"

"Yeah."

"We should sign up," she concluded. "Let's do it when we get back to my house."

I know what you're thinking. Those weren't bad decisions at all, but really, things started to snowball from there.

———

"YOU TWO BE *VERY* CAREFUL TODAY." Mrs. Golden turned around to address us when she dropped us off on our first Saturday in East St. Louis. "Stay with the group. And give Dad as much warning as you can to come pick you up."

She glanced out the window as Rudy pushed the back door open. On the porch of the house she had pulled up beside, three men sat in lawn chairs, smoking cigarettes and watching us.

"Don't walk around by yourselves," she added quickly.

"We won't, mom." Rudy scooted out of the seat and I followed behind her. "Love you."

"Love you too, sweetie," Mrs. Golden smiled. "Proud of you girls!"

She drove away and we walked toward the group gathered around a white banner on the dead lawn of a rundown brick house. All the houses on the street were dilapidated – shingles hanging off the roofs, windows broken out and covered with blue or black pieces of tarp. There were broken beers bottles and wax paper soda cups lying all over the sidewalk. A big, hulking apartment building stood in the middle of the block and a young woman in a baggy t-shirt dragged a wailing child up the crumbling apartment steps. She wasn't wearing a bra.

Mr. Golden had decided it would be better if we didn't drive ourselves; he said we shouldn't leave either of our cars parked there all day. I didn't get it at first.

We approached the group timidly. We were definitely the youngest of anyone there. It wasn't habitat for humanity – Rudy was wrong, they didn't have a St. Louis project for the fall – but we were refinishing two rundown houses. A duplex, actually. It was five after eight in the morning and the project lead, a bald, pot-bellied guy with a kind smile and a tape measure attached to his belt loop, began his welcome speech and an introduction to the work we'd be doing. When he mentioned splitting into groups to tackle separate tasks, I stepped closer to Rudy. I stuck to her like I'd been velcroed on.

Rudy and I got assigned to a group of six who would work on one of the kids' bedrooms. The lady in charge of our group wore a bandana around her short hair and had ashy elbows and knees. She looked like a construction worker, I decided.

"Welcome, team!" She called, waving us over, despite the fact that we were only ten feet away and already heading in her direction.

"Hi." Rudy smiled a polite smile.

"Calissa." The woman held out her hand, first to Rudy and then to me.

"I'm Rudy."

"Jillian." She squeezed my fingers.

A fourth member joined the circle then, extending his arm toward Calissa.

"Jim," he said. He was wearing the kind of shoes that had rubber finger toes. Covertly, I made a face at Rudy.

"Great to have you guys in my group. Is this your first time?"

"Yes," Rudy spoke for us.

"Great, great. Well I'm glad you came out to help. It's really a rewarding experience," Calissa grinned. "So, we should have two more helpers, hmm."

She frowned at a clipboard in her hand. "Looks like we're missing our other gentlemen helpers."

"Anybody know Tank or Benji?" She glanced up at us.

What kinds of names were those?

We shook our heads.

"Okay, then. Well, snooze you lose, right? Let's head in and see what we're working with."

Whatever I'd been expecting, this wasn't it. Inside, there were holes in the walls. Pink and yellow stuffing was falling out of some of the holes and onto the carpet, which was an unappealing dark green and looked like it had been attacked by a pack of rabid dogs. One long tear divided the living room into uneven halves, and one side of it was marked with darker stains. The whole place smelled like cat piss. My nose tingled.

We followed Calissa upstairs.

"Don't worry," she called over her shoulder. "These stairs are okay. They'll get some sprucing up, but they're safe."

The step beneath me creaked. I wasn't sure I believed her.

The bedroom was tiny – it was barely bigger than Rudy's bathroom – and there was a dirty, discarded toy rabbit lying in the corner, his beady black eyes staring up at the ceiling. I wanted to bolt out of the house and back to the Goldens as fast as I could run. Give me a tennis court; give me a trip to the mall. Our lives were so lucky. I fidgeted uncomfortably.

Calissa opened her mouth.

"Is this group seven?" A voice from behind us interrupted.

The four of us turned to see two boys standing in the open doorway. Tank and Benji, presumably.

"Welcome to group seven!" Calissa grinned again. I reevaluated the construction worker angle. She reminded me more of a therapist or an elementary school principal.

"Sorry we're late." The guys shuffled into the room, grinning sheepishly. They were good-looking. Who would have known?

"No problem, you're here just in time."

Calissa divided us into pairs to conquer the repainting, recarpeting, rewiring the lighting, building a shelving system for the tiny closet and a small window seat that would double as a toy chest. I had grabbed Rudy as my partner, and we'd been assigned to strip the old wallpaper and paint. The last time I'd painted was in Boston, when I did a watercolor princess mural on my pink bedroom wall. I was six. My mother had not been pleased.

Calissa and Jim left to get us some solution for the wallpaper and stuff for the guys to remove the old carpet. Once they were gone, I crouched over the rabbit. It was missing its little plastic nose.

"Planning on taking that home with you?" One of the boys teased me.

"Yeah, right."

I pushed it with the toe of my tennis shoe, and a cockroach crawled out from underneath it. I yelped and jumped back against the wall.

"What?" Rudy caught my anxiety. "What is it?"

The boy who had teased me darted across the room and ground his foot into the wriggling bug. "Chill, it's just a bug," he smiled at me. "Look, it's dead now."

He lifted his foot to show me the dead roach, ground into the carpet.

"Thanks," I muttered, blushing.

"I'm Benji." He didn't offer me his hand, so I knew he must be very close to our age.

"I'm Jillian."

He looked to Rudy.

"Ruth Ann. But everybody calls me Rudy."

We both looked at the second boy, who'd yet to speak.

"Tank."

"Is that your real name?" Rudy asked.

He nodded.

"His mom was a crack head when she bestowed him with that," Benji added.

Was he serious? Tank didn't confirm or deny.

"Do you guys go to school here? UMSL or Wash U?"

He thought we were in college. Or, at least, he was pretending to think that. Either way, I was flattered.

"We're from here. We're high school seniors," Rudy fibbed a little.

"That's cool." Benji ran a palm over his brown buzz cut. "Yeah, we go to Wash U. We're sophomores."

Something loud thumped against the wall downstairs and all four of us glanced down at the floor, as if we'd be able to see through it to the level below us. When I looked up, the guys were exchanging a look. I feigned an intense interest in my fingernails.

"So, have you guys done anything like this before?" Rudy soldiered on while I wallowed awkwardly. "This is our first time."

"Same here," Benji said.

"I've done Habitat for Humanity before," Tank added. "Back in Boston."

"You're from Boston?" I perked up. "I moved here from Boston three years ago."

"Oh, yeah? What part?"

"Okay, team." Before I could answer, Calissa was back, her arms full of supplies. "I've got everything you need here. If you run out, just talk to Lou, the project lead. You know, the guy who spoke this morning?"

We nodded.

"Cool." Calissa handed the box to Tank. "Jim and I are going to consult one of the electricians about the wiring work. If you need me, just come find me downstairs. Cool?"

We nodded again.

"Cool," Benji spoke for all of us.

It was hot and stuffy in our little bedroom workspace, and the wallpaper – a dusty burgundy and gold flowered mess that couldn't have looked good even when it was brand new – wasn't coming off of the walls. No matter what we tried, it held on; the best we could do was pull off little chunks at a time, leaving behind a sticky residue. The smell of the solution made me light-headed; after an hour of work, the boys pushed open the only window in the room. Hot, Indian summer air leaked in through the torn screen but there wasn't much of a breeze. By the time we broke for lunch at one, I was mortified to find that the back of my t-shirt was soaked with a spreading circle of sweat.

We'd warmed up to the boys, as it had been the four of us alone all morning long. They were funny, really. And smart, I thought. They were both sociology majors, from Boston and Philadelphia, and they were volunteering as extra credit for one of their semester classes. They definitely weren't preppy, but they were cute. Different, if that's what Rudy was after.

The four of us sat in a line on the curb and unpacked the brown paper bag lunches we'd been provided. I pulled out a flattened turkey and cheese sandwich and a shiny red apple. There was a Little Debbie snack cake at the bottom.

"What kind did you get?" Rudy asked, her hand in her own lunch bag.

"Zebra Cake. You?"

"Star Crunch. Trade?"

I nodded, and we swapped desserts. I set mine beside me on the cement to save for later.

"So, what're you guys doing tonight after this thing's over?" Benji spoke with his mouth full. He'd already finished half of his sandwich while I was still wrestling the plastic wrap off of mine.

"I don't know." I looked to Rudy.

"My dad's supposed to pick us up when we're finished. No real plans after that."

"You need a ride?" Benji looked at Tank.

"We could give you a ride," Tank added, like they'd rehearsed that very line.

Rudy and I shared a glance. 'Do you want to?' her eyes asked. 'I'll do what you do. I'll always do what you do,' was probably how mine responded.

"Yeah, that'd be awesome."

———

TANK'S CAR was an older model convertible with a dent in the front bumper.

"Those don't work," he said, as Rudy and I tugged on the seatbelts in the backseat. "Sorry."

"That's fine." I folded my hands in my lap.

It was a departure from the cars in which we typically bummed rides. In their black converse sneakers, so were Tank and Benji. My heart thumped nervously.

Benji turned up the volume on the car's stereo.

"What kind of music do you guys listen to?"

"We like a lot of different stuff," Rudy said.

The last concert Rudy and I had gone to was Carrie Underwood. Currently, there was a hip-hop c.d. in my car's c.d. player that Rudy and I sang along to, loudly, on our way to school in the morning. I wasn't sure I wanted to reveal either of these things.

"That's cool. You know these guys?" He gestured to the radio, to the song coming from the speakers.

We shook our heads.

"Ah, man, they're pretty good. Really good live. I saw them at a show back home last summer."

We smiled.

"I like them," I added.

"Where do you live again? I don't really know my way

around here that great." Tank turned to look at us in the back-seat. He had pretty eyes under his thick eyebrows. The car drifted to the left a little and someone in the lane beside us honked. My heart leapt. Tank faced forward again.

"Just keep going straight. I'll tell you when you need to exit."

Benji drummed his fingers against the glove compartment.

"So, what do you do with a sociology major?" I asked.

"I want to go into social services. You know, working with welfare recipients and making sure everyone gets what they need to get back on their feet."

We waited for Tank to answer.

"I think I want to do something with drug rehabilitation," he said.

Interesting. Really, they seemed so grown-up and intriguing.

"What about you all? You know what you're majoring in yet?"

I had no clue. Absolutely no ideas, though I knew I wouldn't choose anything math-related.

"I was thinking maybe photography," Rudy said. "Or possibly women's studies. I'd love to be a photojournalist and travel. You know, exposing important issues."

I stared at her. She'd never told me that before. True, I'd never asked – but when did she think about things like that? Was I supposed to be thinking about college now, too? When we were only half finished with high school?

Looking back, that was probably my problem and possibly my saving grace. I didn't think about the future. Not that I was always living in the moment either. Often, like when I was in class, I was living for the very next moment, when I'd be in the hallway talking to my friends. Or when I was talking alone with a boy I liked, I'd be thinking about what came next – when he would reach for my face and kiss me – and what I should do with my own arms, or whether or not I should employ a new kissing technique I'd read about in Cosmo Girl magazine.

Tank let out a low whistle as he pulled up in front of Rudy's house.

"You live here? Damn," Benji added.

At this, Rudy actually blushed.

I had to admit that with the sun setting behind it, the Goldens' mountain of a home, with its immaculate landscaping and big picture windows, looked a little too much. For the first time, I saw a glimpse of it through an outsider's eyes and I felt a touch of embarrassment, especially after spending all day in that tiny bedroom. I understood then why Mr. Golden hadn't let us drive our own vehicles.

"Yeah." Rudy opened the car door. "It's sort of gaudy, huh?"

"Snazzy," Tank said. "Maybe that house will look like this when we're all finished."

Rudy was quiet. I could tell he had stung her.

I climbed out of the backseat behind her.

"Thanks for the ride," I said. "See you next week."

"Yeah, see you."

We were halfway up the pebbled sidewalk when Benji rolled down the car window.

"Hey, you guys want to hang out later tonight? There's this party – well, it's a small get together type thing –off campus," he shouted, sticking his head out the open window.

Rudy smiled and answered – probably too quickly, too eagerly – "Yeah, definitely."

"Cool. We'll call you later," Benji nodded. "Toodle-loo, ladies!"

He stuck his arm out the window, cupped his hand and pageant-waved as they drove off.

———

WHEN RUDY'S phone rang at eight o'clock that night, we'd been ready for an hour and we'd been killing time playing a game of gin rummy on the floor in Rudy's bedroom while we covertly sipped on cans of soda laced with the last of a bottle of vodka. We raced out of the house to meet them, scurrying past Mrs. Golden while she brushed our cheeks with kisses and warned us to be good.

"What time are you getting home," she called as we were flying through the front door.

"Late, mom." Rudy poked her head back through the doorway. I waited on the other side, on the steps of the porch.

We didn't really have a curfew; as long as Mrs. Golden knew where we were going and we promised to call a cab if we needed it, we came home when we pleased.

We told Mrs. Golden the boys were seniors at another private high school in St. Louis County. That's how we were allowed out of Rudy's house that night. It was the first time we'd really lied to her parents, and it left me with a queasy feeling in my stomach that I tried to blame on too much vodka and too little dinner.

"Hey, Jill. Rudy." Benji was back in the front seat of the mustang, the music turned up too loud. He had changed into slim jeans and a faded V neck t-shirt. Rudy and I had agonized over what to wear (how did people dress at an off-campus college party?), and I felt self-conscious in the jeans and top she had carefully selected for me.

"Hey," we said.

It smelled like incense in the back of the car – flavored tobacco, but I didn't know it at the time – and it tickled my nose.

"We should put the top down. Can we do that?"

"Yeah, sure."

Benji showed us how to release the handles and we folded

the top back to let in the cooler night air. And then we were off. To a party. With college guys. My body tingled with jitters.

It was a different type of party, that's for sure.

There were cars lining the street, but the house we pulled up in front of was quaint and quiet. A big, feathered dream catcher hung from a hook beside the front door and the breeze blew it in a slow circle.

Tank knocked, and we waited with our hands in our pockets until a girl answered the door.

"Hey, y'all," she grinned. She was wearing a lumpy grey stocking cap over long red hair. She was tiny, maybe only five feet tall. Mrs. Golden sized. "Come in, come in."

She held the door open for us and Rudy and I followed the boys inside, where it was warm and smelled like beer and weed. I was proud I could identify that scent, at least.

Our arrival elicited nods and quick waves from the scattering of people in the open little living room and kitchen. Most of them were seated on the nubby, mismatched orange and tan couches or around the kitchen table or else on the floor, sitting cross-legged. They were drinking their beer from bottles and cans. A girl in the kitchen was pouring the contents of a big silver tumbler into a line of martini glasses.

The boys weren't up for introductions, it seemed.

"Hi," Rudy introduced herself to the girl who'd opened the door, the de-facto host. "I'm Rudy. This is Jillian."

"Rudy, Jillian," the girl nodded as she repeated our names. "I'm Nat. Nice to meet y'all."

Nat had a little bit of a southern accent. Not like she was from Texas though; Louisiana or Georgia, maybe?

"We were just making some drinks in the kitchen, if y'all want one?"

"Sure," we obliged, following her into the kitchen, where she handed us each a martini glass, now garnished with an olive each.

"What's in this?" I sniffed the glass. It smelled strong.

"It's a vodka martini, dear," the girl said as she kept pouring.

We waited until Nat and the pourer held drinks of their own. We toasted. We sipped.

It was very strong, indeed.

Rudy and I carried our drinks to the living room, where Tank and Benji had taken seats on the floor up against the far wall. Benji patted the carpet beside him. We went and sat, me beside Benji, Rudy beside me.

Off campus college parties, it seemed, were very low-key. Or at least this one was. They just sat like that, talking, the whole evening. Periodically, one of them would light up a cigarette, and Nat would ask them to take it outside to the porch, and they would do so begrudgingly. Once, they passed a few blunts around the circle and my heartbeat quickened. We still didn't know how to smoke. What if it turned me into a mindless idiot in front of these people we didn't even know? But the blunts had crossed around the circle in a random order, and to my relief – and slight disappointment, really – they missed us completely. I took note, however, that Benji and Tank had taken one hit apiece.

The company was interesting, though their conversation bored me. I sat and listened dutifully as they transitioned from local politics to religious expression on campus to which teachers could be bought with a blowjob or an eight ball (they *weren't* talking pool, but I didn't know what it was they actually meant). I was more interested in their odd clothes and hairstyles. The boys wore lots of flannel or soft, worn looking band t-shirts with their jeans. They wore canvas sneakers or regular tennis shoes. One guy wore muddy black combat boots that matched the unkempt black beard that hanging off his face. He sort of scared me. I tried not to make eye contact.

The girls had hair in all colors and lengths. None of them wore skirts or dresses. Two of them wore little silver studs in their nostrils, which looked pretty good on them. My mom would've freaked. Ironically, I thought, Celine would've fit in well, if she could have looked past the drugs.

By the time someone brought out a hookah, I'd managed to force down one of the strong martinis along with two beers Benji had given me.

Rudy nudged me.

"I think I'm going to try it," she whispered.

"Seriously?"

She nodded.

"You don't have to, of course," she added. Always.

"Yeah, I know. I was thinking the same thing. I would have tried the blunt, too, if they'd passed it to us."

Would I? Really, was that what I was thinking?

"You would?" Rudy looked shocked.

I nodded.

"I think I would have, too."

I'd seen a hookah before, in Boston, when I was little. We'd gone to dinner for my grandma's birthday, and we were walking back to where my dad had parked the car. It was sort of late, and we'd had to walk past a crowded bar. People were sitting outside at rickety little tables, with what looked to me like big glass vases sitting between them. My parents averted their eyes. My dad jangled his keys and watched his loafered feet. My mom held her nose up in the air and looked straight ahead.

"Dad." I touched his jacket. "What's that?"

I pointed.

"Jillian, don't point." He looked at me. "It's rude."

"I'm sorry," I said, quietly. "But what are those straw things?"

He waited until the tables and the music and the weird smell were behind us before he answered.

"That's a drug, Jillian," he told me. "People smoke drugs through those hoses."

I had been stricken. "But I thought drugs were illegal."

"Most of them. The worst ones are."

"So, that one's not bad, then?"

He put his hand on my shoulder and stopped me.

"Just because something's legal doesn't mean it's good for you, Jillian. I want you to promise me you'll never touch any drugs, legal or illegal. You've got better things ahead of you."

He had looked so serious. I was only ten years old, but I shook his hand, solemnly.

"I promise," I swore.

The hookah in Nat's living room had four hoses.

"Here, switch places." Benji pulled Rudy to his other side, so that she sat beside Tank. He nudged me with his elbow. "We can share."

He had picked me! I was immensely flattered.

Benji and I took turns from one hose, his mouth covering the spot where mine had been. He really was very cute. His shirt looked good with the greenish color of his eyes.

I didn't feel much, really, except a little light headed. Like I was floating. I wished I'd eaten more dinner at Rudy's house.

More beer and a second hookah later, Benji leaned into me, his leg pressed against my leg.

"Hey," he half-whispered. "Do you want to drive around for a bit?"

Drive around? Drunk? "Huh?"

He laughed. "Do you want to drive around awhile? I think these guys are going out."

It was true; most of the other guests had left in the last hour.

Nat and the rest of the stragglers had tossed around the idea of going to a bar.

"Rudy and Tank, too?"

"Duh, silly," he tapped my head with his open palm. "It's Tank's car."

"Oh, right."

We said good-bye as we headed out the door. My legs were a little like Jell-O below me, but that was okay.

Benji put his arm around my shoulders when we were walking down the sidewalk to the car and my insides melted to goo. Yeah, my legs would be fine.

"You girls doing okay?"

"Yeah," I said. "Why wouldn't we be?"

"Have you smoked before?"

"No."

"Well, that's why."

Tank and Rudy were ahead of us, and they reached the car first. Rudy got into the front seat and Benji climbed in back after me.

"I don't really think I feel anything. What's it supposed to feel like?"

Benji laughed again. Was I really that funny? Was he making fun of me?

"That was just tobacco. It should really just relax you some."

"Oh."

Tank started the car. "Where to, boys and girls?"

"Can we just drive around?" Rudy asked.

"Sure. Whatever you say." Tank grinned.

"Looky what I've got." Benji dug around in the pocket of his jacket. When his hand emerged it held a small glass pipe and a clear baggy of dried green stuff. It looked like miniature brussels sprouts or maybe the green mold that grows on stuff shoved in the back of the fridge for way too long.

"Who'd you get that from, man?" Tank and Rudy twisted around to look.

"Trevor."

Was that the combat boots guy? I couldn't remember.

"Give me some," Tank said.

"Do you want to try it?" Benji asked. He stuck the end of the pipe in his mouth and blew into it.

"What it is?" I asked timidly.

Benji laughed, then quickly straightened up. "Sorry," he said. "That's a legitimate question. It's marijuana."

I nodded quickly to redeem myself. "Okay."

He opened the baggy and picked pieces from it, carefully placing them into the little hole in the end of the pipe. He crumbled another piece from the bag and sprinkled it over the rest. I thought of the labs we did in chemistry. He was taking this so seriously.

"Can I try, too?" Rudy had her elbow propped up on the center console, her chin resting in her palm.

"Yeah, sure." Benji pressed his finger into the hole. "Here. Ladies first."

He held the pipe out to me.

"How do I do it?"

"Let me see your left hand."

I held up my hand. It was sweaty.

"See this? Plug that with your thumb, okay?"

I did it.

"When I light it, just suck in a little. Not too hard. And not too long, especially since it's your first time."

"Whatever you do, don't blow," Tank added.

I nodded solemnly.

"Ready?"

"Yeah." My heart thumped.

He held a lighter over the top of the open bowl. I sucked in through my teeth. It filled my mouth with a weird taste.

When Benji nudged me with his elbow, I pulled my lips from the end of the pipe. He took it from me and handed it to Rudy, who promptly placed it between her freshly glossed lips. From Rudy it went to Tank, then Benji, who put it out with the end of his lighter when he was finished.

"So, how was your first time?"

We'd been sitting on the street in the running car. Tank shifted out of park and started driving.

How was it? I felt lightheaded again, but not much else.

"I don't know," Rudy said.

"You'll feel it in a second. Just give it a couple minutes," Benji said, pocketing the pipe. I wondered how many other girls' lips had been around it.

"I thought you guys were against doing drugs," Rudy said. "I thought you wanted to help people in rehab."

"We consider this to be research," Benji answered. "How can we help somebody if we're not familiar with the issues they're dealing with?"

"Doctors help people with cancer or AIDS when they've never had those diseases."

Why was Rudy arguing with them? We liked them. Or I did, at least.

"Yeah, but that's different. Those are physical illnesses. We're talking about some mental issues here."

They were smart, I thought. Philosophical.

"I guess," Rudy considered. "But don't you worry you'll get addicted or something?"

"Not to pot," – I smirked at Benji's rhyme – "This stuff's not addictive. At least not physically."

"Oh."

Benji was right. Ten minutes later, riding down a busy street (it was only midnight) I was staring at the street lamps as we whizzed past. The taillights on the car in front of us danced.

"Rudy." I leaned forward and put my hand on her shoulder. "It's so pretty here."

She smiled. "I know. I'm glad you moved here."

I sighed as I leaned back into the seat. Benji put his hand on my knee.

"It's hot in here. Are you hot?" Rudy was looking at me. She glanced at Benji's hand on my leg, and she giggled. I laughed, too.

"It is sort of hot in here, man," Benji agreed. "Can you turn the air on?"

"No," I said. An idea popped into my head. I could see it, a big yellow light bulb shining above my forehead. "Let's put the top down."

"Yes," Rudy agreed. "Let's."

The boys were reluctant, but finally they agreed. They indulged us. They had created this situation, after all.

We pulled over in a McDonalds parking lot and the guys pulled back the top while we watched from our seats inside the car.

"I love convertibles. I want a car like this," I said when Benji had climbed back into the seat with me.

"I bet you do," he laughed at me.

"I'm serious."

"I believe you." He pecked me on the mouth when I wasn't expecting it.

We drove down a street with a series of intersections and each time we were forced to stop at a red light, Rudy and I booed and then burst into a fit of giggles. I wanted Benji to kiss me again, this time when I was prepared for it. I poked him in the leg with my index finger but he just winked at me.

"Let's go on the highway," Rudy said. She was speaking

awfully loud, I thought.

"Yes. *Please*," I added.

Again, Tank obliged our desires. On the ramp onto the interstate we started to pick up speed and the wind whipped through my long, loose hair. It felt like ropes flapping out from behind my head.

It smelled great outside, I thought. It smelled like autumn.

"It smells like autumn," I said out loud.

"What?" Rudy shouted. Her hair blew wildly across her face when she turned to look at me.

"It smells like autumn," I yelled over the roar of wind in my ears.

"What?"

"This is *fun*."

———

WHEN WE WOKE up late the next morning, after having crawled into Rudy's bed some time far past one in the morning, my head was pounding harder than my heartbeat. Rudy's eyes were black-ringed with stale mascara, a pink lip-gloss smear on the bottom of her cheek. The inside of my mouth tasted like I had been eating dirt and sweat, and I wanted a drink of water probably more than I'd ever wanted anything before. Neither of us had made the effort to lift our heads up off of our pillows yet; we just lay there underneath the warm covers and I stared at her, mostly because she was the only thing in the room that appeared stationary.

"Cheerio," Rudy said, after five minutes had passed. "Pip, pip cheerio."

She tore the blankets off of her warm body and before I could stop her she was bouncing up and down on the bed.

"Cheerio, pip pip! Cheerio!" The coiled springs of the

mattress didn't strain under her weight but flicked her lightly up into the air. My head thumped against the pillow each time she came back down.

"What the hell are you doing?" I moaned exaggeratedly.

She was skipping now and beaming as she kicked her heels up against her ass.

"Cheerio! Top o' the mornin' to ya." Her feet got tangled in the blankets and she crashed down on top of me, her knee slamming into my hipbone. She burst out laughing – deep, embarrassing belly laughs – with her mouth thrown wide open and a string of sticky saliva clinging to her bottom lip.

"You're fucking nuts," I told her.

Every time I felt like I knew her, she changed, became wild and crazy and did things that I couldn't assign a reason.

Once her laughter had subsided, Rudy rose from the bed and walked across the room to her dresser. Her back to me, she dug around in the drawers until finally she pulled out a bottle of cheap vodka – vanilla flavored, three quarters of the way empty and clearly forgotten years before.

"A throwback to freshman year."

She held the bottle by the neck and thrust it above her head in celebration, grabbing two clear plastic shot glasses from the same dresser drawer.

I sat up in bed, my back braced against Rudy's headboard as waves of nausea rolled like heavy tides through my empty stomach. She set the glasses on the nightstand and poured until each was full, tiny drops of vodka sprinkling the wood finish where she'd missed. She handed me a full shot before lifting her own in a toast.

"To great nights," she said.

"To shitty mornings."

"To college guys."

"To weed."

"Hair of the dog." Her eyes were smiling behind the smudged make-up.

"Hair of the dog." I clinked my glass against hers then threw my head back and tossed the liquor into my mouth, wetting my sandpapery lips and blazing a fire down my hungover throat. I thought for sure I would throw up, but it never happened.

———

OUR VOLUNTEER PROJECT was four weekends long, and that's exactly how much time we spent with Benji and Tank. The boys would drive us home from East St. Louis on Saturday afternoons and we would scarf down dinner with Rudy's parents before we ran up to her bedroom to get ready for our evening outings. We ripped extra holes in two pairs of Rudy's designer jeans, rubbing them with sandpaper around the hems and the knees until they looked sufficiently worn. We raided Kent's closet – how strange it was to be in his bedroom again for the first time since that peculiar night my freshman year – and collected a few vintage t-shirts we tried to wash and dry until they shrunk enough to fit us snugly (that idea hadn't really worked). We didn't get our noses pierced – our mothers would have murdered us – but we wore our second ear piercings proudly. I tried out double silver hoops. Rudy said it looked good on me.

The boys, it turned out, smoked a lot of marijuana. They taught us how to pack a pipe and how to use a bong and what kinds of weed were better than others. And they did other drugs, too – their "get togethers" always featured a buffet of illicit pharmaceuticals, ripe for the taking. Rudy seemed intrigued, but I was petrified, druggy horror stories playing through my brain just like they'd played on the TV screen in my junior high health class. I liked smoking okay, but I thought I preferred the buzz of drinking to the paranoid feeling I got when I was high.

Late one night, when we'd stumbled into Rudy's house, she'd pulled me into the foyer and up the marble staircase. She flipped the light switch that turned on their enormous chandelier.

"Rudy, what are you doing?" I'd whispered harshly. I turned the light off, but she just flipped it on again.

"Aren't they gorgeous?"

"What?"

"The crystals," she said, leaning against the banister and pointing, her index finger shooting an invisible arrow toward the glistening lights. "They're so pretty."

"Yeah."

"You know, when I was little and we moved in here, I always thought it'd be fun to swing on it."

I stood behind her and watched. The prisms were dancing rainbows in my vision.

"It's so close, I bet if I jumped I could reach it."

She leaned out further, and my arm shot out to grab hers.

"Rudy, stop it."

"I'm not going to do it." She laughed. She relaxed in my grip and pulled back from the banister. "Silly."

She patted my cheek.

I didn't think I was being silly. It'd be nice, I thought, if we could just get drunk again. Rudy wasn't so weird when she was only drunk.

Of course, I didn't voice my opinion to anyone. I just went with the flow. Don't rock the boat, you know?

In between those weekends Rudy and I acted like our normal selves, whatever that meant. In her new capacity as a junior yearbook photographer she had to go to soccer games and tennis matches and choir concerts to take pictures, and I went with her and held her big, ugly camera bag while she fiddled with the bulky lenses. We did our homework and I ran on the cross-country team (Rudy had hung up her running shoes when she got the photog position) and we sat with Deena and a table full of other junior girls at lunch. We wore sweatpants and hooded sweatshirts to school most days because, really, who were we trying to impress there? To be fair, I was still trying to impress everyone, but I wore what Rudy wore because it was her I wanted to impress the most.

The Saturday we finished the house, our team went out for ice cream to celebrate. Calissa thanked us for all of our help, and I had to admit, Rudy was right. It really did feel good to see the clean beige carpet, the freshly painted walls, the cute little cubbyhole shelving Jim had built for the closet. We'd scrubbed the windows and with the sun gleaming through the streak-free glass, everything looked really good. I was proud of us.

Benji and Tank took us out to dinner that night, to a funky little sushi restaurant in the Central West End. They wore button-up shirts (untucked though, of course) with their converse sneakers, and they helped us order from the long, foreign menu. Benji let me try his sashimi, dropping a piece into my mouth with his chopsticks from across the tiny table. The boys used their fake IDs to order four sake bombs, and I was proud to drink mine down like a champ. When the waitress returned with our check, Benji and Tank made a show of paying for our meals, and we thanked them with polite smiles before excusing ourselves to the restroom, where I immediately devoured a handful of breath mints.

"Wasn't that good? And even the sake bombs," I said, leaning over the sink and smiling into the dimly lit mirror to inspect my teeth for bits of food. "I didn't think I would like them."

"They were okay," Rudy answered from behind the blue stall door. The toilet flushed, water swirling down into the depths of the floor, and Rudy emerged. She flipped her hair behind her shoulder and squirted soap into her palms.

"They look really good tonight. They dressed up for us." I was an unstoppable force, a gushing geyser of effervescent girliness that evening.

"They do look nice," Rudy smiled, rinsing her hands beneath the faucet while I stood beside her, adjusting the waistband of my jeans.

"Does my breath smell okay?" I asked as she reached for a paper towel.

"Come closer." She motioned with one dripping hand, and I leaned in close to her nose and breathed cautiously into her face.

"Eat another mint," she advised.

I emptied the little box into my mouth.

The boys were waiting for us outside on the sidewalk, their hands thrust into their shorts pockets. As we stepped through the glass door, they looked up at us expectantly. Benji reached for my hand as we began to walk, weaving his stubby fingers through mine, sending warm tingles down my spine.

"Where to now, ladies?" Tank whistled through pursed lips as we made our way down the crowded sidewalk. It was a brisk, beautiful fall evening. Couples were sitting around little aluminum or wrought iron tables outside the restaurants we passed, sipping from wide wine glasses and talking loudly. The sun had just set behind the clouds, and the street lamps flipped on as we passed a frozen yogurt shop with a line of people stretching out the door and down the sidewalk.

"What about a movie?" Rudy glanced back at me and I smiled.

"Nah," Benji frowned. "Nothing good out. Let's go back to the car and drive around for a bit. Maybe stop at a park."

I would have liked seeing a movie, I thought. A tub of popcorn, holding Benji's hand in the dark theater and snuggling up against his shoulder during sad or scary parts.

"Driving sounds fine to me," I said.

We turned off the sidewalk and started down a darker alleyway, between two brick apartment buildings. The pavement was scattered with rocks and grass sprouting up through wide cracks. An overflowing green dumpster sat at the end of the alley, under a single streetlamp that cast a yellowish circle of light over lumpy trash bags tossed haphazardly to the sides of the dumpster. As we came closer, one of the bags shifted, and a shoe appeared, scooting out from under the black plastic.

I screamed. The sound escaped me like a howl, before I could do anything to stop it. Both of the boys jumped back, Benji pulling me with him, and we watched as two sets of dirty fingers tugged at the bag until I could see dark eyes under bushy brown eyebrows. His eyes darted from one of us to the next before he yanked the bag back up over his face. Hiding, like a child.

"Come on," Benji nudged my shoulder with his. "Let's go."

But Rudy was already crouching down beside the man, kneeling in a pile of newspapers.

"Sir?" She spoke softly. "Are you okay?"

At the sound of her voice, the pile twitched. Slowly, she reached one hand toward the lump, resting her palm on the shoulder of his soiled sweatshirt.

"Are you hurt?" Her voice must have been like honey, some sort of golden nectar in his ears, and he lowered the bag, revealing a dirt smudged face. He had a bushy, matted beard that covered the bottom half of his weathered face. There were deep lines in his forehead, under a thick helmet of ratted brown hair. The whites of his eyes were more grey than white, shot through with pale red veins, and his mouth was bleeding, leaving a thin red trail oozing through the tangles of his beard. I averted my eyes.

"Leave him alone, Rudy." Tank stood beside me frowning, his arms crossed over his chest. "Let's get out of here."

Rudy ignored him, touching the man's cheek with her fingers.

"Your lip is bleeding. Do you need to go to the hospital?"

"We're not taking him to hospital."

The man shook his head, his startled eyes meeting Rudy's gaze.

"Are you sure?"

He raised one hand, the fingernails long and pale, dirt trapped underneath and at the cuticle, and he wiped at the blood, exposing a small cut on his bottom lip.

"Spare change?" His voice was softer than I would have guessed – kind, like someone's jolly grandfather. "Can you spare any change?"

Rudy reached into her back pocket and retrieved a neatly folded twenty dollar bill.

"Don't give him that," Benji sneered. "He's an addict. He's just going to spend it on drugs or beer."

"We wouldn't spend it on anything better," Rudy said, without missing a beat. She placed the money in the man's quivering hand and gave his shoulder a quick squeeze before climbing to her feet. There were light circles of dirt covering her knees.

Without another word, the four of us turned out of the alleyway and walked down the street to Tank's car without speaking. Benji reached for the back door and held it open as I climbed inside, hopping in after me. Rudy got into the passenger's seat and closed the door. Tank pulled away from the curb before, finally, Rudy broke the silence.

"Take me home, please." She looked across the console at Tank, her mouth a straight line.

"Huh?" Tank raised his eyebrows.

Huh was right. I was bewildered. Go home? But our big evening, our date night, was just getting started.

She swiveled so that she could look at me in the backseat.

"Jillian can stay, obviously, but I want to go home. Please."

"Why?" Tank pressed. "Because of that homeless guy?"

"I thought you wanted to help people. Isn't that what you're going to school for?"

"Twenty bucks isn't going to save him. What, a fraction of your weekly allowance?" Tank said. "Look, you think you know what that guy needs, but the reality is it's not about him at all. You just want to feel all high and mighty, swooping in from your big shiny house spreading your money, feeling like you're so much better than all those other rich people who look down their noses at anybody who's poor. But you know what kept my mom on drugs? Handouts from people like you. People who didn't really give a shit about anyone other than themselves and their own motives. I'm going to school to help people who're ready to change their lives, and that means getting my hands dirty, not throwing money at the problem then turning my back on it like I solved it."

Beside me in the backseat, Benji clasped his hands over his head and let out a low, whistling sigh. Rudy didn't respond, just stared straight ahead, into the darkness outside the windshield.

"I'll take you home, then," Tank sighed, and we exited the highway toward our neighborhood.

On the ride to Rudy's, all I could think of was how things had gone all wrong. If only we had turned down a different alley, or maybe if I'd been able to suppress my scream. But rolling up to the end of Rudy's driveway – seeing the silhouette of Mrs. Golden watching from one of the front windows as the car idled, I felt relief. The expectations were too high. We had only known them for four weeks.

Rudy got out first, and as she turned to shut the door behind her, I could see tears glistening in her eyes. She stood a few feet away from the car as I pushed open the back door.

"Do you want to hang out again next weekend?" I asked Benji hopefully. Apologetically. Ignorantly.

"Yeah, sure," he said, climbing from the back seat of the convertible and getting into the front.

"Maybe a movie or something?"

"Sure. We'll call you."

They didn't call. But you could have guessed that, right?

———

"How long do you think he's been playing?" Rudy had her head cocked slightly to the left, the viewfinder of the camera pressed up to her eye. She snapped a picture then checked the image on the screen.

"Caleb Rowling?" I looked out onto the soccer field, where the guys were practically indistinguishable from one another aside from their jersey numbers. I could pick him out by the black and white captain's band around his bicep. "Probably since he was little."

"I think he played on a traveling team when we were in fifth grade." She fiddled with the buttons on the side of the screen and lifted the camera to her face again. "He looks sort of like David Beckham."

I promise, we thought about things other than boys. We just spent quite a bit of our time talking about boys. I had my legs stretched out in front of me, and I wiggled my toes free from my black flip-flops, letting them drop onto the grass. I'd just come from cross-country practice, and there was a blister growing on the side of my pinky toe. I needed new tennis shoes.

"He does, sort of."

Caleb Rowling was the senior Rudy had been preoccupied with since the departure of our college boys. He wasn't rugged or quirky or risky, like Benji and Tank had seemed, but he was arguably the best-looking guy in the entire school. Yes, that was how Rudy rebounded.

"I played soccer when I was in kindergarten. Did I tell you that?"

"No," I laughed. "That's hard to imagine."

Rudy was graceful, but she wasn't exactly coordinated when it came to sports.

"Should I tell him that, you think?" she teased.

"I'm sure it would impress him. Maybe you could show him some of your preschool art projects while you're at it."

The sun was going down behind a line of trees just past the soccer field, and with it, the temperature was dropping. I zipped my sweat jacket up to my chin and pulled Rudy's blanket tighter around my shoulders.

I had liked Benji and Tank, but I liked Rudy wanting Caleb Rowling better. It felt so much nicer to stay within the comfort zone of our private school; at least I thought I knew what to expect from the boys at Ogden. If they hurt her, I thought, it wouldn't be as bad.

The action on the soccer field moved down toward the opposing team's goal, and Rudy adjusted her position so she could follow it.

"You should streak naked across the soccer field after the game and ask him to Sadie."

Yes, that Sadie Hawkins. The dance where the girls asked the boys.

"Maybe if they win." She made a face at me and stuck out her tongue.

"Seriously. Do it."

"How about, if they win, you do it for me?"

"Streak across the field? You're insane. I'm not the one trying to ask him out."

"Not streaking. Just asking. Please?" She looked at me with

wounded puppy-dog eyes.

"Don't you want to do it yourself?"

"I'm nervous." She batted her eyelashes and stuck out her bottom lip. "Pretty please?"

"Fine," I relented. "But only if they win."

Ogden's boys' soccer team sucked. We were down two points at the beginning of the second half. It had seemed like a safe deal, but of course, the surest things are the ones about which you should be most worried, and somehow the team pulled it out and managed to win by one goal in overtime.

Rudy and I took our time folding up her blankets and packing up her camera, stalling as the team celebrated. I tried to smooth the hairs on the sides of my head, but my efforts were useless. My drying sweat had made poufs of hair fan out above my ears.

"I'm going to the car. Is that okay? You're okay, right?" Rudy said when the players started walking our way.

"Yeah. Go." I handed her my keys and shoved my hands into my jacket pockets.

My toes were freezing now, exposed in my flip-flops, and my feet probably stunk.

"Caleb," I called when he was within a few feet of me, talking to the sweaty goalie. He turned and looked.

I waved and he headed my direction.

"Hey," he smiled. "Jillian. What's up?"

"Not much. Just came to watch you guys after cross country practice."

"Oh, yeah. I forgot I was talking to the team's star."

"Ha. Hardly," I scoffed. "Congrats on your win though. You played really good."

"Thanks. Did you come to watch me specifically?" He teased, grinning at me.

"Actually, I came with Rudy. She was taking pictures for the yearbook."

"Oh, yeah?" He pulled the bottom of his jersey up to wipe sweat off of his face, giving me an unobstructed view of his toned stomach. "That's cool."

"Yeah." With some difficulty, I averted my eyes. "She had to leave right after the game though."

"Oh." He let his shirt fall back down and I looked at him again. "Can I give you a ride home?"

"Oh, no, my car's here." Just spit it out, I thought.

"Where'd you park? I can walk with you."

"No, that's okay. Actually, I was wondering if you had a date to Sadie yet?"

"Nope." He smiled. "Not yet."

"Cool. Well, I mean, not like that's good that no one asked you yet. Anyway," I stumbled over the words, "do you want to go with Rudy?"

He paused. "With Rudy?"

"Yes. She asked me if I'd ask you. Since she had to leave."

He rubbed the hair on the back of his head.

"Yeah, sure."

"Yes? That's great," I smiled. "I'll tell her."

"Okay. I guess I'll give her a call then?"

"Yeah, that'd be awesome. I guess I'm going to get going then."

"Yeah. Thanks for coming. We don't exactly draw a big crowd." He gave me a sheepish smile.

"No problem." I punched his shoulder lightly with my fist. "Congrats, again, on the win."

"Yeah, thanks. See you later, Jillian."

"See you," I said, then I turned and walked away quickly, hurrying to the car as the bearer of good news.

———

HIGH SCHOOL SORT of revolves around dances, doesn't it? At least Ogden did. It always gets to me now when I see stores pushing their neon, bejeweled prom dresses earlier and earlier each spring. Dances always gave you the easiest excuse to approach the guy or girl you had a crush on. It was a little unfair, really, that the girls only got Sadie Hawkins for the asking (although that rule was never strictly obeyed; plenty of girls asked the boys to Fall Ball or the prom during the years we were there; it just wasn't preferable. Of course you wanted the guy of your current dreams to sweep you off your feet with an elaborate, "Go-to-prom-with-me" gesture). We showed up to dances drunk, holding our tongues and shielding our breaths when we handed our tickets to the teacher guarding the door. We either danced with wild abandon or made a quick sweep around the room between our grand entrances and exits, depending on our dates.

While it was happening, every little detail meant *everything.* Each of my moments was also saturated with self-doubt. Was my date giving me his full attention, or did his gaze sometimes shift toward Rudy? Should I move my arms less and my legs more when I was dancing?

I'd never before been judged by so many people, or judged people so harshly myself. With each year since high school, I've grown less and less shallow and materialistic.

Maybe I was the only one who marked their high school life with school dances. Maybe Caleb measured it with soccer seasons. Maybe Celine measured it by new friends or new schools. Maybe there were guys who marked their time in high school by the girl they were sleeping with, as in, "Yeah, man, the year we lost the state championship basketball game was the year I took Rudy Golden's virginity."

Who could say? I can't.

All I know is that now, all of it seems far away. So very far away.

NOTHING CAME of the Rudy and Caleb thing. Actually, no, "nothing" isn't quite accurate. He turned out to be a pretty good friend. After the dance, we all went back to Caleb's – Rudy, Caleb, my date and I – and watched Children of the Corn in his basement in our pearl-snap shirts and stiff, new cowboy boots. Mid-movie, the boys had paused the TV and retreated upstairs to make some midnight-snack popcorn. When they snuck back downstairs and popped up from behind the couch they scared the living shit out of us. I let out a scream that I couldn't believe had issued from within my body. Rudy fell off the couch, flailing in the tangle of blankets. My screeching woke Mr. Rowling, who rushed downstairs in his bathrobe to check on us. I blushed as red as a sunburn, and the guys could hardly contain their peels of laughter. There was no pressure, real or imagined, that night. It was a ton of fun.

After that, Rudy had continued to pursue Caleb for a few weeks. We became regulars at Ogden's soccer games, even when Rudy wasn't assigned to take yearbook photos. He kept her at just enough distance though that she realized pretty quickly he wasn't interested. We kept going to the soccer games – we even made hand-painted navy sweatshirts with Caleb's number on them to wear on senior night – and we cheered him on, even when it got so cold we had to don earmuffs and scarves and layer sweatshirts beneath our blankets. In return, Caleb cheered for me at all my cross-country meets. At the state championships, he and Rudy joined a handful of my teammates in painting my name across their stomachs. Even though I ended up placing in the bottom half of the pack, I had grinned the whole way through the final stretch when I saw them standing in a line amidst the crowd at the finish line, screaming my name.

10

JUNIOR WINTER

"You in line?" A guy I didn't know – he must've been from another school – nudged me with his elbow. He pushed a little too hard, and I tipped to the side before righting myself, like one of those bobble toys.

"Yeah." I sipped from my plastic cup. He nodded and stood behind us, not bothering to disguise the fact that he was staring at Rudy's butt.

We were waiting for the beer bong at a crowded Thanksgiving party at Deena's house, which under normal conditions would be considered quite large, but for the number of people milling around that particular night, was way too small. Someone bumped into me walking past, and beer sloshed over the lip of my cup and onto the carpet. Oops.

I tapped my fingers against my thigh to the beat of the blaring music as the line crept forward. Someone should've brought another bong, I thought.

"I'm so freaking cold." Rudy shivered beside me. Courteously, the beer bong had been stationed outside on Deena's back deck, so as not to completely ruin the house's tan carpet. The sliding glass door was wide open, and cold air permeated the room where we stood.

"We're almost next."

Outside on the porch a guy from my math class finished his beer and let the hose drop, releasing foam and a trickle of beer. He thumped his chest and let out a long belch. I rolled my eyes.

When it was my turn, the guy holding the funnel end of the beer bong looked me up and down.

"Have you done one of these before?"

"Yes," I said, rolling up my sleeves and tossing my hair behind my shoulders. I touched my wrist. I didn't have a hair tie. "Rudy, can you hold my hair back?"

"Yeah, sure." She brushed wisps of hair back from my face with her fingertips and stood behind me, grasping my hair in her hand.

"Hurry up!" Someone shouted from inside the house. I looked back to see that the line behind us had doubled in size.

"You sure you can handle this? You're a pretty small girl."

"I bet I can do it faster than you."

He laughed exaggeratedly. "Let's see that, sweetheart."

I smiled. In Cancun, Rudy and I had made the surprising discovery that I had an aptitude for bonging beers. I also discovered this talent got me a lot of attention – I wasn't sure if this was good attention or bad attention, but I liked it. I liked proving the cocky beer guys wrong. I liked shrugging off what people expected of me. *I am a petite girl, but I can suck down this beer faster than you, you pudgy asshole.*

I put both of my thumbs – one thumb alone was too small – over the opening of the dirty plastic tube and the beer guy handed him a can, which he promptly popped open and poured into the green funnel.

"You ready?" He asked as the tube filled. He tossed the empty can aside.

I nodded and in one fluid motion – it almost looked choreographed – he raised the funnel above his head and I shoved the tube into my mouth.

I was finished in three seconds flat. I knew because the beer guy had taken the liberty of timing me, yelling the seconds out as they ticked by on his watch.

I dropped the tube and behind me, a cheer erupted.

"Damn." The funnel guy shook my hand as I stood up. I felt a swelling of pride in my chest. "You next?"

Rudy shook her head. "Not unless you want me to spew all over your shoes."

We went to the living room to return to a game of flip cup, but it wasn't long before someone else came to challenge me to a beer bong. Or perhaps they'd just heard I could finish in three seconds and they didn't believe it; they wanted proof. I proved myself three more times in an hour and a half. The fourth time, I fell over mid-bong, the remainder of my beer pouring out of the hose onto my jeans. Somebody caught me by my armpits and carried me off the porch into the grass, amid shouts and murmurs and mumbles. The mumbles, I think, were my own.

I fell to my knees and projectile vomited the contents of my stomach into the grass of Deena's backyard. It was mostly liquid. A chunk of my hair fell onto my face, and I swiped at it. A hand brushed it away, behind my shaking shoulders.

"Rudy?"

I spewed again, a smelly beer fountain beside the flowerbeds. I nearly fit the décor.

"She's inside. Do you need me to get her?"

I tried to nod my head, 'yes', but it must've come out differently, as the person behind me didn't stand to leave. He placed a hand on my back.

I threw up until my stomach was so empty it was nearly flat.

I tried to stand, but immediately I pitched forward toward the bitter smelling pile.

"Whoa," someone steadied me from behind. Again.

"Uhh," I moaned.

"Jill, what happened?"

"Rudy?" She appeared in front of my face, translucent as an angel. The pitch of her voice alarmed me.

"Are you okay?"

"I think that last one got her."

Rudy pushed my hair back behind my ears. Remarkably, it was the first time either of us had drunk so much we got sick.

"Are you okay?"

I nodded.

"I think we should go home. Caleb, can you drive us?"

"Yeah, sure. If you want to stay with her, I'll go bring my car closer."

I heard his footsteps retreating.

"Caleb?"

"He's taking us home. Here, go like this." She wiped the back of her hand across her own mouth. I did the same, and felt wet flecks of vomit clinging to the back of my hand.

"That's disgusting." I wiped my knuckles against the ground.

Rudy knelt behind me in the grass and gathered my hair in her hands. She raked it through her fingers as she wove it into a thick braid and the tips of her short fingernails scratched softly against my scalp, lulling me into a trance. My eyelids drooped.

"There," she said. I felt the braid drop against my spine. "Now it won't get in your way."

In a flash Caleb was back, his car keys jangling in his hand.

"Ready?"

Together they hoisted me up off of the ground, positioning my arms over each of their shoulders. In her heels, Rudy was almost as tall as Caleb. I hung only a little bit lop-sided.

It wasn't working though. I couldn't hold myself up. We stumbled forward a few feet, and then we stopped. I felt my feet being swept off the ground. Then we were moving again, me floating above the ground on strong, warm arms.

"Thanks," I muttered into Caleb's chest.

"No problem," he said into the top of my head. I could feel his breath between the strands of my hair. I felt his lips land, softly and gently and just for a moment, right on the spot where my hair was parted.

Caleb smelled good. Like cologne, I thought, my face pressed into the buttons of his shirt. And then I fell asleep.

EVEN DURING THE peak of our rebellion, Rudy was still the perfect daughter. She had the idea that we should start learning to cook family dinner on Sunday nights, much to Mrs. Golden's delight. She bought her parents thoughtful birthday gifts, while mine were lucky if I remembered to pick up a card at the grocery store. In November, I sat with Mr. and Mrs. Golden in the audience while Rudy was inducted into Ogden's chapter of the National Honor Society. She beamed graciously as she walked across the candlelit stage. She radiated light, and they took it in like lepers who'd been living in a cave. I envied the proud gleam in her parents' eyes.

Her relationship with her parents made things all the more difficult when, just two weeks before Christmas, Mr. Golden suffered a massive heart attack. He lived, thank God, but he spent days recuperating in the hospital. He had to have surgery to clear the blockage in his heart.

The night it happened, Rudy called me sobbing so hysterically I couldn't understand anything she said. Terrified, I had jumped out of my bed and run through the dark in my pajamas and rain boots. The Goldens' front door was unlocked, and I tramped dirty snow through the house on my way up to Rudy's bedroom. When I pushed the door open, she was sitting on top of the covers in her bed, her head buried in her hands.

"It's dad," she sobbed. "What if he doesn't make it?"

I took off my boots and climbed into bed with her.

"It happened so fast. Jill, you should've seen the look on his face. He looked so scared. He...he just fell over."

I swallowed hard. What could you say to that?

"It must be stress. Mom said the stress is too much for him."

"He's going to be okay. It'll all be fine."

"But how do you know that?"

"I just know," I said.

She lay her head in my lap, and I stroked her hair while she cried some more.

Inside, I was shaken. The image of Mr. Golden – the ultimate father figure – in a hospital bed plagued my mind. It felt perverse; a role reversal, with my rock of a best friend crumbling to pieces. I tried to put up a strong front.

"Thank you for coming over. I don't know what I'd do without you," she told me.

For years, I'd been thinking those exact words about her. But, oh, how inadequate I felt when she said she needed me back.

After that, Rudy stopped smoking completely. She stopped going out for a while, too, hovering around her house even when her parents weren't around. I think the heart attack scared some reality into her.

Of course, it doesn't take long for seventeen year olds to regain a sense of invincibility. We were back to our old antics soon enough.

———

THE GRANDEST NEW Year's Eve of my life was celebrated at none other than Caleb Rowling's house. Since then, I've experienced many New Year's celebrations that were happier, but none that have equaled junior year in terms of pure extravagance.

Rudy and I wore glittering cocktail dresses over dark tights and black high heels, and sported red lipstick. We wore our hair in big, glamorous curls. We got Kent, who had been guilted into coming home for the holidays after Mr. Golden's heart attack, to buy us a bottle of Goldschlager to bring to the party. We'd never had it before, but we thought the gold flecks would be classy and cool. My mother let me borrow a pair of her diamond earrings to wear with my silver dress.

We arrived at Caleb's an hour early to help assemble martinis, and he greeted us at the door, a glass of scotch in his hand.

"Happy New Year's, ladies," he smiled.

"Don't you look dapper," I smiled back.

He looked incredibly hot in his tuxedo, with his blonde hair swept back from his face.

"You both look beautiful yourselves."

He led us through the foyer, which was fully decorated in crystals and sequins and glittering garlands, and into the kitchen, where his sister Haley, a sophomore, was unpacking martini glasses from Styrofoam filled cardboard boxes. There must have been a hundred real glasses set out on the kitchen table.

"I like your dresses," she smiled, flattening an empty box and setting it aside.

"Thank you," I said.

"Yours is beautiful, too," Rudy added. "How can we help?"

Rudy and I assigned ourselves the task of mixing the martinis. Who cared if the guests wouldn't arrive for another forty-five minutes? What could you do? We slowly filled each of the glasses.

Caleb's parents had gone to Aruba for the holiday, leaving their children with a multi-thousand dollar limit on their credit cards and instructions to make sure the house was clean when they returned home. No questions asked, just make sure it was clean. Exactly how they had left it.

Obviously Haley had been in charge of most of the party planning. The table in the dining room was covered in silver platters with caviar and crab legs and little cucumber sandwiches. All over the house, little white lights twinkled where they had been hung tactfully from the ceiling, and on the tables sat elaborate silver and crystal centerpieces. There were bags of silver foiled confetti, waiting to be tossed at midnight. I couldn't fathom the mess all those flecks of foil would leave behind in the morning.

Before the first guests arrived, the four of us toasted with shots of Goldschlager.

"To the best year yet," Rudy proclaimed.

I was mesmerized by the flecks swimming around in my glass. We tossed the shots back, each of us grimacing.

"That shit's disgusting," Caleb wiped his mouth with the back of his hand.

"We had no idea." I gagged, the cinnamon taste thick in my mouth. "We thought it'd be festive."

"Oh, god, get me something to wash it down with." Rudy reached for a cup of red punch.

I've always envied those people who can sense when bad things are coming their way. The ones who, before a car crash, can sense their tires hitting ice the moment it happens. The people who have time to try to reverse the situation, or at least pray it won't be as bad as they fear. To brace themselves for the impact.

I, myself, have always been one of the unlucky ones who go through life oblivious. There were signs all around me that winter; I should have been able to read them. I should've paid more attention! Those are the things for which I admonish myself.

If I'm ever in a car accident, I feel sure I'll be caught off-guard, still singing off-key to the radio until the very moment my body jolts forward and my car smashes into a guardrail.

———

AT 11:30 THE party was in full swing. Rudy and I had refilled the martini glasses over and over until all of Caleb's vodka was gone. He'd approached us from behind, throwing an arm around each of our shoulders.

"Nice work," he said, nodding toward the empty bottles.

"The martinis were an awesome idea." I smiled.

"That was all Haley," he said, his cheeks pink. He had loosened his bow tie and shed his jacket hours before. It was so warm I was even sweating a bit in my slinky, sleeveless dress.

Rudy was turning to select a fresh drink when Caleb leaned toward me.

"Hey," he whispered. His breath in my ear sent goose bumps down my arms. "Can I talk to you upstairs real quick?"

I nodded, confused.

He tugged at my elbow, and I followed him. On the stairs I looked back at Rudy. We made eye contact, and she raised a single eyebrow. I shrugged. She sort of smiled, and I continued up the stairs. Just before she was out of eyesight, I thought I saw her toss back her entire martini.

On the second floor, I followed Caleb through a hallway twinkling with little white lights. He pushed one of the doors and led me inside.

I swear, I didn't yet understand. Even then, I was still singing with the radio.

We were in his bedroom. He didn't turn the lights on, but I could make out the shapes of his dresser and his bed and the outlines of soccer posters lining the white walls.

"So, this is your room, huh?" I flipped the light on myself and took in the room. His comforter was navy and light blue striped and his bed was made, though sloppily. In the corner a large black desk was full of papers and books, organized into neat and tidy stacks and his open backpack hung from the corner of the chair by one strap.

"This is it," he said.

"This is where the magic happens," I wiggled my eyebrows exaggeratedly.

"So much magic." He laughed.

Above his desk was a shelf with a small collection of trophies, little gold soccer players in various positions atop engraved plaques. I crossed the room to look closer. Pushed to the back was a larger trophy of a shiny plastic bowling pin. I picked it up and held it out toward Caleb, an inquisitive look on my face.

He shrugged and appeared a tiny bit embarrassed. "I used to bowl in a league."

"Like when you were a little kid?"

"What if I told you it was more like two or three years ago?"

"Who were you in a bowling league with?"

"It was a family league. My parents were big into it. I kind of miss it, but Haley wanted to quit and I didn't really have time anymore with soccer."

I set the trophy back down and peered out the window. It was dark, and I could see the glow of all the main floor lights spilling out onto the grass of the backyard. Caleb came up behind me and looked over my shoulder.

"What're you looking at now?"

"Nothing," I said. "Just looking."

I could feel warmth from his body. I turned toward him – we were a few inches apart, just my martini glass between us.

"I like your hair like that." He reached up and pulled at one of my curls, his fingers grazing my collarbone. I felt little goose bumps rising where he had touched my skin and warmth spread through my torso.

"Thanks," I smiled and he smiled back, and we stood staring at each other like that for a moment.

He sat on the edge of the bed and gestured that I should sit beside him. I did.

"So," I said.

"So." He repeated.

Caleb had left his drink downstairs in the kitchen. I held my martini glass, unsure what to do with it.

"The party turned out pretty cool, huh?"

"For sure. I'm having fun."

I set my drink on the carpet beside the bed.

"Good," Caleb leaned toward me. "I'm really glad."

"But there's no way I'm helping clean up that confetti in the morning," I joked. "That's all you."

"Yeah, I think I can handle that."

He leaned in further and kissed me on the mouth.

I pulled back quickly, leaving him bent over me, his hand on my knee.

"What're you doing," I said.

"I was trying to kiss you." He was still smiling, still in the moment before while I had travelled abruptly to a very different moment.

"I thought you liked Rudy."

At this, he moved away just a little.

"Rudy? No. Not more than a friend. Why would you think that?"

"You went with her to Sadie," I pressed.

"Because you asked me to."

"I don't understand," I said.

He gave me a little smile. He was so cute, so dangerously cute with his hair falling in his face that way. "I thought I'd made it pretty obvious that *you're* the one I like."

"Me." I was having trouble processing what Caleb was saying. Maybe it was the alcohol, I thought. "You're interested in *me*?"

"Yeah. And I thought it seemed like maybe you liked me back, too."

"Why?"

"Why would I think you like me?" His chest seemed to deflate and he leaned away from me.

"No, why would you like me? I mean, over Rudy?"

He blew a stream of air out through the corner of his mouth. "I don't know, Jillian, maybe because you're gorgeous? You're funny. You're a lot of fun to be around."

"But Rudy's all of those things. *More* all of those things."

"Are you serious?" He studied me for a moment with furrowed eyebrows. "Are you really that insecure?"

Sitting on his unmade bed with my long legs sticking out of my short, glittery dress, I wouldn't have considered myself insecure; no, I wouldn't have used that word. It was just that Rudy was the most beautiful girl I could imagine. She was perfect, with her shiny deep brown hair and her light green eyes, her perfect hourglass figure and her skin perpetually the color of a sunkissed tan. Her lips formed a perfect pink heart and even her imperfections served only to enhance her beauty. How was I supposed to compare to that?

I couldn't, I thought. I paled beside her. I sunk below her.

A slimy feeling slid down into my stomach.

"I'm not being insecure. I'm being realistic." I crossed my

arms over my chest. "But I'm not nothing, you know. I'm not just a tool for you to use to make her jealous."

The look he gave me – the perfect blend of desperation and sympathy, predaciousness and protectiveness – permeated my body, holding my vital organs captive, and I wondered for just a second if I was wrong about everything, about the balance between Rudy and I, about the person I imagined myself to be and the interior world where I lived. But the thought was too big – I shoved it away as quickly as it had come.

"I'm not trying to use you. If I wanted to date Rudy, I would have dated her. She doesn't have anything to do with this. This is about you and me."

Below us, I could hear the low rumble of the party continuing in our absence. Looking at his face – his distraught, confused face – I had the perverse urge to laugh. The whole situation was absurd. I stood, and leaned against his desk, needing to put physical distance between us.

"I can't date you. Rudy liked you."

"It was just one dance, Jill. You don't think she can let that go?"

I didn't like the tone of his voice. I wanted to go back downstairs.

"I don't think she'd hold a grudge," I said quietly.

"Then why don't we just try this?" He took a step toward me, looking straight into my eyes. "You do feel the same way, right? That's what it's seemed like over the past few months."

I did like him. I got butterflies in my stomach, especially if I thought about his smile. That's why I had to break eye contact.

"No," I answered.

I heard the countdown start, a unified chant muffled by the floor beneath my feet. I started to walk away, and Caleb caught my wrist.

"Jill, don't leave yet." He wasn't mean when he said it, but still I yanked my arm away from him. I stepped back, and felt my foot knock into the forgotten martini glass, felt the liquid dripping over my shoe and soaking into the carpet.

"Just let me go. Please."

I walked out at the eruption of midnight.

My insides were churning, propelling me down the staircase into the chaotic celebration. Everyone was shrieking, and the air was dense with glinting shards of confetti. Somebody opened a bottle of champagne and the cork whizzed past my ear. Foam splattered the floor.

I found Rudy in the foyer, her arms wrapped around some guy's neck, her mouth pressed against his. She pulled away when I touched her arm. For a split second I saw something weird in her eyes, but it was gone before I could understand it.

"Happy New Year," she squealed, planting a wet kiss where Caleb had kissed me minutes before, right on the center of my lips.

11

JUNIOR SPRING

When track season arrived that spring, I was ready. I'd been running all winter through the dirty sludge left over after snowfalls. Even when we were smoking, I was waking up early the following morning to run. My lungs were resilient.

Still, when Rudy and I pulled into the sports parking lot the morning of the first meet of the year, my stomach was swimming. I bounced one hip against the side of Rudy's car while she pulled her windbreaker over her head.

"They should really consider buying new warm-ups." She sniffed one navy sleeve. "These smell like cheese. And old people home."

I tried to laugh for her, but my nerves were constricting my vocal cords.

"Hey." She elbowed my ribs as we headed toward the track. "Chill out. You're going to do great."

Nervous wasn't in Rudy's vocabulary.

It was just a small meet – we were dueling another private school from across the city – but Coach Kline said they'd be good. They had three senior girl hurdlers. I'd hit the 100m hurdles hard at practice the week before, but I still didn't feel ready.

The energy at a track meet was one of my favorite parts of the sport. It was so different than the relaxed feel before we competed in cross-country. As we passed through the gates to the track, Rudy and I could see the other team running warm up laps, their matching red pants slicking together to make a swooshing sound. To one side of the track, the coaching assistants were assembling the metal pole vault and high jumps standards, and Coach Sampson, the sprinting coach, was calling out stretches to a group of our teammates who lay with their legs spread in the grass. There was a decent crowd shivering in the bleachers. It smelled like popcorn, wafting from the concession stand.

"Crap, I'd better get over there," Rudy started toward the group with Coach Sampson. Thomas Hart, one of the guys on the sprint relay teams, waved to her.

"Good luck," I said to the back of her head.

"I'll try to come find you before you run." She turned back toward me and was jogged backwards while she spoke. "If not, kick ass, okay?" She mouthed the middle of that sentence.

I saluted, and she returned the gesture before jogging off.

In a small strip of grass beside the chute, I sat down, shoved ear buds into my ears and tuned out while I thrust one leg out to the side and bent over my thigh, feeling the stretch down my hamstring.

I was a quarter of the way through my pump-up playlist when I was startled by someone tapping me on the shoulder. I jerked, yanking the wire from one of my ears. It was Coach Kline.

"Hey, Jill. How you feeling?" He had crouched down to my level and spoke to me from behind mirrored aviator sunglasses.

"I'm alright. A little nervous, I guess."

"Don't be. You worked hard in practice the past couple weeks. I know you've got this."

I responded with a closed-mouth smile. Pep talks only made me feel more anxious, but I didn't have the heart to share that with him.

"Just remember, don't change up your steps. Do it just the way we do in practice and you'll be good to go." He clapped me on the shoulder and the wires of my ear buds knocked against his arm. "You've got this, girl. This is your season, I just know it."

When he was gone, scurrying off after someone called for him on his walkie-talkie, I stood and jogged two warm up laps around the crowded track, my legs and arms tingly.

At the first call for the 100-meter hurdles, I was in the chute, the first girl to arrive. Luke Bruggeman, another Ogden hurdler, stood beside me with his under-armored arms crossed over his chest.

"You nervous?"

He rolled his head in a circle, his hair flopping over his forehead, then grabbed at one foot from behind, stretching his quadricep.

"Yeah," I said quietly. I was sizing up my competition, the leggy redhead in particular. She wasn't any taller than me, but her body was two-thirds legs, as impossible as that sounds. I gawked, swallowing the lump in my throat.

"I just don't want to wipe out. I don't even care how I do, as long as I don't eat shit." Luke was bouncing up and down on his toes now, flexing and relaxing his calves. His anxious energy made me want to shake him by the shoulders until he stopped moving.

"Yeah."

When the gun went off for the boys' race, my stomach

churned like an ice cream mixer. They ushered us into the blocks while they adjusted the hurdles. I was in the second lane, sandwiched between the redhead and a shorter black girl. My hands were clammy and cold as I placed my feet in the blocks and positioned my fingers in front of me on the track, the chunky rubber surface pressing into the soft skin of my palms. At the shot of the starting gun, I was out of the blocks and sprinting toward the hurdles. It was a great start.

Coaches always tell you not to look behind you during a race. Just worry about yourself, they say; don't slow yourself down by trying to check up on your opponents. That's easier said than done though. After the sixth hurdle, I glanced slightly to my right but I couldn't see any of the other girls in my periphery.

I finished in sixteen seconds, a full second before the girl in second-place (the leggy red-head finished last; who would have guessed?). I only clipped one of the hurdles. Walking back down the side of the track after the race, my face was flushed.

"Nice race, Jillian."

I turned. It was Caleb Rowling, standing with his friends on the sidelines in jeans and an Ogden sweatshirt, holding a cup of hot chocolate.

"Thanks," I said sincerely.

He gave me a half smile and looked the other direction before I had to say anything more. I accepted two more congratulatory exclamations, one from a girl from the cross-country team and one from my sophomore English teacher, who was manning the concession stand beside the track, when Rudy came running toward me on the sidewalk, her toes lifted so that her spikes didn't scrape the concrete.

"Jill!" She collided against me, wrapping me in a quick hug. "Look at you, turbo. You won by miles."

"Not *miles*," I grinned.

"Metaphorical miles."

The intercom cackled overhead. My organs had settled seconds after the race, and the smell of the concession stand was making my stomach growl.

"I'm supposed to go practice hand-offs with the 4X2 team. I put my stuff over in the shed though. Thomas is watching it for me," Rudy said. During home meets, our team congregated in the old storage shed at the end of the track, laying down blankets and pillows on the cement floor and lounging in our warm-ups while we watched our teammates run. "See you after my race!"

"Good luck!"

I won my second race, the 300-meter hurdles, later that afternoon. When Coach Kline found me at the finish line, he grabbed me in an awkward one-armed hug.

"That's my girl," he grinned. "It's your season; what'd I tell you?"

———

You would think that by April of my junior year of high school, I'd have some idea where I was going to college. Ogden allowed all juniors three excused college visits over the course of the year, but I only took one day to drive to MU with Rudy, where we spent most of the day meandering around the enormous campus observing what the girls were wearing and watching for cute guys before we left to go get frozen custard and drive home.

You could see evidence of the building enthusiasm in the bright new sweatshirts I'd see my classmates wearing: UC Berkeley, NYU, Truman University, Missouri State. I didn't catch their excitement, but, really, I shouldn't have been so surprised that Rudy *was* thinking about her future.

"Guess what?"

"Huh?"

We were sprawled out on the couch in my basement and I was enthralled with the movie on the TV screen.

"I said, guess what," Rudy repeated.

"What?"

She reached for a handful of popcorn from the bowl that sat between our feet, then picked a single kernel from her hand and put it in her mouth.

"My mom said she's going to take me to see the University of Southern California the first week in May. As long as I don't have any finals then."

"Seriously?"

Rudy nodded. "I didn't even ask, she just offered. I think we'll probably go see UCLA too, while we're there."

"Where is USC again?"

"It's in LA."

"Oh." I paused. "That's pretty cool."

"I wish you could come with me. Actually, you probably could. Do you want me to ask my mom?"

Of course I did. College was still fairly inconceivable to me, but I could definitely picture Rudy and me studying together under palm trees on the beach in California.

"That's the week before districts," I said.

"Yeah, you're right. We wanted to go before the semester ended, but maybe I can get mom to move it back."

We? We wanted?

"Maybe." I grabbed a handful of popcorn and shoved the whole thing in my mouth.

———

"Okay, guys, listen up." Coach Kline was yelling above the

rumble in the track and field conference room. Someone had left a stereo on, and rap music echoed through the room below the high-pitched sound of girl chatter. Some guys in the back of the room were laughing like hyenas, trying to do back flips off of the back wall.

"Hey!" Coach let off one sharp whistle blast.

I looked up from where I sat on one end of a wooden bench, tying my shoe. The noise stopped abruptly, except the music.

"Will somebody turn that crap off?" One of the boys shuffled across the room. "Thanks."

"So, we've got districts this weekend, but I hope you were all well aware of that already." He paused. "I won't keep you long because I want you to get the most out of practice this week, but I've got a couple quick things. First, I want to congratulate you all on a spectacular conference meet Saturday. As a team, we had fourteen season bests and seven personal bests, and that's exactly what we need to see going into the end of the season. Individually, I want to congratulate our conference champs, Keegan Lowry in long and triple jump, Justin Jones in the 400, the boys 4X2 team, Whitney Polentry in the 1600 and Jillian Matthews in the 100 and 300 meter hurdles."

I sat up straighter when he looked at me.

"The girls team finished fourth overall, and the boys were second. You did nice work, just remember to keep it up. I know prom's coming up, and graduation for all you seniors," (a few hoots went up from the back of the room), "but don't lose focus just yet. I need everyone to work harder than ever at practice this week. Seriously, I want 110% from all of you. We've got the potential to put a lot of athletes through to sectionals, so don't sell yourselves short." Coach Kline smiled. "Now, get out there and run like you're on fire."

Outside, it was a prime Missouri spring day. The trees in the school courtyard were blooming big white flowers, and I could hear the low buzz of a lawnmower and smell the cut grass somewhere in the distance. The sun was soft and light on my bare arms and legs. I wondered what it was like for Rudy and Mrs. Golden thousands of miles away at USC. Probably amazing, I thought.

"Hey." Luke, my hurdles practice partner, caught up to me on the track. "So, my dad was checking out a track website last night and he said your times from Saturday are the third best in the state this year."

"Really?"

Coach Sampson called for high knees, and Luke and I picked up our knees with the rest of the runners.

"Yeah. I didn't even make the list." He smiled sheepishly. "I'll just be happy as shit to medal this weekend."

"I'm sure you can medal." I breathed deep as we went into lunges. "What was the website?"

"MSHSAA something. Why? You going to go home and Google yourself?" He wiggled his eyebrows at me.

I elbowed him in the gut and he lunged away from me, clutching his stomach dramatically.

"I'm sure you're very familiar with Googling yourself," I said.

"You're *so* funny," he spit back.

That night after practice, I spent hours searching Missouri high school track websites for my own name. Luke was right – or rather, his dad was. I had one of the best times in the state. And I was mentioned a lot on the forums, anonymous people speculating on whether or not I had a shot at winning the state championships, talking about college track and field even. I devoured it all, my chest swelling a little more each time I came across my own name.

I didn't remember I had two pages of Spanish verb conjugations due the next day until I was lying in bed, about to fall asleep. Without Rudy's help, I was up until one in the morning finishing the worksheets.

She'd return from California in just two more days.

———

WE WERE lucky the district meet was being held at Ogden that year (but with a track facility that had been completely redone only five years earlier, complete with the addition of more than five-hundred extra bleacher seats, it was hard to understand why they'd even alternate the location at all). I, for one, was thrilled. I loved to have a big Ogden crowd watching. I loved to hear my classmates chanting my name and getting slapped on the back when I finished my races and to see the younger kids, junior high kids who would go to Ogden in a year or two, looking up to me in admiration.

To say the track was packed that Saturday would be an understatement. It was overflowing, even when Rudy and I arrived, an hour before any of the races would begin.

It would also be an understatement to say I did well that day. Honestly, I'm not just being arrogant when I say I obliterated the competition that day. I won both of my races with times half a second better than my personal bests, even against the stiffest competition I'd seen all year. I was walking on clouds, grinning the entire day.

Mr. and Mrs. Golden took Rudy and me out for Mexican food after the meet was over, and we gorged ourselves on chips and salsa in our warm ups and our wind-blown ponytails while Mrs. Golden showed us pictures she'd taken of our races.

When I got home, the lights were out and neither of my parents' cars was in the driveway. I waited until morning to tell them I was going to sectionals.

RUDY DIDN'T HAVE a lot to say about California other than telling me the schools were huge. They got lost three separate times at UCLA. When I asked her if she wanted to spend four years getting lost on campus, she shrugged it off. "I've got another year to decide, right?" Amid the chaos of the end of another school year, I didn't have much time to contemplate Rudy's college visit anyway. I wore pink lipstick to match my black and pink prom dress. I got one A, four B's and two C's on my finals (the A was in art, where I made a self-portrait out of magazine clippings as my final project). After the sectional track meet, our team numbers dwindled even further. Rudy's relay team didn't make it through to state, and neither did Luke. I stayed late at practice doing drills with Coach Kline until the sun started to set.

Ogden's graduation ceremony was held the Thursday night before the state track meet. Each year, the staff hauled white metal folding chairs out onto the football field, where they were placed in neat rows angling in toward the portable stage that sat on the ten-yard line. The boys wore navy robes, and the girls' robes were white. You could identify the top twenty-five percent of the graduating class because they wore red cords around their necks.

Rudy and I sat in the stands with Deena and we listened as the principal spoke first, then the school board president, then a local businessman. Each year, the class valedictorian was the last to give a speech; this year, it was a guy with glasses who spoke so softly I could hardly hear him, even with the microphone pressed up to his lips.

In the last minutes of sunlight, everything on the field – the soft grass, the feathery tassels hanging from every graduate's hat – glowed, all awash in sepia tones. I still felt the warm hug of afternoon on my shoulders, but the beginning of spring's evening chill whispered against my neck. Next year, we would be the ones who occupied those seats on the field, a stadium of proud eyes cast down upon our heads. I swallowed the soft lump in my throat and turned my gaze away from the stage to Deena and Rudy. Deena was picking at her index finger, her brow furrowed in concentration, using her thumbnail to shave off flecks of chipped blue polish. Beside her, Rudy stared ahead, her dark lashes shining golden in the twilight. Her eyes were solemn, and the corners of her lips turned up slightly in a sad smile, but she wasn't focused on the stage or the blue and white army of robes spread across the field. I tried to follow her line of sight, down the bridge of her nose and off across the field into the distance, but regardless of how I tried, I couldn't see what she saw. When I looked back down at the stage, the valedictorian speech was over and the boy with the soft voice was carried to his seat by a smattering of applause. The ceremony pressed forward.

Afterward, we went down to the field with the rest of the crowd, searching for friends in the mess of smiles and squeals, arms and legs and camera flashes under the bright lights of the field. When we found Caleb, I kissed him on the cheek.

"Congratulations!" I gave him my warmest smile. I hoped I had

been forgiven.

"Thanks." He returned my smile.

He was going to school in Indiana in the fall, miles and miles away.

EVEN ON MY WEDDING DAY, I never felt as nervous as I felt that Friday at the state track meet in Jefferson City. I got lost in the knot of people swarming the track, and I was on the verge of a panic attack, my eyes welling with tears, when finally I found a man in a white official's polo who directed me to the tent where I could sign in. I pinned the paper bib to the front of my jersey, and I could feel the metal of the safety pins against my stomach. During the prelims for the 100, I clipped three hurdles. In the 300 I was slow getting out of the blocks, but I made the finals in each event, which meant I would race again the next day.

Rudy came to watch me on Saturday too, though I wasn't allowed to ride with her. I spent the long bus ride sleeping or listening to my iPod, trying to ignore the tingly sunburn that had developed on my forehead from the day before.

Coach Kline gave me a quick pep talk before my first race, and then he disappeared into the hulking concrete stands, a navy-capped head among thousands of other bobbing, multi-colored heads. I was well rested and irritated with my performance in the prelims. Now that I'd spent a day there, the setting felt familiar. I was calm. I placed third in the 100-meter hurdles, and I stood on the wooden podium with seven other girls as we received our medals, and I just knew I would win the 300 hurdles. Right there, when they hung a bronze medal around my neck, I swear I knew I would do it.

My shoulders were tense as I stood behind the blocks before the last race of my junior season. I didn't realize just how tense until afterward though, when I finally relaxed and felt my muscles melting as the nervous energy left them.

"Runners take your mark."

I positioned my spikes against the back of the blocks and my fingertips at the edge of my lane. Lane three out of eight.

"Set."

In unison, eight butts rose into the air.

At the sound of the gun I was off, flying around the curve of the track, over the first hurdle, then the second, then the third. This time, I really didn't look behind or beside me at the other girls. For once I wasn't competing against anyone but myself. I knew I'd won the moment I crossed the white finish line, and I grinned so hard my face hurt. I threw my arms in the air then immediately lowered them, embarrassed by my own excitement.

The top of the podium was glorious.

———

AND THEN, we were seniors.

THE END

12

SENIOR FALL

I spent the first lunch period of my last year of high school sitting in the yearbook computer lab with Rudy while she edited photos from the first week of fall sports practices. One of the privileges of being a member of the reigning class was that we were free to roam the campus during our lunch hour.

"Did you see the new girls' gym teacher?"

"Huh uh," Rudy grunted, her eyes fixed on a zoomed in portion of a football player's leg. "Why?"

"She looks as young as us. I guess if she just graduated college, she could be only four years older than we are though."

"True. I bet that's weird for her."

"Yeah." I bit into my sandwich and mustard squirted out onto my new skirt. "Shit. Are there paper towels in here?"

"Over there, by the sink in the old dark room."

I licked my finger and dabbed it against the yellow blob. After a few minutes of soap and water application in the dark room, I emerged with just a big wet spot left on the pink linen.

We had agreed to dress up for the first day of school, as was Ogden's senior tradition, but Rudy had already thrown on a sweatshirt over her blouse. The air conditioner was blasting cold air, and the room was an icebox.

"Did it come out?" She asked.

"Yeah, mostly." I abandoned the offending sandwich and opened my bag of chips instead. "What're we doing this weekend? I heard Taylor Kerts is having a party."

"I might have to take pictures at the debate team's first match."

I frowned. "I thought you had other people to do most of that? Don't you just delegate now?"

At the end of the previous school year, Rudy had been elected the photo editor of Ogden's award-winning yearbook. It was an honor, of course, but I thought she was taking the job a bit too seriously.

"Yeah, but this early in the year I want to make sure the photogs know what they're doing. You know?"

"I guess."

She cocked her head at me and smiled.

"Come on." She shoved me playfully. "I'm sure I'll be back in time to go with you to Taylor's."

"Watch your shoving. If you make me get something else on this skirt, I'll have to kill you."

"You wouldn't."

"I'd have to. It's non-negotiable."

She socked me in the shoulder.

"Well, you can have all my crap when I'm dead. I'll write you into my will."

In late September I was sitting beside Deena in Anatomy, my last class of the day, when the intercom clicked on and the voice of the student body president came on over the speaker.

"Good afternoon, Ogden Academy faculty, staff and students," he began. The student body president was a boy in our class who, in my opinion, didn't seem particularly noteworthy for anything other than his voice. He had a voice made for radio, syrupy and smooth. I have no idea what he's doing now, but sometimes when I'm watching a commercial I become convinced it must be that guy who's doing the voiceover.

"As you all know, next week begins the annual Ogden homecoming week." He paused, and a small cheer rang out over the school. You could hear it through the walls in adjacent classrooms. "And this isn't just any homecoming celebration. This year, we're celebrating the 50th anniversary of homecoming at Ogden, which means it will be bigger and better than ever!"

One of the shaggy haired boys sitting in the back of my classroom hooted, and our teacher, a petite older woman who wore pantsuits, narrowed her tiny, angry eyes at him.

"So, here's the information you need. The class spirit competition will begin Monday with hippie day, so make sure you look groovy, guys and gals. Tuesday is nerd day and Wednesday is camouflage day, so dress in your hunting best. Thursday is celebrity look-a-like day and Friday is spirit day so don't come to school if you're not decked in navy and white." He took a deep breath. "Thursday night is the big spirit bonfire, so be there at 7 p.m. or be square. Friday morning we'll have the spirit assembly, and we'll all be released after lunch at 1 p.m. The homecoming parade departs from the front parking lot at 1:30 p.m. and the big football game kicks off at 7 p.m. Friday night, with the coronation ceremony at halftime. Now, what you've all been waiting for." I'd be lying if I didn't admit that I was holding my breath, and my heart rate picked up in anticipation of what I knew was coming next. "The homecoming queen candidates are as follows: Deena Orr," (beside me, Deena squeaked audibly),

"Teegan Westings, LeAnn Tyler, Rudy Golden and Jillian Matthews."

To say I was completely shocked wouldn't be absolutely truthful. This moment had been buried in the back of my mind since the beginning of the school year, and it had slowly begun to emerge as homecoming grew nearer. I had imagined my name being considered as a candidate – the football team nominated and decided upon the five senior girls – but I had also imagined it was unlikely to happen. And if it did, I thought, it would mostly be a testament to Rudy's likability, that it could be so great it would spill over to me.

I was surprised. Not shocked, but genuinely surprised. In my surprise, I had missed the end of the message. The bell rang and around me, my classmates shot out of their seats and out the door.

"Congrats, girl! This is so exciting." Deena grabbed my forearm and squeezed.

"Yeah, congrats to you, too," I smiled.

"We should all go shopping for dresses together this weekend. LeAnn and Teegan, too. I'll talk to them." Deena's excitement was so palpable it was practically oozing out onto me. I wanted to get away from her as soon as possible before it permeated my skin.

"Sure. I'll talk to Rudy about it."

"Awesome!" We walked into the hallway and she squeezed my arm again. "I'll call you guys, okay? I'll see you later!"

She hugged me and headed off down the hallway, almost bouncing.

Rudy was waiting for me when I reached my locker.

"Congratulations, candidate," she smiled.

"Right back at you," I returned her smile two-fold. "Deena asked us to go dress shopping with her this weekend."

Rudy grimaced. "Was she exploding?"

"She was exploding," I whispered, unloading books onto the bottom of my locker.

"Can we just go together? Just you and me? I'll give her an excuse."

"I was thinking the same thing." I grinned.

"Good. I'm glad we're always on the same wavelength."

Me too, I thought. Me too.

———

"O! G! D-E-N! Og-den! Og-den!"

When Rudy and I arrived at the bonfire Thursday night, we heard the cheerleaders chanting in the distance even before we could make out the fiery orange glow against the navy sky. It was twilight, and there was a chill in the air. We wore jackets and jeans and navy, knit beanies pulled on over our heads. As we got closer, our feet crunching the few leaves that had fallen too early, I could make out faces of the people in the crowd. The warmth pulled us in.

"Hey." Thomas Hart, from the track team, grabbed Rudy by the elbow as we were walking past. "Rudy. Jill."

"Hey! How long have you been here? I feel like we're late." Rudy smiled crookedly.

"Nah, it's just getting started, I think. Blake and I got here ten minutes ago."

"Oh, okay. Are you sitting somewhere? We brought a blanket, if you want to sit with us," Rudy gestured toward the over-stuffed bag I was hauling over my shoulder.

"There should be plenty of room. This thing weighs a million pounds," I added.

"Here," he lifted the bag off my arm. "Let me carry it. Lead the way, ladies."

We found an open space, and after Rudy determined the

grass was free of potentially butt-poking debris, Thomas spread out our flannel blanket.

"You know, I feel pretty lucky sitting here with the homecoming queens," Thomas joked. Silhouetted by the blaze behind him, his face was the color of melting chocolate.

"You probably aren't even voting for either of us," I said.

"Yeah." Rudy elbowed him. "Who *are* you voting for?"

"I can't divulge that kind of information in this company."

He would vote for Rudy. He would definitely vote for Rudy.

"Come on. I'll tickle it out of you." Rudy wiggled her fingers to compound the threat.

"Go ahead and try," Thomas grinned.

On the opposite side of the fire, I saw Deena standing on the edge of a group of seniors.

"I'm going to go say hey to Deena," I announced as I stood.

"Jillian!" Courtney Stauder, one of our classmates, saw me first as I approached the group. "You came!"

She leapt forward to give me a hug and a kiss on the cheek. As she pressed up against me, I nearly smirked. The biggest piece of gossip upon our return to school that fall had been the enhancement of Courtney Stauder's boobs, which were clearly two cups sizes bigger than normal. Speculation ran in every direction, but the senior consensus was that Courtney's stepfather had agreed to get her a boob job for her eighteenth birthday, which had fallen sometime that summer.

"Hey," I smiled. "This is pretty cool. I've never actually come to the bonfire before."

"Too cool for school, huh?" Michael Denalby said from across the circle.

"No." I made a face and I heard my own voice take on a sarcastic, flirty girl tone. "Not cool enough, I guess."

"Where's Rudy at?" Deena was looking around, a point and shoot camera swinging from a strap on her wrist.

"She's sitting over there."

Deena glanced behind us. "With Thomas Hart? What's up with that?"

"Nothing." I looked too. "They're just friends."

"Oh. Weird." She swung the camera in a circle and I leaned back, afraid she'd accidentally whack me.

"What's weird about it?"

"I don't know, just weird. I didn't know they were friends."

I watched Rudy from across the lawn. She leaned back on the grass, her legs stretched out in front of her, and laughed with her mouth wide open. Beside her, Thomas was clearly telling a very funny joke.

"They know each other from track."

"That's cool. I was just wondering." Deena smiled and touched my wrist. "Anyway, find me later, okay? And Rudy, too. I want to get a picture of all the candidates tonight."

"Okay."

Deena scurried off, Courtney and another girl following in her wake, leaving me on the empty end of a small circle of senior guys.

I coughed into my hand.

"So, Jillian, the queen voting's tomorrow. What're you going to do to win my vote?" Michael Denalby shoved his hands into his pockets and wiggled his eyebrows at me suggestively.

"I think I can do without your vote." I blushed, in spite of myself. The other guys laughed.

"That's not how Deena answered my proposition." They laughed even harder, seventeen and eighteen year old boys that they were.

"Well I'd hate to put myself through something so traumatizing and then not win after all," I said.

"Oh, come on," Max Briggs, the captain of the lacrosse team, interjected. "You think Deena will win?"

They snickered. I shrugged and turned toward where the cheerleaders had begun to chant again. This time the principal and the Varsity football coach stood beside them, both men dressed in sport coats along with their dark, pressed jeans.

"Can I get everyone's attention please," Dr. Foakley yelled, and gradually the noise died down to a low hush. "Thank you all for coming out tonight, Ogden students, parents, alumni and friends. We're going to get the formal part of the evening started with some spirit from the Varsity cheerleading team and a short word from head football coach, Coach Adams. Afterward, there will be some light refreshments available, courtesy of the Ogden Parent's Association. Again, thanks for supporting our wonderful school tonight, and we hope to see you all again at the 50th annual homecoming game tomorrow night!"

A cheer went up amongst the crowd, and the cheerleaders sprang into action, lifting each other into stunts as Principal Foakley stepped aside. From high in the air they started chanting again, and this time the crowd joined in, fists pumping in the air as the fire crackled.

The week of homecoming was always a special week at Ogden. The teachers didn't assign real homework or tests, the sports teams were more about camaraderie and less about hazing and, the administrators weren't quite so stiff and proper. On the day we dressed as celebrities, the principal came to school wearing a boy band t-shirt and carrying an inflatable microphone. It was cheesy, of course, but we ate it all up. It was just the energy in the air that week; we went nuts for it, for anything out of the ordinary, really.

After the cheerleaders had cheered and the coach had given his quick, impassioned speech, I made my way back to where Rudy and Thomas still sat, stretched out amongst a handful of other crowded blankets and lawn chairs.

"O! G! D-E-N!" Rudy mouthed the words and waved her

arms through the cheerleading motions, probably the only thing we still remembered from our short season as Ogden cheerleaders.

"They were so close to the fire, I was afraid one of them was going to fall in," I added.

"God, that'd be some way to kick off the bonfire."

The three of us sat talking and after awhile, we were joined by Thomas's friend Blake, Deena and Courtney and a couple of guys from the cross-country team, too. Soon, our blanket was overflowing, all of our butts smashed together, each vying for a tiny square of fabric. The sky got darker and you could see all the little pinpricks of stars. When Rudy and I stood to go get hot chocolate, Deena jumped up as well, abandoning her spot on the blanket.

"Wait, let's get a picture really quick before someone leaves!" She ran off, returning with Teegan and LeAnn, the remaining two candidates, following behind her.

We arranged ourselves in a line, arms wrapped around one another, grins on our faces, the bonfire a glowing halo behind our heads, and Thomas took the photo.

———

THE MORNING before a high school assembly is never organized. Rudy and I were sitting in our homeroom class, my stomach flipping nervously as I watched the hands of the clock tick forward. It was ten minutes until the assembly was scheduled to begin and the teacher had yet to dismiss our class. Finally, Rudy and I approached his desk and asked to leave early.

"We have to get seated and stuff. For our speeches," Rudy explained with a wave of her hand.

Two seconds later we were clacking down the tiled hall in our heels, hurrying to the gymnasium. My skirt fluttered around my thighs, and I hoped to hell I wasn't exposing anything as we ran down the stairs.

The gym was already half full, teachers leading their freshman and sophomore classes into empty rows of bleachers while the upperclassmen, allowed to sit unaccompanied, meandered around finding their friends. On the floor of the basketball court, Courtney, Deena and Teegan were already seated in their folding chairs, hands clasped daintily in their laps. All five escorts were sitting in a matching line of seats on the opposite side of an Ogden-crested podium, studying printed copies of their speeches. They all looked nervous, tapping their feet or tugging at their ties.

For my escort, I had chosen Luke Bruggeman, my male counterpart in the hurdles for the past three years. He was smart and cute and well liked, though he was quiet. Rudy had selected Justin Patridge, the senior editor of the yearbook. I waved to Luke as I crossed my legs, and he gave me a crooked smile before returning his gaze to the crisp papers in his lap. I felt a pang for the guys; all we girls had to do was sit there and look pretty.

In the crowd, I found my parents easily, seated beside Rudy's mom and dad. It was the first school event my parents had attended since I'd quit cheerleading my freshman year, unless you counted the Parent Association meetings and fundraisers my mom went to semi-regularly. She grinned and finger-waved to me; next to her, my dad was reading the newspaper, looking bored. I waved back quickly and took a deep breath.

The day was a whirlwind the entire way through. You know how it gets, those situations where, normally, you would be nervous but you aren't because there's literally no time for nerves? That's how the Friday of our senior homecoming game unfolded. The boys gave their five minute speeches, and we all laughed and blushed while they showed blown up posters of our baby pictures and blustered on about our accomplishments. Luke talked about my track championship win and my leadership qualities and my friendliness to everyone (was I that friendly? In these situations you could never really be sure how much was sincere and how much was just a strategy to fill up time). He told the story about me mistakenly drinking from the cup of beer at Rudy's parents' party the first summer after I moved to St. Louis, and everyone chuckled. I glanced inquisitively at Rudy (how else could he have learned that anecdote?), but all she did was smile and clap politely as Luke finished.

Between the assembly and the parade we ended up with a slim twenty-minute window, during which Rudy and I and the other three candidates rushed to change our clothes in the sports lobby bathroom. Rudy and I tugged new blouses over our heads, crammed together in the handicapped stall.

"Wait, you missed a button." Rudy caught me as I was leaving the bathroom. She fastened it, and we applied our lip gloss as we ran across the parking lot bare footed, carrying high heels swinging from our fingertips.

Each girl had a car – shiny convertibles lent by the parents' of Ogden Academy to senior boys who would drive each candidate and her escort. Luke was already seated in the passenger side of a black car, sunglasses on his face. He waved me over and I climbed in back, perching carefully on the top of the backseat. The art classes had painted poster boards for the sides of each car. Mine read, "Ms. Jillian Matthews, Queen Candidate" in fancy black script.

During the twenty minute parade I smiled until my cheeks hurt. I wasn't sure when to wave, and every time I raised my arm to do it I felt stupid and awkward. It was a windy afternoon, and my hair kept blowing into my face and getting stuck in layers of lip-gloss. Mrs. Golden called to me from the sidewalk as we crept past, and I grinned for her as she snapped a photo.

Of course, the biggest event wasn't until later that night. In a display of courteous, friendly "no-hard-feelings-we're-still-friends-no-matter-who-wins" companionship, we all got ready for the game at Deena's house. The mothers made us veggie trays and plates of cheese and crackers, and Deena's mom walked around refilling our glasses of water while we curled our hair and applied makeup. I was careful not to drink much of anything, in part because of how uncomfortable I was being waited on by Mrs. Orr and partially because I didn't want to have to pee when we were out in the middle of the football field.

"Jill, take a picture with me," Rudy said as I replaced the lid on a tube of mascara.

She pressed her face against mine, extended the camera in her arm and took a selfie of the two of us.

"Here, let me take one of you both." Deena's mom jumped up to take the camera, and Rudy and I posed for another photo.

"Oh, mom, take one of the three of us for me, please," Deena sprang up from behind her mother, her fresh curls bouncing against her chest.

Again, we posed. Then with all five of us, over and over with all of our cameras. Then, once our escorts began to arrive in their suits and ties and shiny dress shoes, with the ten of us.

The sun was setting, and my arms were covered in goose bumps by the time the cameras finally disappeared.

"Just wait one more second," Deena's mom stalled, and a moment later we saw why. The parents had hired a limousine to drive us to the game. We all piled in, waving grandly to our parents as we disappeared into the shiny black car. We were supposed to be at the game by the end of the first quarter, but with all of us together that hardly mattered. They couldn't start the show without us.

"You're shivering. Are you cold?" Luke wrapped his arm around me and squished me up against his side.

I nodded.

"Do you want my jacket?"

"No, that's okay." I shook my head. There was no way he'd be able to get his jacket off without knocking someone in the face. We were packed like sardines.

"Rudy, I love your dress," Teegan said, raising her voice above all of the noise. "It seriously fits you perfectly."

"Thank you," Rudy smiled. "You look really pretty, too. Everyone looks so good tonight."

"I'm just ready to get drunk once this is over," Elam, LeAnn's escort said. We all laughed.

"Everybody's going to Harrison's after, right?" Deena glanced around the limo, her index finger raised as if to scold us if we contradicted her. The consensus was a resounding yes. "Good," she said. "This is going to be the best party so far this year."

"No shit, Deena. It's only October." Her escort, Sam, knocked her in the back of the head playfully.

"Don't mess up my hair!" She patted her up-do protectively then grinned and punched Sam in the gut to save face.

In the football stadium parking lot we climbed out of the limo; Luke took my hand as I stepped out gracefully in my sparkling heels.

The stadium lights beamed overhead as we paraded toward the field in two single-file lines, the boys standing at each of our sides. It was a miracle how they transformed from raunchy teenagers to perfect gentlemen with just the addition of some structured clothing. When we stepped onto the track, I teetered in my heels on the uneven surface, and Luke reached out to grab my waist. The side of his finger swiped my boob; with my dress, it was impossible to wear a bra, and he connected, unobstructed, with flesh through thin sequined fabric.

"Sorry." Luke blushed.

"No, it's okay. Thanks for catching me." I blushed, too.

It was odd to be on the track in a formal dress instead of tennis shoes and shorts, everyone's eyes on us as we waited at the end of the field for halftime. We were losing by twelve points already, and you could tell the Ogden crowd was irritated and restless.

At the sound of the halftime whistle, the players started to exit the field while, simultaneously, the JV and freshmen football teams began carrying the stage out onto the grass. Heidi Payne, the senior homecoming liaison, ushered the ten of us into a line of golf carts that had suddenly appeared on the track, driven by male Ogden teachers who were also wearing button up shirts and ties.

"Golden, you're first," Heidi read off the clipboard cradled in her arm. "Then Matthews, Orr, Tyler, Westings. Once around before the coronation, then one more time after for the winner only."

I climbed into the back seat of the cart, and Luke followed behind me. The cushion was cold and stiff. On the back of the driver's seat was a tiny metal placard that read, "Property of St. Louis Country Club".

"I think I'm on your dress." Luke scooted away from me, and I tugged the material out from under him.

"Don't do anything stupid," Heidi said sternly. "Don't forget to smile for the yearbook photos. And good luck, all of you."

We were off at a turtle's pace, crawling along the edge of the track. My teeth were chattering almost audibly, but I grinned and waved and giggled nervously when Luke said anything funny. *Everything* was giddy-funny. I waved some more and on the backside of the track, where there were no bleachers, our driver picked up speed and the wind ruffled my hair and dress.

When we had come full circle, back to the fifty-yard line, we unloaded out onto the AstroTurf beside the opposing team's benches. The other team's players sat there gawking, sweaty and smirking, with their helmets in their laps and plastic water bottles in their hands. One of them hooted and another let out a low whistle and laughed.

Miraculously, the stage was up. The assembly team had disappeared. The cheerleaders (minus LeAnn, their senior captain) and the band stretched out side by side in two long lines across the field, creating a tunnel from us to the stage.

"Ladies and gentlemen, it is my honor to present to you tonight this year's Ogden Academy homecoming queen candidates. These outstanding young women were nominated by the Varsity football team and one winner was selected by a vote of the Ogden student body." The announcer's voice cut through the still night air and my heart pounded. "Without further ado, let me introduce tonight's candidates."

Rudy and Justin stepped forward, poised in position.

"Ms. Ruth Ann Golden, daughter of Charles and Katherine Golden, escorted by Mr. Justin Patridge."

At the sound of her name, Rudy stepped gracefully out onto the field and proceeded through the human tunnel.

"Ms. Golden serves as the secretary of the Ogden chapter of National Honor Society and as Photography editor for the Ogden Academy yearbook. She is a member of the track team, Ogden Cares volunteer organization and the Spanish language club. After she graduates, Ms. Golden plans to attend college and major in photography, sociology or women's studies. Ladies and gentlemen, Ms. Ruth Ann Golden."

The applause was uproarious as Rudy, now a speck at the other side of the field, stepped up onto the platform of the stage. Luke and I moved forward. He wove his arm through mine, and I held my clammy palm in a fist against my ribs.

"Next, Ms. Jillian Marie Matthews, daughter of Todd and Melanie Matthews, escorted by Mr. Luke Bruggeman."

We stepped into the grass. I smiled as we walked through

trumpets and flutes and fluttering pom poms. *Please don't fall, please don't fall*, was the mantra on replay in my head, so loud I didn't hear the rest of my short bio. Suddenly, we weren't walking anymore. Luke helped me up onto the stage.

We stood in our spot, marked by a tiny strip of white tape, on the opposite side of the stage from Rudy. She made eyes at me while Deena was making her way across the field. We applauded at the right places.

Ages later, when all ten of us stood nervously across the platform, the announcer paused. We waited. I drew breath, which is notable, as I hadn't done it much in the fifteen minutes before. I felt my stomach growling and wondered if Luke could hear it.

"It's my pleasure to announce that this year's Ogden Academy homecoming queen is Ms. Jillian Marie Matthews."

Shocked would be an appropriate adjective to use here. So would floored, flabbergasted or horrified. Horrified was appropriate because that's how I felt as my feet stepped forward, possessed by what I assumed was a misguided belief that I had won. I could not have won. Rudy won.

My ears were numb to the applause, and I clung to Luke's arm as he half-drug me down to the lower platform. The student body president handed me a bouquet of white roses, and the football captain presented me with a signed football. Heidi Payne approached me, a jeweled tiara outstretched in her hands, and I squatted awkwardly so she could place it on top of my head. I tried to arrange my facial features into a gracious smile. Around the track again we rode, this time faster.

"Congratulations, Jill." Luke put his arm around my shoulders. "You deserved it."

No, I didn't, I thought, even in that moment. How could you "deserve" something like the title of homecoming queen? You deserved an A on a test when you were up all night studying or you deserved to lose ten pounds when you'd been eating nothing but lettuce and baked chicken for a month. I didn't earn this. I wasn't extra generous or kind, I didn't smile at strangers in the hallway. There was probably at least half of the student population at Ogden to whom I had never spoken. And yet, something about the person I was had compelled them to choose me. I think that was what made it both so unbelievable and so meaningful.

"Thanks." I smiled. As we approached them, I could see the four other couples standing with their arms crossed at the edge of the field, watching us. They came into focus as we got closer. Deena and LeAnn wore polite smiles. They each held a single rose. I felt a small pang; a part of me would've gladly traded places with any one of them while another part of me wanted to beam and do back flips down the track.

"Congratulations, Jill!" They all hugged me lightly, hunching to avoid my armful of trinkets. We posed for photos, Luke and me standing in the center, my tiara glittering in full effect.

And then it was over.

Rudy and I put on sweatpants underneath our dresses and jackets over them and our limbs began their slow thaw. She refused to let me take off the tiara, and so I wore it for the remainder of the game, sitting in the student section of the bleachers, sandwiched between Luke and Justin.

———

WE LOST THE GAME, but that didn't really change the dynamic of the after party.

Rudy and I arrived at midnight, far past fashionably late, drunk and with our escorts in tow. After the coronation, our Homecoming group dynamic had been fractured. We went our separate ways, Rudy and I to Justin's parents' basement, the other girls to who knows where. We were still wearing sweatpants with our dresses, the skirts bunching over top of the thick fleece. Luke was wearing my tiara, and I was watching him carefully, fearful it would disappear.

The first thing our foursome did was to head straight for the keg and fill up our cups. Then we walked the house, collecting congratulations and stares and mingling among our classmates. We smoked, for the first time in months, on the porch with a group of juniors we hardly knew.

At 1:30, Luke pulled me in close. He had relinquished my tiara to Rudy hours before, and now his hair was flattened where it had sat.

"Do you want to go out to my car and talk?"

Talk. He could have at least come up with a better excuse.

I nodded, and he took my hand and led me down the lit sidewalk. We climbed into the back and we kissed, contorting our bodies awkwardly in the small space, and I was especially glad for the bulky fleece barrier my sweatpants created between us because I wasn't ready for anything further just then. After five minutes, my phone rang and it was Rudy.

"What are you guys doing," she whispered coarsely.

"Nothing. Talking in Luke's car." I sat up.

"Like, *talking* or just talking?"

"What?"

"Are you really just talking?"

"Yes," I nodded my head, though she obviously couldn't see me through the phone. "Where are you?"

"I'm outside."

"Outside where?"

"Outside the car." She rapped her knuckles on the tinted back window and Luke jumped. "Can I come in?"

Luke pushed the door open and it hit Rudy in the stomach. She dropped her phone.

"Sorry," she mumbled and bent over to pick it up. My tiara

fell forward, got caught in her hair and hung off the side of her head when she righted herself.

"Sorry for what," Luke muttered under his breath.

"You know, sorry...for whatever." Rudy sighed. "Jilly, can I talk to you?"

"Yeah, sure." I climbed over Luke's lap and out onto the yard. We stumbled a few steps away from the car.

"Are you happy?" She stared at me.

"Yeah. Are you?"

"Of course. I mean, yes. Definitely."

I paused and waited for her to continue.

"Were you guys doing something? You and Luke?"

"Just kissing." I blushed in spite of myself. Was she scolding me?

"I'm sorry."

"It's really not a big deal. He was kind of...slobbery."

Rudy laughed and the tiara clattered onto the sidewalk.

"Oh, God." She scooped it up and examined it. "It's okay; it didn't break."

She set it on top of my head, then patted my cheek.

"Congratulations, homecoming queen. I'm so happy you won."

She wrapped me in a bear hug, lifting me off the ground.

"You should have won," I whispered into her disheveled hair. She couldn't have heard me, but I felt relief just saying it aloud.

"Let's go back inside, okay," she said once she'd put me back down. "I missed you. I was afraid you guys left."

"I wouldn't leave without telling you."

"Yeah. I know."

We linked arms at the elbows and walked back toward Luke's car, but he'd already gone back inside the party.

———

THOMAS HART ASKED Rudy to the Fall Ball. It couldn't have been more obvious – they'd been friendly with each other at track for four years, flirting during warm ups and cheering for each other at meets, and both of them worked on the yearbook staff – but for some reason during the years I was in high school I was under the impression that the most obvious things would always mislead me. I was apprehensive of sure things and distrusting of absolutes. And plus, Rudy hadn't yet confided in me she was interested in Thomas, and how could she come to that conclusion without first discussing it with her best friend?

She told me over homework at her kitchen table.

"Did you say yes?" I asked, tracing the eraser side of my pencil over the page in front of me.

Rudy nodded. "He was really sweet when he asked, too. He came by the house with roses."

"Wow," I said. "What'd your mom say?"

"She was upstairs, so she didn't meet him, but she was impressed with the flowers."

"Do you like him?"

"I'm not sure."

I stared at her. How could you not know if you liked someone?

"I mean, we're great friends. I'm just not sure if I want to chance ruining that by dating him."

"I think you should. If you like him. He'd be a much better boyfriend than Houston was, in my opinion."

"But Houston wasn't Thomas."

Was that a riddle for me to solve? I drummed my eraser in a steady rhythm against the table. Sometimes her vagueness could grate on my nerves.

She chewed her bottom lip. "Anyway, I don't know what I'm going to do about dating him. But I said yes to the dance."

They started dating in October, two weeks after the ball, and

I was right about one thing: Thomas was a better boyfriend than Houston had ever been. He held Rudy's hand in the hallway at school and he called her every night before he went to bed, she gushed to me one cold morning on the drive to school.

"Every night?" That sounded stifling, almost parental. Luke and I had been spending more time together lately, but we spoke on the phone twice per week at most.

Rudy smiled and nodded. "Right before he goes to sleep, so I'm the last person he talks to."

Hm.

"I was thinking about inviting him to Thanksgiving with my family," she added.

"Seriously?" I'd never been invited to the Goldens' for Thanksgiving. Easter, Independence Day and Christmas Eve, but never Thanksgiving dinner. "It's only been a couple of weeks though."

"I know, but I think he's a serious one. He's so interesting to talk to, you know? Did you know he's planning on going to Yale next year? He's already applied early."

"Wow." I reconsidered my first impressions of Thomas. The things I knew about him were largely superficial. He was the fastest sprinter on the track team, he was kind and funny, he was one of the more popular boys in our class, liked by both the students and the faculty, though he wasn't one of the guys who girls usually dated. He was in AP classes, but we all were. I didn't know he was *smart* smart. "That's impressive."

"It's really impressive. Speaking of which, did you send in your UCLA app yet?"

Abruptly, my neutral mood sank.

"No, not yet. I'm still working on the essay."

Since the state track meet the previous spring, I had begun to receive solicitations from colleges about their track programs. I was flattered but also disappointed – the schools that sought me out were schools I'd never heard of and schools I wasn't particularly interested in. I kept the opened letters in a tray on the desk in my bedroom, and they glared at me while I sat in front of my computer screen, ate chips and tried to think of inspired essay topics for my applications to places like UCLA and USC and Boston College, my father's alma mater.

"How far have you gotten?"

"Um, halfway." I had one paragraph written. One shitty paragraph. "What are you going to do if Thomas goes to Yale and you guys are still dating?"

"It would depend on how serious we were then, and whether or not I got into any schools on the east coast."

My heart lurched. "What schools did you apply to on the East coast?"

"Dad wanted me to apply at some private schools out there. Since I know I want to do liberal arts."

I still had no idea what I wanted to study. The only thing I loved was running, but obviously I couldn't major in running and I couldn't stomach the chemistry it took to be an exercise science major.

"But you're still applying to MU, right?"

We had agreed over the summer it would be our safe school. If we didn't share any other acceptance letters, we could at least have Missouri in common. And I didn't think it would be so bad to go there; I would still be a two-hour drive away from my parents, two hours they would probably seldom travel.

"Duh. I sent that one in last week."

"Good," I said as we pulled into the Ogden parking lot. We parked in an empty spot between Deena's Jetta and Justin Patridge's Denali.

The sight of the building, its angular brick exterior, the familiar stone crest over the main entrance, the green vines and pretty fall flowers that crawled up the walls and scattered the front courtyard, set me at ease.

———

NORMALLY I WOULD HAVE JUST LET myself in the side entrance, the one the Goldens' always used, but when I arrived at Rudy's for Thanksgiving dinner, I rang the front doorbell. I could hear it tinkling through the foyer, and I stood and waited patiently in my dress and sweater and boots, until finally the door swung open.

"Hey." It was Kent.

"Hi," I blushed. "Happy Thanksgiving!"

"You, too."

I stepped inside, and he closed the door behind me. The whole house smelled of roasting turkey and melted butter.

"You look nice."

"Thanks." I smiled.

Rudy had asked me to be a buffer for her parents' first time meeting Thomas and though I didn't quite understand it, I had jumped at the chance to spend a holiday with the Golden family. And because I was eighteen and an adult and maybe because I had argued and begged for an entire half hour, my parents agreed to hold our Thanksgiving meal at noon, giving me enough time to celebrate with both families. What I considered both of *my* families.

I followed Kent into the kitchen. Mrs. Golden had her back to us, stirring a huge, steaming pot on the stove. Rudy was wearing a checkered apron and chopping carrots and peppers for a salad.

"Mom's letting me use a knife. Can you believe it?"

"So you're saying prepare for a hospital trip?" I laughed.

"Hello, dear," Mrs. Golden looked over her shoulder and

smiled. Her hair was frizzed over her forehead from the steam.

"Happy Thanksgiving." I took a seat at the island, where Rudy was attacking another carrot. "Can I help with anything?"

"No; no we're just about finished, but thank you for offering," Mrs. Golden spoke into the pot.

Kent had disappeared, and Mr. Golden was nowhere in sight. They were in the den, I suspected. I thought I could hear the sound of televised football.

My stomach growled audibly, but I was the only one who heard it. I'd barely touched my lunch, saving room for what Rudy bragged was the best pumpkin pie on the face of the Earth. Emelda had made two of them the day before she left to spend Thanksgiving with her family in New Mexico.

"Mom, is this enough?" Rudy stepped back and Mrs. Golden leaned over the salad bowl, examining. She nodded.

"Just stir it in. And pour some of the dressing into the glass server, please."

Rudy did as requested and I watched, fiddling with my thumbs.

"Rudy, when is your boyfriend arriving? I thought we'd eat around five. Kent has to drive back to Columbia tonight."

The inflection in her voice was different, but I couldn't determine exactly what the change was. She was still looking into the potatoes.

"He'll be here before then." Rudy untied her apron, wadded it up and set it on the stool beside me. "I'm running upstairs with Jill to change my clothes."

Upstairs in Rudy's room, I sat on the bed, my booted feet swinging off the side, while Rudy undressed.

"Thanks for coming. My parents are kind of freaking out about meeting Thomas." She stood in her open closet in just her beige underwear and a white satin bra, sifting through clothes.

"Really? Your mom seemed fine."

"That's because I blew up at her earlier. She's been bugging me about him since I woke up this morning."

"What about your dad?"

"I don't know. Unreadable, as usual." She stepped into an emerald green dress and pulled it up over her flat stomach.

"Well, I'm ready to buffer. Use me." I spread my arms and gestured the length of my body.

Rudy laughed, but it was stilted.

"I'm so hungry," I said while she put on jewelry. "My mom made this low-carb, no sugar gravy that tasted like ass so I didn't even get to eat good turkey. I'm dying to get my hands on some pumpkin pie."

Rudy didn't respond so I kept talking.

"What does Kent think about Thomas?" It felt devious to bring Kent's name into the conversation that way, but I couldn't help myself. I was still curious about him. "He has an older brother that's Kent's age, right?"

"His brother didn't go to Ogden, though."

"Oh."

Downstairs, the doorbell rang. We heard it chime up through the, stairwell and Rudy froze for a second before rushing down the stairs. I followed, reaching the bottom of the steps just as she was opening the door.

"Hey." Thomas wore a black sweater over his button up and tie. His shoes were so shiny I wondered if they could double as mirrors. He leaned in and pecked Rudy's cheek.

"Hi!" Rudy took his arm and pulled him into the foyer, letting the heavy door slam shut behind him. "We're eating in, like, fifteen minutes. Let me introduce you to my family, and I'll give you a really quick tour of the house before dinner."

They proceeded toward the kitchen, and I followed like a lost puppy.

"Mom." Rudy stood in the threshold of the kitchen. Mrs.

Golden pivoted, a wet serving spoon in her right hand. "This is Thomas. Thomas, this is my mom."

Mrs. Golden's face froze then unfroze in an instant. A speck of gravy dripped off of the spoon and onto the floor.

"Thomas." She swallowed then smiled, setting the spoon on the stovetop. "Very nice to meet you."

"It's nice to meet you, too, Mrs. Golden." He reached out to shake her hand. "Thank you for inviting me."

"It's our pleasure, of course. Rudy," Mrs. Golden tilted her face toward her youngest daughter. "Why don't you introduce Thomas to Daddy while I finish dinner?"

Rudy and her mother locked eyes, but I couldn't read the particular silent language they spoke.

"Jillian, do you mind helping me set the table?"

Me? I shot Rudy a look. Already, I was failing as a lifeline. She didn't meet my gaze.

"Sure, I don't mind."

While I set out china plates and shiny silverware (which side was the fork supposed to go on again?), I questioned my presence in the Golden house that day. Why was I always intruding where I wasn't exactly welcome? Probably, I thought, I should have just stayed at home.

At five past five, we gathered around the table to eat. I sat in the absent Marta's seat between Mrs. Golden and Kent. Thomas sat beside Rudy on the opposite side of the table. Mr. Golden, of course, sat in the chair with the armrests, the head of the table.

"Shall we pray?" Mrs. Golden held out her open palms and I clasped her hand. When I touched Kent's fingers, my heart beat a little faster. *Stop*, I thought. *Just stop.*

We bent over the table, and I closed my eyes while Mr. Golden expressed his gratitude for his blessings, his family and his health. Sometimes, I forgot completely about his heart attack. Then we went around the table one at a time and said aloud one thing we were particularly thankful for this year. Rudy said she was thankful to have a great, caring boyfriend, to which Mr. and Mrs. Golden shared an almost imperceptible worried look. To make up for it, I said I was thankful to have such a wonderful second family, but Mrs. Golden only rewarded my remark with a watered down smile.

If I couldn't buffer successfully, at least I could eat heartily. I dug into the mashed potatoes first, piling them into a steaming mountain on my plate.

"So," Mr. Golden cleared his throat. "Thomas. I'm not sure that I know your parents. What does your father do?"

"My mom is a lawyer. She mostly represents clients in ACLU cases. And my dad runs a bike shop."

"Motorcycles?" Mrs. Golden said, holding her fork aloft.

Thomas shook his head. "Bicycles. He's really involved with triathlons."

"That's cool," Kent interjected. "I've got a buddy at school who just did his first Ironman this past year."

"Rudy's brother is in law school at the University of Missouri." Mrs. Golden smiled indulgently at Kent.

"Nice. How is it? I'm planning to go into law myself."

"Thomas applied to Yale," Rudy countered.

"That's very impressive," Mr. Golden said. He did not sound impressed.

"That's great," Kent said.

I speared a piece of turkey and shoved it into my mouth.

"Law school's been tough. It's a lot of work, but I'm sure you know that already, with your mom being a lawyer. What type of law do you want to practice?"

The conversation went on like that for the entirety of the meal. Kent and Thomas held a polite conversation, while Rudy and her parents interjected intermittently with thinly veiled jabs at one another. I ate enough food for two people. When Mrs.

Golden brought out dessert, I served myself two slices of pie and ate them very, very slowly.

"Rudy," Mrs. Golden said when we were finished. "Will you and Jill please help me clean the table?"

Kent and I were the only ones who had cleaned our plates. Half pieces of pie still remained in front of Thomas, Rudy and Mr. Golden. Mrs. Golden hadn't taken dessert.

"But mom, I have a guest."

"The men can watch television in the den while they wait."

Another eye battle. Rudy looked away first.

"It's no problem," Thomas said agreeably. "Or I can help clean up, if you'd like."

"Thank you for offering, Thomas, but Rudy can do it herself."

In the kitchen, for the first time ever, I wanted nothing more but to teleport back to my own house. I would gladly sit with my parents while my mom frowned upon my large helping of food and my dad peppered me with "helpful suggestions" for my college essays. I would even ask for extra helpings of my mom's crappy gravy. I felt for Thomas, sentenced to spend time in the den with Rudy's dad. At least he had Kent. Between Rudy thrusting dirty dishes in my direction and Mrs. Golden grabbing them, dripping wet from my hands, I had no relief.

I was exhausted when finally, twenty long minutes later, Rudy kissed Thomas goodbye and shut the door behind him, but that was barely the beginning.

"Ruth Ann, what was that about?" Mrs. Golden stood stiffly behind us in the foyer, her arms crossed over her ample bosom. "How could you not at least be courteous enough to prepare us for this evening?"

"I *knew* you'd be like this," Rudy exploded instantly, throwing her hands in the air.

So this is why I'm here, I thought. She'd planned for this all along and dragged me into it on purpose, to soften the blow.

"Be like what, exactly? Be concerned about who you spend time with?"

"What's there to be concerned about, Mom?" Rudy crossed her arms, matching her mother's stance precisely, though she stood several inches taller than Mrs. Golden. "He's a perfect gentleman, he's going to Yale, he's never been in any trouble. Tell me, what's wrong with him."

"Nothing's wrong with him, Rudy. Don't make me the bad guy here, I *never* said anything bad about the boy." Her voice trembled, like she might cry. I stared at the tips of my boots and I stood, invisible in the middle of the foyer, willing the tears back up into Mrs. Golden's tear ducts. "It's just that you have to be careful; you have to be aware of how you're perceived. You're young; you don't understand how the world works yet. I'm sure he's a lovely boy but he's..." Mrs. Golden opened her mouth and paused. "It's just that he's..."

"It's just that he's black, right?" Rudy spit from her mouth, her cheeks pinched like the word had left a bitter taste on her tongue.

I felt my own jaw slacken, the space between my lips open up.

"It's not like that, sweetheart. Don't make it out to be that way." Mrs. Golden reached out her hand and Rudy slapped it away. The slap rang out around us; the shot heard round the world. Mrs. Golden drew her hand into her chest, her mouth open in offense. She looked at Rudy like she was a terrible creature, not the daughter she'd raised from a baby.

"Don't patronize me," Rudy said.

"Ruth Ann, come here. *Now.*" Mr. Golden's voice was loud and firm when it issued from out of the den.

Rudy turned and stormed out of the room, leaving me alone with her mother in the wake of the slap. After a moment, when

Rudy's muffled voice rose above her father's in the den, Mrs. Golden looked up at me, her eyes wounded and sad.

"Jillian, it would probably be best if you went home now," she said softly.

"Right," I mumbled. "Thank you."

———

Do you remember the first time, as a kid, when you realized adults weren't always right? That afternoon was mine. Sure, I could admit my own parents made decisions I disagreed with all of the time, but I trusted Mr. and Mrs. Golden, I *respected* them, and as hard as I tried, I couldn't really formulate a situation where what they'd said – and how they'd acted – that afternoon could be right. Walking back home in the cold chill of nighttime, it was hard to form the word 'racist' in my mind and associate it with Mr. and Mrs. Golden. *Would I date a black guy?* I wondered. I liked Thomas; I thought he was hilarious and sweet, but I couldn't see myself kissing him. I didn't think he was cute. Was *I* being racist? I didn't think so, but suddenly I couldn't be sure.

Rudy never told me the things that were said between she and her parents in the den. I asked, but she always skirted the issue, rolling her eyes and saying how ridiculous her parents had been. But if a little bit of my respect for Rudy's parents disappeared that day, I think it would be fair to say that a lot of Rudy's died. She didn't look at her mom as warmly, and she and her father stopped their subtle joking over the dinner table. There was a hardness, a near-tangible distance between them now. They started to look at her, their youngest daughter, as an adult. They all saw each other through disillusioned eyes.

Rudy didn't break up with Thomas, and her parents never said another bad thing about him in my company, but he didn't come back to her house again.

13

SENIOR WINTER

"Where are you going?" Deena hissed from several feet behind us in the dark parking lot. She was crouching, as if doing so would somehow give her cover in the wide-open space.

"Inside," I whispered.

"I thought Michael had the key?"

From her pocket, Rudy extracted a single, thick golden key. She held it up for Deena to squint at. "Come on." She shrugged one shoulder toward the school and we started walking briskly.

The Ogden senior prank was sort of a tradition. Every year as spring drew nearer, the administrators and teachers began their annual warnings: senior pranks would not be tolerated. All students should behave according to Ogden's etiquette code, especially members of the senior class, as they would soon be departing to the real, adult world (this part I especially didn't understand. This was an elite college preparatory school; we all had at least four more years of partying and coddling and safety ahead of us in college before we were thrust into the reality of adulthood).

Mostly, the tradition of the senior prank was an Ogden legend.

"Everyone's always saying the senior prank's some big thing, but look at the classes before us," Rudy said between bites of her lunch in the yearbook lab one afternoon in December. "Sophomore year they just threw water balloons at us for fifteen minutes."

"Did they even do anything last year?" Deena asked.

No, I thought.

No one else could remember.

"It's stupid," I added. "Nothing ever happens, the senior class just hypes it up to make the underclassmen feel like they have to do something spectacular."

Justin Patridge looked up from whatever he was editing furiously at his desk. "Not true. They used to do awesome pranks, before everybody turned into pussies."

"Like what?" Rudy dotted the question mark in front of her with her fork.

"Well," Justin moved out from behind the desk and scooted toward us in his fancy editor's chair. "My dad went here twenty years ago. When he graduated, their class carried the principal's car from his house to the middle of the student parking lot."

"They *carried* it?"

Justin nodded. "That was back when the principal lived in the Quarters." Years before, the principal of Ogden would live with his family in a pretty, old-fashioned stone house right next to the school. Like a Catholic priest in a rectory. Ten years ago, they converted the Quarters into administrative offices for the school because really, who wanted to live where they worked? "They took off the tires and put it up on blocks and saran wrapped the whole thing. My dad says it was pretty sweet."

"Isn't that illegal?" Deena furrowed her eyebrows. "Did they get arrested?"

"Nobody caught them."

We sat for a moment in quiet admiration.

"That's awesome." Rudy broke the silence. "We should do something like that."

"You want to carry Dr. Foakley's car three miles?" Justin laughed.

"Not that exactly, just something similar. Something as good as that."

She had that spark in her eyes, I noted. That hitchhiking spark from years ago.

"Like what," Deena said. "They have cameras now. We can't exactly show our faces."

"The cameras aren't that good," Rudy said. "They can't ID faces, and we could wear hats."

"And ski masks," I added with a smirk. "Like burglars."

"What if we break into the school?" Rudy perked up.

"And do what?"

"Camp out in the principal's office," Justin said, swiveling back and forth in his chair.

"Yes! That's perfect," Rudy exclaimed.

"What're we going to do, break a freaking window?" Deena, ever the good girl, crossed her arms over her chest defiantly. "That's a terrible idea."

"Maybe we can find someone with a key," I said, aligning myself firmly on Rudy's side.

"That's an idea," Justin said. "I bet I can find someone."

Deena rolled her eyes and shook her head.

"Don't worry, Deena," Rudy reached out to pat her on the head. "We won't make you come."

The idea grew and expanded during the final two weeks of the semester, and on the last day before Christmas break the plan was firmly in place. Michael Denalby, whose aunt was a secretary at the Ogden front office, would secure a key to the building. Thomas researched the school security system and found the cameras weren't monitored when no one was in the building; largely, they were used for figuring out who had side-swiped whom in the student parking lot and for bragging rights on prospective student brochures. The school wasn't even alarmed. Who'd have thunk?

We would wear jeans and our hooded Ogden senior class sweatshirts, for irony and for anonymity. The plan would go down on the last day of winter break, the night before we returned to school for our final semester, and we planned to leave Dr. Foakley a surprise when we left early in the morning, before any school employees arrived.

There were thirty of us committed to the plan. We parked on the school's side street and met in front of the building at precisely 12:30 in the morning.

"God, I thought you'd never fucking show up," one of ten hooded figures whispered huskily when we reached the front doors. It was Michael.

Rudy ignored him, racing up the steps with the rest of us close behind. I was freezing – we all were – in just our sweat-shirts and jeans against the twenty-degree chill. Ice lingered on the edges of the sidewalks and handrails. Rudy's hand was quivering as she jiggled the key in the lock.

"Jesus, hurry up," Deena muttered. "Somebody's going to see us."

At last Rudy got it unlocked, and we shuffled into the school's front lobby. It was dark and eerie and barely warmer than it had been outside. Apparently they turned the ther-mostats way down when the school was closed.

"This is so creepy," Amelia Young, an odd but interesting girl who wore converse sneakers and red lipstick and had been admitted to a top art school for the next year, ran her fingers over the shadowed bust of Frederick Ogden, the school founder.

Someone flicked on the lights and we all froze, squinting and shielding our eyes. Deena squeaked and stumbled back toward the door.

"Chill out," Michael said. "It's me."

"Turn those off," Thomas said. "You could see them from the parking lot."

"You guys are too uptight. Pull the sticks out of your asses," Michael scoffed, but he turned the lights off anyway.

I looked around us, at the blackness of the arched ceiling stories above and the shadowed staircase ahead of us. To my right, the dark depths of the front hallway stretched into oblivion.

"Well, are we going?" An anonymous girl voice whispered. The disguises were working freakishly well. I could hardly recognize anyone – we were just a circle of cult members, our faces shrouded by the hoods of our sweatshirts.

"Let's wait a minute, in case anyone else shows up," Justin said.

They did. In droves, actually. Within five minutes there were forty-two of us crowded into the lobby, squashed onto the three long stone benches or pacing the floor nervously, speaking quietly to one another. I counted heads while I stood beside Rudy, chewing the inside of my cheek.

"What the hell are we going to do with all these people?" I whispered.

"The more the merrier, right," she whispered back. "They can't arrest us all."

At one o'clock, Michael led the parade toward the front offices, the rest of us stepping lightly behind him in the dark. In front of the office we huddled close to one another, shoulder to shoulder.

"Shit." Michael turned the door; it didn't budge. "It's locked."

"There's a keypad," someone whispered.

"Does anybody know the code?"

There was a brief moment of silent contemplation before someone spoke up.

"I was an office aid last year. Try 10-02-58," Eliza Oltman said quietly. "It's Dr. Foakley's birthdate; that way the secretaries remember when to bring him cards."

There was a smattering of nervous laughter.

Why hadn't we consulted an office aid before now, I wondered. Perhaps we hadn't planned as elaborately as we should have.

The code worked. Michael swung the door open, and we all pressed into the small office space. Of course, the principal's office was locked too. We were ill prepared indeed. And there was no keypad for that one. We scoured the office, pulling open every unlocked drawer and searching under the cabinet shelves, behind the doors and on the bottoms of the secretaries' swivel chairs for a spare key, but nothing turned up. We were screwed.

"What the hell do we do now?" Michael said, his voice rising one level above a whisper. Deena shushed him immediately, and he tossed up his middle finger in her direction.

"Let's just do it in here," Rudy said, unzipping the black backpack she held beside her. "It'll still be funny. We have all the stuff anyway."

We all huddled over five bags of supplies: toilet paper, plastic wrap, foil and multi-colored streamers. I grabbed two rolls of toilet paper and began draping the front panel of windows, the ones that opened into the lobby hallway. Beside me, Teegan Westings climbed onto a desk and started hanging streamers from the ceiling fan.

"We should have brought glitter or confetti to put on the tops of the fans," Teegan snickered.

"Agreed."

"They probably wouldn't have turned them on until spring though."

"That might have made it even funnier," I said.

When I finished the front windows, I helped Travis Phelps plastic wrap over the doors to each administrator's office. Thirty minutes later, when we went back for more supplies, the bags were empty; only cardboard tubes and boxes littered the floor. We scooped them up and dumped them into the candy bowl that sat between the secretaries' desks.

"I think we did good work, kids," Michael said when we had finished.

"As long as they don't come in early, they should still be cleaning this up when school starts in the morning," Sam Willoughby laughed.

We were standing, pressed shoulder to shoulder in a huddle around the shrine of the empty backpacks, wearing identical sweatshirts and identical smug expressions on our faces. I had never felt closer to my classmates than I did in that moment; in that hour of exhausted exhilaration, feeling like we'd really accomplished something great together.

I thought about all the knowledge I'd collected about this group of people over the last four years. Kate Yearinger, standing across the circle from me, was the star of the girl's tennis team. She was best friends with Ashley Waters, a pretty junior, and in March of our sophomore year her boyfriend had cheated on her and the Monday morning after it had happened, he made an announcement on the intercom to the entire school asking for her forgiveness. They were still dating, even though he had gone off to college two years ago, and every time I saw Kate I thought about how embarrassed she must have been, and I wondered how she could have forgiven him and been able to trust him miles away. Beside Kate was T.J. Turner. Secretly, T.J. terrified me because he was loud and obnoxious and liked to flirt with girls by embarrassing them; though, in his defense, I don't think he knew he was doing it. Next to T.J. was Sam Willoughby, who had blue eyes and wavy brown hair and a high-pitched voice, for a guy. He had lent me his sweatshirt at a bonfire party back in the fall of our junior year, and I had forgotten to return it. It smelled like outdoors and expensive cologne and for a few weeks after the party the smell and his kindness had been enough to convince me I had a crush on him. But he was dating Yardley Bishop, and even if he wasn't, it was widely known he was a virgin and was saving himself for marriage and the thought of explaining to him the loss of my own virginity made me feel ashamed and dirty. There was Deena, sweet, annoying, Deena, whom I had met the first day of cheerleading tryouts our freshman year when, while we were stretching, she had poked me in the back and asked, desperation in her eyes, if I had a tampon she could use. She had changed since then, I realized suddenly. She had gained weight, but it had made her prettier. She was friendlier and less critical of the people around her and, probably as a direct result, more people seemed to genuinely like her now.

Had I changed, I wondered? Surely, in three and a half years, I had. The physical transformations I had noticed; my boobs had finally materialized, the baby fat had thinned from my face and I was two inches taller, but what about my personality? I wondered what my classmates thought of me. Was I friendly? Did I come across as someone they wanted to know? I was less shy than I had been as a freshman, but I still sometimes felt intimidated, even by these people I'd gone to school with for years. I could know the most intimate things about someone – Michael Denalby had scored a 19 the first time he took the ACT, Teegan Westings's parents met when her father began having an affair with her mom, LeAnn Tyler had cried the first time she hooked up with a guy – and still, the entire time I was having an interaction with them, I would be terrified of how they were perceiving me. The contradictions baffled me.

In just a few months, I thought in that moment, I will probably never see most of these people again. The idea felt strange. It felt sad.

Just then, we saw lights flash in the windows that faced out to the street.

"Shut the light off," someone grunted. We stood silent – rigid – in the pitch dark.

Justin Patridge peeked through the blinds.

"Shit." He turned. You could see the wide whites of his eyes below his hood. "It's the cops."

Abruptly, everyone around me was squealing and wriggling all at once.

"Shut the fuck up," Michael hissed. He shoved his own face into the blinds. "They're in the front parking lot. Everybody go out the cafeteria doors, they'll be unlocked."

How he knew this, I could not fathom.

Like spooked deer, my classmates scrambled out of the office and sprinted down the hall. I stood still for a second, sickening dread sinking into my stomach.

"Where's Rudy?" Deena whisper-shrieked in my ear. "Are you coming?"

Rudy had been missing for the last half hour. I knew what she was doing.

"I have to find her first."

"I'm leaving. Sorry, I'm leaving." Deena hardly glanced back before she took off down the hall toward the cafeteria. She was our ride; so much for the sense of camaraderie.

The last one left in the office, I snatched Rudy's backpack off the floor and left. I paused in the empty hallway before turning and running to the East stairwell. I raced up the steps, my footfalls echoing behind me.

"Rudy?" I hissed as I entered the second floor corridor.

No answer.

I slunk along the wall and the shoulder of my sweatshirt got caught on the edge of a poster board, someone's American history project. I jerked my arm free and peeked into the first classroom. It was empty. I checked the entirety of the second floor, even the girls and boys bathrooms, before I ran – quietly, fearfully – up the stairs to the third floor, panic building in my chest. This was just like her, I thought, always having to go one step further than everyone else. Always making me chase after her. But this was too far. This was reckless and stupid.

At the third floor landing, I thought I heard muffled human noises. I paused, listening, and I heard what was unmistakably the scrape of a chair leg against the floor.

They were in the yearbook classroom. Naturally. I should have checked there first.

"Rudy," I hissed from the doorway.

Through the darkness I saw her head pop up on the other side of the room, behind her photo editor's desk. I couldn't see Thomas at all.

"The cops are here. Come on."

They already had their clothes back on, and they followed me out of the classroom without saying a word, though the look on Thomas's face was one of deep embarrassment. I paused again in the empty hallway, weighing my options. If the police came in the front door, there would probably be one of them waiting there outside. I turned and led us down the central staircase, down toward the cafeteria; the way the rest of our co-conspirators had gone. I knew I'd made the wrong choice when I saw lights at the bottom landing of the stairs. I stepped backward, up the staircase, bumping into Rudy, whose momentum was still carrying her forward.

"Stop." I saw a bald white head above a dark blue uniform. "Don't move."

Two police officers came around the edge of the staircase into full view. My knees trembled.

"Put your hands up." The second officer shined a huge flashlight into Thomas's face. "I said hands up, son!" His hand was at his waist – it was clutching the butt of his gun. I cringed and thrust my arms into the air.

The first officer pushed Rudy and I aside, while the second pulled Thomas to the bottom of the stairs.

"Get down on the ground," he said. "Are you armed? Down on the ground!"

Thomas lowered himself to his stomach on the tile floor, his arms still held out from his body, his hands spread.

"He didn't do anything," Rudy said, her voice thick with tears. "Stop! Please."

"Don't, Rudy," Thomas mumbled into the ground. "Don't."

My face was scalding hot, and my hands were ice cold. The bald officer patted Thomas down while the other stood watch, hand still poised over his gun.

"Do you all know you're trespassing on private property?"

Rudy and I nodded, and I felt a lump building in my throat. *I will not cry, I will not cry, I will not cry*, I chanted in my head.

"You all go to school here?"

Again, we nodded.

"Is there anybody else in here? How'd you get in?"

There was a brief pause when none of us was willing or able to speak. I could hear my own ragged breathing. Thomas was still lying on the floor, his cheek against the bottom of the stairs where everyone stepped, the officer towering over him. Thomas cleared his throat but I couldn't look down at him, not like that.

"We had a key, sir," he said. "It was only us, no one else is here."

The men exchanged looks, and they seemed to consider this information. The bald officer turned and walked down the hallway, reaching for the radio in his back pocket.

I worried what my Dad would say as I was led out the front door of the school building, the bald officer holding one hand on my shoulder. I should have left with Deena, I thought. Or the three of us should have ducked into a bathroom and hidden until they left.

In the back of the police car on the ride to my house, Rudy and I didn't speak, but I think she could feel my anger. I stared straight ahead at the crisscrossed pattern of the metal bars behind the passenger's headrest, and a barrage of thoughts coursed through my brain. At that point, I didn't fear specific consequences – I wasn't thinking of being suspended or expelled from school, of being ineligible to run track in the spring, of losing college scholarships (not that I expected to rack up many of them in the first place). I just felt a pressure in my chest and a weight on my shoulders; the knowledge that I'd done something wrong and I'd been caught. I was afraid of the negative opinions of me people might be forming.

As frightened as I was though, I was curious too. The seats in the back were hard plastic, which I hadn't expected. The back windows were tinted. It smelled like vanilla, which was a far cry from what I might have thought the inside of a cop car would smell like. Nothing about my presence in the vehicle made sense.

When the officer pulled into my driveway, Rudy turned toward me. I could feel her eyes on the side of my face but I didn't turn to meet her gaze.

"Jillian," she said when the policeman got out of the driver's side and walked around the car. "I'm so sorry."

"What for."

She paused. "For going upstairs. You could have left, but you didn't. Thank you."

Then, the back door opened beside me, giving me an excuse to step out of the car without answering her at all.

———

WE WEREN'T ARRESTED – Ogden decided not to press charges. There was probably parental intervention (e.g. money was exchanged) but at the time I wasn't aware of any of the particulars, I was just glad to have exited the whole mess unscathed. No one else was punished; just Thomas, Rudy and I, who were given two days of in-school suspension, where we sat in a windowless room along with two other students – guys who were caught cheating on a math test – and silently completed the work our teachers had sent down to us at the beginning of the day. Thomas and I weren't speaking to Rudy anyway. On the night of the prank, the police had brought Thomas in to the station and held him there until his parents came to pick him up. It wasn't fair, and yet it could have been much worse.

The mess in the office was cleaned up before any students could set foot in the building, but word of our senior prank spread fast. Some of our fellow pranksters had taken pictures before we left, and those made it online. Half of the school criticized us for our failed attempt, and the other half lauded us for our valiant effort at bringing back the senior prank tradition. The junior class was rumored to have already begun planning their own prank, though they had months to go before they were even senior class members. We became quasi-legends before we even left the school for good.

In addition to our in school suspension, my parents grounded me for two weeks, which was fine with me because it meant I had an excuse to stay away from everyone, to hide in my room and stew. For the first three days of my detainment I was still pissed at Rudy, but by the time the long two weeks were up, I couldn't wait to hang out with her again.

———

ON A SATURDAY NIGHT IN JANUARY, I sat on the couch in Skyler Warren's living room, picking chipped polish off of my thumbnail and just barely pretending to be interested in the never-ending story the guy beside me was imposing upon me. I had had just one beer – I was driving, and Rudy said it would be a short visit.

It was that point in the year where winter seems particularly cruel and the school year seems especially daunting. Christmas was over – the decorations and music, the cheer and gifts and festivities were gone and you could still feel their absence in the blank space over the fireplace mantel, the bland streetlights where no more holly hung and the absolute darkness of the neighborhoods around us at night – our community strictly enforced a policy of removing all Christmas lights by the end of the first week of January. All that remained was the bitter cold of winter and five more months of classes, both of which weighed upon me like a dense, suffocating fog.

Next to me, the guy was still going on and on – something about video game graphics – and he mimed the actions with his hands as if he were holding a game controller. I didn't know him from Ogden – he wore expensive jeans and a nice jacket, but his chin was scruffy with dark stubble and I couldn't imagine he was in a class below us. I wondered if he knew Skyler from post-high school life. Skyler had graduated from Ogden the year before. He had enrolled in a community college, which was so far beneath the expectations of an Ogden student that even I felt genuine shock. But he was working a nominal amount of hours at his Dad's company and it was only a matter of time before money and connection improved his circumstances. For Skyler Warren, as for many of my classmates, there were few lasting consequences, just temporary impediments.

I stood up, feeling warm and puffy and irritated. I had left Rudy in the basement playing a game of quarters – it had been nearly an hour (I was counting the minutes), and of course she was nowhere to be found now. The kitchen was empty, the basement was full of stoners and the dining room was a revolving game of beer pong as usual.

As I trudged up the stairs to the second floor, I thought to myself that maybe I was over this – and briefly I marveled at how quickly that moment had arrived, how quickly the things I'd so desired had become unimpressive.

I peeked into room after room, but Rudy was nowhere to be found. As I pushed the last door open, my nostrils filled with the smell of weed and something else, sweet and smoky and chemical. My eyes landed on two shadowy bodies, one straddling the other on top of the overstuffed duvet cover in the dimly lit room – that same dimly lit room where years and lifetimes earlier I'd caught Skyler Warren in the middle of a drug deal - and I got a rush of embarrassment so strong and so familiar it almost knocked me off my feet. The person on top lifted his head and flicked hair away from his face as he glanced up at me. In the dark, my eyes met with Skyler Warren's for a split second.

"Oh sorry, I'm sorry," I mumbled louder than I needed to. I was pulling the door shut again when a muffled voice rose from the bed and stopped me in my tracks.

"Who was that?" I heard Rudy whisper. The door was cracked just wide enough to fit my ear.

"They didn't see anything," Skyler said, his voice thick.

"Are you sure?"

"It was no one."

I heard her sigh, but she didn't say anything more.

I pulled the door shut without a sound and rushed quietly back down the hallway. At the bottom of the stairs, I went straight to the living room couch and let my knees buckle beneath me as I sunk into the cushions. I didn't breathe until the video games guy had started speaking again, and then everything was so much as it was before that it was almost possible for me to believe I had never gone upstairs in the first place.

———

AT TWO IN THE MORNING, we sat next to each other in the front seat on the way back to Rudy's house. My knuckles gripped the steering wheel – ten and two – and I stared ahead at the dark pavement, hoping my concentration would be mistaken for diligent driving and not my reliving what had happened a few hours prior. My mouth was full of half-formed questions and vague concerns, but I just kept pushing forward, my foot heavy on the gas pedal.

"It was you, wasn't it?"

When Rudy finally opened her mouth, I was so used to the silence - the soft rumble of the car and the low whoosh of the heater - that my ears almost didn't register her voice.

"What?"

"Was it you?" She repeated. "Did you go up to Skyler's room tonight?"

So she knew. I had no idea what to make of that.

"Yes," I answered quietly.

She fiddled quietly with the passenger door lock. Locked, unlocked, locked, unlocked.

"It's just temporary, you know."

What was temporary? The drugs? The sex? Why wasn't she speaking in full sentences? Skyler had always left a lingering bad feeling in the pit of my stomach – he was friendly and polite, a good host and a people pleaser, but it seemed there was something darker beneath it. Then again, I was never really a good read of people.

"Does Thomas know?" I asked.

"No." She sighed. "He's been pushing me away, Jilly. I guess I didn't really know what to do, and this just happened."

"How long has it been going on?"

"Not long. And it'll stop really soon. I mean, I have to get serious, right?"

"Yeah."

If there was more to tell, she didn't volunteer it, and as usual, I didn't ask. We drove on in silence, past bald trees and snow crusted lawns and big, black windowed houses. As we pulled into the Golden's driveway and I turned the car off, she finally turned to me again, grabbing my wrist suddenly.

"I'm so sorry, Jill. It's not like I didn't consider telling you." She paused. Her fingers were freezing. "But I couldn't let anyone know."

I thought of that moment with my ear pressed into the crack of the door frame. *It's no one.*

"I know," I said. "I promise, no one will know."

———

IT STOPPED IN MID-MARCH. I knew not because Rudy told me – we'd never spoken about it again – but because Skyler Warren got some kind of vague job working for a tech company in Kansas City and moved into a high rise apartment overlooking the Plaza and the kind of relationship he and Rudy had – which as far as I knew consisted of hooking up over drugs in the shadows at parties – didn't seem like the kind of relationship you held on to long distance. On Rudy's end, I studied her hard for clues – I compared her behavior before and after his departure, I casually peeked inside her purse and in her dresser drawers for some other very large and obvious sign of a problem, but when I found nothing I resolved the mistake must have been Skyler, and now the mistake was gone. She was the same – a little melancholy, a little moodier, but we were eighteen, we were all changing – at her core, I was sure she must be the same as she'd always been.

14
————

SENIOR SPRING

When I was five years old, I wanted to be a doctor when I grew up. For Christmas that year, I begged for and received a dress up kit with a white doctor's coat and a red plastic satchel with one of those white crosses on the sides. Inside it, there were bandages and a blood pressure cuff and a stethoscope that actually worked. I wore the coat every day during Christmas vacation, and I practiced examining and diagnosing my baby cousins, when they would stay still, and my baby dolls when I had no available human patients.

In the fourth grade, when the highly anticipated job-shadowing day rolled around, I had determined education was where my aspirations lay and I spent the day helping my favorite teacher pass out stickers and juice boxes in the kindergarten room at my elementary school in Boston.

When I received my letter of acceptance to the University of Missouri in March of my senior year of high school, I had no idea what I wanted to be when I grew up. I panicked during my first college counseling session at Ogden, when after a solid half hour of Mrs. Stuart, the sweet, Brillo pad haired counselor, prodding me gently about my interests and suggesting majors that might appeal to me, we had yet to come to any conclusions regarding my future. I liked art okay, but I was a terrible artist. I didn't really like kids and teachers were underpaid anyway. I didn't have the endurance to make it through enough school to become a doctor (and to be fair, I probably wasn't smart enough either). Engineering, accounting and agriculture didn't even blip on my radar.

I cried when, two weeks after MU accepted me, I opened my rejection letters from UCLA and USC. In some brutal twist of events, they arrived in the mail on the very same day Rudy received letters of acceptance from both schools.

"You're not going without me, are you?" I could barely choke the words out through my sobs.

Rudy bit her lip and shook her head. "I don't think so."

Warm relief washed through my body. I could breath again.

"You can, you know. It's your dream school. I could visit you on breaks and we could go to the beach." Now that I knew she wouldn't leave me, I could encourage her.

Rudy shook her head more fervently.

"They're not my *dream* schools. They were just nice schools."

By the time Boston College rejected me, I was immune; their letter bounced off my cool exterior. My father, however, was sorely disappointed.

I made mental plans regarding the decorations in the dorm room Rudy and I would inevitably share at MU.

EACH YEAR, in early April, Ogden rewarded the senior class with a break from school during the week when the freshman, sophomore and junior classes were suffering through standardized testing. I think they did it, in equal parts, because the seniors loved it and because it meant they could wash their hands of a bunch of students who would otherwise be flippantly roaming the hallways, distracting the test-takers. Ogden's test scores were a thing of parents' dreams, and they wanted to keep it that way. For our class, Deena had spearheaded a campaign to spend our four-day break taking a class trip to Panama City Beach. She began pushing the trip at class meetings in November, and by the end of February the plane tickets and hotel reservations were booked. Thirty-seven of our class members were going, including Rudy and me, along with five adult chaperones.

On the plane ride, Rudy and I sat together sharing the head-phones to her iPod. She squeezed my hand when we took off and when we landed – plane rides terrified her, though she was far more well-traveled than I was – and as we dragged our rolling suitcases through the crowded airport terminal and out the sliding glass doors once we'd landed in Florida, we were hit with warm, salty air. Loading my bags into the back of a taxi van, I felt stuffy and overheated in the sweatshirt and jeans I'd dressed in back in 40 degree Missouri.

"Isn't it beautiful?" Rudy pushed her nose against the glass of the tinted window in the taxi as the beach came into view for the first time. She pointed at the blue waves rolling into shore and I squinted beside her.

It was. It was gorgeous, the yellow rays of sunlight reflecting off the white tops of the crashing waves, the white-gold curve of the beach stretching down the coast. I felt a pang, of guilt and disappointment, for what we would be missing in California the next four years.

But it didn't last long, thank God. We were on break.

———

"Where do you want to put our towels down? Close to the water or the buildings?" Deena turned around to speak to us, shading her eyes with one arm raised to her forehead.

I shrugged.

"Water," Rudy said.

We followed Deena and Teegan down the beach, kicking up sand like little kids as we went. Once we'd designated the perfect, sun-optimizing spot, we spread our towels and began basting our arms and legs with tanning lotion. I spread it across my stomach then passed the bottle to Rudy.

"Get my back?"

I turned and heard her squirt a glob of lotion onto her palm then massage it into the backs of my shoulders.

"Where are the guys?" Teegan asked when we were all sprawled on our towels, squinting up at the sun overhead.

"Drinking in one of their rooms before they come out," Deena answered. I couldn't see through her dark glasses, but I could tell by the tone of her voice the statement had been accompanied by an eye roll.

"What about Greg's parents?"

When Greg Jennings' parents had volunteered to serve as chaperones, a silent cheer had gone up among the seniors who were booked for the trip. The Jennings were perhaps the most notoriously lenient parents in our class. Not only were they known to provide alcohol to Greg's friends, but it was rumored that once, Mr. Jennings – the manager of our community bank, who wore stiff suits and squeaky black soled shoes and once came to speak to my finance class about the importance of starting a retirement fund in your twenties – had crashed one of Greg's small parties in a bright orange Hawaiian shirt and done shots with all of the boys.

"I'm sure they bought the beer. They're probably drunker than anybody."

It was early in the day, but the beach was already crowded

with bodies and umbrellas. I rolled onto my stomach and propped myself up on my elbows, gazing down the strip of sand.

"Rudy, Thomas is going to Yale next year, right?"

College had been the most popular topic of conversation at Ogden since the regular admission letters began arriving in February and March. It followed me around, hovering around me in the hallways and waiting to pounce onto my back when I entered a classroom full of seniors. I wanted to shove my fingers into my ears and refuse to listen.

"Right." Rudy didn't raise her head off the towel.

"His classes are going to be so tough. He's going to be surrounded by all these brainiacs. Have you decided where you're going yet?" The question was obviously directed at Rudy, but she didn't answer.

"I'm going to Colorado. We finally picked one, last night while I was packing actually," Teegan filled the silence. "It was between that and Kirksville, but I really just want to get out of the bubble, you know?"

"Hey," Deena pointed an accusatory finger in Teegan's direction. "Don't knock Missouri." Deena had been set on the University of Missouri for months; she had an entire collection of emblazoned sweatshirts to prove it. "You're going to Mizzou, too, right Jillian?"

I nodded. "And Rudy."

"Really?" Deena perked up.

"Probably." Rudy shooed a fly away from her nose. "There are a few schools I haven't heard from yet."

I dug my toes into the sand and watched a group of bikini-clad girls pose for a picture by the water. A split second after the picture was taken, a seagull swooped down in front of them and they scattered, squealing with laughter.

"What are you and Thomas going to do when he leaves for Yale? You're not going to stay together, are you?" Deena's lips were pursed together in judgment. I braced myself for her impending rant.

"I don't really know yet."

"Honestly, you don't want to be in a long distance relationship, especially not your first year of college. College is all about freedom and meeting new people. You don't want to be tied to somebody who's a thousand miles away."

"We've talked about it, but we haven't decided anything," Rudy answered quietly, and that seemed like the end of the conversation. I reached into the big straw tote bag Rudy and I had lugged from our hotel and pulled out a magazine, flipping to an article about dressing for your body type.

"What if he cheats on you? You'd never know." Deena was turned toward us, and I could see my distorted reflection in those huge lenses.

Quickly, I looked away, staring holes through the magazine and into the sand. Out of the corner of my eye I saw Teegan gazing intently at her fingernails.

"Not that I'm saying Thomas is that type of guy. But he *is* a guy."

To this, Rudy didn't even respond. Without a word, she flipped over and lay on her stomach, her face turned toward me.

Rudy had been in a funk for the past week or so, and I blamed it on Thomas. The night before we left for Florida, Rudy and I were packing, filling a duffel bag with bikinis and flip flops, when Rudy's phone rang. Her face tightened.

"It's Thomas."

She answered and not even thirty seconds into the conversation, went into her closet and closed the door behind her.

In her bedroom, I kept sifting through the drawer, being as quiet as possible as I strained to hear Rudy on the other side of the wall, then feeling guilty when I caught bits and pieces of the conversation. When the door flew open, I was tilting in the direction of the closet, a pink and white striped bikini top in my hand. I bolted up straight, snapping my head forward and scrutinizing the top in my hands. Rudy's mouth was turned down, her eyebrows furrowed over her glass-green eyes.

I held it up toward her. "Should we pack this one?"

"Sure." She sat back down across from me and picked up where she had left off without saying a word about the phone call. I didn't ask.

After two hours of lying in the sand, the four of us got up and made our way down the beach. Rudy was bubbling over now, exuding something we couldn't help but catch. We giggled along down the boardwalk and she convinced us we should talk some guys into buying us frozen drinks from one of the beachside vendors.

The lucky gentlemen were in a group of four, throwing a football and clutching cans of beer, backward baseball caps pulled down over all of their heads. The one in blue and white swim trunks was cute, I decided, as he lofted the ball over his head. None of us wanted to approach them, and after two rounds of rock, paper, scissors, Deena was appointed our less-than-willing messenger.

They took our cash and returned with green plastic souvenir glasses, brimming with strawberry daiquiris. They told us they were on spring break from Ohio State University, and we told them the names of the colleges we'd be attending in the fall, in an attempt to distract from the fact that we were still in technically in high school. Late in the afternoon, when we departed, we exchanged phone numbers and made plans to meet up with them that evening. We trudged back to the hotel, dehydrated and tipsy from the alcohol and the sun.

Back in our room, Rudy fixed my hair while I sat on the gaudy floral bedspread and applied make-up over my pink cheeks, squinting into a hand mirror propped up against my bent knees. I wore a dress of Deena's that was a little too big around my hips and Teegan borrowed the pink high heels my mom gave me for Christmas. We had all severely over packed, the contents of our stiff new suitcases overflowing out onto the dingy carpet.

We met up with the rest of the Ogden group in the dimly lit hotel lobby and we walked next door for dinner at a seafood restaurant with cushioned red seats and an enormous lobster tank in the middle of the dining room. I ordered crab, Rudy ordered shrimp, and we picked off of each other's plates.

At nine o'clock, we left for a dance club in a pack of twelve. Rudy and Thomas walked on opposite sides of the group, but I was too excited for the night ahead of us to worry about their relationship. I was tired of the tedious drama. I was ready to let loose and have fun, and I was ready to find the football tossing guy from the beach.

Inside the club the air was hot and stale; the walls pulsed with music from the huge speakers at the DJ booth. Green and blue and pink lights swiveled from the ceiling over the middle of the dance floor, shooting strobes of color across the crowded room. Near the bar where they'd promised to meet us, Deena spotted our drink-buying friends from that afternoon and we made our way toward them through the throngs of tanned bodies. They proudly brandished their neon-braceleted wrists and slipped cash across the sticky bar counter and were rewarded with full cups of beer, which they handed off to each of us once we were out of the bartenders' view. The boys from Ogden had disappeared as soon as we'd entered the club.

We stood in a tight circle and drank quickly while the guys from the beach recounted a story about their long drive from Ohio. Two quick beers later, we were dragging them onto the dance floor, moving to the beat of the music while the guys put their arms around our waists and tried to follow our motions.

The guy I was dancing with wasn't particularly good looking, but Rudy's partner had striking features and nice green eyes and arm muscles that bulged beneath the sleeves of his white polo. Of course Rudy got the best-looking guys, even when she had a boyfriend, I thought with a pang of jealousy.

I twisted my neck and looked for Thomas in the crowd, but I couldn't spot any of the guys from our class. I wondered what he would think if he saw Rudy with this hot college guy – not that she was doing anything wrong, really. I guess. For a second, I thought of the night I'd walked in on her at Skyler Warren's. I wondered what was going through her mind while she moved across the dance floor.

My toes were aching, pinched into a pair of Rudy's half-size-too-small heels, and my new dance partner, the guy who had been dancing with Teegan earlier, wrapped a sweaty arm around me. I pulled away and gestured to Rudy, nodding my head toward the bar. She was smiling and glistening with the faintest layer of perspiration across her forehead.

We perched on two sticky, ripped stools at the end of the counter, and I rested my tired feet against the metal bar at the bottom of the stool. Once I had caught my breath, I turned to talk to Rudy, but she was staring daggers across the room, her jaw clenched and her arms folded across her chest. I followed her gaze over all the swaying bodies until it landed on the far side of the dance floor, where Thomas was wiping sweat off his forehead while he danced with his body pressed up against a girl I didn't know. Before I could say anything, the guys we'd been dancing with appeared at our sides.

"You girls want some shots?" One of them yelled over the pounding of the music.

I nodded without looking to Rudy first. I wanted a shot. I didn't want this trip, my senior trip, to end with me soberly following along as the third wheel to Rudy's crashing relationship.

He passed a plastic shot glass, overflowing with yellow liquid, into my hands and some of it dripped onto Deena's dress. The four of us lifted our shots to cheers and threw them back. It was good, lemon something. Before I could wipe my mouth, they were handing us another shot each, which we promptly tossed back as well.

I'm sure you can guess where things went from there – downhill very quickly. I had barely eaten in the past two days, irrationally afraid of stomach bloat and looking fat beside my friends in my swimsuit on the beach. It didn't take long before the shots – and the beers that followed them – had me swaying side to side on my barstool, leaning into one of the guys who had plied us with those shots in the first place, probably with this exact scenario in mind.

I was twirling, watching my dress billow and fall, when Rudy pulled me close and whispered in my ear. "Let's go hang out somewhere else."

"You want to leave? Just you and me?" I half-whispered, half-shouted into her ear.

"They invited us to their room."

"*Rudy.*" I turned to look at her and pressed my face close to hers.

"What?" She feigned innocence. Or ignorance. Or maybe it was an honest question.

"We can't."

"Nothing's going to go on," she said firmly.

I stared at her. "Why do you want to?"

"Free drinks. And the music is too loud anyway."

She was hurting. I could see sadness in the corners of her eyes, and I could tell by the firm line of her jaw that for whatever reason, she was adamant about this venture. I could feel myself capitulating already to what she needed from me.

As we stumbled out of the club, ushered by the two boys – what were their names? Oh, God, I knew them, but in that instant I couldn't remember – who were steadying us by the crooks of our elbows, I glanced back over my shoulder, looking to make eye contact with Deena or Teegan, but neither of them was on the dance floor where we'd left them. I hoped someone would see us, would stop us, but then I was out on the sidewalk, away from the doorway and the thumping of the music and it seemed like the moment when I could have changed my mind had passed. Whatever was happening now, I would go along with it, because there seemed to be no other choice.

"This way?" Rudy pointed straight ahead down the street, her arm outstretched, the tip of her yellow painted fingernail a light to guide us.

"Yeah, like two blocks." The boy on Rudy's arm nodded.

"Ours is that way, too," she added.

The ocean breeze outside was cool against my skin, and it ruffled the bottom of my dress. I held on to the hem with both hands as I teetered along the uneven sidewalk, preventing it from blowing up around my waist, though the wind wasn't nearly that strong. Strands of my hair blew across my face and got stuck in my lip-gloss, and I tried to spit them out of my mouth while still grasping at the dress with both hands. The boy beside me laughed, then smoothed the hair behind my ear.

Standing outside the hotel lobby door, it took the guys three tries before they were able to successfully swipe their key card. Once inside, my heels clacked noisily on the tiled lobby floor. We all stood quietly with our arms crossed over our chests, avoiding awkward eye contact as we waited for the elevator to make its way back down to the first floor, and when the button lit up and the doors parted, one of the boys swept his arm in front of the open space.

"Ladies first," he winked. Ew, I thought. Winks.

Rudy and I stepped inside, leaning up against the silver metal handrails in the tiny square box. One of the boys punched the number four.

Inside the guys' room it smelled strongly like beer and weed. There were two low beds with a wicker nightstand in the middle – one was strewn with a few empty pizza boxes and Cheetos bags, orange dust streaked across the wrinkled turquoise bedspread and the other held two open duffel bags, clothes spilling out. The trashcan was overflowing with empty beer cans. On the far side of the room, the door to the balcony was open and salty ocean breeze blew the curtains. My eyes stung.

"Sorry about the mess," one of the guys quickly swept everything off the beds and onto the floor, which didn't really seem much better in my opinion.

"Want to sit down?" He gestured toward the seat he'd cleared and timidly, I sat beside him, the wicker poking into the backs of my bare shoulders. They turned the TV on and got us each a can of warm Bud Light, and I wished so hard to be back at the club. I checked my phone, but there were no messages from the other girls.

On the other bed, Rudy had her legs stretched out and crossed at the ankles, and the guy had his arm propped up on the headboard behind her, though it wasn't touching her at all.

Before long, the beers were gone, and I was tired.

"Do you have any vodka?" Rudy asked. I had thought maybe we could leave, but it seemed I was wrong.

"Yeah," the guy beside her sat up. He exchanged a quick glance with the guy next to me – really, I should have remembered their names. "Do you want me to mix you a drink," he asked her.

"Sure," Rudy shrugged. "Please."

The guy next to me leaned forward and tapped my knee. "How about you?"

"Okay," I said.

They stood at the bathroom counter with their backs to us, and I shot Rudy a look. She pretended not to understand. The guys returned with paper coffee cups filled to the brim with dark soda and vodka.

I took a sip; it was disgustingly strong. Rudy had already tossed back half of hers. I set it on the floor beside the bed and stared at the TV, feigning intense interest in an old episode of a reality show, wishing I was almost anywhere else.

———

A LITTLE WHILE later I woke up shivering, my brain pounding against my skull. The balcony door was still open and the curtains billowed in the cool breeze. I sat up, alarmed and disoriented – the guy next to me was slumped against the pillow snoring. The other bed was empty and the TV cast blue light across the sheets, playing for no one. I scrambled to my feet, panic spreading through my body. The bathroom was dark and unoccupied, and the door to the hallway stood slightly ajar – bright light peered in through the crack. What had happened? Where could Rudy have gone? I grabbed my shoes and phone with trembling hands and fled from the room, my heart pounding in my chest.

The hallway was empty, and I paused, unsure where to go next. One of the lights flickered behind a seashell shaped sconce, and down the hallway I could hear the hum of the ice machine. Then, as I wondered what to do, I heard a muffled cry. I turned and ran, clutching my things to my chest. When I reached the end of the hallway I found her, sobbing against the wall behind the ice machine, her legs bent up to her chest, her arms wrapped around her knees. One of her dress straps hung off her shoulder and her eyes were pressed into her kneecaps as she cried into her legs. I was equal parts terrified and relieved.

I knelt on the carpet and put my arms around her. I pressed the side of my face to hers and I felt her tears on my cheek.

"Are you okay?" I said.

She didn't answer, but she reached up to hug me, her fingers gripping the backs of my arms.

"Let's get out of here," I whispered, and I could feel her head bob up and down as she nodded.

But there was more. Walking back to our hotel, my arm wrapped around Rudy's waist, we crossed the parking lot at exactly the same time another group was approaching from the opposite side. It was a group of our classmates - Deena, Michael Denalby and at the back of the group, Thomas.

I tried not to make eye contact, to slip in the side entrance, but Michael saw us and called out my name.

"Hey, Jillian," he yelled, his hand cupped over his mouth. "Where have you guys been. Wait up."

They were drunk and Rudy was still crying, and I was an unqualified intermediary standing between them. I attempted to bridge the gulf safely; leaned against my shoulder, Rudy still felt as fragile as glass.

"Just headed back to our room," I smiled a tight smile.

"Oh my God, did you all leave with those dudes from the club?" Deena asked loudly. "They were hot."

I glanced at Thomas and saw his face tighten. Leave it to Deena.

"Rudy! What happened?" Deena stepped toward us, her arms spread motheringly. She turned toward me, as if Rudy couldn't speak for herself. "Oh my God I didn't even realize she was crying."

"Probably nothing she didn't ask for," Michael said. He said it under his breath, but it wasn't difficult to hear.

I could barely breathe.

"What did you say?" I whispered.

He shrugged on an additional layer of courage and said louder this time, "She probably asked for it. It's not like nobody knows about her and Skyler Warren."

"Fuck you," Rudy said. Her voice quivered and there was snot in the corner of her nostril, but she stood up a little taller. "You don't know what you're talking about."

"Seriously," I added as sincerely as I could muster. "Just shut up."

I wanted to tell him how wrong he was about her, but I couldn't get my mouth to open again. It seemed like a very flimsy gesture anyway, one that would probably do more harm than good.

I think maybe she expected someone else to defend her, to fill in the gap with reassurance that she wasn't that type of girl, whatever type it was exactly Michael was accusing her of being. The cheating type? The slutty type? The druggy type? But as I looked around the circle, no one made eye contact – they all knew. Every single one of them.

"Just defending my friend, man." Michael slung his arm over Thomas's shoulder, who in his defense looked as if it was an unwanted burden at that moment. "You really fucked him over, Rudy."

Did Thomas know? His face was heavy. He was looking at Rudy and Rudy was looking directly into his eyes expectantly, but he didn't stand up for her either; then he shrugged off Michael's arm and looked away.

"Did you ever even care about me in the first place?" She searched Thomas's face and her voice cracked. "Or was I just a convenient excuse to lose your virginity before college?"

"You're a bitch." Michael reached out and pushed her away from Thomas. It wasn't hard, but it was unexpected and she fell, her face naked with surprise as her backside hit the ground. One of her shoes flew off her foot, landing with a smack against the pavement.

"You're an asshole!" I lunged at Michael but the other boys were already pulling him away.

Behind me, Rudy had scrambled to her feet again and stormed off across the parking lot.

"Aren't you going to say something?" I grabbed Thomas's arm.

His eyes were dark and full. Guilt, I realized, they were full of pity and guilt.

"I broke up with her last week," he said quietly.

———

I RETRIEVED HER SANDALS – the first she'd lost when Michael pushed her and the second she'd kicked off as she ran – and I ran after her, leaving everyone in our wake. I chased her all the way out to the beach, where she ran down the sand while I screamed her name. If she heard me, she refused to turn and look back in my direction. She didn't stop until she had run directly into the ocean, all the way out until the fingers of the dark waves reached up to soak the bottom of her shorts.

I was panting when I caught up to her.

"Rudy, what the hell?"

Her face was wet, and the breeze was cool against my bare skin. The waves lapped at my knees.

"What's wrong?" I said. "What happened tonight? What's going on with you?"

She just shook her head and wiped at the tears on her face. "I just don't get it. I don't understand what's wrong with me."

"There's nothing at all wrong with you," I offered quietly.

"I'm never going to be good enough. I fuck everything up. What am I supposed to do?"

In the dark, her skin glowed translucently, the veins in her forearms blue beneath the surface. Her eyes were wide, searching pools. I couldn't hold their gaze.

If only she had asked a question I could answer. Something more along the lines of, "We shouldn't have gone to that hotel, right?" or "Michael Denalby's the worst, isn't he?" For those, I could have agreed with her. With fervor, I would have rushed to her defense. For the question she asked, I was at a loss.

Between us, the waves were flowing in and out, dragging sand with them each time, leaving the shoreline damp and perfectly smooth. Rudy stared out at the dark expanse of water. It was impossible to see where the ocean ended and the sky began. I shivered.

"We should go for a swim," she said after a long time.

"A night swim," I said, but I didn't move. I thought back to the hot, carefree summer afternoons when we used to dive topless into the Goldens' backyard pool after a long, sweaty run. I smiled.

"But it's too late for that now, huh," Rudy said, backing slowly out of the water and up onto the sand, her footprints leaving soft imprints on its surface.

"Yeah," I said. "Yeah, you're probably right."

———

THE REST of our time in Panama City unfolded with little drama but with little innocent fun either. The next morning, the sun was bright and warm and all of the events from the night before seemed as unreal as a bad dream. Rudy went down to the lobby to get coffee, and whether or not I actually believed the cheerful façade she presented to us when she came back into the room where Deena, Teegan and I were tying on our bikinis and gathering our magazines and beach towels, I told myself she was fine. I recited in my mind that Rudy was happy: she was beautiful, she was loved, she would find other boys who would be more than willing to have her heart if Thomas wasn't. If she didn't want to dwell on what had happened, who was I to bring it up? In this way, I was able to convince myself that everything with Rudy was okay.

"We're going to the beach," I said when she sat down on the bed, coffee in hand. "You're still coming, right?"

She nodded, rubbing a piece of her loose hair across her lips.

"You can wear my blue bikini," I said. It was the only thing of mine she'd ever asked to borrow.

I held it out to her, two tiny scraps of bright blue spandex, like it was the best thing I could offer her. Like it was the only thing she needed from me in that moment.

———

"Jill," Rudy said over the phone. "You have to come over. I've got big news."

There was a bubble of happiness in her voice.

"What? Just tell me."

I was in the middle of watching a two-hour long TV special on Britney Spears' life story and I was still wearing my pajamas, though it was almost one o'clock on Sunday afternoon.

"I want to tell you in person. Please?"

I groaned, but I got up. I changed into a pair of sweatpants and walked out of the house, yelling good-bye to my parents as I shut the door behind me.

Three weeks had passed since our senior weekend in Florida. In that time, I had been named co-captain of the girls' track team, and I was at the top of my game in the hurdles – I was faster and more agile than ever. Coach Kline had mapped out an even more rigid training schedule for me this year, and I wanted not only to win two more state championships but to set records.

We'd just had our senior prom, the most extravagant dance yet, and Rudy and I had gone together, in sparkling black and white dresses that complemented each other perfectly. I bought her a red tipped white rose, and I made an elaborate show, bending down on one knee to slip it over her hand while she laughed and Mrs. Golden's camera clicked in our ears. The state track meet was a month away and before it arrived, Rudy and I were planning a spectacular, outrageous party at her house while her parents were away visiting Marta in New York. They would be gone for three nights – plenty of time to hold the party, get everyone out and get the place cleaned up – before they returned, with Marta in tow, for our graduation ceremony. We had been planning in secret for weeks, lining up our alcohol purchases and scouring the mall for the perfect dresses. We were going to go out with a bang.

Weeks before, it had been hard for me to imagine we would only be at Ogden for another month, but now our departure felt necessary and imminent. It buzzed around the air at school, an extra current in addition to the usual teenage drama. Our graduation robes and tassels had arrived in the mail two weeks earlier.

The trees in my parents' yard – the same trees that lined the middle of all the streets in our subdivision – were in full bloom. Big, fat white flowers hung from the spindly branches and gave off a faint, perfumy fragrance. It was a warm April day, the sky a shade of light cerulean. A slight breeze ruffled my hair, and I smiled to myself.

It was a good day. The perfect spring day. We should go to the park or something, I thought as I ran up the steps of Rudy's front porch.

She opened the door in a pretty lavender skirt and sandals.

"Hey!" She leapt at me, wrapping her arms around my neck.

"Hi," I breathed into her hair, which smelled like her rosy shampoo. The same shampoo I'd been buying since the first summer I spent at her house.

"Mom, we'll be back in a second. We're going to walk," she called behind her. She didn't even remember to shut the front door behind us, she was pulling me down the sidewalk so quickly.

"Why're you so dressed up?"

"We just got back from celebrating. We had lunch at The Boathouse. I got the salmon this time, like you said, and you're right, it was amazing."

"Celebrating?" I raised an eyebrow. "Celebrating what?"

We had made it to the end of her driveway, where the brick drive met the pavement of the street. She stopped and turned to face me.

"Well," she said. "That's what I wanted to tell you about. I got into Sarah Lawrence!"

My stomach clenched. There was a long pause, during which I considered her face. Her lovely, happy, face.

"Sarah Lawrence? Like the school on the East coast?"

She nodded enthusiastically, like a bobble-head doll on a dashboard.

"Are you *going*?"

"Yes!" She was still visibly excited; my reaction had yet to puncture her bubble and the juxtaposition of our energies made me cringe.

"Why?"

"It's a great school." Her voice went down an octave. "My parents are really happy."

I thought of Mr. and Mrs. Golden, with their Ivy League degrees and their lavish expectations, glowing at the thought of their youngest daughter tucked away at school on the east coast. They could frame her acceptance letter and hang it in the hallway beside a photo of the three of them, squeezed together in front of the school's historic buildings, smiling gleefully, tears in Mrs. Golden's eyes as they dropped Rudy off for her first semester so far away from home and so far away from me.

"MU's a good school, too."

"Well, yeah, but Sarah Lawrence is a really great liberal arts school, Jill. It's really competitive. I'm lucky I got in."

"That doesn't mean you have to go," I crossed my arms over my chest defensively. "All girls?"

"It's co-ed. And it's small and the programs are so cool and individualized. Plus, it's only half an hour from Manhattan! I'll have the best of both worlds."

She sounded like a college brochure. I could see her in a cable-knit wool sweater, sitting beneath a grand old tree in a bed of crunchy red and golden autumn leaves, a textbook spread open in front of her, and her lips parted in laughter as she studied joyfully with another handsome, sweater-clad, Sarah Lawrence caliber student.

"I'm sorry," I said, harshly. "Am I supposed to be excited for you?"

Her face crumpled. "I thought you would be."

"*I* thought you were going to school with me next year, but I guess you've been hiding things from me this whole time."

"I didn't hide anything from you. I was waiting to make a decision until I knew what all my options were."

"Right. You were waiting for a better option than me." I knew she wanted the argument to end – we never argued, not about anything that mattered anyway – but I was just warming up. Old feelings, feelings I'd ignored for years, were churning in my chest, and my self-pity was indulgent.

"That's not it at all." She drew a deep breath. "This is probably the hardest decision I've ever had to make. You're my best friend, and you know I wish we could go to school together, but I have to make a serious decision on this. We can't follow each other forever."

"And it's so convenient that I've been following you for years and now when I need you, when I trusted that you'd be there for me, because I have to move to another place where I don't know a single person, where not a single person will notice me, you bail on me. I'm so sick of living in your shadow, but I did it because you're my best friend, and I thought – for some reason, I thought, that I was your best friend, too."

"You *are* my best friend. You're the track star, Jill. They picked you as the homecoming queen. You've never been in my shadow."

"Don't you get it, though? None of that matters. In the fall, no one will give a shit that I was good at track in high school. And homecoming was a fluke. What you've got *counts* – your perfect grades and perfect looks and perfect family," I could hear hysterics in my own voice. "Why can't you stop being so selfish for once?"

"Don't you know my life's not perfect? Out of everyone in the world, I thought you were the one person who could see that - who could understand me." Rudy's mouth sagged at the corners, and I could tell by the way the tip of her nose twitched that she was about to cry. "You can come visit me in New York, and I'll come visit you in Columbia," she said weakly. "Please. I know you don't mean all that crap." She gave me a sad half-smile.

I squared my jaw and looked at her injured face. I could feel the spot inside me that was beginning to give, the spot that was already starting to rearrange my life to defer to Rudy's. Maybe I'd make friends easier if I had a random college roommate. She might turn out to be great; I would go to parties with her on the weekends and I'd meet her other friends and over Thanksgiving break I would ask to go visit Rudy in New York. We'd ride in yellow taxis and wear cashmere scarves against the East coast chill, and she'd be impressed with how much I'd changed without her. But I didn't want to give in to her logic; I felt I had yielded too much already. At eighteen years old, don't we all feel we never get our way, that the world is unfair and vindictive toward us in particular? I locked the soft part of me away in a dungeon, and I dug into my own wound, pressing on in anger.

"I'm sure your life in New York will be perfect. I just don't want to be part of it."

When I said it, I felt the tears rush to my eyes and I turned and fled down the driveway before she could see them. She didn't chase after me, and I didn't turn around to see what she did instead. I don't know if she stood at the end of the driveway and watched me go or if she went straight back inside her house. I don't know exactly what she was thinking – how badly my words injured her.

But they were just *words*, I thought at the time. And *I* was angry and hurt, too. I knew she was smart, that she had better grades and better test scores than I did, but wasn't college college? Couldn't she get an education and be my roommate simultaneously? It's not like I would have held her back, I thought. Though the possibility had been lingering in our lives for the past year, I realized in that moment I'd never thought she would actually leave me. And I was embarrassed I had been so naïve.

If I could say something to myself in this moment, I would shout and scream at eighteen-year-old Jillian to go back. To apologize. You didn't mean it, I would yell.

You didn't mean it.

Even then, I knew I didn't mean it. But sometimes, no matter how hard you beat yourself up, there are things you just can't take back.

———

SHE TRIED to talk to me before class the next day, but I skill-fully avoided her. It wasn't difficult. We had finals that week, and the normalcy of our days had been interrupted, replaced with rigid test schedules. I arrived at Ogden just before the bell rang, I focused on the black text on sheet after sheet of exams, I ate lunch with a group of girls from the track team and if Rudy approached me, I would simply get up and leave the table.

That Friday, at the culmination of finals week, was supposed to be our party. I wondered if Rudy would go through with it without me. On Friday morning, when I heard whispers about it before the bell rang in my math class, I knew that she would. With or without me, apparently, the celebration would go on. I sulked.

On Friday night my new dress stared at me from where it hung on the back of my bedroom door, the tag still poking out from under the armpit. Out the window I could see a few cars already parked in front of Rudy's house. I closed my curtains and turned up the music and lay in my bed with a fat magazine spread open over my face. I held it up until my eyelids grew heavy, then I set it down beside me on top of the sheets and closed my eyes and tried to think of nothing at all.

At eleven thirty, I turned out my lamp and went to sleep, and I didn't stir until nearly noon the next day.

———

THEY SAID no one found her until 3 a.m., when it was far too late to do anything to help her. She lay in the middle of the foyer, her almond arms woven between shattered gold and crystal pieces, her thighs smashed against the grey and white marble. A twisted pile of shimmery opulence, ready to be swept from the floor.

Everyone was there that night; every boy we'd kissed, every girl we knew and every single person who had ever received a wink or a smile or a nod from Rudy as we crossed paths in a crowded hallway. Everyone was there, everyone except me.

They said Rudy was out of control. She was clearly several shots in when the first guests arrived, and when she struggled to open the heavy front door, her hair fell in big, chocolate-gold curls in front of her face. They said she was the life of the party that night, throwing off her shoes to dance on her family's formal dining room table. Cartwheeling down the length of it, her bare feet slapping against the shiny wood.

They said that by midnight she couldn't walk; she just sat at the foot of the marble entryway stairs, rooms away from where the party was raging. The grand staircase, with its grand chandelier and its grand fucking elevator music piping in through the walls. Several people said they sat on the stairs and talked to her. Someone told someone else she was upset; she was crying and she was in complete hysterics. Someone told someone who told someone else she was puking her guts up, which I know is a lie because I'd never seen her throw up a single time in my life. No one was there when she made her way to the top of the staircase, or when she reached over the railing toward that stupid chandelier.

An ambulance came at 3:30 in the morning. My bedroom window faced the street, but I didn't hear the wailing siren or see the red and blue lights through my curtains. Almost everyone had fled the scene and the ones who stayed paced the living room or sat with their heads in their hands. Someone threw up. No one held her hand.

The paramedics burst in and carted her off – I can see it all unfolding in slow motion in my mind, even though I never saw it at all – but it was too late. Maybe it had been too late for a while now.

She didn't see just who she was. Maybe I never did either.

———

I WOKE LATE that morning with a good feeling in my gut. It was one of those mornings where the sun was warm outside my window and birds were chirping quietly while they built nests in the trees outside. I lay for twenty minutes with my head against the pillow, enjoying the feeling of my soft sheets and the warm cocoon my body had made, wrapped up in the comforter. Through the floor, I could hear my parents' hushed voices downstairs and the click of them opening and closing drawers in the kitchen as my mom made herself lunch. I think about that morning often now, those last conscious minutes before I knew. Before my world turned upside down. I wish I could remember what I was thinking while I lay there, but maybe it's not important that I know after all.

At noon, I crawled from the sheets and went straight to my bathroom. In the shower I sang along to the radio, and I brushed my teeth while I conditioned my hair. After, I dressed in jeans and a tank top and bounded down the stairs into the kitchen.

"Mom." Her back was turned – she was standing over the kitchen sink – and I started to tell her I was going to Rudy's for lunch. I was ready to apologize. When my mother turned, the look in her eyes stopped me dead in my tracks. They were red-rimmed and bare, and they sagged at their wrinkle-less corners. She looked old and serious in that instant, and it struck me with paralyzing fear.

"Jill."

She exchanged a look with my father, who was seated at the kitchen table. He didn't have the newspaper like he usually did.

His hands were folded on the tabletop beside his empty coffee mug.

"What's wrong?" I said, and my mother broke into tears, stepping toward me with her arms outstretched. "What happened?"

My father cleared his throat and he met my eyes for only a brief second before looking back down.

"Jillian," he began, softly. "There was an accident last night. Ruth Ann passed away in an accident at her house."

His voice tunneled in my ears; it distorted and became a strange echo against my brain. My mother had closed the distance between us and had wrapped me in her arms, crying with her face against my shoulder.

"What accident?" A shrill voice cut through my mother's sobs. It was my voice, I realized with a jolt.

"Jilly, we're so sorry." My mother rubbed her palm in a circle against my back. I shuddered.

"What accident," I repeated. "I don't understand."

My father stood.

"We don't know exactly what happened, but she passed away early this morning. If you need to talk about –"

"Why didn't you wake me up? I should have been over there. I need to be with her!" I was shouting.

"She's gone, Jill. It's terrible, but Ruth Ann is gone."

My mother hugged me tighter and I was smothering, my chest collapsing into my lungs. I could feel my damp ponytail where it hung against my back, leaving a wet spot spreading across my shirt. I could smell the mint toothpaste on my own breath, and I could feel the little hairs on my mother's arms pressed up against my triceps. My father started to speak again, but his words jumbled and his face blurred in my vision and for a second I didn't know why.

Tears.

There were hot tears in my eyes; that's why I couldn't see.

————

It wasn't at Rudy's funeral where I felt things the hardest but at our graduation ceremony, one week after her death. We were all crowded inside the gymnasium, this huge herd of navy blue and white robes, with teachers-as-shepherds dispersed among us, yelling above our low rumblings, trying to direct us into straight lines. No one paid any attention to me, aside from the occasional sideways glance or tight smile. At the time, I felt I was invisible to them without Rudy by my side – no one wants to finish watching a movie once the hero's been killed off – but I've gained perspective since that time. How could I expect my eighteen year-old classmates to know what words to say in the wake of my best friend's death? Fifteen years later, I still don't know how to approach it.

The year before, when Rudy and I were juniors, a senior had been killed in a car accident one snowy evening in February. He was on the tennis team and was secretary of the student council, and we had smoked weed with him once, on someone's back patio while we rubbed at the goosebumps on our biceps and froze our asses off. We didn't even really know him, but when word of his death had trickled through the school, Rudy and I had joined the rest of the upperclassmen in the auditorium. We bawled our eyes out, hugging each other and pressing our wet cheeks to other friends' shoulders. The whole school was a mess of tears, and I caught myself thinking, how are these broken down girls, red eyed with muddled blush caked on their cheeks the same girls who never stepped outside without mascara? I felt acutely aware of my weight resting against the shoulder of the girl beside me as we all pressed together, and I can remember thinking maybe this was the most you could love someone you didn't really know – huddling shoulder to shoulder with them, connected by the loss of one of your own. I felt calmed, and at the same time I felt disturbed by the queer unreality of the whole situation. When Rudy died, I thought back to this afternoon and I tried not to cry at all. I avoided the theatrics and pity of tears; tears were a cheap form of currency I did not want. They made things about me instead of her, and I didn't want to steal anything more from her, especially not this moment. I deferred to Rudy, even in death.

I stayed publicly dry-eyed through the visitation, the funeral and my final school days at Ogden, but I cried endlessly at home in front of my mother, and in my own bed at night, shaking underneath the covers.

The evening of graduation, I walked with my classmates out onto the grounds of the football field, the girls' heels sinking gently into the soft ground as we strode out in neat lines under the fading light of dusk. We made our way to our seats – folding chairs covered in crisp white linens and arranged in rows across the grass. Around me, my classmates grinned and whispered excitedly to one another and bobbled their heads so that their tassels would shake from side to side. They waved up at their parents in the football stands. I did not know where my mother and father were sitting, and I did not attempt to find them.

As the ceremony began, I felt my face flush, blood rushing to my cheeks and my forehead. My eyes felt swollen. The principal spoke first, then the guest speaker – a Missouri state senator – and mid-way through his speech the lights above the bleachers flipped on, adding illumination as the sun disappeared behind the horizon and the sky darkened. Everyone's eyes darted from the stage up toward the lights, and I could see the principal frown at this untimely distraction, this blemish that revealed Ogden to be just shy of the perfect presentation it strove for, and its students to be exactly what we were – still kids, distracted by flashing lights and sounds. So much of life, it occurred to me then, though I think the realization had been lingering in my mind for many years, depended heavily on appearances. The senator continued, unfazed. During the part where Rudy would have spoken as our class valedictorian, the class president stood at the podium instead and looked both sad and uncomfortable as Mr. and Mrs. Golden came forward, Mr. Golden's arms around Mrs. Golden's shoulders, holding her up as she shook and cried, and they received Rudy's diploma. My heart ached.

We filed across the stage – all 147 of us – received our diplomas, shook hands with Dr. Foakley and endured hugs from each of the teachers in line to congratulate us as we made our way back to our seats.

At the end, we were led out of our chairs and encircled the football field, as we'd practiced the morning before, our arms outstretched to hold the hands of the people beside us. The band played the school song. Everyone around me sang, but I didn't even attempt to mouth the words. At the very end, fireworks erupted up into the sky behind the podium, raining gold and blue and purple sparks down from above. We threw our caps high into the air, and everyone was cheering, shrieking with joy. The boys clapped one another on the shoulders and the girls squeezed each other in tight hugs. The air sizzled with excitement and as I stood there, not moving, not speaking, I could feel the pit of my stomach drop and all of the energy in my body drain to my fingertips. I would never again feel her absence as acutely as I did in that very moment. I burst into tears.

———

EACH TIME I tell someone my high school story – my Rudy story – I can feel the questions rolling around in their heads. I know I shouldn't tell this story, or at the very least I should tell the abridged version, with less longing breaking through in my voice. Because it's been fifteen freaking years, and so many things have happened in my life that haven't included Rudy at all.

I have two children now, five and two years old. I worry constantly about the mistakes I'm sure I'm making with them – am I allowing them too much freedom, am I too soft when I punish them for throwing tantrums or bickering with each other, do I give them enough kisses and tell them often enough how fervently I love them – and I wonder what missteps the Goldens made, what missteps my own parents made with my upbringing. I wonder how different my life would be if she'd never been in it. I wonder how I changed her life. I wonder what would have happened if I'd been there to catch her that night.

Rudy's photo, our first photo together, the photo of the two of us on the staircase before we became inseparable, sits on the entertainment center in our living room, where I pass by it daily while I get ready for work and pick up after the kids. I still feel eclipsed by her presence, by the unfulfilled potential of the bright light inside her. She was the person who always knew me best, and yet I wonder if I ever truly knew her at all.

During the first year of our marriage my husband, a high school counselor, suggested I go see a therapist to talk things over, things that still haunt me daily. After three meetings with the woman, she told me – to put it quite simply – that I had to move on. I had to stop idealizing Rudy and the friendship we had, because years had gone by and even if Rudy had lived, things would have changed so drastically since then. Rudy would be thirty-two years old today; she would have children and a job and she would forget to take out the garbage and she would have love handles and she would fight with her husband. Or maybe she wouldn't. And the reality of it is we probably would have grown apart somewhere during those fifteen years since high school. But that's just the problem. She isn't here. She never had the chance to change another person's life. We never got the chance to grow apart.

————

ON THE LAST day of our first summer together, as we lay beneath the chandelier with our entire lives spread out in front of us, Rudy turned to me, her eyes sparkling with the reflection of the crystals. She reached for my limp hand and wove her warm fingers through mine.

"You're the best friend I've ever had." She said it solemnly. Seriously – like an oath.

Before I could respond, she was bounding to her feet, her bare toes slapping the cold floor as she ran through the house and dove into the pool, leaving me disoriented and alone as I watched her from the foyer.

"You're my best friend, too!" I called after her, but she didn't hear me, her head engulfed in the wake of her splash, her hair a cape flowing out from behind her. She was smiling, the little squares of her teeth white behind a delicate waterfall. She was always smiling – maybe I imagined that part. But on that day, she was her best – the purest form of beauty, a diamond excavated from the dark depths of the Earth, cleaned and shined and put under the bright display lights for everyone in the world to see.

And in my mind she's always going to live, forever, that perfect, shining, innocent girl.

Rudy.

ACKNOWLEDGMENTS

I'd like to thank my parents, for the use of their typewriter when I wrote my first book in elementary school, for their blessing when I decided to forgo Journalism and instead pursue a degree in Creative Writing and for their never-ending love and support in all aspects of my life for the last thirty years.

To all my wonderful friends, who have read early drafts and been sounding boards for story ideas. To Mallory Parsons, who did an amazing job as my cover designer. And to Reid and Danielle Garcia - without you both and our summer trip to Zion Canyon, I'm convinced this book would still be a draft right now.

To my forever favorite aunt, Laura Maxwell, who edited my words and has always made me believe I'm capable of anything.

To my kids, who are my heart and my motivation. I hope that years from now when you're actually able to read, you'll be as proud of your mom "the writer" as I am of everything you do.

And to my husband, Ryan, who has watched our babies while I worked, encouraged every wild dream I've ever chased and treated my writing as if it were as important as the work he does day in and day out. You are the best and none of my dreams would be the same without you by my side.

ABOUT THE AUTHOR

Andrea Dickherber was born and raised in Missouri, graduating with honors from the University of Missouri with a degree in English. She considers herself a road trip addict, an amateur home improver, a sort of runner and drink of all the coffees. She lives in Los Angeles with her husband, Ryan, and her children, Knox, Quinn and Rooney. Golden is her first novel.

Find her online at her website www.sincerelya.com or on Instagram.

instagram.com/andrea.dickherber.writes